REX RIDERS™

By
J.P. Carlson

Illustrated by
J. Calafiore

AN IMPRINT OF MONSTROSITIES INC.

Rex Riders

Copyright © 2010 by J.P. Carlson
Cover illustration by Fabio Pastori copyright © 2010 by Monstrosities Inc.
Illustrations by J. Calafiore copyright © 2010 by Monstrosities Inc.
Published by Monstrosities Inc.
The Monstrosities logo is a trademark of Monstrosities Inc.

Publisher's Cataloging-In-Publication Data

Carlson, J.P.
    Rex Riders / by J.P. Carlson – 1st ed.
        p.   cm.
    Summary: a group of cowboys travel to a prehistoric planet in the company of a rex-riding stranger to stop a cattleman from bringing a herd of triceratops back to Texas.
    ISBN-13: 978-0-982-57963-3
    [1. Dinosaurs-Fiction.   2. Action & Adventure-Fiction.   3. Science Fiction.
4. Cowboys-Fiction.   5. Texas-Fiction.]   I. Title
PZ7.C375Re 2010   2009939914
[Fic]-dc22

Printed in the U.S.A.

This book is dedicated to everyone
who ever looked at a dinosaur skeleton
or a picture of a dinosaur and wondered,
and to Kaiyodo, the company
that made dinosaur dreams come true
for people around the world

Contents

REX RIDERS

Prologue

Patagonia: The Cretaceous Era

The smell of death was in the air. It wasn't the putrid stench of a decaying carcass that had been lying out in the sun too long, but rather the delicious scent of an animal that had died just a few hours before and hadn't yet begun to decompose. It was so faint it could only be detected by the creatures that fed on the flesh of the dead. Insects, scavengers, vermin and opportunistic predators smelled the body of the lifeless, long-necked dinosaur and began to gather and nibble at its ample carcass almost immediately after it took its last breath.

The female Tyrannosaurus rex was a quarter of a mile away when she first smelled the carcass and began to lead her two offspring toward the fresh meat. But now—fifty yards from the body—she stopped in her tracks and stared at the scene before her. Her nostrils twitched as she tried to decide whether to move any closer. It wasn't the small animals that had reached the body ahead of her that caused her to pause. She recognized most of them. They were no match for a full grown T-rex and would scatter when she got closer to stake her claim. No, there was something else that was strange about what lay in front of her, but she couldn't quite figure it out.

The body of the diplodocus was lying on a circular platform one hundred yards across that was constructed of metal and stone. Richly detailed carvings of prehistoric animals were inlaid on its top and sides. Three gently sloping walkways, set equally apart, led to the top of the platform. On the platform's outer edge stood three huge metal statues that resembled sauropods standing on their hind legs, as if they were straining to reach the delicate leaves atop a tall tree.

The big T-rex snorted once she'd made up her mind. The scene may have been unfamiliar, but she wouldn't let that stop her from feeding her young. She strode up the walkway toward the sauropod with her offspring in tow. The smaller animals fled, just as she'd expected. The youngsters chased after the stragglers until a growl from their mother returned them to her side.

Now it was time to inspect the body. The juveniles hung back and waited as their mother leaned down and sniffed the carcass. It smelled fresh, and the T-rex began to salivate. Then she licked it several times. Yes, this was a meal fit for the king of the dinosaurs, and without the risk of a fight nor

Prologue

the possibility of injury! She reared back and roared twice as a warning to nearby predators to stay away while she and her brood fed on the body. Then she waited and listened. When no other dinosaur roared back to challenge her, she tore into the carcass with gusto, followed by her young.

The T-rex and her offspring never noticed the alien scientists who were hovering nearby, waiting patiently for this moment before they activated the platform. The hungry rexes were too busy feasting to pay attention to the rising drone of the generator that was buried underneath them as it recharged the teleporter. And when they rematerialized on a similar platform in the middle of a habitat that recreated their environment on Earth, they had no idea they were on a different planet.

The transition had been seamless, and it was a tribute to the technological prowess of this otherworldly race that the many prehistoric animals they had collected for study thrived in their new environment, light years from Earth. But technology cannot ensure the survival of a society and even the most advanced civilizations can encounter challenges that technology cannot overcome.

So it happened that when this alien civilization observed a cluster of meteors heading toward their world eons after they began their exploration of infant Earth, they decided that the safest course was to leave their home and relocate to another planet. And since rebuilding their civilization required every available resource, they reluctantly left behind the creatures they had gathered for study with the intention of rebuilding their collection from scratch on a new world.

Rex Riders

The meteors slammed into the planet and filled the atmosphere with the choking dust of an element unknown on Earth. But something unexpected happened to the dinosaurs. Instead of dying out as they did on Earth when a similar catastrophic event occurred, the creatures on the alien homeworld survived. T-rex returned to the top of the food chain, and the evolution of dinosaurs and other intelligent life forms that were entirely different from those that evolved on Earth was set into motion.

Chapter
One

Dos Locos, Texas: August, 1881

The trouble started with a horse. It didn't end with a horse, but that's where it all began. Zeke Calhoun knew exactly who this particular horse belonged to. Heck, anyone from Dos Locos would have recognized the horse in an instant. Midnight was a black Andalusian stallion that was born and bred in Spain for bullfighting, and there wasn't another like him in all of Southern Texas. And there he was, miles away from his corral at the Crossed Swords Ranch, grazing on scrub grass, enjoying his new-found freedom.

Midnight's owner was Dante D'Allesandro, the richest man in Dos Locos. D'Allesandro bought the horse from a breeder in Spain and had him shipped halfway around the world at great expense to his ranch in Texas. Even though Midnight was reputed to be one tough horse, D'Allesandro babied him. The only time anyone ever saw D'Allesandro ride Midnight was at parades and special events.

Zeke was fourteen years old and couldn't relate to this at all. What was the point of owning a beautiful stallion like Midnight if you didn't ride him, and ride him hard? If Midnight could have spoken for himself, Zeke was sure the horse would have said that he was tired of all that soft living, asking instead to be taken for a ride. Not that Zeke had any firsthand experience with owning a horse. The sorrel he was riding was one his Uncle Jesse only allowed him to use whenever he'd finished his chores. Even then, Uncle Jesse sometimes forbade him from taking her out.

Still, Zeke should have known better than to go near Midnight. Anything that had to do with the D'Allesandro family was trouble. The D'Allesandros were the first settlers in this part of Texas, and Dante's grandfather and great uncle built the town themselves. They named it "Dos Locos" to thumb their noses at everyone who told them they were crazy to settle there. Local legend had it that the D'Allesandros were related to a Spanish conquistador who deserted his countrymen after stealing a wagon full of Incan gold; then traveled north into the territory that would later became Texas. He supposedly hid the gold in the mountains surrounding Dos Locos, and it was that gold that became the source of the D'Allesandro family's great wealth.

Dante D'Allesandro scoffed at the stories and insisted that his family was descended from Spanish nobility who earned their money from cattle ranching in Spain, but no one in town believed him. Zeke's uncle Jesse used to say that Dante

Chapter One

was kind of like a rattlesnake with its tail cut off: sneaky, silent and deadly. The bottom line was this: if something belonged to D'Allesandro, you stayed away from it.

Besides, everyone knew that it was never okay to ride another person's horse without first asking permission. That was part of the unwritten code of the West, like being neighborly or making sure that you fed and watered your horse before you got yourself a meal.

As Zeke rode closer to Midnight he was impressed by what he saw. Midnight was clearly a different breed of horse. He was taller, his chest was fuller, and he actually looked stronger than the other horses Zeke had seen around Dos Locos. Even more remarkable, Midnight was wearing a saddle.

Zeke was within ten feet of Midnight now, and the horse was watching him, waiting to see what Zeke was up to. Zeke knew that he should head back to his Uncle Jesse's ranch, tell him exactly where he found Midnight, and let Uncle Jesse take care of it. Uncle Jesse knew D'Allesandro, and he'd know exactly how to handle it. Yes, that was definitely the best thing to do.

Zeke got down from his horse and moved slowly toward Midnight. He decided he would try to do the best thing starting tomorrow. Today, he'd see if Midnight would let him take a ride. If the horse did, Zeke would return the Andalusian himself. Worst case: Midnight would run off; then Zeke could still go back and tell Uncle Jesse where he'd last seen the big stallion. So either way, everything would work out fine!

Midnight stared at Zeke as the boy inched toward him, but the horse didn't run. Zeke held his breath as he reached out ever so slowly to grab hold of Midnight's reins. A moment later Zeke was up in the saddle and feeling very proud of himself. He reached down and took the reins of his own horse. He'd tie her up first and then take Midnight for a little ride. The stallion could use some exercise for a change.

While Zeke was out having fun with Midnight, Shorty Stevens was sitting on his bed in the bunkhouse at the Crossed Swords Ranch turning his battered, old civil war hat over and over in his hands, as he agonized over the best way to break the news to Mr. D'Allesandro that Midnight had run off. Shorty was responsible for taking care of his boss's prized possession, and that included feeding, grooming and exercising the horse. The trouble with Midnight was that he was a typical Andalusian: intelligent, headstrong and ill-tempered, just like his owner.

Earlier that morning, Shorty was hand-walking Midnight after a brief ride when he accidentally stepped on a rattler. The snake startled both man and horse, and when Midnight reared up, he knocked Shorty over. Shorty lost his grip on the reins and Midnight was gone.

So now Shorty had a problem. If he quit and walked off the job without telling anyone what happened—which he was tempted to do—D'Allesandro would assume that Shorty had stolen Midnight and send the law after him. That most certainly meant jail time . . . *or worse*. Horse stealing was a serious enough crime, but D'Allesandro would personally see to it that Shorty was prosecuted to the fullest extent of the law, regardless of what really happened. That was just the way D'Allesandro was.

On the other hand, if Shorty remained to face D'Allesandro,

Chapter One

he risked a beating at the hands of D'Allesandro's nasty trail boss, Cable Cooper. And that was just as bad. Just thinking about Cable Cooper sent a shiver down Shorty's spine. Cooper had a terrible temper and was one scary guy. He exuded a frightening aura of violence and unpredictability. One second Cooper could be laughing and happy and the next moment his temper was out of control. You never knew what might set him off. Grown men avoided Cooper's glance for fear they would look at him the wrong way and inadvertently provoke him. And when he walked down the street, people crossed to the other side.

Shorty knew it wouldn't be long before someone noticed that Midnight was missing and come looking for the horse, so he had to make up his mind quickly. It was an awful predicament and Shorty's stomach was in knots. He was concentrating so hard that he didn't hear the sound of boot steps and jingle of spurs on the wooden floor of the bunkhouse.

"Where's Midnight?"

The sudden sound of Cable Cooper's voice in the doorway nearly caused Shorty to hit his head on the upper bunk. Cooper glared at him ominously.

Shorty was so startled he could barely speak. "He . . . I mean, I . . . There was this snake, see, and . . ."

Before he could finish what he was saying, Cooper sprung on him like a bear trap and yanked him to his feet.

"I asked you a question. Now you answer me, boy."

But Shorty's nerves had gotten the better of him and all he could get out was, "I . . ."

Cooper released Shorty's shirt with his right hand and socked him in the jaw. Shorty's head lurched backward from the impact of the blow, and the back of his head struck the upper bunk above his bed. Cooper jerked him forward and shook him.

"Tell me where that horse is now, or so help me I'll kill you."

Tears welled up in Shorty's eyes. He couldn't help it. Shorty was in a state of panic and his emotions were out of control. "He— he ran off. There was a snake, and I fell, and he ran off. That's all. He ran off. I'm sure we can find him. I'll go right now."

"You're going nowhere," spat Cooper. "You're coming with me."

Cooper dragged Shorty out of the bunkhouse into the bright sunlight. Some of the men had crowded around the doorway when Cooper began shouting, but no one had dared enter. Shorty's appearance startled them. His nose was bleeding, his face was red, and his cheeks were streaked with tears.

Cooper flung Shorty to the ground. Then, talking to no one in particular, he started barking orders.

"Take this piece of cow manure and tie him up in the barn where he belongs. Mr. D'Allesandro's horse is missing. Shorty stole him and hid him somewhere."

He pointed at One-Eyed Jack, Thom Jackson and Tall Bill. "You three are going with me. Saddle up and meet me out front. And bring my horse. I have to see Mr. D'Allesandro."

Cooper looked at Shorty with contempt and kicked him. "If we don't find that horse, you'll hang. And I'll put the rope around your neck myself." Cooper wheeled around and headed in the direction of D'Allesandro's palatial Spanish-style house.

Cooper was the only one of the men who was allowed into D'Allesandro's house without an invitation, and that was a

Chapter One

privilege that Cooper never took for granted. As he stood outside the closed door to D'Allesandro's study, he removed his hat, then knocked quietly and waited for D'Allesandro to bid him enter. Holding his hat in his hands, Cooper stared at his feet as he approached his boss.

"Excuse me, Mr. D'Allesandro. I just thought you might want to know that Midnight's gone. Me and the boys are going out to bring him back."

D'Allesandro looked up at Cooper from behind a large, ornately carved teak desk. His expression was impassive. "I see," he said calmly with a hint of a Spanish accent. "Who is responsible for this?"

"Shorty."

"And?"

"He got part of what he deserved," Cooper confirmed. "But he's got more coming."

"Good. Make sure the men know what happened to Shorty. Where is he now?"

"We got him tied up in the barn."

"Do what you feel is appropriate Mr. Cooper. I leave this to you. Let me know when Midnight is back. I would like to see him for myself. If he has been harmed in any way, Shorty must make amends."

"Oh, he will, Mr. D'Allesandro," Cooper said with a grim little chuckle. "He will."

Zeke had run Midnight pretty hard that morning, and now the horse needed time to cool down and rest. He hadn't been run so hard since he left Spain for the Crossed Swords Ranch, and both teen and horse had worked up a sweat. Zeke understood why D'Allesandro had wanted an Andalusian. Midnight was an exceptional creature and responded well to Zeke's touch. He was fast and surefooted, with quick reflexes. It was no wonder Andalusians were used in bull fights!

They had stopped for a drink at a stream. As Midnight drank his fill of the cool, fresh water, Zeke saw Cooper and his men off in the distance. *Good timing,* Zeke thought. They weren't far from where hed left the sorrel, so he could turn Midnight over to Cooper and wouldn't have that far to walk to retrieve her.

"There he is!" One-Eyed Jack cried. "There's Midnight! Who's that with him?"

"That's Zeke Calhoun, Jesse McCain's nephew," Thom said.

Cooper's eyes narrowed. "So he's the one that stole Mr. D'Allesandro's horse."

"What are you talking about?" Tall Bill asked. "Back at the ranch you said Shorty stole the horse. I heard you."

"Shut your mouth!" Cooper shouted angrily. "Calhoun stole that horse. You can see for yourself." Cooper fingered his whip. "And he's gonna pay. Let's get him! Come on!"

Zeke remounted Midnight and rode toward Cooper and his men, expecting a friendly chat about what a hero Zeke was for finding Midnight and turning the big horse over to them. As Zeke rode along, he rehearsed what he was going to say. He'd tell them how he found Midnight out in a field and managed to catch him before he ran off. They were lucky Zeke was on the ball!

Zeke would miss Midnight, but he was glad he had the chance to ride the Andalusian. Maybe he could visit the horse

Chapter One

some time. Hey, there might even be a reward, and he'd get a couple of dollars! D'Allesandro could certainly afford it. Now that would be something. He could buy a lot of great things at the General Store with even just one dollar, and there was plenty he'd had his eye on. But Zeke wouldn't spend it all. No, he'd save some of that money for a rainy day. Although why he would need money for a rainy day was beyond him.

As Zeke's mind wandered from one thought to the next, it suddenly occurred to him that there was something strange about the way Cooper and his men were riding toward him. The speed of their horses, the way the riders were leaning forward, their tight formation; something didn't look right.

Then it dawned on him: they weren't coming to meet him; they were out to catch him. It made no sense, but whatever was going on, Zeke wanted no part of it. He wheeled Midnight around and took off in the opposite direction.

"Look! He's trying to get away," Cooper shouted. "I told you he stole that horse! Come on!"

Although Zeke had given Midnight a lot of exercise that morning, it hadn't tired the great beast at all. It only seemed to warm him up for the chase. Zeke and the stallion had a good lead on Cooper and his men, and the teen had a hunch that Midnight could easily outrun them in a race. But Zeke would need help to get out of whatever trouble he was in, so he headed straight back to Uncle Jesse's Double R Ranch.

As the Double R came into sight, Zeke called out for his uncle, but there was no response. Then he remembered—Uncle Jesse had gone into town with Stumpy and Bull! Now Zeke had a decision to make: should he ride toward town in the hope of meeting Uncle Jesse on the road or stay near the ranch and wait for his uncle to return? Zeke knew every inch of the place and thought maybe if he hid out in the barn, Cooper and his men would take Midnight and leave. The only problem was that if Zeke slowed down they might catch up to him.

As Cooper followed Zeke toward the Double R, he knew he was courting trouble. It wasn't considered trespassing to follow someone onto their land to recover a stolen horse, but accusing Zeke of stealing Midnight was a risky play. To pull it off, he'd need to get his story straight when he saw Zeke's uncle. He'd also have to deal with Shorty when he got back to the Crossed Swords. It would be tricky but it was worth the risk if he could take Jesse McCain down a notch or two in the eyes of the townspeople. And having a horse thief in the family would definitely stain the great Jesse McCain's reputation.

When Cooper heard Zeke calling his uncle's name, it dawned on Cooper that the ranch might be deserted, which opened the door to several new possibilities. Cooper unhooked the bullwhip he carried on his belt with his right hand, letting it drop to his side. Cattle could be stubborn, and the cracking sound that a whip made was often enough to get a herd moving again. But Cooper had something different in mind.

"He's heading toward the main house. Go 'round the other side, and me and Jack'll head toward the front. We'll cut him off," Cooper shouted to Tall Bill and Thom.

Zeke didn't notice that two of Cooper's men had split off. He was worried about his next move, and without realizing it, was slowing Midnight down as Cooper and One-Eyed Jack spurred their horses to catch up to him.

Chapter One

As Zeke rode toward the front of the ranch, Tall Bill and Thom cut him off from the opposite side of the house. Zeke pulled on the reins to reverse Midnight's direction just as Cooper and One-Eyed Jack closed in from behind.

Cooper's right arm was up in a flash, followed by a loud crack as the whip hit Midnight's flank. The searing pain caused the horse to lurch sideways and lose its balance exactly as Cooper had planned. Midnight hit the ground hard, and Zeke was catapulted off her back. Zeke relaxed his body and rolled just like he'd been taught by his uncle to avoid getting hurt, but Midnight stood up favoring his right foreleg.

"No!" Zeke yelled as he ran toward the limping stallion. Before he could reach Midnight, however, Cooper and his men jumped down from their horses and circled him. Zeke was trapped!

"Don't let him out," Cooper ordered, climbing off his horse with his whip in hand. "Why'd you do it, Calhoun?" he asked Zeke as the bull whip's thong dropped to the ground.

Zeke gulped. He'd been in a few scrapes before with other boys his age, and even had his backside tanned by his mother once when he was little, but he'd never been whipped.

Cooper snapped the bullwhip, menacingly.

"I don't know what you're talking about," Zeke cried as he circled away from Cooper.

"You know what I'm talking about. You stole that horse."

"I did not!" Zeke responded, indignantly. "I found him and I was bringing him back."

"Oh, yeah? Then why'd you run?" Cooper snapped the whip again, and the sound sent a chill down Zeke's back. Zeke turned and tried to escape between Tall Bill and Thom, but they shoved him back toward Cooper. They were all laughing now, enjoying Zeke's rising state of panic.

"Looks like he's scared," Tall Bill said.

"Yup. Scared of a little whip? Imagine that," One-Eyed Jack said. "Nothing to be scared of Calhoun. You'll get used to sleeping on your stomach till your back heals up—in a couple of months." The laughter continued.

Off in the distance, Uncle Jesse was driving his buckboard back toward the Double R Ranch. On one end of the bench sat his husky right-hand man, Milo Pluribus Whitman, who (mercifully) went by the nickname "Bull," and on the opposite side was the old camp cook, Stumpy Gibbons. The men had gone into town to pick up supplies and were in no particular rush to get back.

"Wonder what Zeke's up to," Bull said to no one in particular as he struggled to stay awake in the afternoon heat.

"What did you say?" Stumpy asked. The old cook was slightly hard of hearing, but it was difficult to tell which ear gave him trouble.

"He said he wonders what Zeke is up to," Uncle Jesse replied more loudly.

"You don't have to shout," Stumpy answered, grumpily. "He's probably finishing his chores."

Uncle Jesse grunted. "Not likely."

As they rounded the bend in the trail that led to the ranch, Uncle Jesse saw Zeke inside the circle of men and recognized Cooper from the bullwhip he was snapping.

Chapter One

"What the heck is going on?" Uncle Jesse said angrily. "That's Cable Cooper. What's he doing on my property? And what's he doing with that whip?" All three men instantly tensed and felt a surge of adrenaline when they realized that Zeke was in danger. Urging on the horses, Uncle Jesse steered the buckboard directly toward the group of men and ordered Stumpy to take the reins. As the two men changed places, Uncle Jesse exchanged a quick glance with Bull. This was going to get messy.

"Why don't you stop running, Calhoun? You ain't making it any easier for yourself," said Cooper as the buckboard bore down on them.

Two images burned themselves into Zeke's memory that day. The first was the image of Uncle Jesse standing on the seat of the bouncing buckboard, yelling at the top of his lungs, fists clenched at his sides. Second was Uncle Jesse launching himself at Cooper and tackling him to the ground as Stumpy drove the wagon through the circle.

Cooper's goons piled on top of the two struggling men, and Zeke bravely joined the fray with fists swinging to help his uncle. One-Eyed Jack made the mistake of taking a poke at Zeke and wound up flat on his back, courtesy of Bull's fist. Then Uncle Jesse's powerful right-hand man grabbed Cooper's other two men and tossed them aside like they were sacks of flour, while Uncle Jesse and Cooper continued to roll around on the ground.

This wasn't the first time that these two had squared off, but in the past it hadn't actually come to blows. Cooper was a bully who was used to intimidating people, and neither Uncle

Jesse nor Bull would have any of it. Cooper hated that about them. He was itching to find a way to show up Uncle Jesse and now the opportunity had presented itself.

For Uncle Jesse, it was equally personal. In town, he'd seen Cooper humiliate men who were too afraid to stand up to him, and Uncle Jesse promised himself that if Cooper ever tried that nonsense with him, he'd put Cooper in his place. Bull felt the same way, but this was Uncle Jesse's fight, so Bull made no effort to intervene.

As the two men wrestled, the rage that had welled up in them found expression in the blows they struck at each other. No words were spoken by either man as they struck with all their might. After several minutes of pounding, both men struggled to their feet.

"I ain't done with you, McCain," Cooper said as he tried to catch his breath.

"Good. Saves me the trouble of chasing you down," a panting McCain replied. Suddenly, Cooper noticed his bull-whip lying on the ground. He had dropped it when Uncle Jesse tackled him and this was his chance to get it back. Uncle Jesse saw where Cooper's attention had shifted, but it was too late. Cooper dove and had the whip in his hands before Uncle Jesse could react. "Still want to chase me down, McCain? Come and get me, you coward."

It was ironic that a man using a whip in a fist fight would call his unarmed opponent a coward, but that was pure Cooper; not a lick of sense. Uncle Jesse knew Cooper was just baiting him, so instead of rushing inside the range of the whip, he circled Cooper and bided his time.

Chapter One

Cooper shot his right hand forward and the end of the whip caught Zeke's uncle on the shoulder. Uncle Jesse cried out as the tip of the lash ripped through his long-sleeved shirt and cut through his skin. The pain was intense and Uncle Jesse's shoulder throbbed, but it spurred him back into action. If Uncle Jesse couldn't stay out of range, he'd have to move inside the whip's arc so it wouldn't be effective!

Uncle Jesse charged Cooper with his arms in front of him to protect his face. Cooper brought the whip down again, but Uncle Jesse was too fast and had too much momentum to be stopped. He ducked beneath the lash of the bullwhip and plowed into Cooper, sending him tumbling to the ground. Then Uncle Jesse dropped his knee hard on Cooper's right arm, forcing the whip from his hand. As Uncle Jesse jumped to his feet, Stumpy tossed him a hunting knife, which Uncle Jesse used to cut off the handle of the lash in one smooth motion. Then he cut the long leather thong in half and flung all three pieces to the ground.

"Thanks," Uncle Jesse said as he handed the hunting knife back to Stumpy.

Cooper flew into a rage and reached for his gun, but before he could pull it out of its holster, Stumpy fired a warning shot over Cooper's head.

"Get your horse and get off this ranch, Cooper!" Stumpy shouted. "And take these saddle tramps with you. You're trespassing on Double R land."

"What about Mr. D'Allesandro's horse? That thief stole him, and now the animal's lame! Look at him!"

Sure enough, the stallion continued to favor its right foreleg.

"You think he's getting away with that?" Cooper cried as he pointed at Zeke.

Stumpy gave no reply. His gun remained leveled at Cooper, while both Uncle Jesse and Bull stood unmoving with their arms folded against their chests, separating Zeke from Cooper and his men.

"We'll be back, McCain," Cooper finally said. "Only next time we'll have the law with us."

Cooper dusted himself off and deliberately took his time walking back to his horse. Then the four men galloped away with Midnight in tow.

Uncle Jesse, Bull and Stumpy waited for D'Allesandro's men to disappear over the horizon before confronting Zeke. He and his uncle had taken some pretty hard shots, and Bull's hand was a little sore from slugging One-Eyed Jack. But this was no time to sit around and organize a crying party.

"What's going on, Zeke? When we left for town, you were out on the porch and said you'd likely go for a ride after finishing your chores. What happened?"

"Well, that's exactly what I did, Uncle Jesse. I was out riding and saw Midnight out by himself. I figured he got free somehow. I was going to get you, but when I saw he was saddled, I thought I'd return him."

"Okay, fair enough. So what were you doing riding him? You didn't have to ride him to return him."

"Well, I just thought it would be better that way."

"I don't think so. You know better than to ride another man's horse without permission. That ain't the way things are done in these parts."

Chapter One

"I know. I just thought . . ."

"And if you were out on Midnight, what happened to my sorrel? You didn't just up and leave her somewhere, I hope."

"Well, actually I did . . ." Zeke voice drifted off as he struggled to think of some way to justify his actions. "But I was planning to go right back and get her after I returned Midnight."

Uncle Jesse tried to remain calm, but leaving a horse out on the range was too much. "You know, the more you keep talking, the less sense this story makes. I would like to know what made you do something so stupid?"

Zeke was shocked by Uncle Jesse's question. "I didn't think it was so stupid to want to return a valuable horse," he shouted in response. "Midnight is worth ten times more than any of the broken down nags you have around this place! That's a real horse!"

"That pampered prima donna would be lucky to do half the work my worst horse can do," Uncle Jesse yelled in reply.

But Zeke was so caught up in his own emotions, he didn't seem to hear. "And so what if I abandoned your precious horse? Maybe if you trusted me enough to take her out when I wanted, without having to beg you every time, I'd care a little more!

"So *that's* what this is about?!" shouted Uncle Jesse. "Maybe if you showed more responsibility doing your chores and taking charge of some of the other jobs around here without my asking you all the time, I'd allow you to have a horse of your own."

Zeke started to interrupt, but Uncle Jesse would have none of it.

"You get your butt out there and bring my sorrel back from wherever you left her. If you're going to treat a horse that way, you don't deserve to have one. Now, *git*, before I lose my temper and say something I'll regret."

Zeke, furious at being called stupid, stood staring at his uncle and strained to think of something hurtful he could spit back at him. In point of fact, Uncle Jesse hadn't actually called Zeke stupid, but that was the way Zeke heard it.

"I can't talk to you," Zeke finally blurted before abruptly turning and walking away, leaving Uncle Jesse alone on the porch.

Zeke felt the blood pulse in his ears, and they burned bright red. He couldn't get over it; how dare his uncle call him stupid! He wasn't stupid. All he did was try to do a good deed. How could that be a bad thing? Besides, Cooper attacked him, and then tried to whip him! All Uncle Jesse could think about was why he was riding Midnight! What difference did that make? He was trying to do the neighborly thing and return a valuable horse! A horse, by the way, that was worth way more than anything Uncle Jesse had on the whole Double R. That was a fact. This place was a big dump. Okay, he hadn't brought Uncle Jesse's horse back yet, but he was planning to, if everything hadn't happened with Cooper.

It wasn't that Zeke hadn't tried to do all the right things. He wanted to fit in but nothing he did seemed to work. Bull and Uncle Jesse had been friends for years and didn't need words to communicate. A glance, a grunt or a nod spoke volumes. It worked for them. But Zeke felt left out and uncomfortable. It was like Uncle Jesse and Bull had a code or a secret language, and Zeke couldn't crack it. Zeke even studied them to try to imitate their gestures, but his efforts were ignored and didn't

Chapter One

work. Now he was being called stupid over a dumb horse! Zeke took a deep breath and shook his head. It just wasn't right.

Uncle Jesse stared at Zeke and shook his head, as the boy walked across the field on his way to find the sorrel. Zeke had been living at the Double R for close to a year now since his mother died, and they still hadn't clicked. There were all kinds of reasons. First off, the boy was a talker, full of questions about all sorts of things, and Uncle Jesse never saw the use in needless chatter. Maybe it was all the time he'd spent out on the range by himself long before Zeke arrived, but there were times when Uncle Jesse didn't feel like answering all those questions and they irritated him.

Uncle Jesse was also one of those stoical sorts who took a lot of pride in the fact that he never complained about anything. It wasn't that Uncle Jesse never got upset—he actually did . . . *quite a bit*. He just didn't complain about it out loud. Instead, Uncle Jesse would clench his jaw, causing the muscles in his cheeks to bulge. Zeke figured his uncle got mad a lot since he had the most well-developed cheek muscles of anybody he'd ever met.

The problem came from the fact that Uncle Jesse expected everyone else to be just as unemotional as he was. Zeke wasn't used to cowboy life and complained about a lot of things: sore feet, sore butt, sunburn, bug bites, bee stings, blisters, splinters, turned ankle, headache, stomachache—the list went on and on. Uncle Jesse never complained about those things when he was younger. Why should Zeke?

On top of that, the last thing Uncle Jesse needed right now

was a run-in with D'Allesandro. The Double R was in a sad state of repair but it couldn't be helped. For several seasons the ranch had earned enough money to support a small crew and turn a modest profit. But a couple of bad seasons had drained his savings, and he was forced to lay off everyone, except Bull and Stumpy. The spring rains had been good and things looked like they might be coming together. And now this.

Expecting things would escalate, Bull had discretely tiptoed away when Uncle Jesse began to raise his voice at Zeke, and the argument had been so loud Bull could hear the shouting from behind the barn. Stumpy had gone inside so he wouldn't appear to be nosy, but was doing his best to eavesdrop, which wasn't so hard, even with his hearing difficulties, given the volume.

Bull wasn't sure what to make of it all. Cowboys could be critical and dismissive of outsiders, and it was easy to write Zeke off as a soft city kid. But Bull understood that life in the West took time to get used to, and Zeke had a good heart. He was sure Zeke had the makings of a good cowboy and would turn out okay if Jess gave him a chance.

Stumpy hadn't known Uncle Jesse as long as Bull had, but Stumpy felt he knew him long enough to judge him. Men like Jesse were proud and stubborn. But Jesse's relationship to Zeke seemed out of character from the first day the boy arrived to stay with him, and Stumpy was disappointed that Jesse hadn't made much of an effort to get to know Zeke better. Maybe Stumpy had softened as he got older, but at this point in his life, Stumpy couldn't see why Jesse had to be so hard on the boy.

* * *

Chapter One

A couple of hours after Zeke left to find his horse, the three men were sitting around the kitchen table drinking coffee when Sheriff Healy rode up and delivered the bad news that D'Allesandro had sworn out a warrant for the boy's arrest. Zeke hadn't yet returned with the sorrel, but that didn't worry Uncle Jesse. He assumed Zeke was moping around somewhere stewing over the argument they'd had, and he'd come back sooner or later. Of course if something happened to his horse there'd be hell to pay, but there was no need to think about that right now.

Uncle Jesse asked the Sheriff to step outside so the two of them could discuss the matter in private. He hoped that maybe he could convince the Sheriff that there wasn't any substance to the case against Zeke, but the Sheriff didn't need any convincing.

"Before you say anything, McCain, I want you to know that I don't believe Zeke stole that horse," the Sheriff explained as they strolled along. "Problem is, Cooper swore he saw Zeke do it, and there's several witnesses that saw the boy on the horse gallop away when Cooper tried to confront him. You take those facts together, and there's enough for a warrant. Of course the key is Cooper saying he saw Zeke take the horse."

"What about Shorty Stevens? Ain't he responsible for taking care of that horse? What does he say about all this?"

"D'Allesandro says Shorty's gone missing. I asked around, and no one knows where he went to."

"Well, ain't that convenient," Uncle Jesse said sarcastically. "Looks like I've got a problem."

"I'm afraid that isn't the only problem. Midnight was

injured while Zeke was riding him and supposedly lame. Since your Zeke's kin, that makes you responsible."

"Lordy," Uncle Jesse exclaimed, as he clenched his jaw. "I saw the horse limping, but he didn't look like he was hurt that bad."

"I don't have to tell you there's no way to know how bad the horse was hurt without taking a closer look at him," the Sheriff explained, "and that isn't going to happen. Besides, any-body over there could fix it so the horse is lame by the time we get the chance."

Uncle Jesse shook his head ruefully. The question of whether a horse was lame was often the subject of disagree-ment. An animal that was limping one day might recover completely. On the other hand, if Midnight were proven to be truly injured, Uncle Jesse would have to reimburse D'Allesandro for its value. Since D'Allesandro had the Andalusian back in his hands, he could order any one of his henchmen to deliberately hurt the horse in order to prove his claim in court without anyone being able to prove otherwise.

"What's D'Allesandro claim the horse is worth?" Uncle Jesse asked.

"A thousand dollars," the Sheriff answered grimly.

"A thousand dollars! I don't have that kind of money," Uncle Jesse exclaimed. "I'm not the one with a cave full of gold in the mountains."

"D'Allesandro knows that, so he's willing to make you an offer," Sheriff Healy explained. "Now, don't get mad. Let me say it first, and then we'll talk about it." The Sheriff hesitated before continuing. "If you agree to send Zeke back East,

Chapter One

D'Allesandro will agree to drop the charges."

"And that would square it?"

"Not quite. That's only the first part. D'Allesandro also says that if you agree to turn over the deed to the Double R, he'll forgive the debt for Midnight and rent the place back to you. And as a gesture of good faith, he'll give you the horse. Says he has no use for an injured Andalusian."

"So he takes my ranch, and I get a lame horse. Do I have that right?" Uncle Jesse asked, seething. Before the Sheriff could answer, an explosion of bad language and threats cut him off. Uncle Jesse's patience had finally reached its limit.

From the main house Stumpy and Bull could hear every word, though Uncle Jesse and Sheriff Healy had walked a few dozen yards away.

"I had a feeling that was coming," Stumpy said, as he calmly sipped his coffee.

"You were able to hear that?" Bull asked skeptically.

"I ain't deaf you know," Stumpy snapped.

"Now Jesse, I knew you'd have that reaction," the Sheriff said, as he tried to calm down Uncle Jesse. "And I don't blame you, I don't blame you a bit."

"You don't, huh?" Uncle Jesse shouted.

"Let's take this one piece at a time," Sheriff Healy calmly explained. "I agree D'Allesandro's proposal is outrageous, but you know the courts around here. D'Allesandro's a powerful man in these parts and he has a lot of friends in high places. I can't promise you that Zeke will win at a trial or even receive a fair one! But if you agree to send Zeke back east, he can avoid the matter entirely.

"You want to keep Zeke out of jail and save this place?" the Sheriff asked. "I suggest you go along with this. It's the best thing for everyone. There's a stage coming to town tomorrow afternoon. You agree to have Zeke on it, and I'll be part way to getting rid of these problems for you."

"What about the horse?"

"One thing at a time. We get this done, and I'll tell D'Allesandro that you'll let him know about the Double R. Maybe we can parley with him. What do you say?"

Uncle Jesse clenched his jaw until the muscles in his cheeks looked like they'd explode. His mind was flooded with conflicting thoughts and emotions. "Okay. I'll do it. I'll make the arrangements, and have Zeke on that stage."

"Good, good," the Sheriff said. "I ain't saying it's right. You know me. I don't take anybody's side. I'm only saying it's the best thing for now. Shake?" He extended his hand. Uncle Jesse hesitated before taking it. He was angry, but Sheriff Healy wasn't to blame. The Sheriff was just doing his job the best he could.

Stumpy was in the middle of serving dinner, when Uncle Jesse broke the news that he was sending Zeke to live with relatives back East, and the old cook couldn't hide his anger.

"I never thought I'd see the day when you'd give in to that bum, D'Allesandro," he said in disgust. "You know what? I ain't surprised. You been against Zeke since the day the boy first got here. I'd sure like to know what you got against him."

Chapter One

"That's my business," Uncle Jesse snapped as he rose to his feet. "And I don't appreciate your prying into it." The room fell silent while Stumpy and Uncle Jesse glared at each other. Uncle Jesse was hard to beat in a staring contest, and Stumpy blinked first. He stomped his foot on the floor and slammed the cast iron skillet he was holding against the stove in frustration.

"You got anything to say about all this?" Uncle Jesse demanded, looking at Bull.

Bull simply shook his head sadly. "When you gonna tell Zeke?" he asked.

"Soon as he gets back," Uncle Jesse snarled, defiantly. "And don't give me that look like I did something wrong. Zeke brought this on himself."

"No need," Zeke said quietly from the doorway to the kitchen. "I already know." The men could hear the boy choke back a sob as he trudged to his room. Uncle Jesse's face grew red in response to Bull's accusing stare.

"Well, it looks like everything's gonna work out just fine," Stumpy said sarcastically.

Stumpy fixed a plate of food for Zeke and when he had it piled up just right, he walked it through the small sitting room to the bedrooms in the back of the house. He banged on the boy's door until it opened and shoved the plate into Zeke's hands. "Eat this; then get your boots on and meet me out front when you're done," he said. "But don't use the front door. We're going for a walk. And no more crying. We got some talking to do."

After Zeke finished his meal, he climbed out the window and ran around to the front porch where Stumpy was waiting for him. The moon was near full and its glow lit up the night sky close to daylight. They walked in silence for a while as Stumpy gathered his thoughts.

"Son, I wanted to give you a little advice. I know you ain't asked for any, but I'm a little bit older than you and I figure that my advanced age gives me the right." Stumpy cleared his throat and spit.

"Hey, that landed on my pants," Zeke exclaimed in surprise.

"That's your first lesson: Don't walk too close to a man with a limp."

Zeke laughed. Stumpy's odd sayings never made much sense, but they were funny and always served to lighten the mood. "Stumpy, I didn't steal Midnight. I found him and rode him. But I didn't steal him. Honest."

"I know you didn't, son. And so does the Sheriff. The problem isn't the horse. It's the owner. D'Allesandro's family carries a lot of weight in town, and he has a history with your uncle. D'Allesandro's been trying to find a way to rile him, and this horse problem just happened to come along."

"But it isn't right," Zeke said.

"No, it ain't," Stumpy replied. "But sometimes it doesn't matter who's right or wrong. D'Allesandro has a witness and swears you stole Midnight."

"Does Uncle Jesse think I stole him?" Zeke asked.

"No, he doesn't," Stumpy answered.

"Then why is he making me leave?"

"D'Allesandro told the Sheriff that he was going to press charges against you. But Sheriff Healy talked him out of it. He told D'Allesandro that he'd speak to your Uncle Jesse about

Chapter One

sending you back East if D'Allesandro agreed not to press charges. Your uncle was madder than I've seen him in years. Maybe ever! But he didn't want to see you put in jail with the chance that the local circuit judge might find you guilty."

"Guilty? How could I be guilty? I didn't steal anything! People have to tell the truth in court, right? They make you swear."

"That's true. But sometimes people lie anyway."

"So Uncle Jesse thought D'Allesandro would lie?"

"Not D'Allesandro. He'd never testify unless he had to. Cable Cooper would be the main witness against you and he'll say anything."

"But that isn't fair!" Zeke cried.

"I know, son. I know. Problem is, life ain't fair." Stumpy slapped his bad leg a couple of times. Stumpy was on a first name basis with bad luck and knew that life didn't always work out the way you planned. Stumpy had worked as a cowhand for thirty years and was darn good at it. But a broken leg that hadn't healed right after he'd suffered a freak fall left him with one leg shorter than the other and a pronounced limp.

When Stumpy tried to return to his old job, the injury would ache from long hours spent in the saddle until his eyes filled with tears from the pain. He knew his days of riding the range for a living had come to a close. But Stumpy was a fighter and wasn't ready to give up the life of a cowboy, so he turned to cooking for the men.

He began as a helper to a camp cook. The men teased him at first, but Stumpy caught on quickly. And as his cooking improved, the teasing died off. After all, it's never a good idea to make fun of the person who's preparing your food! He met Zeke's uncle during the good years at the Double R, when Uncle Jesse was looking to hire a cook. Stumpy had stayed on with him ever since.

"Isn't there some way I could stay?" Zeke pleaded. "Maybe if I talk to him."

"Not likely," Stumpy answered. "You said too much already and made things worse when you argued with him. Now, he won't back down. Your Uncle Jesse's a stubborn cuss."

"But he said some things that made me mad! He called me stupid!" Zeke said indignantly.

Stumpy rolled his eyes in exasperation. "That may be, son, but let me ask you something. Have you ever seen a man convince a mule to do something the mule doesn't want to do by yelling at it? Losing your temper and yelling at a mule is a waste of time. You need to figure out a way to make that mule want to do what you want it to. And that temper of yours is only getting in the way. Trust me; it'll only bring you grief."

"I'm not the only one who gets upset around here," Zeke snapped defensively. "Uncle Jesse has a pretty good temper himself. I've seen it plenty of times."

"That's true," Stumpy admitted. "And he's the proof of what I just said."

"Huh?" Zeke said.

Stumpy sighed and shook his head. Young people! One minute they had all the answers and the next minute they needed everything explained to them. Of course if you did that, it would defeat the whole purpose of these talks!

Chapter One

"You just think about what I said. A man has to learn to control his anger. Not the other way around."

Zeke felt a whole lot better discussing things with someone who was on his side for a change. When he and Stumpy returned from their walk, they heard Uncle Jesse and Bull sitting in the kitchen talking quietly. Zeke thought about saying something to Uncle Jesse but changed his mind. It wouldn't do any good, so why bother?

Instead he went around to the rear of the house and climbed back through his bedroom window. He sat down on the edge of the bed and slowly looked around the small room, studying every detail. He wanted to remember things exactly as they were. Then, he undressed and climbed into bed. Tomorrow would be a long day, and he needed to rest.

Zeke stared at the ceiling. He took a deep breath and exhaled slowly. His mind was racing. It was hard to believe that tonight would be his last night at the Double R Ranch. How could this have happened? Everything had changed in just one day! If he could have done it all over again, he would have. But all he could do now was lie there and wait for morning.

He closed his eyes, squeezing them tight. "Please, please let me stay," he whispered. And with that, he fell asleep and began to dream. But his dreams brought no comfort. Zeke saw himself riding across a field of green clover in a state of panic. He was looking back over his shoulder at someone or something that was chasing him, but he couldn't see what it was. Suddenly, he was at the edge of a cliff with no escape. He pulled on the reins of his horse and whirled around to face his pursuer, but all he could see was a huge black shape coming closer and closer until it swallowed him up and he was engulfed in darkness.

Zeke shot up in bed. His heart was racing, and he was covered in sweat. He shook his head and looked around the room to get his bearings. After a few moments he lay back down and tried to sleep. Tomorrow would be a very long day.

Chapter
Two

The Double R was up for business a little past five A.M., and Zeke was exhausted. His strange dreams the night before had kept him tossing and turning, and he'd hardly slept.

Stumpy cooked Zeke's favorite breakfast of steak, flapjacks, pan-fried ham, grits, biscuits and gravy, but the boy wasn't in the mood to eat and just picked at his food. Stumpy was disappointed that Zeke didn't have his usual appetite, but he was even more annoyed at the whole turn of events. So he made a big show of slamming down the plates in front of Bull and Uncle Jesse, which had a chilling effect on the conversation, and everyone ate their breakfast in silence.

Uncle Jesse felt awful on the inside, but refused to let it show. He remained stone-faced throughout the meal, and all that tension made eating difficult for Zeke. No wonder he wasn't hungry!

Rex Riders

When breakfast was over, Zeke packed up his few belongings in a beat-up suitcase his mother had bought for him. It was one of the few things he had left that reminded him of her. He thought about the horse that caused all his problems and wondered how Midnight was doing. This so-called accident may have been Cable Cooper's fault, but Zeke felt terrible about it. If only he'd left Midnight alone, none of this would have happened. He promised himself he would never make the same mistake again.

Stumpy hadn't told Zeke about D'Allesandro's demand that Uncle Jesse pay him back for the stallion or the possibility that his uncle could lose the Double R. The boy had enough trouble on his shoulders, and it was a problem the men would solve together. Besides, Stumpy didn't want Zeke sneaking over to D'Allesandro's ranch to find out the condition of the horse. With Zeke you couldn't be too careful.

The stage was due sometime in the early afternoon, and the trip to town from the Double R took a good hour by buckboard, so getting Zeke on his way would take up the better part of the work day. Uncle Jesse figured that after the boy left, it might be hard to go back to work, so he planned on giving Stumpy the night off and having dinner in town with Bull.

Zeke said goodbye to the sorrel Uncle Jesse had let him ride. Only now, with the prospect of never seeing her again, did Zeke realize how much he loved the horse. It made his actions from the day before all the more regrettable. The three men took their usual places in the front of the buckboard with Zeke in the back with his valise. As they rode away, Zeke waved goodbye to the Double R. It hadn't been easy adjusting to Uncle Jesse's way of

Chapter Two

doing things, but the ranch felt like home just the same. He'd miss the place.

Meanwhile, similar preparations were underway at the Crossed Swords Ranch. D'Allesandro looked forward to seeing Zeke shipped back east. Although he was still fuming over Midnight's injury, the chance to hurt Jesse McCain and seize control of the Double R lessened some of the anger he felt over the harm done to his purebred Andalusian.

Cooper heaped the blame for the horse's injuries on the boy, leaving out his own involvement entirely. But blaming McCain's nephew for stealing the horse had created a new problem: how to deal with Shorty. It wasn't enough to get rid of Zeke. Shorty was a potential witness in the dispute. It was important to "persuade" Shorty not to say anything that would contradict Cooper's account of how Midnight was "stolen." And if Shorty couldn't be persuaded, Cooper would have to find a way to silence him.

D'Allesandro accompanied Cooper toward the back of the barn where Shorty was tied up. A glance at his pocket watch confirmed that D'Allesandro had an hour before he had to leave for town, plenty of time for him and Cooper to have a word with Shorty. But when they arrived at the spot where Cooper hog-tied him, they discovered that Shorty was gone.

"Calhoun! It's got to be," cried Cooper. "That little sneak must have come out here to snoop around after the Sheriff served the warrant. And right under our noses, too."

D'Allesandro glared at Cooper. "Calhoun is the least of our worries Mr. Cooper. Have a couple of the men keep an eye on the

Sheriff and that deputy of his for the next several days. If Shorty tries to speak to either of them, make sure he does not succeed. Do you understand?"

Cooper nodded.

"And Mr. Cooper, please confirm whether it was Calhoun who helped Shorty. It is very important that something like this never happens again."

When the buckboard carrying Zeke and the others from the Double R arrived in town, Uncle Jesse tied the horses to the hitching post in front of the general store. The town of Dos Locos had grown considerably even in the short time since Zeke had arrived. In addition to the general store, there was now a bank, a hotel, a saloon, a dance hall, a blacksmith, a jailhouse, and several small businesses. And that didn't take into account some of the professionals like the town's doctor, who didn't have a storefront shop, but rather practiced their trades out of offices in their homes.

Uncle Jesse's first stop was the bank to withdraw the money he needed to pay for Zeke's passage back east. Bull headed over to the blacksmith to pick up some supplies, while Stumpy and Zeke wandered into *Johnson's* General Store.

The store was stocked with a wide variety of basic goods for farmers, ranchers, and travelers, as well as things of interest to young people and children. Zeke had a sweet tooth and liked to look at the jars of hard candy that were behind the counter. He was especially fond of ribbon candy, and Stumpy had promised to buy him several pieces as a going away present.

Johnson's general store was owned by Henry B. Johnson

Chapter Two

and adjoined *The Longhorn* saloon, which was owned by Henry's identical twin brother, Benjamin H. Johnson. It was so confusing people just called them Mr. H and Mr. B.

Both businesses shared one large building which was also owned by the Johnson brothers. The wall that divided them had two swinging doors that allowed customers to go back and forth between the general store and *The Longhorn*, and many an upstanding family man was able to enjoy a stiff drink at the saloon and never be seen entering or leaving through the front door.

The Longhorn was Mr. B's pride and joy and he was particularly proud of an ornately-etched, Parisian mirror that was hung behind the beautiful oak bar that ran the length of the building. It was a small miracle that the heavy glass mirror arrived in Dos Locos unbroken and Mr. B made it sparkle.

Hanging on the wall above the mirror was an unusual animal horn that was around four and a half feet in length. It fascinated Zeke and he never missed a chance to get a look at it from inside the general store when he was in town. And like a lot of things in Dos Locos, there was a story connected to it.

Many years before, a prospector came to town with a wild story about discovering the skeleton of a gigantic, horned beast in a cave in the mountains. He claimed that the creature's skull was so big he couldn't handle it by himself, so he pried off one of its horns as proof of what he'd found. When he reached Dos Locos he offered to take anybody who was interested back to the cave to help him retrieve the rest of the animal's remains. He even offered to split whatever they could sell the skeleton for, fifty-fifty, but he couldn't get any takers.

Rex Riders

The largest animal skull that any of the townsfolk had ever seen in that part of the country belonged to a bison, and even though it was large, it was fairly easy for a grown man to lift and carry. The idea that this prospector had found an animal skull that was more than six feet long sounded like a lot of non-sense.

When the prospector offered to sell the horn to Mr. B in ex-change for a night's room and board, the saloon keeper laughed. Trying to sell an animal horn in Texas longhorn country was like trying to sell an omelet to a chicken farmer. There was no shortage of steer in Dos locos and Mr. B had no need for a horn! On the other hand, there was a big pile of wood in the back of the saloon that needed splitting.

The prospector took care of the wood, earning himself a bed for the night, but was so disgusted that no one believed his story he departed the next morning leaving the big horn behind.

Mr. B considered throwing the horn away but there was something strange about it, so he hung it over the bar as a con-versation piece next to a mount of a sun-bleached steer's skull and horns. As it turned out, no one had ever seen a horn quite like it, which was great for business! The local cattle ranchers, cowboys and farmers who came to *The Longhorn* for a drink were just as fascinated by the horn as Zeke was, and it inspired quite a few lively debates, occasionally punctuated by a punch or two.

The ranchers were sure the horn hadn't come from a bull or a steer. A bull's horn had an entirely different shape, and a horn from a longhorn steer had a curved tip that was different from the horn above the bar.

Like everyone else, Zeke wondered what kind of animal grew

Chapter Two

such an unusual horn, but no one believed the prospector's story or was interested in trying to find the cave where the man claimed he'd found it. So the mystery remained unsolved until that afternoon.

Several miles away, Micah Fitzsimmons was driving the westbound stagecoach to town at a slow but steady pace. The day was hot, and he was in no particular rush. The stage was due in Dos Locos at midday, but that was plus or minus a couple of hours. A schedule was posted, but there was no telling how long the journey from one town to the next would take over the harsh, unsettled landscape. Basically, whenever it got there, it got there. And in the August heat, it was best not to overwork the horses. Dos Locos was Micah's last stop on this run. He'd see that the horses were watered and fed, and then he'd rest for a few hours before picking up any passengers and heading back east with a fresh team. This was the stage that Zeke was supposed to leave on.

On this particular day the stage had only two passengers: Dante D'Allesandro's younger sister, Maria Del Fuego, and her teenage daughter, Angelina. The two ladies were coming for an extended stay at the Crossed Swords Ranch following the death of Maria's husband, and they were two days ahead of schedule. The trip west had taken them more than a week during the hottest month of the year. Seven days traveling in the sweltering heat with nothing to do but stare out the window at the harsh landscape while trying to stay cool had taken their toll. They were both exhausted from the journey and eager for it to be over.

Rex Riders

Angelina had never been to Dos Locos, but she had heard all about the town and its people from her mother. She was so thrilled about her visit that she asked Micah to tell her when the town was in sight. The last leg of the route had taken them through some rugged territory, but as they emerged from a wooded area, Dos Locos came into view.

"There she is, Miss Del Fuego!" Micah cried, as he leaned over and banged on the side of the stagecoach door.

It was hard to say who was more excited. Angelina stuck her head out the window while her mom did the same on the opposite side.

"It's a lot bigger than I remembered," Maria shouted, excitedly.

"I can't wait to get there!" Angelina replied. "Uncle Dante is going to be . . ." Angelina's voice trailed off, and her expression suddenly changed.

"What's the matter?" Maria asked.

"What's that?" Angelina said, pointing.

"I'm not sure," Maria answered uneasily.

In the distance, a full-grown male triceratops was grazing on scrub brush. It was an old male and bore the scars of territorial battles with other males and assorted predators. Its tail was a foot shorter than it would have been if it hadn't met up with an adult T-rex in its younger days. This old boy was big—more than twenty feet long—and its head was massive. The noise and dust kicked up by the stage had caught its attention, and instinctively the beast began to charge at the trespasser on its territory.

"Mother, it's heading toward us!"

Chapter Two

In the six years that Micah Fitzsimmons had been driving the stagecoach he had faced flash floods, fires, highwaymen, rockslides, broken wheels, sick horses, ornery steer and a bad case of the flu. But one thing he hadn't encountered was an angry dinosaur that mistook his stagecoach for an enemy that had to be gored, or head-butted if goring it wasn't possible. And although Micah Fitzsimmons wasn't afraid of man or beast, when he saw how big the trike was and considered the effect those horns would have on the stagecoach and the horses, he knew they had to move a lot faster.

"Hang on, ladies," he shouted as he put the lash to the horses. The stagecoach lurched forward, throwing Maria back into her seat.

The trike wasn't as fast as the stagecoach and couldn't run at top speed for very long, but the dirt road that the stage was on would take them right alongside the beast if it continued running in the same direction. Taking the stage off the dirt road was possible but it was very dangerous at high speed. If the stage struck a rock or a pothole at the speed they were going, there was a good chance they would break a wheel or an axle and the stage would topple over. If that happened, it was likely everyone would be killed. That left Micah with only one option: he would have to stay on the road and try to outrun the trike.

As the stagecoach hurtled along, the driver tried to frighten the animal off by firing into the air with his revolver, but the loud noise had no effect. The wagon creaked and groaned as it lurched from side to side while Micah struggled to keep it on the twisting road. It was a bruising ride and Angelina and her mother clung to each other. They had no hope of staying seated, because every time the stage hit a bump, they were tossed in the air, and came down hard on the thinly padded seats. Angelina tried to look out the window to see what was happening but the stage hit a rock and sent her flying upward, throwing her head against the top of the window frame, and she cried out in pain.

The trike angled its approach and was now running alongside the stage. Only Micah's heroic driving had kept the horned beast from meeting them head on. But it now threatened to push the stage off the narrow, dusty road. The triceratops was just outside, within inches of Angelina and her mother, who huddled against the far side of the cabin, when it swung its enormous head and hit the side of the stage. The women screamed as the wheels lifted off the ground and the coach teetered for a moment.

Micah pulled on the reins to veer away from the trike, but the beast slammed its body into the rear wheel, knocking it out of balance. Micah felt the difference immediately. The stagecoach began to slow down and pull to one side. This was bad. With a bum wheel he couldn't outrun the trike.

Micah knew he was seconds away from help if he could just keep the wagon upright. He decided to take a chance: if outrunning the trike was no longer an option, he'd try the opposite.

As he entered Main Street, Micah pulled back hard on the reins hoping the triceratops would have too much momentum to stop and would run past them. It might have worked, too, if the rear wheel hadn't chosen that moment to collapse.

The stagecoach began to topple and the trike rammed it again, shattering the front wheel. Micah jumped off as the coach slid down the dirt street on its side, dragging the horses down with it.

Chapter Two

* * *

Zeke was just leaving *Johnson's* general store after watching Stumpy haggle with Mr. H over the price of a sack of dried pinto beans for what seemed like an eternity. When he couldn't take it anymore, he told Stumpy he'd wait for him outside and immediately started rummaging through a bag of candy he had purchased for his trip. He was so intent on getting just the right piece, he didn't notice the commotion that was building in the street until a man running past him nearly knocked the bag out of his hands. He looked up just in time to witness the damaged stagecoach fly past on its side, followed by the trike.

The sounds of the crashing stagecoach and the horses' frightened neighs brought the townspeople of Dos Locos out of their homes and businesses, and they lined the street to see what was happening. The sight that greeted them didn't seem real. A twenty-foot–long monster stood in the middle of the street swinging its massive head and bellowing in rage at a stagecoach, which was lying on its side. The stage may have been out of commission but to that trike, the battle had just begun.

Inside the cabin, Maria and Angelina were too stunned to move. Miraculously, they'd escaped with only minor cuts and bruises.

"Mother, are you alright?" Angelina asked.

"I think so," Maria answered. "What happened?"

"I think that animal—"

Before Angelina could answer, the triceratops slammed into the fallen stagecoach. Its massive horns burst into the cabin, barely missing the two passengers, and showered them with fragments of wood and bits of stuffing from the tufted leather upholstery. Angelina and her mother screamed in unison as the horns passed by their heads. The townspeople gasped when they realized there were still people inside but no one made a move to help. No one except Zeke.

The trike tried to pull its horns out but they were stuck, and the big animal dragged the stagecoach down the street as it struggled to free itself. Inside, Angelina screamed, "Get out!" as she struck at one of the horns with a piece of the seat.

Rocking the cabin from side to side, the triceratops finally succeeded in ripping its horns out with such force the coach skidded several feet in Zeke's direction. The trike roared, then slowly turned and walked away, satisfied it had vanquished its enemy.

Now was the time to act! Zeke ran over to the wrecked coach, leapt on top, and pulled on the handle with all his might to get the door open.

"It's stuck!" Zeke shouted as he struggled. Maria and Angelina pushed as hard as they could from inside the cab, but it was no use.

"The window," Maria shouted. "Go through the window." Angelina popped her head and torso through the opening and began to lift herself out when her skirt got caught on a jagged piece of wood.

"Mother, I can't . . .," she cried.

"I'll get it." As Maria struggled to free the dress, the triceratops turned toward the noise coming from the "creature" it thought it had disposed of and saw the two young people.

"Come on, hurry!" Zeke urged.

"I'm trying," Maria answered desperately, but the fabric was caught fast.

Chapter Two

An ominous growl caused Zeke to look over his shoulder, and he saw the trike preparing to charge the stagecoach again.

"Let me try," he said, reaching down and ripping Angelina's skirt free. "Got it. Let's go!"

Angelina and Zeke jumped off just as the animal struck, sending the vehicle spinning across the street with Maria still trapped inside. Zeke grabbed Angelina's hand to pull her to safety, but instead of running, she turned and faced the coach.

The underside of the cab was caved in from the trike's blows and they could see the large holes torn into its sides where the dinosaur's horns had penetrated. The broken wheel was long gone, and one of the remaining wheels barely hung on. It was obvious to Angelina that the cabin couldn't withstand another blow. Unless her mother got out immediately, she'd be killed.

"Hey!" Angelina screamed at the trike. "Here we are!"

"What are you doing? Stop! Are you crazy?" Zeke cried as he tried pulling her away.

"Get away from me," Angelina said, struggling free. "Go ahead and run!" She stepped closer and kept right on yelling and waving her arms. "You! Over here! Come and get me!"

Zeke was stunned. Here he thought he was saving the girl from this weird animal and now she was running toward it. Then it dawned on him what she was doing. How could he have been so stupid?

"Come on, you ole . . . son of a gun!" Zeke yelled as he stepped beside Angelina. She looked at him in surprise, and he gave her a nod. "Over here!"

The trike stared at the two teens for a moment, and then started walking toward them.

"It's working," Angelina said to Zeke before continuing. "C'mon, you big, dumb beast!"

"What are you waiting for?" Zeke screamed as he picked up a rock and threw it at the creature. Zeke's aim was pretty good and the rock definitely got its attention. The triceratops was trotting now, picking up speed as it ran toward them. Zeke was ready to run but Angelina hadn't moved from where she stood.

"I think we should go now," said Zeke nervously.

"We're over here!" she cried, waving her arms.

"Oh no, we aren't!" Zeke shouted as he finally succeeded in pulling her away. The two teens took off toward *Johnson's* general store with the trike in pursuit.

The folks inside, watching through the big picture window, streamed out the door when they saw Zeke and Angelina running in their direction with the great beast in pursuit.

"I think it worked," Angelina said, grinning.

"Yeah, I'd say it worked," Zeke said, looking over his shoulder at the charging dinosaur. He stopped at the hitching post just long enough to untie Uncle Jesse's horses, which were already straining to escape and gave them a smack on the rump to send them on their way.

"Always take care of the horses first!" he shouted.

They flew through Johnson's open door, and Zeke ran back to close it. "Always close the door; keeps the flies . . ."

The dinosaur crashed through the picture window before Zeke could finish that bit of homespun wisdom and both teens dove to the floor. So much for keeping the flies out.

"Are you okay?" Zeke whispered.

"I think so," Angelina answered.

Chapter Two

"My name's Zeke. What's yours?"

"Angelina."

"Glad to meet you." They shook hands as a couple of hard candies rolled by. Zeke dusted off one and offered it to Angelina. "Peppermint?"

While the triceratops rampaged through Johnson's, Uncle Jesse and Bull ran over to the battered stagecoach and helped Maria out of the wreckage.

"My daughter! Where is my daughter? Is she alright?"

"Don't worry ma'am, she's with Zeke," Bull replied.

"Zeke?" Uncle Jesse shouted in surprise. "How'd she end up with Zeke?"

"He pulled her out; probably saved her life," Bull said. "I saw it myself as I was coming back from the blacksmith's. Then Zeke and the girl managed to keep that critter from hitting the stage again. They saved this lady's life."

"A couple of brave kids," added a bystander who had come to lend a hand.

Uncle Jesse was incredulous. "Are we talking about the same Zeke?"

"Is something wrong? Would somebody please tell me who Zeke is?" Maria asked.

"Everything's fine, ma'am," Uncle Jesse replied. "It just seems my nephew can't stay out of trouble. Did anybody see where he and the girl went?"

"*Johnson's*," Bull said, pointing to what was left of the store's façade. "Critter went in after them. And by the sound of it, I'd say he's still looking for them."

"Oh my God," Maria cried when she saw the wreckage and heard the sounds of destruction coming from inside. "Someone, please do something!"

"Let's go, Bull." And the two men took off.

Inside the store, the triceratops was raging out of control. A ladies corset and a pair of red long johns were strung across the beast's horns and hung down in front of its eyes making it difficult for the animal to see. But that didn't mean Zeke and Angelina were out of danger. The trike was determined to get the clothes off and every time it swung its massive, frilled head, something else crashed to the floor. And that wasn't all. While the wooden floor of *Johnson's* was sturdy, it wasn't built to support the weight of an animal that big. As the trike stomped around the room, the floor boards buckled, threatening to give way.

Zeke realized time was running out. He motioned to Angelina to stay where she was and started crawling on his stomach toward the entrance. If he could just get there, maybe he could lure the triceratops back outside and save her.

Zeke was halfway across the floor when he noticed something red, white and wavy lying off to the side. He checked his pockets and realized that the brand new piece of ribbon candy Stumpy bought him had fallen out when he dove to the floor. And that ticked him off. Luckily, it was only a couple of feet away.

He almost had a hand on it when the triceratops suddenly backed up over him, nearly squashing his arm. Zeke curled up into a ball on his back and stared at the animal's huge belly and heaving chest. *It doesn't know I'm here,* he thought.

Zeke flipped over onto all fours and noted the position of each

Chapter Two

of the creature's massive feet. It was a tricky situation. If Zeke was going to get out alive, his timing would have to be just right. Every time that trike took a step, Zeke was right there with him, crawling underneath. The teen was concentrating so hard, he didn't realize the bag of candy Stumpy bought him had also fallen on the floor and was lying in front of his left knee.

CRUNCH!

The dinosaur suddenly stopped in its tracks and listened. Zeke froze. He looked down at a broken container of ladies bath powder. A cloud of dust swirled in the air and Zeke took a sniff. The nice, fresh smell reminded him of his mother, but the darn stuff tickled his nose and he found himself fighting an uncontrollable urge to sneeze. Angelina pantomimed holding her nose closed with two fingers but it was too late. A sneeze was on its way, and Zeke couldn't stop it.

Angelina was frantic. She grabbed hold of a fallen masonry jar and threw it as hard as she could to the far corner of the store just as Zeke let loose with a tremendous *"Achoo!"* Her timing was perfect. The dinosaur couldn't hear Zeke's sneeze over the sound of the breaking jar and lumbered off to investigate the crash.

Zeke grabbed the striped candy, held it up and winked. Angelina rolled her eyes and shook her head. All that for a piece of candy! That boy needed a talking to.

Zeke knew that running away from an animal was often the worst thing you could do, because some animals—like bears—instinctively gave chase. And sometimes if you played dead, an animal would leave you alone and go away. But the store was too small for a full grown trike and if that beast stepped on one of them while they were playing dead, they'd actually *be* dead.

That left them with only one option.

Are you ready to run? Zeke mouthed.

Angelina nodded.

Zeke held up three fingers, dropping each in sequence as he mouthed the countdown. *One . . . two . . . three!*

Zeke leapt to his feet and grabbed Angelina's hand, and the teens took off for the swinging doors that led to the saloon. As they dodged the broken shelves and vaulted over the racks of work clothes and bolts of fabric lying on the floor, it occurred to Zeke that this was turning out to be a pretty good day, after all. He was holding hands with a gutsy girl who was really pretty, and they were running for their lives from a giant monster. If these were his last moments in Dos Locos, at least they were going to be memorable!

As soon as the trike heard them running, it turned around and charged in the direction of the sound.

"How old are you?" Zeke asked breathlessly as he and Angelina zigzagged around the debris.

"Fourteen," Angelina answered. "You?"

"Fifteen," Zeke responded, exaggerating slightly by moving his birthday up a couple of months.

"Would you like to go riding some time?"

"Sure," Zeke replied. "Only I'm supposed to go back east today."

"Oh, that's too bad," Angelina said, trying not to sound disappointed.

Sheriff Healy and Deputy Burton joined Uncle Jesse and Bull as they ran toward the gaping hole in the front of *Johnson's*. The men could see a large, moving shadow and heard the sound of things breaking.

"How in the heck did a buffalo get inside the general store?" Sheriff Healy asked.

"That's no buffalo," Uncle Jesse replied.

"Then what is it?" the Sheriff asked.

A loud crash was followed by a thunderous bellow that shook the saloon's picture window.

"Darned if I know," Uncle Jesse said.

"Coming through," Zeke shouted as he and Angelina dashed through the saloon's swinging doors and ran past Mr. B toward the entrance to the saloon that fronted Main Street.

The trike burst through the wall and would have skewered Mr. B if a couple of the regulars hadn't tackled him. The piano was tossed into the air and landed on top of the bar before it crashed into Mr. B's prized mirror. Tables, chairs and glasses flew in every direction as the dinosaur continued its rampage. And when it reached the other side of the room, it crashed through the wall and continued straight through into the lobby of the adjoining boarding house.

Guns drawn, Uncle Jesse and the boys stepped inside *Johnson's* and picked their way through the debris to the gaping hole in the wall that adjoined *The Longhorn*. A cloud of dust greeted them when they entered. As it settled, the scene that emerged looked like Armageddon.

Mr. B's prize oak bar was ripped in two, and the fancy Parisian mirror and every bottle and shelf that fronted it were destroyed.

Rex Riders

Nothing could have survived this, Uncle Jesse thought as he and the other men made their way through the devastation.

The sound of coughing from the far end of the bar proved him wrong. Slowly the figures of the two customers who saved Mr. B and now helped him to his feet came into view.

"We couldn't abide the thought of a barkeeper as fine as you ending up on one of those horns," the first man said.

"Hope you don't mind us knocking you over," the other added.

"You look like you need a drink," the first suggested.

From where the men were standing, you could see all the way through to the boarding house, but the trike was nowhere to be seen.

"It must have crashed out onto the street through the front of the boarding house," Uncle Jesse said.

"Good grief," the Sheriff said.

Uncle Jesse turned to Bull. "Who's got a hunting rifle?"

"Johnson's got some," Mr. B volunteered.

"Sheriff, get Doc and see who needs help. Somebody has to stop that thing or it'll destroy the whole town. Bull, let's find a rifle."

Sheriff Healy looked at Jesse "You're a good man, McCain. Good luck."

As Sheriff Healy and Deputy Burton ran to find the town doctor, Bull and Uncle Jesse foraged through the wreckage of the general store looking for a hunting rifle and some ammunition. Most of the guns were damaged, but Bull managed to find a good one and handed it to Uncle Jesse with a box of cartridges.

Chapter Two

"I'm coming too," Bull said.

"No," Uncle Jesse said. "Find Zeke and make sure Stumpy's okay. He can't run too well with that bum leg of his. And see if you can find our horses. It's a long walk back to the Double R."

The triceratops was standing in front of the hotel. It seemed confused. Uncle Jesse stepped into the street and fired a shot in the air to get its attention. The trike looked at him for a second before shaking its head and bellowing. Uncle Jesse stood his ground, aimed his rifle and waited. The creature roared again, lowered its horns and charged. Uncle Jesse calmly waited for the animal to get within range. Finally, he slowly squeezed the trigger.

Nothing.

"Okay. That's not good," Uncle Jesse said. Beads of sweat appeared on his face and neck, and he tried again . . . and again. Each time the hammer struck the shell but nothing happened.

Uncle Jesse threw the rifle aside and in one smooth motion lifted his revolver out of its holster and squeezed off six shots, but the beast kept coming. He clenched his jaw and winced, expecting to wind up on the end of one of those horns, when the triceratops collapsed inches from his boots and expired. *That was close,* Uncle Jesse thought as he closed his eyes and exhaled.

It had all happened so quickly. In a matter of minutes, a single animal had decimated a chunk of the town. The townspeople stepped out from their hiding places and looked around. Some gathered about the body of the trike while others walked up and down the street in shock surveying the devastation.

D'Allesandro's business with Shorty back at the Crossed

Rex Riders

Swords had delayed his trip into town, and he arrived just in time to witness the showdown between Uncle Jesse and the prehistoric beast. He walked over to the body of the fallen dinosaur, joining a crowd of people who were pushing and shoving each other to get a better look and touch the body.

D'Allesandro walked around the animal several times and took in the commotion that was swirling around him. The powerful effect the dead animal exerted over the townsfolk was not lost on the savvy businessman. And all the while, his mind churned with possibilities.

Here was a creature of unimaginable power, the likes of which no one had ever seen before. What was it? Where did it come from? And how could it be used to his advantage? D'Allesandro needed time to consider all of the ways he could capitalize on this new opportunity, and to do that, he'd have to gain control of the carcass.

He stepped away from the triceratops and clapped his hands several times to quiet the crowd.

"May I have your attention, please?" D'Allesandro said. "I have an announcement to make. My friends, my grandfather and my great uncle founded this town almost sixty years ago. To me, Dos Locos is more than my home. My family's roots are deep here. What has happened today is not the end of Dos Locos. You have my word that the D'Allesandro family will do whatever is needed to rebuild. If it is men, my family will provide them. If it is money, my family will lend it.

"For now, the first step is to remove the remains of the beast that has caused so much harm to our buildings and businesses. I promise you that I will dispose of this brute. I do this for you."

Chapter Two

There was a smattering of applause, and murmurs of approval rippled through the small crowd. Uncle Jesse had wandered off to be by himself after the animal collapsed. It was such a close call he needed a moment to compose himself. But seeing and hearing D'Allesandro's speech ended his moment of contemplation. He walked to the front of the crowd and looked D'Allesandro in the eye.

"That critter belongs to me," Uncle Jesse said matter-of-factly. "He ain't yours to take."

"What do you mean?" D'Allesandro said in surprise.

"I killed him, so he's mine, plain and simple."

"He's right," Sheriff Healy said as he stepped through the crowd and stood alongside Uncle Jesse. "No different than if he'd shot a bear or a coyote. It's his to claim unless he says otherwise. Now, if you want to buy it from him, maybe he'll sell it to you."

D'Allesandro was stunned. Uncle Jesse and Sheriff Healy were right, of course. How could he have been so stupid? D'Allesandro could not claim ownership of an animal that another man shot unless the beast belonged to D'Allesandro or it was shot on his land. McCain shot the creature on a public street, so the trike belonged to him. This was one of the most fundamental laws of the the old west.

"Then perhaps we can speak in private, Mr. McCain," D'Allesandro said, smiling broadly.

"You want to make me an offer, you can make it here and now," Uncle Jesse said.

"Very well. I will pay you a hundred dollars and remove the beast from the street at my expense with no further bother to you."

Uncle Jesse frowned. "Mr. H, how much do you reckon your inventory is worth?"

"I don't know offhand," Henry Johnson replied. "I suppose it might be worth around two thousand."

"And what about *The Longhorn*?" Uncle Jesse asked.

"I'd say another thousand," Ben Johnson answered.

Then, addressing the crowd, Uncle Jesse furthered, "Anybody else?"

"You don't expect me to pay these merchants for their losses, do you?" D'Allesandro asked, incredulously.

"No, I don't," Uncle Jesse replied. "I expect you to pay me what this dead critter's worth, which I figure is whatever it's going to cost these folks to rebuild. And to show my good faith, you can keep all of the goods that are replaced, regardless of whether they're damaged. Anybody have a problem with that?" The brothers Johnson and the other merchants shook their heads.

"One more thing," Uncle Jesse said to D'Allesandro, his eyes narrowing. "You agree to cancel the debt for Midnight, and I get the horse or there's no deal. You have no need for a lame stallion. You said so yourself. I'll take the burden off your hands."

D'Allesandro laughed. "And if I say no to your offer, how will you dispose of the brute? You haven't a proper crew at the Double R, and you can't do it with the two ranch hands you do have. In this heat, the beast will begin to rot in a few hours, and the smell will be unbearable. The streets will be crawling with wolves and coyotes once the sun sets. I suggest you accept my offer or I'll withdraw it, and this town will suffer because of your greed." D'Allesandro gave Uncle Jesse a smug smile and

Chapter Two

looked back at the crowd for their support.

Mr B was the first person to step forward. "I'll help you get rid of it, Mr. McCain," he volunteered.

"I will too," Mr. H added. "Anybody else?"

Hands rose in the air, and dozens of townsfolk who were willing to lend a hand stepped forward. D'Allesandro had underestimated the people's willingness to come together as a community and help one another.

"My offer stands. Take it or leave it," Uncle Jesse said as he folded his arms across his chest.

All eyes were glued on D'Allesandro, and the crowd grew silent. It was rare for anyone to get the best of the powerful businessman, but Uncle Jesse's strategy seemed to be working. Of course, it all depended upon how badly D'Allesandro wanted the remains. The fact that no one understood why he wanted them so badly didn't matter. All the townspeople knew for sure was that he did.

The crowd was so focused on what D'Allesandro's response would be that no one noticed Shorty Stevens quietly slipping through the crowd toward the Sheriff.

D'Allesandro took a breath. "Done."

Everyone cheered as Sheriff Healy walked over to D'Allesandro and put his hand on his shoulder.

"There's one more piece of business that needs to be dealt with Mr. D'Allesandro," he said firmly. "I know you had some trouble at your ranch yesterday, and one of your men accused Zeke Calhoun of stealing your horse, Midnight. Shorty, would you step forward."

As Shorty emerged from the crowd holding his old civil war

hat in his hands, D'Allesandro's eyes narrowed and bore a hole into Shorty's chest.

"Do you have something to say?" the Sheriff asked.

Shorty hesitated and stared at the ground, afraid to look D'Allesandro in the eye. "Yeah. Calhoun didn't steal Midnight. The horse ran off when I stepped on a rattlesnake and lost my balance. It was my fault Midnight got loose."

D'Allesandro was caught and knew it. First McCain, and now a good-for-nothing hired lackey had outmaneuvered him! He had no alternative other than to force a smile and run with it.

"Then I see there was no basis for an arrest warrant. The facts are not as they were represented to me. Justice demands that the warrant naming Master Calhoun be dismissed!" D'Allesandro said, with fake magnanimity.

"I thought you'd see it that way," Sheriff Healy replied coolly. "McCain, there's no need for young Zeke to go back east unless you still want to send him."

Now it was Uncle Jesse's turn to be surprised. He looked at the Sheriff and broke out into a big smile. "No, I reckon we'll let him stay awhile."

From the back of the crowd Stumpy and Bull let out a big cheer as they made their way to Uncle Jesse's side. "Either of you know where the boy is?" Uncle Jesse asked.

"Last I saw, he was with the daughter of that woman who we helped out of the stage," said Bull.

As the crowd dispersed, D'Allesandro turned to Uncle Jesse. "Mr. McCain, I will have my representative contact you about the payment we agreed to and arrange for delivery of Midnight. I assume that is acceptable."

Chapter Two

"Yup." McCain nodded as he shook D'Allesandro's hand. "I'm glad we could come to a fair arrangement."

"Yes, I'm pleased as well," D'Allesandro said. "I would like to continue this discussion, but for now, I must say adios."

Before D'Allesandro could leave, however, his sister Maria rushed up and kissed him on the cheek. "My dear brother, I am so glad to see you," she gushed.

"Maria, what are you doing here?" D'Allesandro asked, confused.

"I was on the stagecoach that was attacked by the beast."

"My God, I had no idea! Are you alright?"

"Yes, I'm fine, Dante," Maria reassured. "These men came to my rescue. And this young man rescued Angelina from the horrible beast," Maria continued as she ushered Zeke and Angelina in front of D'Allesandro.

There was an uncomfortable silence as the men regarded one another with astonishment. Neither Maria nor Angelina knew what to make of their bewildered expressions.

"I didn't have a chance to thank you for helping me, Mr. . . .?" Maria began.

"McCain, ma'am. Jesse McCain," Uncle Jesse said as if someone had just hit him over the head.

"And I want to thank your nephew, Zeke, for saving my daughter," Maria added, nodding in the boy's direction. "He is a fine young man. I am sure you must be very proud of him."

"Mother, would it be all right if Zeke and I went riding some time," Angelina asked.

"Of course," Maria said. "Provided it's all right with you, Mr. McCain."

"Um, yes ma'am, of course. No problem. Well, um, we better be going," Uncle Jesse stammered.

Uncle Jesse backed up and almost fell over Bull. "We'll be seeing you D'Allesandro. I mean, Mr. D'Allesandro."

"Yes, I'll—I mean—*we'll* be seeing you, Mr. McCain," D'Allesandro replied as Maria and Angelina excitedly waved goodbye.

There was stunned silence as Uncle Jesse, Zeke, Bull and Stumpy walked away from the D'Allesandros.

"Uncle Jesse, I didn't know she was a D'Allesandro," Zeke said. "If I had . . ."

Before he could continue, Uncle Jesse interrupted. "I heard what you did, Zeke. And I'm proud of you. It doesn't matter if it's a D'Allesandro or not. If a neighbor's in trouble, you help 'em. Anybody know what happened to my buckboard and horses?"

"I unhitched them before that critter tore into the general store," Zeke replied hesitantly.

Uncle Jesse nodded gravely before his smile returned. "Now that's using your head," he said. "You go find them, Zeke, and I'll put this money back in the bank. You won't be needing fare for any trips east. I'd like to thank Shorty, too, for coming forward. I wonder where he went to."

Zeke took off down the street and was so happily preoccupied that he didn't notice Cable Cooper hiding in the shadows of an alleyway he was passing.

"Calhoun," Cooper called.

"What?" Zeke stopped for a second, startled to hear his name. Cooper grabbed Zeke's arm and jerked him into the alley.

Chapter Two

Then, he shoved the boy against the side of the building and stood directly in his face.

"You got away with it this time Calhoun, but that won't happen again. I'll make sure of it."

"Let me go! I didn't do anything," Zeke shouted, trying to get away. But Cooper pushed him back.

"I don't know how you got into the barn and cut Shorty free, but I know it was you that done it," Cooper said.

"Cut Shorty free? I don't know what you're talking about. Let me go," Zeke cried as he struggled to free himself from Cooper's powerful grip.

"You remember what I said Calhoun. Shorty ain't getting away with it and neither are you." With that, Cooper released Zeke and disappeared into the shadows.

"Jerk," Zeke muttered under his breath. *What is with that guy?* he thought. *What did I ever do to him?*

In the weeks after the triceratops tore up the town, August gave way to September, things settled down, and the folks in Dos Locos resumed their routines. Hitching posts were mended, buildings were restored and bumps and bruises healed. But things were far from normal. It was a miracle that no one was hurt in the trike's rampage, and people found themselves looking over their shoulders and jumping at any unfamiliar sound.

D'Allesandro was good to his word and delivered a check for the agreed amount to Uncle Jesse, who distributed the money to the local merchants. In return, they turned over their inventory to D'Allesandro.

It took a team of horses and plenty of men to move the

carcass onto a wagon that D'Allesandro had specially built for that job. The challenge was constructing a wagon that was light enough to be pulled by a team of horses when loaded with the body, yet strong enough to support its weight. It was a tribute to D'Allesandro's ambition and ingenuity that he succeeded.

It seemed strange to the practical-minded people of Dos Locos that someone would go to the trouble of building such a massive wagon for only one job, but then buying the remains of the animal seemed pretty strange in and of itself. No one knew exactly why D'Allesandro wanted the carcass so badly, and neither he nor the trike were talking, so it remained a mystery.

Shorty was never seen or heard from again, and people assumed he'd left town after telling the Sheriff what happened to Midnight.

Some odd things happened, too.

The horn that was hanging over the bar in *The Longhorn* disappeared one day. Mr. B said someone bought it, and he refused to talk about it.

Strangers started coming into town fairly regularly. They'd arrive, ask for directions, and head off to the Crossed Swords. The odd part was that no one ever saw them return. It seemed like they came to town and then fell off the face of the Earth. The few people who were nosy enough to ask D'Allesandro where they went, received the same well-rehearsed answer: "They are all busy working on my behalf. Their exact location is unimportant." And that was as much as he would say.

Chapter
Three

I *can't wait to get out of here,* thought Zeke as he stared out the window of the one-room schoolhouse. It was a mild spring day, and Zeke was planning to go for a ride with Stumpy after school. It was hard to believe that six months had passed since the incident with the triceratops. Angelina's invitation to go riding never materialized for reasons outside their control, but Zeke stayed on the lookout for her whenever he was in town.

On one of the few occasions their paths did cross briefly outside of school, Zeke was too nervous to speak to Angelina and resorted to stuffing his hands in his pockets and trying to appear cool and aloof.

Angelina wanted to speak to Zeke, but was perplexed by his strange behavior, so she said nothing. This only heightened Zeke's anxiety about speaking to her, starting a whole vicious cycle.

Rex Riders

Angelina's mother made her start school in September, but as far as Zeke was concerned it was a complete waste of time. Angelina was so far ahead of the other students there wasn't much reason for her to bother going. Sometimes it seemed like the girl knew as much as the teacher, even though Angelina was modest and never showed off or did anything to make the other students feel uncomfortable.

When class was finally dismissed Zeke bolted for the door.

"Hey, Zeke," Angelina shouted. "Wait a second."

Zeke looked down at his boots as he waited for Angelina to catch up to him.

"I heard there's a square dance next week. Are you going?"

"I might," Zeke said shyly.

"Well, I'm going," Angelina said. "Maybe I'll see you there."

"Okay," Zeke said.

"Tell your Uncle to go, too," she added. "I think my mom's going."

Zeke watched her walk away. He wasn't really sure about square-dancing, but it sounded like fun. He was also unsure whether Uncle Jesse square-danced or not. It didn't seem like the kind of thing he'd be interested in. That would be a good thing to ask Stumpy about.

When Zeke got back to the Double R, he tossed his books on the bed and joined Stumpy for an afternoon ride on the sorrel. Zeke didn't bother asking Uncle Jesse if he could ride Midnight. Though the Andalusian was Uncles Jesse's horse now, it was definitely off limits.

D'Allesandro's claim that the big stallion was lame turned

Chapter Three

out to be a lot of hokum, and Midnight made a complete recovery from his injuries. Uncle Jesse rode him a lot more than D'Allesandro ever did, and Midnight proved to be the finest horse Uncle Jesse ever owned, just like Zeke had said. Of course, Zeke didn't dare remind Uncle Jesse that he'd told him so.

Stumpy told Zeke to stow his rain gear in his saddlebag because a storm was coming, but Zeke argued that it was nice out, and he didn't need it. The ache in Stump's bad leg told him differently and he insisted. Sure enough, they were only out for about an hour when clouds started rolling in and they heard the distant sound of thunder. They were standing atop a ridge overlooking Small's Stream and were about to turn back home when Zeke thought he saw something in the dry riverbed far below.

"Hey Stumpy, do you have your glass with you?" Zeke said. "Take a look down there. What is that?"

Stumpy took a small spyglass out of his bag and opened it up to its full length. "Looks like a pack of wolves."

"I know that!" Zeke declared. "What's that other animal; the one standing over the man?"

"Hmm . . . I'm not sure," Stumpy replied. "My eyes ain't that good. Let's go down and take a look."

Stumpy and Zeke left the horses behind and hid behind a group of large rocks no more than a few dozen feet from the action. They saw what appeared to be a man lying face down on the ground with a pack of hungry gray wolves circling him. These were the days when the gray wolf was still plentiful in Texas. The wolves flourished, preying on the cattle the ranchers introduced into the animals' environment. Some of them were six feet long and weighed as much as 130 pounds. Ranchers hated the beasts because they threatened their livelihoods.

What made this scene different was the strange looking creature that stood between the body and the wolves. It was about seventeen feet long from nose to tail and stood on two powerful legs. Its long, thick neck supported a large head, which was dominated by massive jaws stuffed with dagger-like teeth. Its arms were spindly and grossly underdeveloped in relation to its body. Stumpy and Zeke had no idea they were looking at a juvenile Tyrannosaurus rex.

Even though the T-rex was a dangerous predator, the wolves were unfamiliar with it, so they were willing to challenge the dinosaur. The dead body of one wolf already lay nearby. As they awaited an opening, the six remaining wolves circled the rex.

The wolves focused their attack on the rear legs and tail of the dinosaur, a strategy that worked well with cattle and other creatures the wolves preyed on like bison and elk. With herd animals, a pack would methodically separate the young, weak or sick from the group, then pursue them until they tired. The wolves would attack from the rear and drag their target to the ground before devouring it.

The largest member of the hunting pack, the lead wolf, tried to distract the T-rex by racing back and forth in front of it. At the same time, five smaller wolves darted in and out from behind, trying to grab hold of the dinosaur's legs without being hit by its massive tail.

Then it happened!

One of the smaller wolves managed to latch on to an ankle. But before the wolf's companions could seize the advantage, the

Chapter Three

T-rex opened its jaws wider than Zeke thought possible and clamped them around the animal's torso. The wolf yelped in pain and the dinosaur jerked it off the ground and swung it violently from side to side, killing it almost instantly.

As two more wolves rushed in, the T-rex flung the dead wolf aside and attacked them both in a blur of snapping jaws. The wolves were unprepared for the ferocity of the strange creature's attack and turned tail and fled with the rest of the pack trailing close behind.

Stumpy and Zeke watched unmoving as the T-rex turned its attention away from its vanquished foes to the figure on the ground. Then the dinosaur paused and sniffed the air. Slowly, it turned its head toward the rocks where Stumpy and Zeke were hiding. Its eyes narrowed.

"You don't suppose it knows we're here," Zeke whispered.

Before Stumpy could answer, the T-rex let loose with an angry roar and charged. Stumpy jumped back in surprise and would have fallen over if Zeke hadn't caught him. They ran back up the hill but stopped about midway when they realized the creature was not following them.

"I never saw anything like that," Zeke said. "What is it?"

"I don't know," Stumpy gasped, trying to catch his breath. "That big critter killed that poor fella and now it's protecting its dinner. But I'm gonna make sure it doesn't kill again." Stumpy removed the hunting rifle slung on his back and raised it to his shoulder. But Zeke grabbed the gun barrel and pointed it toward the ground.

"What did you do that for?" Stumpy yelled. "That thing's a killer."

Rex Riders

"That critter didn't kill the man, Stumpy. I don't see any bite marks on him, and there isn't any blood. You saw what its teeth can do. I think it's trying to protect him. And another thing—I'm pretty sure I saw some kind of bridle in its mouth . . . and reins."

"Son, that's crazy. That wasn't a bridle. It was a lasso. The man tried to rope the critter, and it attacked him."

"I bet you're wrong," Zeke declared. "And I'll prove it."

The boy found himself a good size stick; then cautiously crept toward the body of one of the dead wolves, ready to take off if the creature started toward him.

"Zeke, get back here!"

"Don't worry. I know what I'm doing. I'm just going to take a quick look. I'll be right back, I promise."

Stumpy shook his head and muttered a few choice words under his breath as he again raised his rifle. He knew something like this was going to happen! That boy never listened.

Zeke turned and saw Stumpy aiming his gun. "Don't shoot unless I say so, okay? Nothing's going to happen."

"You just go and take a look. I'll take care of the shooting."

Flies swarmed around the dead wolf as Zeke poked it with the stick. He wanted to see what kind of damage that strange animal was capable of. The wolf's neck and upper chest were crushed and matted with blood where the rex had grabbed it. That took tremendous biting strength!

"I'm going to see if that guy's still alive," Zeke shouted, taking several small steps toward the unconscious figure. He was about eight feet away now and had a better view of the body and the dinosaur. Yes, that was a bridle and those were reins. *I knew it*, Zeke thought. That meant it could be ridden!

Chapter Three

"You're close enough. Stop right there."

Zeke looked at the fearsome creature and held the branch out in front of him like it was a spear. "You stay back now." But this only served to anger the beast further, and it drew to its full height, releasing a thunderous roar.

Zeke was terrified. He stared at the T-rex and it stared back. Was it possible the animal thought that Zeke was going to hurt the man on the ground with the stick? Maybe it was defending him. He decided to take a chance. It was crazy but he threw the stick aside.

Stumpy groaned. What was that boy doing?!

Then Zeke slowly inched his way closer until he was right next to the rider.

"He's been shot," he shouted to Stumpy.

"Dead?"

"I can't tell. Come here and help me turn him over."

Stumpy thought to himself that he never would have done any of this if he'd been alone. He brandished his rifle at the T-rex as he hobbled to Zeke. "You better not move or I'll shoot ya'," he told the animal.

The rex snarled at him.

"Put that down and give me a hand. You're just making it mad," Zeke said as he tried to turn the man over.

Stumpy reluctantly laid his gun on the ground and grabbed hold. But the rider was too heavy for them to lift. They had barely raised one of the fallen man's shoulders, when the T-rex lowered its head between them and wedged its snout in the gap between the rider and the ground. With a snap of its neck it flipped him onto his back.

"Well, I'll be danged," Stumpy said.

Zeke moved closer to get a better look at the rider's face and couldn't believe what he saw. "Whoa!" The boy was so startled he jumped back, tripped over a rock and wound up on his butt.

"Ah, he ain't so bad," Stumpy said. "I saw a cowboy eating a taco down in Mexico who had half his face eaten off by red ants."

"Ew, that's disgusting!" Zeke said from a safe distance.

"There's nothing wrong with tacos, son," Stumpy reproached.

"I wasn't talking about the taco and you know it."

The funny thing about people is that no matter how gross something may seem at first, after the initial shock wears off, they want to get a better look, and Zeke was no exception. The boy got back up and rejoined Stumpy.

The rider was more than eight feet tall. His skin was a tan color—more like the color of exposed rock than human flesh—with a texture similar to a horned toad's, full of bumps and spikes.

The top of his head had numerous lumps that came to blunt points. A bony ridge spanned his brow, and his nostrils were large and flat against his face. He had a massive jaw with two small horns on the end of his chin that curved under like a horseshoe. His neck was so compact, it appeared as if his head sprouted from his upper chest between his wide, square shoulders, all of which were covered in a hard shell. Around what there was of a neck was a strip of leather threaded through a large white bone in the shape of a knife blade. Zeke noticed it was hollow and had a serrated edge.

The rider's upper arms were long and muscular and ended in hands sporting three huge fingers, each tipped with a thick, blunt nail. Running along the outside of the arms and shoulders were

Chapter Three

more rigid plates, and a row of short spikes protruded from each forearm. On one wrist he wore a metal bracelet.

Stumpy tapped on a plate covering one of the creature's shoulders. It was hard like the shell of a turtle.

The rider wore leather chaps adorned with strange designs that were held up by a belt, from which hung an empty leather pouch. His hips were wide and his legs were bowed. He had one large, clawed toe on each corner of his bare feet and his ankles sat in the middle of his feet, instead of the ends.

"That ain't no man," Stumpy said finally.

"What do you reckon we ought to do with him?" Zeke asked.

Stumpy stroked his chin as he considered the possibilities.

"If we leave him here, he'll most likely die when the stream floods from the rains. I'd say we've got no choice. We have to bring him back with us."

"Hot dog!" Zeke shouted. "But how do we get him out? He's too heavy to lift, and there's no time to get a wagon in here before it starts to rain."

Stumpy eyed the T-rex. For some reason the animal had calmed down. Though it watched closely as Stumpy and Zeke examined the rider, it was no longer behaving in a menacing manner.

"Don't need one. That critter carried him in here, and it'll carry him out. All we have to do is get his rider on top. Besides, if that thing can be ridden, it must have been broke by this fella. Toss me my rope and see if you can get the varmint to sidle on next to him. Just make sure it doesn't bite your head off. Not that it would make any difference," Stumpy teased.

While Stumpy struggled to tie one end of the rope around the creature's shoulders, Zeke cautiously approached the T-rex. The animal shook its head and snorted, but didn't move. Zeke slowly reached out and took the reins. Then he gave them a gentle tug. To his surprise, the dinosaur obediently moved toward him.

"There you go," Zeke said, soothingly as he squatted down to look at the rex's ankle. It was bleeding. Zeke removed his neckerchief and tied it around the wound. "You come along now," he said, leading the animal to the side of its rider.

A few minutes later, Zeke had Stumpy's rope in place just as the old ranch hand returned with the horses in tow.

"Now, hold him still," Stumpy ordered. "Toss me the free end of the rope and I'll tie it on to my saddle. We'll use my horse to hoist him up."

"That ought to work," Zeke agreed.

"Keep him steady," Stumpy said, gesturing toward the rex. He nudged the horse forward, and the rider slowly rose off the ground.

While Stumpy secured the body to the back of the T-rex, Zeke returned to the area where they'd found the rider to take a final look around. He had a hunch that whatever had been in the rider's leather pouch fell out when he toppled off his ride, so it was probably somewhere nearby. There was a flash of lightning, and Zeke thought he saw something shiny out of the corner of his eye in a cluster of low-lying shrubs.

The boy trotted over and pulled out a strange metal object. It was about fourteen inches long and had a heavy, solid feel to it, like an iron bar. In the center were a series of indentations designed for gripping, provided you had a hand as big as a baseball glove, and a row of buttons down the side. Zeke pressed

Chapter Three

them, but nothing happened. He held the object up to his ear and shook it. Nothing.

"Come on," Stumpy yelled. "We've got to move before the rain gets here."

"I'll be right there," Zeke called. He ran back to his horse and stashed the strange object into his saddle bag. This was something he figured he'd keep to himself for a while.

While Zeke and the old cook prepared to leave, the T-rex wandered over to the body of one of the dead wolves and sniffed the carcass. Then it placed a clawed foot on the dead animal, tore off a big chunk and swallowed it. Three bites later, the body was gone. It was a chilling sight. Neither Stumpy nor Zeke had ever seen a creature that could tear apart an animal the size of a wolf and devour it like that!

When the T-rex finished, it walked over to the body of the second wolf, picked the limp carcass up in its jaws and carried it back to where Zeke and Stumpy were standing.

The T-rex dropped the carcass at their feet and nudged it toward them with its snout. It was giving them the second wolf! Zeke looked up at Stumpy.

"Well, I guess it eats wolf," Zeke said weakly. "Too bad we don't have any back at the ranch."

"Yeah, too bad," Stumpy replied dryly. "I think I'll keep my rifle handy just in case it eats something besides wolf."

Less than a half mile from the spot where Stumpy and Zeke discovered the T-rex and its rider, Cable Cooper led a group of three men on horseback. Thom Jackson crouched down on the ground to study a series of large three-toed tracks. "They lead this way," he said, pointing up a steep hill.

"Come on," Cable snarled. "We've got to find him before the rains start or we'll lose the trail."

"This is a waste of time," Tall Bill said. "He's dead."

"Then how come we ain't seen any blood?" Cable growled.

"But we all couldn't have missed him. Not at that range," One-Eyed Jack insisted. "He's dead."

"I don't care if he is dead," Cooper growled. "He's got something Mr. D'Allesandro wants. And we're getting it. Let's go." He charged up the hill with the others in line behind him.

Stumpy was sitting on his horse when the first rain drops splattered against the hard riverbed. The storm had arrived and sheets of rain were sweeping over the nearby mountains.

"Zeke! We have to go!" The rain was coming down hard now, and Stumpy urged his horse out of the gulch.

Zeke took the T-rex's reins and tugged. "Come on," he said. To his surprise, the animal obeyed and walked with him, and Stumpy and Zeke began the trek back to the Double R with the dinosaur and its unconscious rider in tow.

By the time Cooper and his men reached the riverbed, Stumpy and Zeke were out of sight, and water was already streaming through the area, washing away any trace of the rider.

"Where's the trail?" Cooper demanded.

Thom Jackson dismounted and studied the wet ground. "I can't tell. The trail ends here."

Cooper surveyed the area, vainly searching for any sign of the T-rex and its rider, but it was too late. Cooper cursed and spat.

Chapter Three

Then he got back on his horse and led the men out of the gulch back toward the Crossed Swords Ranch.

It was dark by the time Stumpy and Zeke arrived at the Double R. The rain had stopped pouring but continued in a light drizzle, and they were soaked to the skin. Jesse and Bull had finished dinner and were playing cards at the kitchen table when they heard Stumpy and Zeke return. Zeke was bursting to tell his uncle and Bull what happened.

"Uncle Jesse! Bull! Come out and take a look at what we found!"

"It's about time you two got back. What kept you?" Uncle Jesse asked as he studied the cards in his hand, barely paying attention to Zeke's invitation.

"Zeke found something," Stumpy shouted. "You best come out here and take a look."

Jesse and Bull looked at each other and shrugged. Poker could wait.

It was a curious sight that greeted the two men when they stepped outside. The back of the T-rex was covered with a blanket, soaked by the rain, and it was obvious there was something big underneath. The dinosaur was calm and its demeanor gave no hint of how dangerous it could be. The only light came from the big kitchen window that overlooked the porch so Uncle Jesse and Bull couldn't see too well. Then a cloud covering the moon drifted out of the way.

"Lordy, lordy, where'd you find that thing?" Uncle Jesse asked, pointing to the T-rex.

"Out by Small's Stream," Zeke replied, beaming. "And

look . . ." He pulled back the blanket covering the rider.

Uncle Jesse and Bull stepped down off the porch and moved in closer to get a better view.

"Whoa, he's a big one. Are those spikes part of him?" Bull said, pointing at the bony ridges that covered the rider's head.

Uncle Jesse stepped closer to the unconscious figure and pressed the palm of his hand against one of the spikes. It was hard. He made a fist and pretended to throw a punch toward the spike in slow motion.

"You wouldn't want to hit this guy in the head. You'd break your hand," he muttered to himself, as he made a mental note.

"He's been shot," Zeke volunteered.

"Shot? Who did it?" Uncle Jesse asked. "Did you see what happened?"

"We didn't see anything," Stumpy interrupted. "We found him in that spot where Small's Stream makes a turn; a bit south of the big rock that looks like a goat."

"You mean that black rock with the part that sticks out like a nose?" Bull asked.

"No. I'm talking about the gray one that looks like a ram's horn, next to the brownish one that looks like a manure pile."

"Next to the whitish one—?"

"Okay, that's enough," Uncle Jesse interrupted. "I know the spot. Now, finish the darn story."

"Anyhow, as I was saying," Stumpy continued, "we found the body lying out there in the river bed. With the rain coming I knew the area would flood, and he'd drown if we didn't move him."

"True enough," Uncle Jesse said. "Did anybody see you?"

"No, there was no one out there but us," Stumpy said.

Chapter Three

Zeke's uncle eyed the motionless body. "Is he alive?"

"Hard to tell," Stumpy said. "I think so. Every so often his leg twitches."

"That doesn't mean anything," Uncle Jesse said. "Hmm . . ." Uncle Jesse rubbed his chin as he walked around the T-rex, considering what to do next.

Finally he looked at Bull. "I've got a plan," he said. "Bull, you're going to ride into town and get Doc."

"What should I tell him?" Bull asked.

"Tell him someone got shot, but don't tell him who. Just get him out here alone. And make sure he doesn't go running to the sheriff. But first, you and I need to get this big fella out of sight."

"Where are we going to put him?" Bull continued.

"We'll stick him in the spare bedroom in the back of the house," Uncle Jesse said.

Stumpy frowned. This sounded risky. "How do you figure on doing that?"

"Carry him, of course," Uncle Jesse answered, like that was the dumbest thing he'd ever been asked.

Stumpy rolled his eyes. "He weighs a ton. You two ain't gonna be able to carry him by yourselves. Why don't you let Zeke lead this critter into the back room and do the work for you?"

"I'm not letting that thing into my house. I don't even know what it is," Uncle Jesse said flatly. "Anyhow, Bull and I got it handled."

"Suit yourself. *Stubbornnnn . . .*," Stumpy muttered under his breath.

"You say something?" Uncle Jesse asked sharply.

"Nothing you could hear," Stumpy mumbled.

"What do we do with the critter?" Bull asked.

"After we get the rider off him," Uncle Jess said, "Zeke can hide it in the barn until we figure out what's going on. Is that thing dangerous?"

"Naw, tame as an old nag," Stumpy replied. "He won't give you any trouble as long as he ain't riled up. Might want to keep the wolves away, though."

"What's that supposed to mean?" Uncle Jesse asked.

"He doesn't mean anything, Uncle Jesse," Zeke added quickly. "He's just joking. You know Stumpy." He laughed weakly.

Uncle Jesse looked at Stumpy and then back at Zeke. "Okay. Do you think you can handle him?" he asked Zeke.

"Yessir," the boy quickly replied. "No problem at all."

"Then hop to it. Okay, Bull, let's get this big fella inside."

Uncle Jesse was what some people call "country strong." This kind of strength doesn't come from a gym or lifting weights. It comes from the heavy work that ranchers and farmers do. Bull, on the other hand, was "naturally strong." He was born strong the way that some people are born fast, and all the hard work he did on the ranch just made him stronger. So you can understand why Uncle Jesse was confident that he and Bull could carry the rider the short distance from the front porch into the back room.

What Zeke's uncle didn't realize was that the rider weighed considerably more than his size would indicate if he'd been an ordinary man. The strange being was more than 400 pounds, and Uncle Jesse and Bull didn't have anything resembling a stretcher to help carry him. Their only saving grace was that much of the rider's body was covered with hard body plates which made him easier to hold on to. The downside was that those hard plates dug

Chapter Three

into the men's skin when they tried to lift him and they hurt something awful.

Still, the rider had to be moved and Uncle Jesse was too mule-headed to even entertain the idea that he and Bull couldn't do it by themselves. The two men draped the creature's arms around their shoulders, and grabbed each others' wrists behind its back. Then they pulled the rider off the T-rex. They paused a moment to make sure each had a solid grip, but as they supported his weight, the bony protuberances on the rider's skin dug into their arms and shoulders. And the pain was excruciating!

"Wow, is he heavy," Uncle Jesse said. "Those thingamajigs on his skin are killing me."

"Me, too," Bull said as they dragged the rider through the house followed by Stumpy.

"Easy, easy . . . All right," Uncle Jesse groaned as he and Bull lowered the body onto the bed. "Now let's swing the legs up."

Jesse and Bull each took a leg. "On a count of three. One . . . two . . . three!" They heaved the legs onto the bed.

As they stood back to take a breather, they looked at the odd figure they'd just moved. The rider was so big that a good part of his lower legs stuck out over the edge of the bed. Uncle Jesse looked at Stumpy with a smug look on his face.

"Like I told you, we got it handled."

Suddenly, there was a loud cracking noise from the bottom of the bed as the wooden support slats gave way under the weight of the rider and he crashed to the floor, leaving the outside of the bed frame intact.

"Yep. You handled it about as well as I expected," Stumpy said.

"He's going to have to fix that," Bull said, gesturing toward the unconscious guest.

Uncle Jesse glared at Stumpy for an instant and then stomped out of the room. He returned a moment later and tossed a blanket on top of the rider and looked at Stumpy.

"Cover him up so he stays warm," he said. "Bull, get along into town. I'll go out to the barn and check on Zeke. Maybe one of these days something around here will go the way I planned."

"I doubt it," Stumpy muttered.

Before Uncle Jesse could respond, a tremendous *BWAP!* erupted from the unconscious figure.

"You hear something?" Uncle Jesse asked. The men looked at one another and then turned toward the rider. Within seconds a foul odor filled the room.

"What's that smell?" Bull said, nearly gagging.

"Smells like a cow burp," Stumpy said.

"Wrong end," Uncle Jesse corrected. "Better keep this door closed."

"Well, if you don't need me, I think I'll head into town," Bull said, as he hurried out the door to get away from the stinky smell.

"You get going," Stumpy called after him, slapping Uncle Jesse on the back. "Jess here has it handled."

"Like I said before, I'm going outside to check on Zeke," Uncle Jesse snapped. "And make sure you close that door when you leave."

Stumpy chuckled to himself. There was nothing funnier than seeing Uncle Jesse having a bad day, unless Stumpy was the cause of that bad day. Then it wasn't funny at all.

* * *

Chapter Three

Uncle Jesse had barely stepped outside when he heard a mix of shouts, roars, neighs and moos coming from the barn. "I was having a nice game of cards until those two came home."

He ran to the barn and flung open the doors. The T-rex stood in the center of the floor, roaring at the horses and cows, which kicked, neighed and mooed, while Zeke yelled for them to stop.

"What's going on in here?" Jesse shouted angrily as he stormed over to Zeke and grabbed the rex's reins. "You calm those horses down," he barked at the boy. Then, looking the dinosaur in the eye, "And you shut up!"

Surprisingly, the creature quieted down, shaking his massive head a few times.

Uncle Jesse walked the T-rex to the farthest stall in the rear corner of the barn away from the other animals and looped its reins around a front post. The animal eyed him curiously, but made no effort to break free. But when Uncle Jesse tried to remove the bridle from the T-rex's mouth, the dinosaur growled and bared its teeth in disapproval, forcing Uncle Jesse to take a different approach. He tied a loop at one end of a rope and gently placed it around the creature's jaws, tightening it in place. Now the T-rex was unable to open its mouth.

Although it may seem strange, one remarkable fact about animals—and humans—is that the muscles used to open the jaws are much weaker than the ones used for biting down on things. This is why a person of average strength can hold shut the powerful jaws of an alligator with just two hands.

Next, Uncle Jesse blindfolded the T-rex with a scarf and a length of rope. He often used blindfolds to control horses in stressful situations where the animals might become frightened and hurt themselves or their handlers. This maneuver occasionally backfired, though, with some horses reacting violently, but most accepted a blindfold and calmed down when it was applied gently. Fortunately, the T-rex didn't fight it.

Once it was in place, Uncle Jesse felt more comfortable that the T-rex couldn't attack him. Finally, Uncle Jesse secured the rex with two lengths of rope; each looped around the animal's neck and tied on opposite sides of the stall.

"There, that ought to hold you," Uncle Jesse said with a sense of satisfaction, confident that he had taken all the right steps to control the dinosaur. It never occurred to him that the techniques that worked on a horse might not work on this animal.

An hour later the storm cleared, the moon shone and things began to dry out. Uncle Jesse and Zeke were on the porch when Bull returned with the doctor, a tall, thin man in his early fifties. Some years before Doc was passing through town on his way west when he was called upon to help a boy who had suffered a broken arm in a fall. Doc set the bone, but it became infected, and he remained in town caring for the boy until the arm healed properly. By that time, Doc had gotten to know not only the boy's family and neighbors, but also darn near everyone in Dos Locos. So he decided to put down roots and stay.

"Now, what's all this about someone getting shot?" Doc demanded as he shook Uncle Jesse's hand. "Your man here wouldn't say who it was. You certainly look all right." He took a step back and observed Zeke. "Your nephew, too. What about that piece of rawhide you call a cook?"

"I heard that," Stumpy shouted from inside the kitchen

Chapter Three

where he was brewing a pot of coffee. "Just because I'm old don't mean I can't hear!"

"We're all fine Doc," Uncle Jesse said "But we have somebody in the back bedroom who needs your help."

He led Doc through the house and paused outside the door where the rider lay unconscious. "Doc, before you go in there, I think I ought to warn you . . ."

"I've seen men shot before, Jesse McCain. More than I care to remember. Now stand aside," Doc said impatiently as he stepped around Uncle Jesse.

"Suit yourself." Uncle Jesse turned his head away and held his breath as he pushed the door open. Once Doc was inside the dimly lit room, Uncle Jesse closed the door and waved his arms wildly trying to disperse the smell that escaped.

Inside, Doc's nose twitched a couple of times as the odor began to register. But foul smells were common in the medical profession and Doc wasn't fazed by them. He simply removed a white neckerchief from his bag and tied it around his head and over his nose so he resembled an outlaw.

"Whew! That is quite a smell!" Doc shouted from inside the bedroom.

"I tried to warn you," Jesse replied from the non-smelly side of the door.

"Then why don't you open the door and air the place out?" Doc asked.

"And stink up the whole house? No way!"

"No wonder it smells in here," Doc said as he approached the body. "He's all swelled up to twice normal size. You didn't tell me he was dead."

"That's because he ain't." Uncle Jesse corrected.

"How can you tell?" Doc asked.

"Every so often his leg twitches."

"That doesn't mean anything. What's he doing on the floor?"

"Don't ask."

"Okay, I won't." Doc knelt down, pulled the blanket aside and took stock of his patient. "Good lord. What happened to his face?"

"Nothing. He was just born ugly," Uncle Jess said.

"Well, he's not the only one."

For the next ten minutes Doc examined the rider. He prodded and probed; listened for a heartbeat; attempted to find a pulse; and looked down his patient's throat. He also tried examining the metal bracelet the rider was wearing, but when he tried to slip it off, the bracelet re-sized itself more tightly, so it couldn't be removed. *Now that's a neat little trick*, Doc thought. *I wonder how that thingamajig works.*

"Looks like he's been shot in the front at least three times," Doc called.

"Four more in the back," Uncle Jesse explained as he finally entered the room, holding his nose. "You look good in that," he said, noticing Doc's neckerchief.

"I don't have time to discuss my looks," Doc grumbled. "I've got work to do. Go tell young Zeke to heat up some water and get me a wash basin."

"I'm on it," Zeke shouted from outside the room.

"And while you're at it, get me a clothespin," Doc added.

"Are you fixing to do some laundry?" Uncle Jesse asked.

"I'm fixing to wash my hands and close my nose. It stinks in

Chapter Three

here. Have Zeke light a couple more candles to burn off some of this smell" Doc reached into his bag and took out a small flask.

"I don't think he'll be needing any of that pain medicine," Uncle Jesse observed. "He's out cold."

"I wasn't thinking of offering him any. This is for me." Doc took a swig from the flask. "Well, I've got a patient to take care of. You wait in the other room. I'll call if I need help."

Fortunately for Doc, the human nose has an amazing capacity to adjust to even the foulest odors, so it wasn't long before he hardly noticed the stench.

An hour later, Doc called for Uncle Jesse and Bull to help him turn over the rider so he could remove the bullets embedded in his back. That wound up being even more difficult than getting him into the bed!

It was another hour before Doc came out of the room with a metal pan holding seven bullets and declared that he'd done everything he could. He washed up and joined Uncle Jesse on the porch. As the two men leaned against the railing, Doc held his jacket up to his nose and sniffed. "If I can't get this smell out of my jacket, I'll have to burn it, he said. "And you'll get the bill."

"Will he live?" Uncle Jesse asked.

"I expect so," Doc replied. "His skin is tougher than boot leather, and he's got a kind of hard shell covering parts of his body. None of those bullets was in too deep. I doubt they had much effect on him."

"You saying those bullets didn't knock him out?"

"Yep."

"So what did?"

"Hard to say. But I doubt it was those bullets. He would've felt them, but his hide's so thick they wouldn't have stopped him."

"Huh. Imagine that. Shoot a fella seven times and he barely feels it. Good man to have in a fight. Especially if things get a little rough."

"Since we're on the subject of things getting rough, what are you planning to do when that fella wakes up? Assuming he does."

Uncle Jesse leaned back and thought for a moment. "Reckon I'll just say howdy."

"Better hope he says howdy back. May I make a small suggestion?"

"Sure."

"You may want to tie him down to what's left of the bed, just to be on the safe side. But I'll leave that to your good judgment."

"I'll keep that in mind. Did Bull happen to mention that he wasn't alone when the boys found him?" Uncle Jesse asked nonchalantly.

"Don't tell me there's another one of these things around here? Where'd you put it? The outhouse?"

"Not exactly. Come out back, Doc. Let me show you."

Uncle Jesse reached for a lantern and led Doc out to the barn. Doc stopped him short of opening the door.

"What's this one smell like?" he said.

Uncle Jesse laughed. "Better go back and get your clothespin," he said as Doc's face took on a look of horror. "No, I'm just fooling with you. This one doesn't stink nearly as bad."

As they stepped inside and walked toward the back where the T-rex was being kept, the lantern cast a shadow of the creature's tail on the rear wall. Doc shook his head in disbelief.

"Look at that!" he gasped.

"Wait until you see him up close," Uncle Jesse declared.

"Well, I'll be," Doc said as he put on his glasses. "Looks like you've got yourselves some kind of a dragon. Better make sure it doesn't set the barn on fire. The boys find this with the other one?"

"Yup. They came as a package. Only this one wasn't lying face down. You really think it's a dragon?" Uncle Jesse asked.

"I have no idea. But I wouldn't want to get too close. It looks like it could take your arm off," Doc observed.

"Aw, he's no trouble," Uncle Jesse said. "Stumpy and Zeke say he's as tame as an old hound. I tied its jaws shut after it started making a racket and scaring the horses. He looks a lot worse than he really is. Oh, I almost forgot. Did I mention that somebody broke him?"

"Broke him? Are you suggesting that fellow back in the house rides this thing like a horse?"

"It looks that way, although I wouldn't want to try," Uncle Jesse replied. "It had a bridle in its mouth when the boys found it. Still does. I tried to get it off but it wouldn't let me."

"Interesting," Doc said. "What does it eat?"

"Don't know," Uncle Jesse said. "I asked Zeke and he mentioned something about rabbits and squirrels."

Doc looked at Uncle Jesse skeptically. "Is that what Zeke told you? You better doublecheck to make sure that rabbits and squirrels are all it eats."

The two men started back to the main house.

"So what do you make of all this?" Doc asked.

"I'd say that strange looking fella inside was riding that thing in the barn, and got himself ambushed."

"Any thoughts on who did it?"

"Oh, I've got my suspicions," Uncle Jesse said.

Doc laughed. "I'm sure you do. Care to share them?" Doc asked, taking the bait.

"Where does most of the trouble around Dos Locos begin and end? I figure it's got something to do with D'Allesandro. Our friend must have said something that D'Allesandro and his boys didn't like."

Doc nodded in agreement. "I still haven't forgotten that long-horned animal that busted up the town. And now these two. It makes you wonder where they're coming from and what might be next."

Uncle Jesse remained quiet for a moment, letting Doc's words sink in. "Say, Doc. That fella in the back room—he's not human, is he."

"No, he's not. Whatever he is, he's not human."

The two men stopped and looked at one another. "Maybe it's best we keep this a secret between us," Uncle Jesse said.

"I was thinking the same thing," Doc said. "Whoever shot your guest might not take too kindly to you fixing him up. They may try to finish the job if they know he survived. That would mean paying the Double R a visit, and you don't need that kind of trouble. Not with the boy around. You know, Jess, it might have been better if Stumpy and Zeke had left those two where they found them. You could find yourself in a situation."

"Heck, Doc, 'situations' are what make life interesting. It's been slow around here. I could use a little excitement."

Chapter Three

"Around here, 'situations' are what make people dead. I try to avoid them, myself," Doc said.

"You're getting old," Uncle Jesse teased.

Doc started laughing. "I'm not getting old—I am old! And if I stay out of 'situations,' I may manage to get a little older."

"Hey, Doc. When was the last time you were out to D'Allesandro's place, anyway?"

Doc thought for a moment. "It's been a while. The closest I came to the Crossed Swords was a couple of months ago when I patched up a fellow who looked at Cable Cooper the wrong way. Cable hurt the man pretty bad and then dumped him on the road into town. The Sheriff found him and brought him to me. Of course, there weren't any witnesses, and the fellow refused to press charges. He left town not long after. At least I think he left. He certainly hasn't been seen since."

"The talk in town is that D'Allesandro's been doing a lot of building on his property," Uncle Jesse said. "I was thinking maybe I'd take a ride out there and see for myself."

"If you do, take your man Bull with you. You shouldn't go out there alone," Doc cautioned.

"Shucks, Doc. D'Allesandro and I are old friends. You know that."

"It's not D'Allesandro I'm worried about. It's that lunatic he's got working for him."

"Aw, I can handle Cable Cooper with my eyes closed," Uncle Jesse said.

"He'd like you to try. But I wouldn't recommend it."

"You worry too much, Doc," Uncle Jesse said with a laugh. "What could go wrong?"

Rex Riders

* * *

As Uncle Jesse and Doc talked, Zeke was in his room examining the strange silver pipe he'd found near the rider. It was pretty heavy, and Zeke thought it might be a club. At least, you could hurt someone with the thing if you hit them over the head with it. Maybe buttons opened it up.

For the next hour Zeke lay on his bed, pressing the buttons in different combinations, but nothing much happened except that his eyes got heavy, and he started to doze off. He opened them with a start, and the rod was making a humming sound and emitting a greenish light that lit up every corner of the room.

Zeke got out of bed and looked around. It was spooky. The glow cast no shadows, but rather filled every bump and curve of the walls, ceiling and floor. Maybe it's some kind of magic lamp, the boy thought.

He pressed his finger against a knot in the wall, but couldn't feel it. There seemed to be something clear and smooth over it, almost like glass. In fact, the entire perimeter of his room felt like it was covered with something smooth. Yet, when Zeke knocked on the wall, it made the usual sound.

Stumpy heard the rapping from the kitchen, and when he walked over to the boy's room to check on him, he saw a strange light at the bottom of the door. "Zeke, you okay?" he whispered.

Zeke was momentarily startled. "Yeah, I'm okay."

"Mind if I come in?" Stumpy said, pushing against the door. "No, I'm—"

"Oomph!" The sound of Stumpy's efforts forced Zeke to pause and stare at the entrance to his room. *I don't remember locking the door,* he thought. But as hard as Stumpy tried, he

Chapter Three

couldn't open the door. It just didn't move. "You got something up against this door?" he said.

"No, no, I'm just changing," Zeke replied.

Zeke got out of bed and rushed to the door. He could grasp the handle, but it wouldn't budge.

"You sure you're okay?" Stumpy asked, concerned.

"I'm fine. Really."

"Well, I'm going to bed," Stumpy said, giving up. "I'd like you to do the same. I'll see you in the morning."

Zeke picked up the silver object and started frantically pushing the buttons. *How the heck do I shut this thing off?* His answer came seconds later. The humming abruptly stopped, and the green light faded, leaving the room in darkness.

Stumpy saw the light go out, too, and was surprised to find that when he tried the door again, it easily swung open. "What the heck are you doing in here?"

"Nothing," Zeke said, pulling the covers over his head. "Just trying to fall asleep, that's all. Good night."

Stumpy peered at him in the dark. "Goodnight, son," he said, closing the door "See you in the morning."

As soon as Zeke heard the old cook's footsteps fade along the hallway, he rolled over and carefully stuffed the object under the mattress. The boy wondered if he could get it to work again. He was pretty sure he remembered the sequence of buttons he'd pressed. It would have to wait until tomorrow. That was enough for one night.

Chapter
Four

The following morning found Zeke sitting across the kitchen table from Uncle Jesse with his hands folded in front of him and a serious expression on his face. Despite his best attempts, he had hardly slept the night before because of everything that had happened, and who could blame him?

At this particular moment, the boy was struggling to stifle a yawn and appear interested while Uncle Jesse launched into the latest plan he'd come up with. Uncle Jesse was the kind of a person who took it personally if you yawned while he was speaking, but the harder Zeke worked at suppressing the yawn that was growing inside him, the bigger and more uncontrollable that urge became.

"Am I boring you?" Uncle Jesse asked sharply.

"No sir," Zeke answered with a yawn.

His uncle frowned. "Try to stay awake while I talk to you."

"Yes, sir," the boy replied as another yawn managed to escape.

"Now look, Zeke, while you're at school, the three of us are going into town. After we drop off Stumpy at the general store, Bull and I are heading over to D'Allesandro's to nose around a bit. When you get back, I want you to remain here and keep out of trouble. And that means staying out of the back room and away from that animal in the barn. Bull and I tied that fella down just in case he wakes up before we get back so he won't give you any trouble. If anything happens, ride into town and get us. Understand?"

"Yes sir."

"Then that's settled. I'll get Bull and Stumpy and we'll be on our way."

Uncle Jesse met Bull outside and the two men walked to the smokehouse around back where they were met by the crusty old cook who was tending to the meat. Smoking and drying meats was an important part of life out west because there wasn't any ice available to keep food fresh. Since a grown steer yielded more edible meat than an average-size family could eat before it spoiled, smoking was used to preserve the meat by removing moisture. It also gave the meat a unique flavor. One of Stumpy's specialties was beef jerky, and the old cook always made sure to have plenty on hand whenever he or the men left the ranch. Stumpy was just loading up the men's saddlebags for the trip when they arrived.

"It's about time you two showed up," he said.

Uncle Jesse smiled. It wouldn't be a proper start to the day without Stumpy griping about something.

Chapter Four

The three men piled onto the buckboard and rode around to the front of the house where Zeke was sitting in a rocking chair on the porch.

"You know what to do, right?" Uncle Jesse called.

"Ah, leave him alone," Stumpy said, hitting Uncle Jesse with his hat.

"I'm okay, Uncle Jesse," Zeke answered. "If there are any problems, I'll head into town. I promise."

"Good man." Uncle Jesse looked at Bull and nodded slightly. Everything was going according to plan.

An hour later, Uncle Jesse was pulling up to *Johnson's* general store. "Remember what I told you, Stumpy. See what you can find out, but don't make it too obvious. And don't tell anyone what you and Zeke found. Not a word."

"I heard you the first dozen times you told me," Stumpy grumbled, as he climbed off the buckboard.

"When we're done, we'll circle back and pick you up. Bull, did I miss anything?"

Bull cleared his throat. "While you're inside, see if they have any of that dark-colored maple syrup. I noticed we're running low at breakfast. Also, see if they have any brown sugar. We ain't had baked beans in a while and—"

"I'm not talking about your grocery list," Uncle Jesse snapped. "I'm talking about who shot that fella back at the house."

"No, I think you got that covered Jess."

Stumpy liked spending time in town. He'd lived in Dos Locos for years and knew almost everyone within a twenty mile radius.

Of course there weren't many people within a twenty mile radius.

After ordering the supplies at *Johnson's*, Stumpy was on his way to the boarding house for a bite to eat when he saw a man dressed head to toe in animal skins and furs sweating profusely by the stables. The man looked lost, so Stumpy decided to strike up a conversation.

"Howdy stranger," he said.

"Howdy yourself," the man sneered. He had a thick French accent and eyed Stumpy suspiciously.

"You're not from around these parts, are you? You look like you might need directions. Where are you headed?"

"I am looking for the Crossed Swords Ranch," the stranger answered. "I have business with Monsieur D'Allesandro. Do you know this man? Where can I find him?"

"Know him? I'm practically kin," Stumpy said. "Be happy to help you. But first, you look like you could use a meal and a cool drink. I was about to get something myself. Let me show you the way."

As the two men walked, Stumpy reached into his pocket and pulled out a thick piece of beef jerky and offered it to the stranger. The man looked at it skeptically, but a small nibble was followed by a reasonable bite and then another.

"Thees is magnifique!" the man raved. "I am most grateful. What do they call you, monsieur . . . ?"

"Stumpy. Stumpy Gibbons."

"I am Jean-Claude Pinchot."

"Glad to meet you Mr. Pin-cho," Stumpy said, shaking the man's hand. "What kind of business do you have at the Crossed Swords?"

Chapter Four

"Monsieur D'Allesandro has need of a trapper and I am the greatest trapper in all of Quebec."

"You don't say. Are you gonna be trapping around here?"

"The Monsieur did not say. Only that the prey is beeg."

"Big, you say?"

"Very beeg."

Stumpy thought for a moment. The biggest animals in that part of the country were deer, antelope, bison, bear and wildcat. But nobody needed a trapper all the way from Quebec to deal with any of those animals.

"Tell me more, friend," Stumpy said with a big smile as they reached the boarding house. "I'm very interested."

While Stumpy plied Jean-Claude with food and drink, Uncle Jesse and Bull were nearing the edge of D'Allesandro's property. They had been making small talk about what happened the night before, but Bull had something more serious on his mind.

"You could sell out you know," Bull said abruptly after a lull in the conversation.

"What? You mean sell out to D'Allesandro?" a surprised Uncle Jesse asked.

"He'd pay you a fair price. Maybe get our old jobs back. Or we could head down to Mexico. Start over."

"I've thought about it, Bull, but I can't do it. It would be like I was giving up and he won."

"That may be more in your mind than his. Which bothers you more? The you-giving-up part, or the him-winning part?"

Uncle Jesse sighed. Leave it to Bull to get straight to the heart of the matter. It was a fair question, but Bull was the only person who could've asked it without getting his head bitten off.

"If it wasn't for D'Allesandro, I'd have given up a long time ago and left Dos Locos for good. I wanted to prove he was wrong. That I could start my own ranch and be successful. Be an owner instead of just a hired hand. I guess I'm just not cut out for the job."

"You're a hell of a cowboy, Jess. But an owner has to have a head for business."

"Are you saying I don't have a head for business?" Uncle Jesse asked.

"No," Bull replied calmly. "I'm just saying they're two different things."

As they reached the edge of D'Allesandro's property, they stopped and looked up at a massive oak sign that read CROSSED SWORDS RANCH hanging over the trail. The words were burned into the wood underneath two shiny swords. It was hard to believe, but D'Allesandro actually had a man polish those swords periodically so they didn't rust out.

"It's been a long time, hasn't it, Bull?" Uncle Jesse commented as they passed underneath

They continued down the dirt road until they saw an odd-looking wooden tower in the distance.

"What do you think that's for?" Bull asked.

"I have no idea," Uncle Jesse said. "But since we're out here, we may as well take a look."

When Jesse and Bull reached the structure, they climbed off the buckboard and studied the tower's construction from every angle. The base was built out of three huge logs that crisscrossed to form a giant tripod. The logs supported an enclosed platform

Chapter Four

that was encircled by a catwalk. At least fifty feet up, a rope ladder led to a trap door on the underside of the base.

The roof was shaped like a cone and sat atop the supports positioned on the inside of the platform away from the railing. A cast iron church bell hung from the center of its ceiling. This design allowed a person to walk completely around the outside of the platform without encountering any obstruction.

"Looks new," Jesse observed. "The wood isn't weathered."

"It doesn't look like it's been used, either," Bull said.

"I don't think anybody's home," Uncle Jesse said.

"Then you may as well check it out," Bull suggested. "I don't see anybody around to stop you."

Uncle Jesse climbed the ladder to the platform, while Bull stayed below with the horses. The view was superb from that height and the catwalk provided a full 360-degree view of the surrounding area. Uncle Jesse looked out over a broad expanse of prime grazing land.

"D'Allesandro's been busy," Uncle Jesse called to Bull. "I count three more towers and several other new buildings. Can't tell what they're for, but they're big. Looks like the rumors were true."

"There's only one way to find out," Bull said.

Soon the two men pulled up to an enormous Spanish-style mansion that was easily several times the size of the Double R ranchhouse. D'Allesandro's men had seen the dust kicked up by the buckboard and alerted their boss that he had visitors. So D'Allesandro was on the front porch waiting for them.

"Mr. McCain. Mr. Whitman. To what do I owe the pleasure?" D'Allesandro asked pleasantly.

Uncle Jesse wasn't sure what kind of reception to expect from

Rex Riders

the rancher after everything that had happened between them. He'd expected at least a bit of suspicion, even hostility, at his visit. D'Allesandro's welcome was the last thing he'd anticipated.

Equally surprising was the change in D'Allesandro's appearance. He'd lost a considerable amount of weight since Uncle Jesse last saw him, but looked remarkably fit. In fact, he looked thinner than Uncle Jesse could ever recall seeing him, which was strange since D'Allesandro rarely exerted himself.

"We were passing by and thought we'd pay you a social call," replied Uncle Jesse.

"That's quite a coincidence," D'Allesandro said. "I was just remarking to Maria this morning that we've seen so little of you in town. I'm surprised our paths don't cross more frequently."

"It's been a while," Uncle Jesse agreed. "It looks like you've done some work to the place since I was last here." He pointed to the newly-expanded barn. There were quite a few men working on the structure and the air was filled with the sounds of hammers and saws.

"Yes. We are always looking for ways to improve our business, Mr. McCain. Progress demands it."

"Well, well, look who's here," Cable Cooper said, walking out onto the porch. "How's that horse thief of yours, McCain?"

D'Allesandro gritted his teeth and continued looking directly at Uncle Jesse. Cooper had no business interrupting him.

"Mr. McCain, you know Mr. Cooper," D'Allesandro said evenly.

Uncle Jesse was startled to see three fresh scars running parallel down the right side of Cooper's face from his temple to his jaw. It appeared as if he'd been viciously raked by someone—or some*thing*!

Chapter Four

Still, Uncle Jesse remained unfazed. "I'm afraid so," he replied coolly as Cable glared at him.

"Mr. Cooper, I would like you to check the men's progress on the barn. It's important that they remain on schedule. If you find they need some motivation, I will leave it to you to provide it."

"Whatever you say, Mr. D'Allesandro," Cable said, smiling. "Maybe I'll see you later, McCain."

"Not if I see you first," Uncle Jesse answered with a friendly tip of his hat.

Cooper took a step, and then spun around and stared at McCain with a confused expression. "Huh?"

"Mr. Cooper . . . the barn . . . ," D'Allesandro said firmly.

D'Allesandro's order ended Cable's stare-down with Uncle Jesse, and he headed toward the barn.

"Good employees are so hard to find, Mr. McCain," D'Allesandro said. "That's why losing men of your caliber was such a blow. But that's all in the past. You are the owner of a cattle ranch yourself now and know what I'm talking about. Why don't you join me? I'll show you around."

For the next hour, D'Allesandro escorted Uncle Jesse and Bull around the grounds of the Crossed Swords Ranch. It was an eye-opener. There was a log corral, with posts at least ten feet high, and water troughs big enough to take a swim in.

The last stop on their tour was the expanded barn and it was far larger than any barn the men had ever seen. The original building was several times larger than a traditional barn, but it looked as though D'Allesandro was doubling its size!

As they walked closer they noticed strange-looking skulls of varying sizes and shapes hanging over the barn doors. They bore no resemblance to the animals that were common in the area. Besides being a good deal larger, they sported abnormally long snouts, unfamiliar beaks and oddly-shaped horns. And you couldn't miss the rows of razor-sharp teeth—even from a distance. Bull raised an eyebrow and gave Uncle Jesse a sideways glance. Both men wondered where D'Allesandro had gotten them.

The interior of the barn was cavernous and everything in it was oversized, from the stalls, to the hay loft and feed containers, to the wagon that D'Allesandro had used to remove the trike's remains. Everything was proportionately sized—just bigger. In fact, when Uncle Jesse and Bull first entered the barn, it looked as though someone had placed miniature versions of horses and cows in the stalls.

Off in the back corner of the barn was a wooden structure that looked like a shed. It was windowless and had a single door that was securely bolted. Leaning against its side were six sharp pikes of the type used by loggers.

"Nice tool shed," Uncle Jesse said.

"Shed?" D'Allesandro seemed to have no idea what Uncle Jesse was talking about.

"In the corner," Jesse said, pointing.

"Oh, yes . . . the shed. Yes, it is nice. Thank you."

"We've been thinking of building a new one ourselves, but haven't gotten around to it. Mind if I take a look at yours?"

"Another time perhaps," D'Allesandro said.

"It'll only take a second," Uncle Jesse insisted as he moved toward the structure.

D'Allesandro blocked him before he could take a second step. "Maria has refreshments waiting for us. She'll be wondering

Chapter Four

where we are. Come, let's go inside."

The ranch owner put his arms around Uncle Jesse and Bull, as he ushered them to the front of the barn. "Besides, if you see everything today, you'll have no reason to come back. And you and Mr. Whitman are most welcome any time."

"We don't want to put you to any trouble," Uncle Jesse said.

"It's no trouble, I assure you."

Uncle Jesse and Bull exchanged glances. The force of D'Allessandro's arms about their shoulders said it all. He wasn't so much leading them, as pushing them away from the shed. But what could the rancher be hiding? It didn't make any sense.

The foyer in the main house was as elegant and beautiful as Uncle Jesse and Bull remembered it. The floor was made of finely-chiseled stone, and suspended from the ceiling was an elaborate chandelier made from dozens of antelope antlers. Maria greeted them holding a tray of fresh lemonade in two crystal pitchers, and everyone retired to the parlor.

The lemonade was a refreshing respite from the heat outside and helped Uncle Jesse and Bull momentarily forget their host's strange behavior a few moments before.

D'Allesandro was his usual commanding self and spoke at length about the latest ranching methods and new varieties of cattle that were making their way west. After a few minutes, he stood up.

"Maria will you excuse us? I have something to show our guests."

"Of course," Maria replied.

Rex Riders

"Gentlemen, would you join me in the study?"

D'Allesandro led Uncle Jesse and Bull from the sitting room across the hallway to a pair of ornately-carved mahogany doors. "I think you will find this interesting," he said, as he unlocked them. "I recently had the entrance to this room expanded. You'll see why in a moment."

The walls of the study were lined with twelve-foot high bookcases, mounted with a track and rolling ladder that enabled easy access to the books on the uppermost shelves. Even though Uncle Jesse and Bull didn't spend a lot of time reading, they were impressed by the size of the collection and what it suggested about D'Allesandro's education.

Above the cases hung antlers from deer and antelope that D'Allesandro's ranch hands had shot over the years. There were several handsome nail-head, leather chairs covered in steer hide and a teak desk that must have been eight feet long. It was a magnificent room and the men were taken by its beauty.

But that wasn't all.

In the center of the room stood a slab of polished marble, mounted with the skull of the triceratops that Uncle Jesse had killed. An elaborate metal armature raised the massive skull eighteen inches off the base and held its jaws open. It was stripped clean of flesh and muscle, and was bleached white. A full-grown bear's skull was placed beside the trike's to provide perspective. It looked like a peanut next to the dinosaur head! The effect was overwhelming and exerted a hypnotic effect upon Uncle Jesse and Bull.

"Is that . . . ," Uncle Jesse began, as he stared at the skull from across the room.

Chapter Four

"Yes it is," D'Allesandro answered proudly. "Magnificent, isn't it? Please, take a closer look. I thought you might want to see it."

D'Allesandro couldn't have been more right. The skull was far bigger than any animal skull they had ever seen. Uncle Jesse and Bull walked around the mount several times, stopping at different points to study it.

"The only flaw is the hole over the eye socket," D'Allesandro observed, pointing to the spot where the bullets fired by Uncle Jesse had struck. "You're an excellent shot, Mr. McCain. All the bullets entered the skull within an area no larger than a silver dollar. But even with this slight imperfection I've had several sizeable offers from buyers interested in purchasing the skull as well as the remainder of the skeleton."

Bull touched the bone. It was remarkably smooth. "How'd you get it so clean? Left it out in the sun did you?"

D'Allesandro hesitated before answering: "Exactly right. The sun dried the skin, and nature did the rest."

"That must have taken a while," Bull grunted.

"Less time than you would think."

"It's amazing," Jesse said, shaking his head in awe.

"We're lucky it didn't eat anybody," Bull said. "Look at the jaws on that thing."

D'Allesandro chuckled. "There was no danger of anyone being eaten, Mr. Whitman. This specimen is known as a triceratops. Triceratops were plant eaters and normally quite placid unless disturbed."

"I hear what you're saying," Bull replied. "But I still wouldn't stick my hand near its mouth."

Rex Riders

"Let me assure you, Señor D'Allesandro is quite correct."

Uncle Jesse and Bull spun around to see a distinguished-looking man, wearing an ill-fitting, tweed riding suit, at the doorway to the study. By the way his clothing hung so loosely on him, it was obvious he'd lost a considerable amount of weight. That coupled with the unhealthy pallor of his skin and sunken eyes and cheeks suggested that he was a very sick man.

"Gentlemen, I don't believe we've met. I am Professor Wesley Kornbluth," he said, extending a his hand.

"Glad to know you, Professor," Uncle Jesse said as he and Bull took turns shaking Dr. Kornbluth's hand. "What do you do around here?"

"I am a scientist, Mr. McCain. My areas of specialization are the flora and fauna of prehistory, the ancient plants and creatures of bygone times believed to be extinct."

Bull leaned toward Uncle Jesse and whispered, "What the heck is he talking about?"

"You mean dead critters?" Uncle Jesse asked slowly.

"Three months ago I would have answered 'yes' without qualification. But with the appearance of this triceratops, it was clear that not all prehistoric animals are dead. Señor D'Allesandro has a theory that some of the myths and legends of the indigenous peoples might have some basis in scientific fact. I came here for the purpose of—" But before he could finish, D'Allesandro broke in.

"Dr. Kornbluth is assisting me in our work here. Triceratops is a member of a group of animals known as 'dinosaurs,' which lived on Earth millions of years ago and believed to be extinct. But as we all know from bitter experience, this brute was all

Chapter Four

too alive. I asked Dr. Kornbluth to join me here at the ranch to help determine the origin of this creature and assess the future risk to Dos Locos. After all, our livelihoods depend upon the health and prosperity of the town."

"Mighty neighborly," Uncle Jesse commented.

"But if all you're doing is trying to figure out if there are any more of these tri-whatchamcallits, why did you build such a big corral?" Bull asked.

"An excellent question, Mr. Whitman. I think you'll agree it would be a shame to destroy possible future specimens merely because we lack the facilities to house them properly. Dr. Kornbluth has been enormously helpful in designing appropriate enclosures to care for such beasts."

"What about the towers Bull and I spotted on the way in," Uncle Jesse asked.

"Merely lookout stations, outfitted to sound a warning to the townspeople, should such creatures appear again. Fortunately, all my efforts are proving to be in vain. My men have scoured the area and no more of the animals have been found."

"How much you figure a live one is worth?" Uncle Jesse asked.

D'Allesandro looked as though the thought had never occurred to him. "Hmm . . . a live one? I have no idea. As I mentioned, my interest is purely scientific. Will you join us for lunch, gentlemen?" D'Allesandro asked, changing the subject.

"Oh yes, please do, Mr. McCain," Maria implored from the study's entranceway.

"Thank you, ma'am," Uncle Jesse replied. "But we better get going. Stumpy's waiting for us back in town."

"Let me show you the way out," D'Allesandro offered.

The ranch owner seemed oddly quiet as he led Uncle Jesse and Bull onto the porch.

"There is one thing you could do for me, Mr. McCain," D'Allesandro said, breaking the silence.

"What's that?" Uncle Jesse asked.

"I am looking for someone," D'Allesandro answered hesitantly. "He has something that is of great value to me."

"And he wants it back." Cable Cooper added with an edge in his voice from the far end of the porch. He came out of nowhere and seemed to know exactly what D'Allesandro was referring to, even though he hadn't been part of the conversation .

"You don't say. And what might that be?" Uncle Jesse said.

"None of your business," Cooper snapped without thinking.

"Then how am I supposed to help get it back?" Uncle Jesse replied.

Dr. Kornbluth tried to stifle a chuckle, and Cable looked around with a scowl on his face to see who was laughing.

"Calm down, Cable," D'Allesandro said before returning his attention to Uncle Jesse. "The 'fellow' I'm looking for is not like us. He assaulted several of my men before they wounded him in self-defense. Unfortunately, he managed to escape. My men tracked him to an area near Small's Stream, but yesterday's storm interrupted their search and washed away the trail they were following. I believe he was drowned, which is all to the good since he had a violent temperament. You know that area quite well. If I can recover what I am looking for, I will make it worth your while."

"Tell me more," Uncle Jesse said with great interest.

"It's a metal cylinder; a pipe about fifteen inches long,"

Chapter Four

D'Allesandro continued. "If you should find it, I would greatly appreciate your returning it. I'm offering a substantial reward."

"If I find it, I will let you know," Uncle Jesse assured.

"One more thing." D'Allesandro hesitated and glanced at Dr. Kornbluth before continuing. "This 'fellow' was not riding a horse. He rides a two-legged creature, unknown to these parts, called Tyrannosaurus rex. The name means *tyrant lizard king*. It's also a dinosaur, but unlike triceratops, this 'T-rex,' as it's often called, is a vicious beast with a voracious appetite for flesh. It eats incessantly. It will lie in wait until the moment is right, then strike without mercy. This particular specimen is small— perhaps sixteen feet long from nose to tail—but it is supremely powerful. In the hands of a rider who can control it, the creature is virtually unstoppable. My men are under orders to destroy it on sight. It is . . . much more than it seems."

"And this fella you're talking about; he can control this T-rex?"

"Yes. Where he comes from he is called the Rider, the *Rex Rider*. If you encounter this beast or its master, I recommend that you deal with them the same way you dealt with the animal in my study: with a well-placed bullet in the head."

"I'll keep that in mind," Uncle Jesse said soberly. "I'm obliged for all your hospitality. And we'll keep an eye out for that metal pipe you're looking for."

"Thank you, Mr. McCain. I know I can trust you to keep our discussion confidential. I have no desire to worry the towns-people. They have suffered enough."

"This stays between us," Uncle Jesse confirmed, and Bull nodded in agreement.

Rex Riders

"I never properly thanked you or your nephew for coming to the aid of my sister, Maria, and my niece—"

"It was nothing," Uncle Jesse interrupted.

"Perhaps next time you'll stay for lunch, Mr. McCain," Maria said.

"That would be lovely, ma'am," Uncle Jesse replied, tipping his hat.

"I do hope we will see more of you," she said. "Next time, I will make sangria. Will you be going to the square dance?"

"Hadn't thought about it," Uncle Jesse said. "But now that you mention it, I may go. Will you be there, ma'am?"

"I will. It's been many years since I went to a square dance in town. I'm looking forward to it."

"Then maybe I'll see you there. Adios."

Bull nudged Uncle Jesse as they walked toward the buckboard. "Looks like she might be interested in getting to know you better," he said with a grin.

Uncle Jesse looked troubled. "We have to get back to the ranch. I never should've let Stumpy and Zeke put that thing in the barn. Doc warned me, but I didn't listen." He shook his head in disgust at his stubbornness. "I don't know what I was thinking."

"You're worrying yourself over nothing," Bull said. "That Rex Rider's out cold and you tied up his mount in the barn pretty good. I don't understand what's bothering you."

"One word: Zeke."

"Aw, you told Zeke to stay away from the both of them. I heard you."

"I know what I told him. And I also know that boy. Let's get going." Uncle Jesse took his seat on the buckboard, and with Bull

Chapter Four

beside him, urged the horses into a gallop.

D'Allesandro watched intently from the porch. "Strange. They didn't seem to be in a rush a moment ago," he observed.

"Your story about that tyrano-thing probably spooked him," Cable sneered.

"I doubt that very much, Mr. Cooper. In my experience, Mr. McCain and Mr. Whitman do not 'spook' easily."

While Uncle Jesse and Bull rode back toward town, Zeke stood outside the doors to the barn, saddle in hand. His heart beat so fast he felt a little light-headed. The boy took a deep breath. Once again, Uncle's Jesse's instructions had gone in one ear and straight out the other. All Zeke could think about was that he had to act fast before they came back. If that strange animal in the barn could be ridden, he was going to try.

Zeke peeked into the barn to see where the T-rex was, but it was so bright outside that his eyes had trouble adjusting to the shadowy darkness inside. He pressed his ear against the space between the doors, but heard nothing. Holding the saddle with both hands he stuck the toe of his boot in the space and nudged a door open. It creaked so loudly that Zeke couldn't help but look around to make sure no one was watching. All was quiet except for the sound of birds and insects. Beams of sunlight streamed into the barn, and Zeke could see particles of dust floating in the air.

He took a step inside, stopping to give his eyes time to adjust. The T-rex was tied up just as they'd left him: blindfolded, rope around its jaws, with two thicker ropes looped around its neck and tied to posts on opposite sides of the stall, its big tail sticking out the back.

Rex Riders

Zeke crept toward the dinosaur. It turned its head in the boy's direction and let out a low growl. In spite of the thickness of its neck and size of its head, the animal was surprisingly flexible, and its range of motion was far greater than a horse's.

Zeke gulped. The rex couldn't possibly see through the blindfold, yet seemed to be looking right at him. This was unexpected. Last night the animal seemed friendly—tame even. Now it was back to behaving like it did when he and Stumpy first found it.

For a moment Zeke wondered if this was a good idea. He glanced over at Midnight tied up in a stall on the opposite side of the barn. All kinds of thoughts flashed through his mind. He was back in Uncle Jesse's good graces, and things were going better. Hadn't he promised himself he wouldn't make the same mistake he'd made with D'Allesandro's horse? Why jeopardize everything? There was a perfectly good sorrel he was allowed to ride.

The T-rex had seemed tame, but that didn't mean it would let Zeke ride it. What if the creature got loose and ran off? What if the men who shot the Rider saw Zeke on the animal? Would they follow Zeke back to the ranch to finish the job? What if the beast threw him and he got hurt? Even worse, what if Uncle Jesse came back sooner than Zeke expected and he got caught? What then?

Aw, if a man let every little thing that might happen stop him, he'd never accomplish anything! Zeke took another step closer on tiptoes, trying not to make a sound.

"*Shhh* . . . quiet boy. I'm not going to hurt you."

Zeke finally reached the T-rex. He tentatively reached out and stroked the animal's side. Its skin was tan and streaked with brown. It was about a foot taller than a horse at the hip, and its chest was fuller. Its skin was leathery and covered with a

Chapter Four

stubbly, coarse hair. The animal seemed to quiet down as Zeke stroked its side.

"There, there," Zeke said softly.

Zeke figured that since the T-rex had been broken, it could be ridden by anyone. With horses that would have been a safe bet. But a T-rex bonded with only one rider, and that was the only person who could ride it with few exceptions. It was one of the main differences between a horse and a rex: you get on another man's horse and the worst that would happen is it would throw you, and you wound up on your butt. In the case of a T-rex, you could wind up as dinner.

Zeke hoisted the saddle onto the dinosaur's back with one easy swing and crouched to cinch the straps that held it in place. While he worked, Zeke quietly went over each step, as if checking each item off a list, unaware that the creature was deliberately moving its head to test the strength of the ropes.

"There we go," Zeke said as he secured the last buckle. The straps barely fit under the T-rex's thick chest. Zeke stood up, pleased with himself. Then he grabbed hold of the pommel, slipped his left foot into the stirrup, and was up in the saddle in an instant.

"Well, that wasn't so hard."

It was right about then that the rex decided it was through being cooperative. The animal began to swing its head from side to side, jerking against the ropes to get free. Zeke leaned forward and stroked the creature's neck to calm it down, but the more resistance it felt from the ropes, the more violently the T-rex swung its head. Somehow the ropes held strong, but a board one of the the ropes was tied to came loose and went flying, barely missing Zeke's leg. The rex bent its head and pawed at the rope around its jaws until it came off. It performed the same feat with the blindfold. Now that was something a horse couldn't do!

The T-rex looked around to get its bearings; then slowly turned its head to see who was sitting on its back. When the dinosaur saw that it was Zeke and not its master, it let out a roar.

Zeke gulped.

Suddenly, the angry beast took a step to the right, and slammed its side against the stall, trying to throw Zeke. The boy anticipated the move and swung his right leg to the rear of the saddle just in time.

"You'll have to do better than that!" Zeke cried.

The rex snorted and moved the other way, slamming into the opposite side of the paddock. But once again Zeke was ready. When that didn't work, it backed out of the stall and surveyed the inside of the barn.

Zeke pulled hard on the reins to show the T-rex who was boss, which caught the dinosaur by surprise, jerking its head back. The creature roared angrily and thrust its head forward with such force that Zeke was nearly pulled out of the saddle. Zeke loosened his grip on the reins for an instant to regain his balance, then pulled hard to his right and dug his heels into the beast's sides to prod it into motion.

Zeke got what he wanted, and the T-rex launched into action. *Now that's more like it,* Zeke thought.

But instead of moving in the direction that Zeke had in mind, the dinosaur headed straight toward the low-hanging hay loft on the opposite side of the barn. There was barely enough clearance for the T-rex, never mind a rider, and all Zeke could do was throw

Chapter Four

himself forward, grab the animal's neck with both arms and close his eyes. Every low hanging winch, tool and doo-dad hit Zeke's back as the rex raced underneath.

When the animal emerged from under the hay loft and Zeke was still in the saddle, it switched to plan B. It charged at a post supporting the barn's roof and barreled into it with its shoulder. The roof groaned as the rex backed up and shook its head.

Zeke was confused. Did the beast just do that on purpose or was it an accident? This animal is crazy! What on Earth is it doing now?

The dinosaur clamped its jaws on the post and braced its legs. The muscles in its neck strained as it shook its head and tried to rip the post out of the ground, all the while growling furiously.

Zeke panicked when he realized what the animal was trying to do. "Hey! Stop that, stop!" he cried.

The boy jerked back on the reins with all his might, but it was hopeless. The rex was immovable! The post drifted back an inch, then two . . . There was a terrible creaking noise like the sound of a rusty door hinge only much louder, and suddenly the bottom of the post was free. Zeke hunched his shoulders and cringed expecting the roof to cave in any second but nothing happened.

The T-rex roared in frustration and raced toward a second post, hitting it full force. Then the animal whirled, smashing the support with its tail. The support creaked, and began to bow from the weight of the roof. Zeke looked up to see the roof start to sag.

"Oh lord," he said. This was not going the way he'd planned!

Again the dinosaur struck the beam with its massive tail, and the remaining roof supports all seemed to collapse at once. The T-rex let out a triumphant roar as the roof began to fall inward.

Rex Riders

Zeke pulled furiously on the reins to move the T-rex in the direction of the barn doors but the beast was oblivious to the mayhem that was unfolding around it. Zeke was paralyzed with fear and indecision. Should he hop down and make a run to safety or trust that the animal's inborn survival instincts would drive it out of the barn in time? His mind went blank and he had no idea what to do. Fortunately, the T-rex decided for him.

The dinosaur lowered its head and crashed into the barn doors, bursting through just as the roof collapsed. A pair of chickens, scratching around, flew up in the air, and the rex lunged at one and then the other, catching each in midair. Zeke made a few mental notes: likes to eat chickens and wolves; swallows chickens whole; keep hands away from mouth!

The rex took off toward a nearby wooded area and plunged into the brush. But in its headlong flight it ran into a fallen tree and smacked its head.

"Ha! That'll teach you, you ole—*Auggh!*"

Zeke never saw it coming. As he turned his attention to taunting the rex, the beast veered in the direction of a low-hanging branch. The limb hit Zeke in the chest and clotheslined him from the saddle, knocking the wind out of the boy. Zeke was lucky he landed on a grassy patch of ground so no serious harm was done.

You might wonder how a horse reacts when its rider accidentally falls to the ground. There is no single answer that applies to every animal. It depends a lot on the creature's temperament and how it was trained.

This T-rex was not the forgiving kind. And Zeke had done what no one should ever do. He rode someone else's rex. When

Chapter Four

the dinosaur realized it had finally thrown the pesky teenager, it was payback time, and the beast wanted its pound of flesh—literally!

Zeke struggled to his feet and dusted himself off. A low guttural snarl stopped him. He slowly raised his head and came face-to-face with the rex, who stood a few feet away. The animal drew to its full height. The nails on its claws clicked together as the beast opened and closed them in anticipation of the attack.

Zeke was no dinosaur expert, but he knew the rex was angry and about to charge. But what to do? Pick up a stick or rock? Wave his arms and shout? Or turn and run? Zeke decided to run.

And for a second, Zeke thought it might work. Then he heard a roar, followed by the clomping sound of the rex's clawed feet as they hit the ground directly behind him.

At that moment, Zeke knew that fleeing was a mistake and he'd never be able to outrun the beast. So he sprinted toward the closest tree as fast as he could until his chest ached and his legs burned from the exertion.

When he reached the tree he leapt for a branch that was high enough so he'd be out of range of the rex's jaws. Unfortunately, Zeke was no gymnast. As he grabbed the limb, the best he could manage was to swing his legs up and wrap his feet around it so his butt hung down.

The rex snapped at him, and Zeke lashed out with his legs, kicking the beast in the nose with no effect. It wasn't long before Zeke lost his grip and dropped to the ground.

Zeke scrambled backward against a tree trunk. He shoved his hands into his pockets desperate for something he could use as a weapon to keep the rex away, and pulled out a hunk of Stumpy's beef jerky.

"Back, back!" Zeke shouted, as he kicked with his legs and brandished the jerky like it was club. The rex snapped its jaws as Zeke swung the dried meat back and forth before its nostrils. The rex's nose twitched as it got a whiff of the savory treat. Suddenly, it stopped snarling. It licked its lips and leaned in to get closer to the jerky.

Noticing the change in the rex"s demeanor, Zeke held out the jerky. The animal was now focused completely on the meat. It would be risky, but Zeke slowly stretched out his arm, and the rex licked the meat several times with its large pink tongue.

"Yuck." Zeke tossed the jerky to the ground at the creature's feet. The big animal sniffed and licked the meat again to make sure it was edible, before swallowing it. The rex seemed calmer.

Zeke held out the rest of the jerky. The beast took a step toward the prize just as calm as could be. With his free hand Zeke reached out and took the bridle. This time the rex made no move to get away. Its attention was fixed on the treat.

Zeke took a step toward the rex's side and considered the empty saddle. All of a sudden the stirrup seemed really far away.

Do I try this again? he thought. *Or do I drop the meat and head back to the ranch while I have the chance?*

Zeke sighed.

He fed the last piece of jerky to the T-rex and got back in the saddle. A cowboy doesn't quit! And with that, he gently urged the newly-obedient rex forward.

* * *

Rex Riders

Back in town, Uncle Jesse and Bull picked up Stumpy and told the old cook everything they had learned. Stumpy's meal with Jean-Claude had also gone well, but Jean-Claude knew very little about what he was needed for other than that the game he was hired to trap would be big.

By the time they finished their meal, the two men were fast friends, and Jean-Claude promised he would visit Monsieur Stumpy and prepare his famous beaver l'orange, assuming he could trap a beaver and obtain some oranges, which seemed questionable given the locale.

The men agreed that D'Allesandro was up to something. But what? Parts of his story made sense on the surface but others sounded crazy. The trike was dead and the idea that more of them might be around was ridiculous. Yet, every sign pointed to the rancher getting his spread ready for some really big animals just like Slim had said.

There was no question his men had shot the stranger but his story about the Rex Rider stealing something that belonged to D'Allesandro sounded like a lie. D'Allesandro was after something valuable and wasn't going to tell them what it was.

As they neared the Double R, Bull turned to Uncle Jesse with a puzzled expression. "Hey Jess, remember when we left this morning?"

"Yeah."

"The barn was still there, right?"

"What?!"

Uncle Jesse leapt to his feet while the buckboard was still moving and fell backward. "Stop this thing, darn it all!" he yelled.

Chapter Four

He stood on the seat to get a better view of the barn, and sure enough, the roof had caved in! He threw his hat on the ground and turned to Stumpy.

"I should've known better than to let you talk me into bringing that Rider into the house! When am I going to learn my lesson?"

"Me?!" Stumpy sputtered. "Are you accusing me of talking you into something? I haven't been able to talk you into anything since the day I met you! That was your idea!"

Uncle Jesse clenched his jaw and stared at Stumpy. "Bull, let's get moving. We have to see if that boy is okay. Lord help me if he isn't!"

From a high ridge, Zeke looked down at Dos Locos from atop the T-rex and gently stroked its neck. He had run out of jerky but the animal seemed as tame as one of Uncle Jesse's horses.

"The town's in that direction," he said. "The Double R is over there, and that's where I come from"—he pointed to a range of mountains in the east—"a long way from here. I bet nobody ever saw anything like you back home. I wonder where you're from."

He and the dinosaur stood for a while, contentedly staring at the sun setting over the mountains.

"Well, we better be getting back. It'll be dark soon, and everyone will be wondering where we went to."

When the three men arrived at the main house, Uncle Jesse jumped off the buckboard. "Stumpy, you and Bull check the barn," he cried, running inside. "See if that dragon thing is still tied up."

Rex Riders

Uncle Jesse took out his gun and silently looked inside each room, cursing himself for leaving Zeke behind. He was relieved when he saw the Rex Rider was right where he'd left him, but there was no sign of the boy.

And then it hit him.

"If Zeke took off on that critter, there'll be hell to pay!"

He raced out of the house to join Stumpy and Bull as they poked through the wreckage of the barn. Fortunately, although the center of the structure had collapsed, the four exterior walls remained intact, so there weren't any casualties among the live-stock, except for a couple of missing chickens.

"Well?" Uncle Jesse cried.

"Near as we can tell, the critter ain't here," Stumpy said. "And neither is Zeke."

"Oh, I'll bet you Zeke had something to do with this! I told that boy to stay away from it!" Uncle Jesse shouted.

"Take it easy, Jess," Bull said, trying to calm him down. "We don't know what happened. Maybe the animal got out by itself and did all this."

"Maybe it ate him," Stumpy offered, before realizing what he said.

Uncle Jesse glared at Stumpy. "That'll be the least of that boy's problems when I get my hands on him," Uncle Jesse replied. "I should have known better than to leave him here alone! Spread out and look for tracks."

"I got some here!" Bull yelled. "They lead that way." He pointed in a southwesterly direction.

"Bull, get the horses and meet me back at the house," Uncle Jesse said. "I'm going to get my rifle."

Chapter Four

"It's going to be dark soon, Jess," Bull said. "Maybe we should wait—"

"I know it's getting dark," Uncle Jesse said sharply. "But I can't leave Zeke out there all night. I've got to try to find him."

Zeke rode the T-rex back to the ranch at a leisurely pace, while humming a cowboy song his mother used to sing to him when he was a baby. At one point a bear stood and watched them but kept its distance.

The closer the boy got, the more excited he became about telling everyone what had happened and temporarily forgot that the rex had torn down the barn. It's funny how a little thing like that can slip your mind when you're having fun.

When Zeke finally saw the main house, he realized he hadn't eaten anything in hours and began to imagine how great it would be to have dinner with Uncle Jesse, Bull and Stumpy, while sharing his experiences from the day. The boy was sure they'd be impressed with his resourcefulness.

"Hey, everybody!" Zeke shouted, beaming with pride as he approached the house. "Take a look at this!"

Stumpy's selective hearing was in full force, and he was the first to hear the boy's call in the distance.

"Zeke's back!" the old cook yelled. "And it looks like he went and tamed it!"

Uncle Jesse was loading his rifle in the kitchen when he heard Zeke's voice. He closed his eyes and let out a huge sigh. But his feeling of relief was quickly replaced by anger. Zeke had disobeyed his order to stay away from the creature. This was a problem he intended to fix . . . *permanently*.

"Darn it all, Zeke! I told you to leave that animal alone!" Uncle Jesse cried angrily as he stepped from the porch.

"But Uncle Jesse, wait until I tell you what happened," Zeke said excitedly.

"I can see what happened! My barn is wrecked, and you're riding the very same critter I told you to stay away from. Am I talking to myself around here?"

Uncle Jesse raised his rifle and pointed it at the T-rex. "Now, get down from there."

"Uncle Jesse, what are you doing? He's tame. I swear it," Zeke shouted. "Stumpy, tell him."

"I can see how tame it is for myself. I don't need you to tell me! Now get down!" Uncle Jesse cocked the trigger.

The T-rex growled menacingly, as it leveled its gaze at Zeke's uncle.

"You don't know what you're talking about!" Zeke cried. "I'm not getting down! You'll have to shoot me, too!"

There was a loud crash from inside the house. Uncle Jesse clenched his jaw and yelled to Bull. "Tie up those horses and go see what that noise was. I ain't done yelling at Zeke and I've got some business here I need to finish."

Bull grunted and rushed off.

"Like I was saying before I lost my place—" Uncle Jesse began, before being interrupted by another loud crash.

"Hey, Jess!" Bull called from inside the house. "You know that fella that was sleeping in the back room?"

"Yeah."

"He's awake. And he don't look happy!"

Chapter
Five

"Zeke, you take that critter back to what's left of the barn and stay out of sight," Uncle Jesse ordered. "I'll deal with you and that thing later. Stumpy, come with me."

The Rex Rider stood swaying in the doorway to the back room. He was rubbing his eyes and had the groggy expression of someone who had just awakened from a deep sleep. Tying him to the bed frame hadn't accomplished very much. Uncle Jesse had left some slack in the ropes, since the stranger was recovering from gunshot wounds, and he'd easily freed himself.

"I got him covered, Jess. He ain't going anywhere," Bull said as he waved a pistol at the Rider.

"Put that thing down, Bull," Uncle Jesse urged. "You'd just be wasting your bullets."

Although Uncle Jesse wouldn't have admitted it, the Rider

was one scary-looking figure. The light in the hallway was poor, and in the half-shadows, he looked like a monster out of a nightmare. He was so broad that he filled up the doorway. Everywhere you looked he had some kind of bony scute, plate, bump or horn. On those areas of his body that weren't covered by body armor, his skin hung on him more loosely than a human being's, and his muscles rippled and flexed with every movement in a way that reminded Uncle Jesse of a muscular animal like a horse. His three-fingered hands reached down almost to his knees, and when he leaned back and yawned he had the worst morning breath imaginable.

"Whew! He smells just as bad standing up as he did lying down," Bull commented as he waved a hand in front of his nose in a useless attempt to dispel the stench. "And that breath; that's just nasty."

"Let me try to talk to him," Stumpy volunteered. He cleared his throat and stepped forward. "You speak English?" he asked slowly emphasizing each word. When his question failed to get a response, Stumpy tried a variety of Native American languages and even threw in some sign language, but the Rider gave no indication that he understood anything Stumpy was saying.

"Well, that didn't work. I seem to remember you saying something about a plan a while back," Stumpy said, looking at Uncle Jesse.

"I'm thinking," Uncle Jesse snapped, as he tightened his jaw.

"We got it under control," Bull said, eyeing the Rider. "He won't try anything funny if he knows what's good for him. It's three against one. He doesn't stand a chance."

Bull smacked his fist into the palm of his hand to show he

Chapter Five

meant business. The Rider may have been disoriented, but he understood Bull's gesture meant the cowboy was spoiling for a fight, and if that was what these men wanted, he'd give them one!

The Rider's eyes narrowed, struggling to focus as he stared at Bull. He reached for the leather pouch that hung from his belt. When he discovered it empty, he angrily muttered something unintelligible under his breath. Then he turned toward the door frame and ripped out a four-foot chunk of wood and nails. It was an impressive display of raw strength and wasn't lost on the boys.

"Now that ain't right," Bull moaned . "He's gonna have to fix that."

The Rider tapped the makeshift club into his palm as he stepped toward the men who simultaneously took a step back.

"Let's take this outside, boys," Uncle Jesse said.

While Uncle Jesse and company backpedaled toward the front door, Zeke rode the rex back to the barn as Uncle Jesse had ordered. He'd been so caught up in trying to stay in the saddle when the animal ran amok inside the barn that he hadn't fully appreciated the extent of the damage caused while it was happening. But now, his heart sank as he assayed the situation. The barn was a disaster! This was going to be impossible to explain. Fortunately, although the rex had knocked out the central supports causing the roof to collapse, the walls and smaller beams were still intact.

Zeke ducked his head as he steered the rex through the broken barn doors. He was relieved to hear the ranch animals make their usual commotion as the dinosaur approached. It sounded as though none of them was harmed! That was a stroke of luck. The best thing to do now was to light a lantern and wait until Uncle Jesse called or somebody came for him.

Inside the house, the Rider plodded unsteadily toward the three men, threatening them with the hunk of torn door frame.

"Stumpy, get out of here and make sure Zeke is safe," Uncle Jesse ordered. "Leave the fighting to Bull and me."

Stumpy knew better than to argue in a time of crisis, so he slipped out and headed for the barn. The old cook was no coward, but the days were long past when he settled arguments with his fists. That was for younger men.

Bull ducked out next. He positioned himself against the wall on one side of the doorway with a weathered rocking chair close by. Then, stripping out of his shirt, he tore off its long sleeves, wrapping them around each hand to protect his knuckles, the way boxers do.

As Uncle Jesse backed out onto the porch, he closed the door behind him to conceal his movements from the rider. Picking up a small table made from a couple of boards and some tree limbs, he positioned himself on the side of the doorway opposite Bull. The two men glanced at one another. The trap was set. As soon as that rider came through the door, they'd ambush him and regain control of the situation.

The Rider shattered the top of the front door with a single blow from his massive fist. A second blow sent the door flying off its hinges and cartwheeling off the porch.

As he continued through the doorway, Bull swung the rock-

Chapter Five

ing chair, striking him squarely across the back. But the chair bounced off like a rubber arrow and the Rider barely budged. He merely shook his head, then wheeled around to face his attacker. Bull tossed the chair aside, lowered his shoulder and plowed into his adversary's midsection, fists flailing.

Now it was Uncle Jesse's turn. While Bull pummeled the Rider with his fists, Uncle Jesse swung the small table over his head and brought it down on the Rider's neck and head. The force of the blow destroyed that rickety table, but didn't faze his opponent one bit. Instead, the Rider locked his long arms around Bull's waist. Then, in one motion, he jerked the brawny ranch hand off his feet and over his shoulder. Bull landed atop Uncle Jesse, who was taken completely by surprise! The two men crashed to the porch in a heap. So much for the trap.

Zeke was pacing when Stumpy reached the barn. "What's going on? Is everything okay?" he asked.

"Everything's under control," Stumpy said reassuringly. "That fella your uncle tied up in the back of the house woke up on the wrong side of the bed, and Jesse and Bull are trying to calm him down."

"Is it working?"

"That's hard to say. Last I saw, the front door flew off and that fella was coming after them with a hunk of wood about four feet long and full of nails."

"What?!" Zeke exclaimed. "Stumpy, we have to help them!"

"Son, we're going to give them a couple of minutes to get to know one another and sort things out," Stumpy said calmly. "Then we'll ride out front and see if they need us."

"But what if we're too late?" Zeke asked.

"We won't be too late," Stumpy answered firmly. "Those boys know how to defend themselves. They've been in a lot of scrapes together and seen it all. You can trust me on that."

As Bull and Uncle Jesse struggled to untangle themselves and get back on their feet, Uncle Jesse shook his head in disbelief.

"We ain't doing so well," he said.

"He's a tough one," Bull agreed.

The Rider looked like he'd recovered his faculties, which was a bad sign since the battle hadn't gone too well when he was plainly woozy. But a cowboy never quits, so even though Uncle Jesse and Bull shared a sinking feeling this was a losing proposition, they refused to give up.

Uncle Jesse put up his dukes and assumed the stance of a prize fighter while Bull egged him on. Perhaps skill could succeed where brute force had not.

"Okay Jess. Take your time, take your time."

The Rider responded in kind by raising his hands in front of him. But instead of clenching them into fists, he kept them open.

Uncle Jesse had been in enough fist fights to know better than to start swinging without first taking the measure of an opponent. And the Rider's fighting ability had so surprised him, he decided to proceed extra cautiously.

As Uncle Jesse circled, he feinted a few times to test the Rider's reflexes. Each time, the Rider tried to catch Uncle Jesse's hand, something no human opponent had ever tried to do.

"That ain't fair! Fight like a man!" Bull shouted. "You got him, Jess. That's it! He can't get you, you're too fast. Draw him

Chapter Five

in and get inside those arms, then let him have it."

Uncle Jesse threw a series of jabs that were deliberately short of the mark, and when the Rider lunged to catch his fist, Uncle Jesse stepped inside his opponent's long arms and let loose with a crisp right cross that caught him flush on the two small horns at the bottom of his chin. It was perfectly timed and executed, but the blow had no effect on the Rider. Uncle Jesse, however, felt like he'd just punched a rock!

Bull winced when he heard the solid thunk of Uncle Jesse's fist landing on the Rider's bony chin, "*Ooooh, that didn't sound good."

"*Yow!*" Uncle Jesse screamed, as he leapt around the porch in pain, massaging his aching hand.

The Rider grabbed the back of Uncle Jesse's shirt while he was in mid-hop, spun him around and unloaded on him. The last thing Uncle Jesse saw before everything went dark was a big three-fingered fist hurtling toward him.

It was all up to Bull now. The burly rancher glanced around the porch for something to use as a weapon and settled on Stumpy's old rocker. For an instant he considered whether to take a different one, but he never liked the ratty, old piece of junk, anyway. So he hoisted the heavy oak chair over his head and swung it at the Rider.

The blow never reached its mark. The revitalized Rider plucked the chair out of Bull's hands before it hit him and threw it out of reach. Then he grabbed the front of Bull's shirt with one hand, lifting the stunned cowboy off the floor, and slapped him across the face.

"Put me down!" Bull shouted, blood trickling from his nose

as he struggled to free himself from his opponent's iron grip.

The Rider smiled slightly and stepped toward the railing to oblige Bull and threw him off the porch with such force that Bull actually bounced a couple of times upon hitting the ground.

When Bull came to a stop he was out cold.

The Rider looked at one man and then the other. They were no longer a threat. He remembered seeing a third man—an older one —but he was gone. The Rider raised his hands over his head and exulted with a roaring cry that echoed across the silent fields surrounding the ranch.

"Stumpy, did you hear that?" Zeke whispered.

"I heard it," Stumpy said.

"It sounded like someone screamed *D'Allesandro*," Zeke said.

"I think you're hearing things, son," Stumpy said.

"What do we do now?"

"Well, it looks like it's up to you and me," Stumpy said.

"So we're going into town to get help, right?" Zeke asked nervously.

"Heck, no! We're taking him on," Stumpy replied, slapping Zeke on the shoulder.

"What?" Zeke exclaimed as his heart started beating faster. "How are we gonna stop him if Uncle Jesse and Bull couldn't?"

"Son, if you wanted to catch a long horn steer, would you try to wrestle him with your bare hands or rope him?"

"Rope him, of course."

"Exactly. No sensible man would try to wrestle a steer if he had a rope. You'd get yourself killed. So go get your rope, and saddle up."

Chapter Five

"Should I take the sorrel or this critter?" Zeke asked, gesturing to the rex.

Stumpy rubbed his chin as he considered the question. "Don't know for sure." He put his hand on Zeke's shoulder and looked the boy in the eye. "Son, you showed me something in town a while back when that three-horn went loco. I'm going to leave this decision to you. Saddle up quick and meet me out front. I'll abide by whatever you decide."

With that, Stumpy mounted his palomino and rode out of the barn with his rifle and his pistol to wait for Zeke.

Zeke thought this was a heck of a time for people to start trusting his judgment. Couldn't they have started with something easier like what to have for dinner? The boy looked at the rex. He was barely acquainted with the animal, but there was something special about it. In a weird way, the whole episode in the barn had convinced Zeke that the animal had a high level of intelligence, and maybe that would be a help to them in whatever they were about to face out there. Then again the dinosaur was unpredictable, and Zeke had no more beef jerky. His sorrel knew him and responded to his touch without fail. They'd gotten out of lots of predicaments together.

"Hurry up, Zeke!" Stumpy called in a hushed whisper.

"I'm coming," Zeke yelled; then under his breath, "I just don't want to screw up again."

He took a deep breath and grabbed his rope. Time to choose!

The Rex Rider looked around the porch, getting his bearings. The fog he was in when he awoke had lifted, and he was feeling more like his old self. Still, he had no idea how long he'd been unconscious, where he was or how he got here. The last thing he could remember was feeling dizzy and falling off his T-rex. He didn't recognize the men he just fought, and worst of all, he didn't know where his rex was. The Rider sighed. Since the first day he arrived in this bizarre place things had gone from bad to worse, and now he'd lost his rex!

As the Rider walked around the porch and stretched his muscles, he noticed how achy and sore he was from the gunshot wounds. For the first time he realized that someone had treated them, though some of the bandages had fallen off during the fight.

He gently examined the wounds. All of the bullets had been removed! But who did it? Surely not D'Allesandro's men; they had been trying to kill him. Maybe it was the men he'd just fought. They weren't part of the group that bushwhacked him back at the creek bed. But then why did they just attack him?

None of it made any sense. There were too many questions and no answers. The Rider went back inside the house to make sure there were no men hiding in wait for him.

Stumpy had his rifle ready and his eyes locked on the house, as he waited for Zeke outside the barn. *Where was that boy?* he thought.

Zeke appeared through the doors astride the T-rex.

"Steady," Stumpy said to his horse. "He ain't nothing to be afraid of."

The old cook's soothing words seemed to do the trick, and both horse and T-rex proceeded toward the main house.

"Zeke, hold your rope like I taught you, and grab the reins

Chapter Five

with your free hand. We're going to come at that hombre from different sides. If one us manages to lasso him, we'll drag him around the barn. That should take some of the fight out of him."

Zeke shuddered. Getting dragged by a horse was awful! But what Stumpy said made sense. If Uncle Jesse and Bull weren't strong enough to take him, they should use the animals to fight the stranger.

The Rider heard voices in the distance and realized reinforcements were coming just as he feared. He had to get out of there. No warrior could defeat an army single-handedly. There was no time to waste; he needed his rex!

The Rider reached for the large, hollowed-out tooth that hung from his neck and blew. It emitted a high-pitched sound that was hard on the ears, like the sound of fingernails scraping a blackboard. If his T-rex was anywhere nearby, it would come when called. Maybe it would know the way home. But even if it didn't, it could still carry him to a safe place to hide and recover while he tried to figure out what to do next.

When Stumpy and Zeke heard the sound they knew it was a signal, but they weren't sure who or what it might be signaling.

"I hope he isn't calling for reinforcements," Stumpy said. "One of him is enough."

The T-rex became stock-still. Only its eyes moved, and they darted back in forth as if trying to pinpoint something.

Stumpy and Zeke noticed the change in the dinosaur's demeanor and looked at each other. Maybe bringing the rex wasn't such a good idea, after all. People trained dogs to respond to whistles, and the same was also true of horses. Why not strange, two-legged critters with lots of big teeth?

"What is it, boy?" Zeke asked in a low voice. "What's the matter?"

The Rider blew into the tooth again. *Where is he?* he thought impatiently. If he couldn't find his rex, escape would be more difficult. There was no way he could find his way out of this place on his own and these men would surely try to kill him. For the first time it struck him that the rex might be lost, or worse, dead. He took a deep breath.

Upon hearing the whistle for a second time, the rex growled and started toward the house, but Zeke pulled back on the reins and restrained him.

"Stumpy, what should I do?"

Stumpy grabbed his rope and smiled. "Too late in the game to change horses, son! Stay close, and watch me. If I go down, ride into town and get help! Don't try to take him by yourself. Now, let's ride! *Yee-hah!*"

The old cook looked over at Zeke as they galloped toward the house. *It was a lot to ask from a greenhorn,* he thought, *but that boy was a game one!*

The Rider heard Stumpy's cry as he stepped out onto the porch. He glanced around for something with which to defend himself. The guns the men used were deadly, but useless because they were too small for his large hands to manipulate. He considered grabbing the porch railing to use as a battering ram or the beat-

Chapter Five

up old chair that was lying next to him as a missile. The Rider tugged on the railing to test how hard it would be to rip free and dislodged it easily. He changed his mind and stuck it back. For now, he'd stick with the chair. At least until he saw what the men intended to use against him.

As Stumpy and Zeke rode toward the house, Stumpy collected his thoughts. He knew bullets wouldn't work against the Rider, and wasn't surprised he'd beaten Uncle Jesse and Bull. Those young bucks thought that brute strength was the answer for everything! Getting old had taught Stumpy otherwise. He chuckled to himself as he thought about all the plans Uncle Jesse had concocted over the years that had gone awry!

Zeke shouted a warning when he saw the Rider on the porch, preparing to hurl a chair at them. Stumpy ducked low on his horse to make himself a smaller target. Then he noticed that the chair the Rider was using as a weapon was his old rocker, and that sent him over the edge.

"Put that down!" he shouted. "I got a bad back! That's the only chair in this gol-darn place that's broken in!"

Stumpy's shouts went unheard. When the Rider saw Zeke riding his T-rex, he couldn't believe his eyes! No one had ever ridden his animal before! How was this possible?

Stumpy let his lariat fly, and it looped around the curved legs of the old rocker. In the blink of an eye, he tied the end of the rope around his saddle horn and yanked it away, but the Rider barely noticed. He was mesmerized by the sight of Zeke riding his rex.

Zeke saw Stumpy's success in disarming the Rider as the

perfect opportunity for him to attack. He charged from a different angle, expecting to pull the Rider off his feet in dramatic style after roping him.

The boy's throw was right on the mark, his lasso dropping around the Rider's shoulders just as he'd planned. But when Zeke spurred the T-rex into a gallop away from the Rider, the dinosaur abruptly slowed and, instead, proceeded in a friendly trot toward him!

"Git," Zeke shouted, but the T-rex continued on its course.

I knew I should have taken the sorrel, he thought.

Zeke was sure this was the end, but instead of yanking him off the rex and pounding him, the Rider wrapped his long arms around the animal's head, ignoring the boy completely. He gently scratched the rex under its chin, and whispered something to it in a language Zeke had never heard before. Then the Rider looked at Zeke and smiled.

"Who are you?" he asked in a deep, raspy voice.

For a moment Zeke was speechless. "I'm Zeke. Zeke Calhoun. You speak . . . *English,*" he said in amazement.

"I speak many languages," the Rider explained. "How did you ride my yerka?"

"Yer-what?"

"Yer-*ka,*" the Rider explained. "The beast you sit upon."

"Oh, that's what you call it." Zeke just shrugged. "I don't know. I just rode him."

The Rider looked puzzled; then his face grew dark. "Where is the one called 'D'Allesandro'?" he demanded. "We have business that is not finished."

"He isn't here," Stumpy said as he sidled up beside Zeke.

Chapter Five

"You're at the Double R Ranch. D'Allesandro's spread is about five miles away from here . . . that way."

"How did I get here?" the Rider asked. "Did D'Allesandro's men bring me?"

"No. Zeke found you and your ride out by Small's Stream a couple of days ago just before it started raining. You were shot up, and your critter was protecting you from a pack of wolves. If Zeke and I hadn't pulled you out, there's a good chance you would've drowned."

"You were shot about seven times," Zeke continued. "My Uncle Jesse said it was okay to put you in the back room, and Bull went into town and got Doc. He's the one that took all the bullets out."

The Rider couldn't follow all of the unfamiliar names, but he understood the gist of it.

"I am grateful for all you have done for me, and I am sorry about the others. I thought they were friends of D'Allesandro."

Stumpy laughed. "Friends? That's a first. No, they ain't friends. And we know all about D'Allesandro." He spat on the ground in contempt.

Then the old cook turned to Zeke. "Son, I think it's time we made sure your Uncle Jesse and Bull are okay."

Zeke got down off the T-rex and handed the reins to the Rider.

"Let me help you," the Rider said. He commanded the rex to "stay," then noticed the neckerchief that Zeke had tied around the animal's leg.

"He got bit by a wolf. It didn't hurt him much—he's tough. I don't think he even noticed. I put that on to stop the bleeding."

The Rider squatted down and examined the injury. "Does

D'Allesandro know I'm here?" he asked.

"You can put your mind at ease," Stumpy said. "No one knows you're here except us."

"And Doc," Zeke added.

"What is your name, ancient one?" the Rider asked.

"I'm Stumpy Gibbons, and I'd appreciate it if you didn't call me 'ancient one,' thank you very much."

The Rider showed no sign he'd heard Stumpy's request. "Are you the chief of this tribe?"

"Not exactly," Stumpy responded with a chuckle. "Although I probably ought to be, seeing as how I'm the smartest. I do the cooking around here. The man lying on the porch owns this place. He's Jesse McCain. And that big fella lying over there on the ground is Bull. What do they call you, friend?" Stumpy asked.

"Friend," the Rider repeated. He'd heard the word before, but it hadn't meant much in this place. Still, these men seemed different.

"I am a Tarngatharn. My yerka is called Gixkarnu," he declared, patting the T-rex on the neck.

Stumpy cleared his throat and considered both names for a moment. "How about we call you 'Slim' and we call your ride 'Hellfire'?"

The Rider was surprised by the request. "All right," he finally replied.

"Then I'm glad to make your acquaintance, Slim." Stumpy reached out to shake the Rider's hand.

Slim hesitated. He was vaguely familiar with the gesture, but this was the first time it had been offered to him. He accepted the old cook's hand and it vanished inside his huge mitt.

Chapter Five

"Let me introduce you to Jesse McCain," Stumpy said.

Although it may sound strange, it never occurred to Stumpy that Uncle Jesse or Bull would have any lasting animosity toward Slim once they had a chance to sit down together and the misunderstanding was explained to them. Fist fights were a part of life on cattle ranches where groups of men worked together shoulder to shoulder for months at a time and sometimes rubbed one another the wrong way. Brawls didn't happen often, but when they did, they were quickly forgotten by the participants, who rarely bore a grudge. After all, a cowboy takes his lumps and doesn't complain.

Uncle Jesse had recovered and was sitting on the floor of the porch examining his sore hand when Zeke, Stumpy and Slim approached.

"Let me help you up," Slim said as he offered his hand to Uncle Jesse.

Uncle Jesse's mouth fell open when he heard the Rider speak.

"Better take my other hand. That head of yours is as hard as a rock," Uncle Jesse said, as Slim helped him to his feet. "I never should have taken a poke at you."

"I thought you were with D'Allesandro," Slim said. "If I had known the truth, I never would have hit you."

"Well, that's good to know," Uncle Jesse said. "Where's Bull? Is he okay?"

"He's lying out there, Uncle Jesse," Zeke said, pointing to an area off in the dark.

"Hey, Bull. You okay?"

Bull was lying on his back, looking at the stars. "Yeah, I'm all right except for my head. Who are you talking to?"

"We're talking to Slim, the big fella that knocked you for a loop," Stumpy replied. "Go inside and get yourself cleaned up, unless you're planning to spend the night out here. I've got to fix you boys some dinner."

"You tell that Slim that he's gonna have to pay for this shirt," Bull shouted.

"Tell him yourself; I got work to do."

"I will."

"Good luck collecting it," Stumpy muttered under his breath as he headed inside the house.

"Slim," Uncle Jesse began as he massaged his sore hand, "why don't you come in and we'll get better acquainted."

"Yeah!" Zeke exclaimed. "And I can help you with Hellfire. We've been keeping him in the barn. He loves it here! Come with me. I'll show you."

Slim thought for a moment. Should he trust these men? Then he laughed as Zeke ran back to where Hellfire was standing and took hold of the yerka's reins. The boy had no fear of the animal and reminded Slim of himself when he was young.

"Go with Zeke while we tidy up," Uncle Jesse said. "He'll take care of you. When you're done, come back to the house."

Zeke bombarded Slim with questions the whole time it took to bed Hellfire down for the night in the barn. When they returned, Slim was carrying the front door under his arm.

"Uncle Jesse, Slim found the front door and he's gonna put it back on for us," Zeke said.

"Well, that's mighty neighborly," Uncle Jesse said politely, as he bit his tongue. "But there's no need to do that tonight, Slim.

Chapter Five

Why don't you just stick the door in the corner for now and we'll fix it tomorrow. And pull up a chair while you're at it."

Slim set the door down and picked out the strongest looking chair to sit on, next to Zeke.

"I see that your barn is crumbling," Slim observed.

Uncle Jesse shot Zeke a look. "Yeah, that's a good way to describe it: 'crumbling,' That happened a little earlier today while I was in town. I was gonna ask Zeke how it happened but didn't get around to it. I have a feeling Hellfire might have been involved, too."

"Then I am responsible as well," Slim said. "Perhaps, I can help you to fix it." Just then Bull walked into the kitchen looking like he had the world's worst headache.

"Pull up a chair and say howdy to Slim," Uncle Jesse said.

"I think I'll stand, thank you," Bull said as he eyed Slim warily.

"Suit yourself," Uncle Jesse said, then turned his attention back to his guest. "We've never seen anyone like you or Hellfire before. Where do you call home?"

Slim looked at Uncle Jesse with a puzzled expression.

"Where did you come from?" Zeke asked, trying to be helpful.

"I am from a place called Ismalis," Slim replied.

"I think I've heard of it. That near England?" Bull asked.

Uncle Jesse rolled his eyes. "Help me out, Slim. Where exactly is this Ismalis in relation to Dos Locos?"

Slim hesitated for a moment. "I do not know," he said finally.

Uncle Jesse leaned forward. "Then how did you get here?"

"D'Allesandro brought me."

"So you're saying D'Allesandro brought you here from

Ismalis, but you don't know where it is. Is that right?"

"Yes." Slim looked at Uncle Jesse and Bull and could see they didn't believe him.

"Do you think me a liar?" he asked.

Stumpy cleared his throat. This conversation was heading in the wrong direction. One fight per evening was more than enough for him. "Slim, it ain't none of our business, and I know these two won't ask you straight out, so I will. How did you come to get involved with D'Allesandro and how did you get yourself shot up?"

"D'Allesandro is planning to move a herd of thurgs onto his land," Slim answered. "If he does that, he will start a war with the Cragnon. They will never let him take their thurgs without a fight. I came here to try to convince D'Allesandro not to."

"What's a thurg?" Uncle Jesse asked.

"They are large beasts—grass eaters. They have two horns on their heads and one on their snout."

"Uncle Jesse!" Zeke exclaimed.

Uncle Jesse nodded. "I know, son. Slim, I think we may have seen one of them thurgs, but nobody knew where it came from."

"Let me see if I understand you," Stumpy said. "You're saying D'Allesandro is going to rustle a few of these critters from a tribe that calls themselves the Cragnon and bring them back to Dos Locos. And if he does that, the Cragnon are gonna go on the warpath?"

"More than just a few," Slim explained. "Hundreds. And that is just the beginning."

"That's crazy," Bull said with a laugh. "He'd need an army to move that many of them."

Chapter Five

"He has one," Slim said.

Uncle Jesse leaned back in his chair and glanced at Bull. The pieces were falling into place.

"When is he planning to make his play?" he asked.

"I don't know, but I think it will be soon," Slim said.

"Why did D'Allesandro's men shoot you?" Stumpy asked.

"I told D'Allesandro that if he did not agree to drop his plan, I would do everything I could to stop him. These Cragnon are warriors. They will slaughter everyone and burn your villages to the ground. No one will be left alive, and no building left standing. This is what D'Allesandro brings upon you. You must warn your people."

Uncle Jesse, Stumpy and Bull looked at one another. Cowboys don't take threats well, and they had a hard time believing Slim's prediction. Dos Locos would never be destroyed. Her citizens would rally together as a community and do whatever it took to defend themselves.

Still, Slim had been shot multiple times and didn't die. Then he beat the stuffing out of them the first day he got out of bed. Not only that, Hellfire single-handedly defeated a wolf pack and nearly tore the barn down. If these Cragnon were anything like Slim and Hellfire, maybe they could destroy Dos Locos!

Uncle Jesse turned to Zeke. "Son, maybe you better go to your room."

"Let him stay," Stumpy said. "He's proven he's man enough."

Uncle Jesse sized up his nephew. "You're right," he finally agreed. "But don't think you're off the hook with that barn."

"No, sir," Zeke said.

"Slim, these Cragnon you're talking about, are they like you?"

"No, they live on the plains and they ride the u'hars."

"What's a 'you-har'?" Bull asked. "Are they anything like Hellfire?"

"No, they are not like yerka. They are like . . ."—Slim paused as he struggled to think of a comparison—"they are like your chickens, only bigger. D'Allesandro's men call them warbirds."

"Well that doesn't sound too bad. What's a giant chicken gonna do? Lay an egg on you?" Bull said with a laugh. "How much bigger are we talking about?"

Slim held a hand a couple of feet over his head.

"Wait a minute," Uncle Jesse said. "You're telling us they ride on chickens that are taller than you?"

"That don't sound right," Bull said.

"These Cragnon . . . do they have guns?" Stumpy asked.

"No," Slim replied. "They are an ancient race, and cling to the old ways. Their weapons are from the ground."

"You said that D'Allesandro brought you here," Uncle Jesse said. "But I still don't get it. How did he get you here?"

"He used a machine that was buried deep in the forest of Khuradar. You have one in your land. If we can find it, I can return home."

"A machine," Uncle Jesse repeated. "Where is it?"

"Somewhere in the mountains. My yerka may know the way."

"Maybe we can help. Bull knows these mountains and so does Stumpy. Let me sleep on what to do and talk it over with the boys tomorrow morning. In the meantime, you're gonna need a place to stay until we can find this contraption. You can sleep in the back room, and Hellfire can stay in the barn."

"The horses are getting to know him and they aren't scared of

Chapter Five

him anymore," Zeke said excitedly.

"Thank you, but I must get home," Slim said. "There is much that needs to be done."

"Slim, we aren't gonna try to stop you if you've made up your mind to go," Stumpy said. "But you just fought a heck of a fight, and aren't healed up yet. Why don't you give yourself a day or two to regain your strength before you take on D'Allesandro. You said yourself he's got an army. And they aren't gonna show you any quarter. Besides, D'Allesandro's at his ranch; Jesse here was there today."

"What!" Slim cried as he rose to his feet. "Why didn't you tell me?"

"Now hold on, Slim," Uncle Jesse said. "I wasn't trying to hide anything. I was just listening to what you had to say. You're in no shape to take on D'Allesandro, especially at his ranch. He's got the place built up like a fortress, and his men have orders to kill you as soon as they lay eyes on you. D'Allesandro told me as much. But as long as he's at the Crossed Swords, he can't be rustling those critters you were talking about."

Slim looked at the faces of the men and the boy. What they said made sense, and they seemed sincere. The fight with Uncle Jesse and Bull had greatly fatigued him, and there was something about the air that made him sluggish. He needed time to recuperate from his wounds if he was going to go up against D'Allesandro and his men. It had only been one day since Doc removed the bullets, and the wounds weren't fully healed. A good night's sleep would do him good.

"I am grateful," Slim said. "I will stay, but only for a day or two."

"Then, it's settled," Uncle Jesse said. "Slim, a big boy like you probably has a big appetite. Well, you're in for a treat. Stumpy here is the best cook north of the Rio Grande. Stumpy, how soon 'til we eat?"

"Another couple of minutes. I threw something together before we went to town and it's almost done," Stumpy said as he stirred a pot, which emitted a delicious aroma that filled the kitchen.

Slim apologized to Uncle Jesse and Bull again for walloping them, and the men took it in good humor. They even had a laugh about the broken door.

Stumpy tasted a spoonful of stew and smiled. "Tastes just right!" Then, he carried the pot to the table and ladled a nice size portion into a bowl for Slim. Everyone waited while their guest maneuvered the fork into his bowl and took a taste.

"Blehh!" Slim exclaimed as he spit the food back into his bowl. "This is food for a yerka!"

"Then Hellfire will eat your portion," Stumpy said matter-of-factly.

"Slim, what can I offer you?" Uncle Jesse asked. "Would a steak suit you better? What kind of food do you eat? You're welcome to anything we have."

"I'll be right back," Slim said.

The Tarngatharn carried his bowl of stew to the barn for Hellfire and returned with one of the horse's feedbags, full of hay and oats. To the men, it looked disgusting and smelled bad, but as Slim contentedly chewed, Zeke thought it suited him. Slim went back to refill the bag several times before he declared himself full.

Chapter Five

After the meal was over and the table cleared, Stumpy brewed up a pot of coffee, and everyone retired to the porch.

"You know, Slim, I've been thinking," Uncle Jesse began. "What's your stake in all this? Are you some kind of lawman?" Unfortunately, Uncle Jesse happened to sit back on the same section of railing that Slim had pulled loose during the fight and it gave way under his weight, sending him tumbling backward off the porch.

Stumpy had to work hard to keep from laughing, while Zeke held his breath expecting a big explosion. But when Uncle Jesse got back on his feet, instead of being furious like he usually was when something like that happened, he just looked determined.

"Slim, as long as you're gonna be here for the next couple of days, I think I may take you up on your offer to help. First thing tomorrow morning we start fixing this place. We can start with this railing."

Before he could continue, a loud noise pierced the air, followed by a foul smell, and all eyes turned toward Slim.

Stumpy pretended to yawn. "Well, I'll see you boys in the morning bright and early for breakfast. We're getting an early start, so I'm going to bed."

"Me too," Zeke said, jumping to his feet and hurrying after the old cook. "Good night everybody."

Uncle Jesse leaned over to Bull who had pinched his nose with his fingers. "I think Slim and I need to have a little talk about his manners."

"Good idea."

Chapter
Six

The following morning, Uncle Jesse got up even earlier than usual. His right hand was throbbing, the knuckles so badly bruised it was painful for him to flex. But nothing was broken so he considered himself lucky. He wanted to talk to Stumpy and Bull in private before Slim woke up, so he quietly dressed and made his way to the kitchen, where Stumpy was already busy fixing breakfast and Bull was enjoying a cup of coffee. They were expecting him.

"Better pour me a cup, pronto; I'm dragging," Uncle Jesse said. He looked at the dark bluish bruise under Bull's eye and the red lump on the bridge of his nose, and raised a tin mug in salute. "Here's to you, young fella. You look like you've been in a fight. How do you feel?"

"Okay, I guess," Bull answered. "I'm lucky he only hit me on the head. How's your hand?"

"Sore," Uncle Jesse said, massaging his knuckles. "Next time I'll wrap my hands like you did before I hit someone made of rocks. I'm paying the price today."

"That was quite a story Slim came out with last night," Stumpy said.

"It sure was," Uncle Jesse agreed.

"I'm still having trouble believing he can speak English," Bull said. "Do you think we can trust him?"

"I spent the night thinking about it and I'm still not sure," Uncle Jesse said. "But a lot of what Slim said about D'Allesandro makes sense."

"I'm not surprised," Bull said. "We all knew D'Allesandro was up to something."

"The question is what do we do about the Cragnon? We can't just ride into town and tell folks they're gonna be attacked. That would be like saying the crops are going to fail because of a drought next summer or there's going to be a bad winter two years from now. People won't take it seriously.

"None of us has ever seen or heard of them Cragnon," the old cook continued. "So when people start asking questions, we won't be able to answer. We don't even know where Slim comes from."

"I wouldn't mention the giant chickens, either," Bull interjected.

"You're right," Uncle Jesse said, shaking his head in frustration.

"We could bring Slim into town and have him speak for himself," Bull said. "Heck, he speaks English better than I do."

Chapter Six

"That seems too risky to me," Uncle Jesse said. "Who are the townspeople gonna believe, D'Allesandro or Slim? We already know what D'Allesandro will say about Slim and Hellfire. He'll twist the story around and make it out they're monsters, and some people will believe him simply based on how they look. And if D'Allesandro finds out that Slim is staying with us, he'll send his men over to finish him off. I don't want that trouble here."

"We could do nothing," Bull offered.

"But if what Slim told us turns out to be true, we'd be responsible for placing the whole town at risk," Uncle Jesse said.

"I don't think you have much of a choice," Stumpy said. "You have to go back with Slim and see things with your own eyes. D'Allesandro's a shrewd one. You can't go up against him without knowing all the facts."

"You think we ought to bring Doc into this . . . or the Sheriff?" Bull asked.

"Not yet," Uncle Jesse said. "Not until we have a better idea of what's really going on."

"You can always call on them later," Stumpy agreed.

"Then it's decided," Uncle Jesse said. "Bull and I will tell Slim as soon as he wakes up."

"Tell me what?" Slim asked.

The men turned their heads in surprise to see Slim standing in the doorway to the kitchen. How long had he been there? For a big fellow he moved very quietly.

"Bull and I are going with you to size up the situation," Uncle Jesse said. "Maybe we can talk some sense into D'Allesandro and get him to stop. It's worth a try."

"Good," Slim said, nodding his head. "There is wisdom in your decision. I am pleased. Perhaps you will have more success than I did."

"I'd like to leave first thing, tomorrow morning," Uncle Jesse said.

"What's wrong with today?" Slim asked in a tone that sounded more like a demand than a question.

Uncle Jesse shifted in his chair and looked Slim in the eye. "I'd rather wait," he said firmly. "That will give me today to get things in order and make some repairs around here. I can't run this place without a barn and right now my barn is wrecked."

"Bull, why don't you get Zeke out of bed, and we'll have some breakfast and get started," Stumpy said, as he stirred a pot full of boiling water and hay. "Slim, I cooked something I think you'll like. I call it hay soup. Take a seat and tell me what you think."

Slim seemed a bit peeved when he sat down, but his attitude changed as soon as Stumpy set a bowl of his steamy concoction on the table in front of him. It smelled like wet horse and looked awful, but when Slim gave it a sniff, he broke into a smile.

"Yuckash!" he said.

"I'll take that as a compliment," Stumpy said, winking at Slim. "Just a little something I came up with last night. And I have a brand new recipe for pan-fried hay that I'd like to try out before you leave."

Then the old cook turned to Uncle Jesse and Bull. "You boys want to try some?"

Before they could tell him no, Zeke stumbled into the kitchen and looked into the pot Stumpy was holding.

"What's that?"

Chapter Six

"Hay soup. Your Uncle and his partner over there ain't interested. You want a bowl?"

"Sure," Zeke said, and Stumpy poured a serving.

"Slim, did you ever go to a barn-raising?" Uncle Jesse asked.

"No," Slim said between slurps.

"Well, there's a first time for everything. It's sort of a big celebration where folks come together to build a barn. It's a hard job for one family to do alone, but a group can do it in under a week. I have a hunch that with your help, we'll be able to repair the barn and a few other things that need fixing around here, and still make the square dance tonight. I'm not that interested myself, of course, but there's somebody sitting at this table who wants to go pretty badly."

Uncle Jesse nodded his head in Zeke's direction.

"I don't know who you're talking about," Zeke said defensively as he drank his soup. "I only mentioned it once or twice. Hey, Stumpy, this is good."

"Once or twice?" Bull said.

"Okay, a few times," Zeke admitted. "It's just that we don't have them that often, and they're fun."

"Which reminds me," Uncle Jesse said. "In all the commotion around here yesterday, I never got around to asking you how the barn fell. Why don't you enlighten us."

"Well . . ." Zeke began slowly. "Hellfire got kind of upset about something and pulled out a few of the supports. The next thing I knew, the roof caved in."

"Uh-huh." Uncle Jesse gave Zeke one of those looks that said, *you've got to be kidding me*. "I suspect there's a little more to what happened than that."

"Not really," Zeke said as he dug into his soup, keeping his head down. "That's about it."

"And how did your saddle wind up on Hellfire's back with you in it?" his uncle continued. "Did that part happen before or after Hellfire got 'upset'?"

"Oh. I guess I left that part out," Zeke said.

"How about you fill that part in."

"Are we gonna keep jawing here all day?" Stumpy interrupted, rising to his feet. "We have work to do. You have a barn to raise, chairs and railings to fix, and I got vittles to prepare for the square dance tonight. And ain't nothing gonna get done while you're yakkin' about ancient history.'"

Stumpy grabbed Slim's empty bowl and hobbled to the sink, winking at Zeke along the way.

"Zeke, if you're finished, start clearing this table," he said.

Zeke jumped to his feet and carried his dishes to the sink. No one had ever seen the boy move so quickly to do housework before.

"I mean to get to the bottom of this," Uncle Jesse grumbled. "And if I don't do it before Bull and I leave with Slim, I'll do it when I get back. You understand, son? I'm not forgetting about this."

"Yessir," Zeke said from the sink.

Uncle Jesse, Bull and Slim left to inspect the damage to the barn, leaving Zeke and Stumpy to straighten up the kitchen.

"He's just giving you a hard time," Stumpy said with a chuckle.

"I know," Zeke said, laughing. "I'm getting used to it."

* * *

Chapter Six

Later inside the barn, Uncle Jesse knelt down and inspected one of the broken supports that was lying on the dirt floor.

"The base has been chewed up pretty badly," he remarked.

"But it broke farther up," Bull observed, pointing to a spot by the roof.

"It looks like Hellfire pulled it out of position at the base, and the weight of the roof snapped it. It'll have to be replaced. For now, let's see if we can prop up the roof with what's left while we check the rest of the damage."

Meanwhile, Slim did his own reconnaissance, walking around the barn, pushing a strut here, pulling a beam there. After a few minutes, he rejoined Uncle Jesse and Bull.

"What do you think, Slim?" Uncle Jesse asked.

"It can be fixed," the Tarngatharn said optimistically.

The men looked at one another and then at Slim. "You game to try?" Uncle Jesse asked.

Slim simply nodded.

"Then let's get started," Uncle Jesse said, slapping Slim on the back. "Yow, that hurts!" he cried. "And that was my good hand! Bull, remind me not to do that again . . . *with either hand.*"

For the next several hours they worked together. Slim was able to do the work of a team of men. His great strength enabled him to lift and position logs that would have taken several to move. Occasionally, he felt short of breath and had to rest—the only sign that he wasn't completely healed from his injuries. But he recovered quickly.

Zeke joined them after he finished helping Stumpy in the kitchen, and Stumpy wandered over a bit later to offer a running

Rex Riders

commentary about what they were doing wrong. It was hard for Zeke not to laugh. When Stumpy wasn't telling them how he'd do everything differently—if only he didn't have a bad leg—the old cook regaled them with anecdotes about barn-raisings he'd been involved with in the past. Neither Bull nor Slim paid any attention, but Stumpy knew just what to say to get under Uncle Jesse's skin.

"Why are you putting that support over there?" he asked.

"'Cause this is where it goes," Uncle Jesse answered as he began hammering the nails that secured the wooden beam.

"Hmm . . . seems to me you'd be better off moving it over about five feet," Stumpy said.

"Well, I'm not putting it there," Uncle Jesse said firmly.

"Fine. Do it your way. It's your barn, but I'd move the support over about five feet."

Uncle Jesse took his eyes off the spot he was hammering. "Look, you old coot, I know what I'm do— *Yow!*" The hammer landed squarely on Uncle Jesse's good thumb.

"You should really watch what you're doing," Stumpy advised as Uncle Jesse hopped around the barn holding his sore hand.

"Why don't you mind your own—" Uncle Jesse whirled around and bumped his head on a low hanging rafter.

"And watch your head," Stumpy said.

"Out! Get out!" Uncle Jesse screamed. "And take your bad leg with you!"

"I come in here to help with my considerable experience and wisdom, and get nothing but grief for my efforts. I can tell my help is not wanted. I'm going back inside and fix something for

Chapter Six

you boys to eat. If I have time, maybe I'll get your saddlebags ready for tomorrow," Stumpy said with all the indignance he could muster.

By the time Stumpy had finished his speech, Uncle Jesse looked like steam was going to come out of his ears, while Zeke was almost doubled over in pain from trying not to laugh out loud.

Once the old cook had left, Bull looked at Uncle Jesse. "You think maybe he was right about the support, Jess?"

Uncle Jesse glared at him.

"You're right. This is the spot."

By the time the midday meal was ready, the boys had successfully raised the collapsed roof and restored the original roofline. It wasn't a permanent fix, but it was good enough for the short run and it opened up the floor of the barn, giving them more room to work. By mid-afternoon they'd fixed the barn door, the entrance to the ranch house and the porch railing.

"Not bad for a half-day's work," Uncle Jesse said, looking pleased. "Now I think it's time to get ready for tonight."

As much as the men teased Zeke about wanting to go to the square dance, everyone had been looking forward to it. Community dances provided an opportunity for the people of Dos Locos and the surrounding area to put aside their work for an evening of socializing, eating and fun.

A banquet of food would be set out on long tables, buffet style, and every family and ranch contributed a dish they were proud of. Although most of the food was southwestern, the westward expansion over the years guaranteed a variety of unusual foods of different nationalities that the men had never seen or tasted before.

Stumpy prepared a big pail of pork and beans and buried it in the ground over a bed of hot coals to ensure the fat, molasses and other seasonings blended together.

Pork and beans was a favorite of working men and considered a meal all by itself. Stumpy never scrimped on the ingredients when he prepared the dish for the men at the Double R. But for special occasions he went all out and made it richer than ever. There may have been fancier foods but few were as deeply satisfying.

Of course you couldn't have a square dance without music and someone to call the steps, and Stumpy was both a harmonica player and a square-dance caller. He planned to sit in with Mr. B, who played the fiddle, and his brother, Mr. G, who played the guitar, and the three men would take turns calling the dance.

Stumpy had fooled around with a harmonica when he was a boy, but it wasn't until he became a cowboy that he taught himself how to play. It was common for cowboys on cattle drives to bring along musical instruments for entertainment around the campfire at night. Harmonicas were favored because they were both portable and durable.

Cowboys were also good at improvising songs and poems on the fly, and entertaining one another with tall tales and amusing stories. Calling a square dance was a different skill that involved presenting cues to the dancers which told them what steps to make, but it wasn't hard to master.

Zeke had attended a couple of square dances since he arrived

Chapter Six

in Dos Locos, but he hadn't paid any attention to the actual dancing. He ran around having fun with his friends from school, doing things like catching fireflies.

Angelina's invitation put a different spin on things, and as the day of the dance drew closer, he started to feel nervous. All of a sudden Zeke felt this pressure to act a certain way and say the right things. It wasn't anything specific Angelina had said to him—they hadn't even talked about the dance since her invite—but for the first time in his life, Zeke cared about what a girl might think of him, and he didn't want to embarrass himself by saying or doing the wrong thing.

So instead of looking forward to the dance, he started to dread it. It even crossed his mind that maybe it'd be easier if he just stayed home and told her he'd gotten sick. There wouldn't be any way for her to check up on him, and Uncle Jesse wouldn't ask any questions.

Stumpy noticed the change in Zeke's mood as the night of the square dance approached and suspected it had something to do with Angelina. He also figured the boy was reluctant to speak to either his Uncle Jesse or Bull because of all the teasing he'd have to endure. So the old cook casually asked Zeke if he'd mind helping him with the calls he was working on. In the process, Stumpy walked the boy through the basics of square dancing. And by the time they'd finished, Zeke's confidence had grown, and the boy felt like he'd be able to hold his own on the big night.

While Zeke spent hours fretting over seeing Angelina at the dance, Uncle Jesse was very blasé over Maria Con Fuego's interest in seeing him. He was flattered by Maria's invitation, and Angelina's mother was attractive, but the ranch owner wasn't interested in courting her.

For some men Maria's proximity to the D'Allesandro fortune would have been a powerful aphrodisiac, but Uncle Jesse was cut from a different cloth. He didn't have any interest in getting a hold of money he didn't earn with his own two hands, let alone D'Allesandro's. Besides, Zeke's uncle wasn't ready to get married and put down roots. He wasn't sure he wanted the responsibility of running the Double R, and getting serious with a fancy lady like Maria would tie him down. Yet, when it came time to get dressed, Uncle Jesse looked cleaner, sharper and more handsome than anyone could recall seeing him in a long time.

"Now that's some get-up," Stumpy said when he saw Uncle Jesse's fancy shirt and jeans, and spit-shined boots.

Zeke had never seen his uncle dressed up before and was shocked. Even Bull took note and remarked that Uncle Jesse looked "better'n a tater in a beef stew." Coming from the burly ranch hand, that was high praise indeed.

Bull wasn't one for socializing, himself. He didn't go in for dancing or making small talk with the ladies. But he did look forward to seeing his friends from other ranches and farms and swapping stories with them. Most of them also preferred to stand on the sidelines and observe the festivities. So Bull wasn't in any danger of being bored or lonely. And the food was something he'd been thinking about for weeks.

When it was nearly time to leave for town, Slim approached Uncle Jesse.

"Do you mind if I go for a ride while you're gone?" the Tarngatharn asked.

Chapter Six

"I don't see why not," Uncle Jesse said. "I doubt anyone will be coming out to the Double R tonight. Everyone's going to be in town. Just wait until after sundown to be safe.

Slim nodded.

"There is one thing, though," Uncle Jesse added. "I'd rather you didn't take Hellfire. It's not that I don't trust your good judgment, but someone might come across his tracks and follow them back to the Double R. I want to leave here tomorrow morning without any trouble. No one knows you're here, except for us and Doc. If it's all the same with you, I'd like it to stay that way."

"Then how will I ride?" Slim asked.

"You'll take my horse."

That raised a couple of eyebrows. "Your horse?!" Bull, Stumpy and Zeke exclaimed at once. Even Slim seemed more than a little surprised.

"Let's take a walk out to the barn," Uncle Jesse said putting his arm around the Rider's shoulder. "You come too, Zeke."

The way Slim reacted, Uncle Jesse was half expecting he'd put up an argument, but he didn't say a word. Slim just walked out to the barn and wondered to himself how this was going to work out.

"Ordinarily, finding a horse strong enough to handle someone your size would be tricky, but Midnight isn't from around here. He's bigger and sturdier than other horses. And since we'll be traveling to town on the buckboard, I won't need him tonight."

As Slim maneuvered his giant foot into Midnight's stirrup, Hellfire growled

"I think he's jealous," Zeke said.

"Ah, just ignore him," Uncle Jesse replied. "Slim, you get on up there."

The Rider swung himself into the saddle and Hellfire's response was frightening to see. The dinosaur roared and pulled wildly on his restraints.

"Maybe this isn't such a good idea," Zeke cried nervously. The boy was no stranger to what the great beast could do when it was upset.

This was Uncle Jesse's first exposure to the rex's fury, and he couldn't help wondering how his young nephew was able to handle the creature. *That boy's got guts,* he thought. *No question about it.*

"Zeke may be right, Slim," Uncle Jesse shouted. "I'm not looking to have my barn knocked down again. It ain't worth it. Not after all the work we put into repairing it."

Slim didn't seem to hear. He was in a world of his own as he stroked Midnight's neck. The Tarngatharn had never ridden a horse before and wondered how the experience would compare to riding a yerka. But when Hellfire's tantrum grew louder and more violent, Slim got down off Midnight and walked over to Hellfire just as calm as could be.

Uncle Jesse was sure the angry T-rex was going to take a bite out of his master, but Slim gently stroked Hellfire and spoke to him in a low voice. Soon the creature calmed down. It was an amazing sight: one moment Hellfire seemed out of control, the next he was purring like a house cat. Then Slim got back on the big stallion like nothing happened.

"You feel okay up there?" Uncle Jesse asked as he kept an eye on Hellfire.

Chapter Six

Slim nodded. There was no mistaking the Tarngatharn's way with animals. Midnight took to him immediately. Hellfire started growling again, but Slim growled right back.

"Did you ever ride a horse before?" Zeke asked excitedly.

Slim shook his head with a laugh.

"Go on and take him around the barn a couple of times," Uncle Jesse said. "It may take a minute to get used to him."

That was all the encouragement Slim needed. He rode Midnight straight out the barn door with Zeke running behind. After only one trip he stopped, but the usually stoic Tarngatharn was smiling from ear to ear.

"He'll do," Slim said. "He'll do nicely."

Soon it was time to leave for the dance. Stumpy stowed his big metal pail of baked beans in the buckboard and everyone took their usual place. Zeke waved goodbye as Slim watched them depart from the porch.

They had ridden only a short distance when Uncle Jesse looked back over his shoulder to see that Slim was already gone.

He didn't waste any time, Uncle Jesse thought. *I wonder what he's up to.*

Uncle Jesse continued to roll that question around his head all the way to the dance. Whatever Slim was doing, Uncle Jesse hoped it didn't involve any more damage to the Double R.

The party was just getting started when the boys arrived. People were strolling around greeting each other and the buffet tables were beginning to fill up.

Zeke had rehearsed what he intended say to Angelina during the trip into town so he'd appear cool and calm, and give off just the right air of confident self-assurance when he saw her. He figured he'd find Angelina near the bandstand, so while Uncle Jesse tied up the horses, that's where he headed.

Sure enough, Angelina was watching the musicians tune their instruments, along with a group of other kids from the schoolhouse. She was wearing a vest over a pretty white dress, and her long hair was done up with ribbons under her cowboy hat.

Angelina didn't notice Zeke at first, giving the boy a good opportunity to admire her from a distance. *She's beautiful,* he thought.

Then she turned around.

"It's about time you got here," Angelina called as she started walking toward him. "I thought maybe you weren't coming."

Zeke gulped. In spite of the fact that they were classmates and knew one another fairly well, he felt himself getting warmer. Zeke was literally speechless and might have stayed that way if Uncle Jesse hadn't come up from behind and given him a friendly slap on the back.

"Evening, Angelina," Uncle Jesse said, tipping his hat. "Where's your ma?"

"Over by the buffet table talking to some people," Angelina replied.

"Thanks." Uncle Jesse noticed the terrified look on Zeke's face. "You okay, son?"

Zeke nodded.

"All right then. You kids have a good time, now."

But Zeke's strange, frozen expression remained.

"Hey," Angelina said with concern. "You okay?"

"Oh . . . uh . . . yeah . . . fine," Zeke stammered.

Chapter Six

"When did you get here?"

"Uh . . . just a few minutes ago," Zeke said woodenly, as he slowly recovered the power of speech.

"You want to go for a walk?" Angelina asked.

"Okay."

Although the conversation was awkward at first, and there were plenty of long pauses, Angelina managed to keep it going. And the longer they walked and talked, the more Zeke loosened up and started acting like his old self.

"So how do you like it here?" Zeke asked.

"Very much," Angelina said. "It's different from back east. Isn't that where you're from?"

"Yeah," Zeke said. "After my mom died, I came out here."

"I'm sorry," Angelina said, biting her lip. "Do you like living with your Uncle?" she continued, quickly changing the subject.

"I guess so." Zeke laughed. "Like you said, it's different. My dad left when I was still a baby, so growing up, it was just my mom and me. I never even knew I had an uncle; my mom never mentioned him."

"When you get older, do you think you'll stay here?"

"I'm not sure. I kind of like being a cowboy. What about you?"

"My mother wants me to go to college back east, but I prefer it here."

"You should think about college," Zeke said. "You're smart."

"You are too," Angelina said, blushing.

"Nah," Zeke said. "I'm no brain. The good thing is, out here that doesn't make much of a difference. A man can make his way without being book smart. Look at my uncle. He's got his own ranch; he's doing pretty well."

Rex Riders

"My uncle says the world is changing, and it's going to be important to get an education, whether folks like it or not, and there won't be any cowboys in the future."

Zeke said nothing. He'd heard this kind of talk before. The West was changing, and the old ways were threatened by forces that people in small, out-of-the-way towns like Dos Locos couldn't control. Of course, if there weren't any cowboys, where did that leave Zeke and his plans for the future?

"Yeah, well, your uncle can't see into the future." Zeke sniffed. "Nobody knows what's going to happen. My uncle says that cowboys will always be around. A man who knows how to work with his hands will always have a job. He can't be replaced."

"My uncle says that if he could find a way to see into the future, he'd be a millionaire."

Zeke laughed. "A millionaire? That's crazy. Nobody in Dos Locos could be a millionaire."

"Maybe not," Angelina said. "But what if you could?"

"That's a good question . . ." But before Zeke could answer, Angelina let out a squeal.

"Hey, the food's ready! Let's get something to eat!" she cried, taking off toward the buffet. "Come on!"

Zeke couldn't help but notice that even wearing boots and a dress, Angelina was pretty darn fast. "Wait for me," he yelled, running after her.

Meanwhile, Uncle Jesse was taking a leisurely stroll in the same direction. He was in no particular hurry, and it was just as well. You would have thought he was running for office what with

Chapter Six

all the men who stopped to say hello and the ladies who tipped their hats and made small talk as he leisurely strolled toward the buffet.

Slim's grave warning about a possible attack was on Uncle Jesse's mind, and he was on the lookout for any sign of D'Allesandro or his men. If the opportunity presented itself, he intended to speak to the rancher about what Slim said the night before. But Uncle Jesse hadn't seen more than one or two cowboys he recognized from the Crossed Swords. *That was typical,* he thought. D'Allesandro's men never seemed to be around. You would've thought the rancher would have given his men the night off, and they'd all be here.

Uncle Jesse caught sight of Maria in the distance, chatting and laughing with a group of people he recognized. There seemed to be a glow about her.

Like mother like daughter, Uncle Jesse thought. *No wonder Zeke was acting funny!*

As Uncle Jesse considered whether to approach the group or wait until Maria was alone, she caught sight of him and waved. Uncle Jesse took his hat off and walked over to where they were standing.

"Mind if I join you folks?" he said.

"Mr. McCain," Maria said, "I was hoping to see you and your nephew this evening! Did you bring Zeke along? Angelina was looking forward to seeing him."

"I saw them together a few minutes ago by the dance floor," Uncle Jesse said. "Of course they could be anywhere by now."

Maria turned to the group. "Mr. McCain was at my family's ranch yesterday on business with my brother, Dante."

"Business, you say?" Henry Poole asked suspiciously. "What kind of business?"

Uncle Jesse was a surprised by Henry's tone. It almost sounded like he was accusing Uncle Jesse of wrongdoing by talking to D'Allesandro.

"Just a friendly visit," he replied. "We were catching up on the cattle business. I hadn't been out to the Crossed Swords Ranch in quite a while—a couple of years at least. Nothing more than that."

"Mrs. Con Fuego here was telling us about her brother's plans to expand his holdings," Henry continued. "He's looking to build his cattle business and making offers to buy land. You're not thinking of selling the Double R, are you?"

"No, the subject never came up," Uncle Jesse said.

"Strange," Henry said skeptically. But Uncle Jesse refused to discuss it further, knowing that more denials would only fuel Henry's suspicions. After a few more minutes of chatting, Maria and Uncle Jesse excused themselves and strolled off.

"I hope I didn't overstep my bounds back there by mentioning you'd been out to the Crossed Swords," Maria said when they were out of earshot.

"No, not at all," Uncle Jess said reassuringly. "You know small towns. Everybody knows everybody else's business. Sometimes people let their imaginations run away with them, and they start reading into things. Saying I was talking business with your brother, people start assuming I'm selling out to him."

"I'm sorry if I gave them that impression," Maria said. "I didn't mean to."

"Don't give it a thought. Anyway, I straightened it out."

Chapter Six

"Do you square dance, Mr. McCain?" Maria asked, changing the subject.

"I've done a little square dancing in my time," Uncle Jesse admitted.

"Then perhaps you'll show me how it's done," Maria said playfully. "I'm a little rusty."

"It'd be my pleasure ma'am," Uncle Jesse replied, bowing deeply.

Uncle Jesse and Maria joined the dancers, and it turned out that Uncle Jesse more than held his own. Although they were both too modest to admit it, they were among the best dancers on the floor!

"I haven't done this since I left Dos Locos," Maria said as they stepped away to take a break. "I missed this life . . . and the west. It's a different world out here."

"It surely is. You grew up out here. What made you leave?"

"After I was married, I moved back east with my husband, where his family ran a large business."

Uncle Jesse was curious about what happened to Maria's husband, but realized it would be rude to ask, so he wisely steered the conversation in a different direction..

"I haven't seen your brother this evening." he said. "There's something I wanted to speak to him about".

"Dante couldn't make it tonight and sends his regrets," Maria explained. "He left town on business this morning."

The news surprised Uncle Jesse.

"Mind if I ask where he went?" he asked as casually as possible.

"New Mexico. My brother went to check on a new breed of

cattle, much bigger than the long horns we're accustomed to raising in this part of the country. A rancher in Santa Fe has a small herd, and Dante went to take a look. He says they're the future of ranching."

"I'm sure they are," Uncle Jesse said, studying Maria's face. He wondered what she knew about her brother's plans. After all, she lived under the same roof and had to know what was going on. Was it possible she was telling the truth, and D'Allesandro had gone to New Mexico to inspect cattle?

"Santa Fe's a nice town. I've been there myself a few times. Say, would you like some dessert? What are you partial to?"

"Some apple pie sounds good."

"It's *mighty* good," declared the unmistakable voice of Doc Simpson, who had worked his way across the room to speak with Uncle Jesse. "I just had a slice."

"Well, fancy meeting you here," Uncle Jesse replied. "Maria, you know Doc."

"Of course. Everyone knows Doctor Simpson," she said.

"So he's got you calling him *'Doctor'* Simpson, eh?" Uncle Jesse teased.

"Don't listen to him, Mrs. Con Fuego. I appreciate good manners, but *Doc* is just fine." He gave Uncle Jesse a playful glance.

"If you'll excuse me, *Doc*," Maria said. "I was just on my way to get us a couple of pieces of that wonderful pie you so highly recommend."

Doc waited until he was sure Maria was out of earshot.

"I've been meaning to ask you, Mr. McCain. How's your house guest feeling?"

Chapter Six

"He's doing a lot better," Uncle Jesse said. "You did a good job patchin' him up."

"Did he head back home yet?"

"He'll be heading back tomorrow."

"That so? And what about that unusual horse of his?"

"Left him purring like a kitten in the barn."

"Good. I'm pleased to hear it," Doc said. "Perhaps we can get together some time soon, and you can tell me all about it."

"Not too soon, Doc. I'll be going away for a couple of days," Uncle Jesse said. "We can get together when I get back?"

"Mr. McCain, you didn't mention you were going out of town," said Maria as she handed him a slice of pie. "On business?"

"It's just a little hunting trip, ma'am. I'm going with Bull. It will only be for a couple of days."

"When you get back, stop by," Doc interjected. "I'm eager to hear all about it." He reached out to shake Uncle Jesse's hand, but Uncle Jesse declined.

"Better not Doc, this one's a little sore." Uncle Jesse held up his right hand and showed Doc his bruised knuckles.

"Mr. McCain, that looks painful," Maria exclaimed.

"It's all right, ma'am," Uncle Jesse said. "Hardly worth mentioning, except Doc here has a handshake like a vice."

"More like a marshmallow," Doc said as he examined the injury. "Make a fist for me, please. *Hmm* . . . nothing seems to be broken; just badly bruised. Still, I would stay away from any strenuous activity for a few days. If you don't mind my asking, how did it happen?"

"Oh, just a little roughhousing. Nothing too serious."

"Yes, I understand," Doc said, smirking. "Well, it's time for

Rex Riders

this old timer to go to bed. It was nice seeing you again, Mrs. Con Fuego. Adios."

Doc tipped his hat and bowed.

"Adios, Doc," Maria said.

High upon a bluff overlooking Small's Stream, Slim sat on Midnight, seething with anger as he recalled the sequence of events that brought him here, culminating in the ambush that left him near dead.

D'Allesandro had wanted the force generator the Rex Rider carried, and now it was missing. Slim wasn't sure if the rancher's men had gotten it or if it had fallen out of its holster during the fight, but he was going to get it back either way.

As the Tarngatharn neared the stream bed, he pressed a button on the metal bracelet he was wearing. A broad beam of light shone over the area. At first, the scanner gave no indication of the generator's whereabouts, but then Slim noticed a faint trace of red by one of the bushes a dozen yards away. The device confirmed the generator had been in that spot.

Slim pressed another button and a three-dimensional grid appeared showing Slim's location in relation to the missing generator. What he discovered made him check his calibrations. It was back at the Double R!

It was nearly midnight by the time Uncle Jesse and Zeke bid goodbye to Maria and Angelina; late by country standards since farm work started before sunrise, and cowboys were accustomed to going to bed early.

Uncle Jesse offered to escort Maria and her daughter back to

Chapter Six

the Crossed Swords, but Maria politely declined, explaining that her brother had arranged a ride for them after the party. Satisfied they'd be safe, Uncle Jesse and the boys said their final goodnights and went on their way.

On the ride home, all Zeke could think about was the dance. This was one of those rare times when something he was looking forward to actually exceeded his expectations, and he wasn't alone in feeling that way.

"That was some party," Uncle Jesse said as the buckboard bounced along. "It looked like you boys had yourselves a good time."

"I feel bloated," Bull groaned. "I think I ate too much."

"What a surprise," Stumpy said, rolling his eyes. "That never happened before. Did anybody else get to try the beans I brought or did you eat them all?"

"I managed to get a spoonful," Zeke said. "That's all that was left by the time I got to them, but it was the best spoonful of beans I'd ever tasted."

"I saw you high-stepping it with Mrs. Con Fuego," Stumpy said to Uncle Jesse. "You did a pretty good imitation of somebody who knows how to dance."

"I've done a little square dancing in my time," Uncle Jesse said.

"It shows," Stumpy said, teasingly. "And I saw young Zeke out there too, with the prettiest girl in Dos Locos."

"I made it out of there alive," Zeke said, who was suddenly red in the face, although no one could tell in the dark.

"Anybody see D'Allesandro?" Bull asked. "I looked but I never saw him."

"Me, neither," Stumpy said.

"He's in New Mexico," Uncle Jesse said.

"New Mexico? What's he doing there?" Stumpy asked.

"Looking at cattle."

"What?! Who told you that?"

"Maria Con Fuego. Says he's interested in a new breed in Santa Fe that's bigger than ordinary longhorns. And Henry Poole told me that D'Allesandro's been looking to buy more property. He wants to increase his holdings."

Bull grunted while Stumpy remained quiet.

"Angelina said her uncle left with a group of men early this morning," Zeke volunteered, trying to be helpful. "But she didn't know where he was going."

When Uncle Jesse heard Zeke mention what Angelina had told him about D'Allesandro, he instantly regretted discussing the rancher in front of the boy. "Son, this doesn't involve you or Angelina," he said. "I don't want you asking her anything more about her uncle."

"But I didn't ask her," Zeke tried to explain. "We were just talking and she brought it up."

"I understand," Uncle Jesse said. "And if she brings it up, that's okay. But I don't want you two in the middle of this. It's not your concern and I don't want you taking advantage of her trust."

"But I wouldn't do that," Zeke insisted.

"I know you wouldn't," Uncle Jesse assured.

"He wouldn't have needed his men to go to Santa Fe," Stumpy said.

"Why don't we talk about that later," suggested Uncle Jesse.

Chapter Six

"Right now, I want to hear more about what everybody did at the party."

Zeke was asleep in the back of the buckboard when it pulled up to the main house of the Double R. There was lamp burning in the kitchen, and Uncle Jesse was glad to see the place was still standing.

Slim was munching on a big bowl of hay when they walked in, chewing in that slow deliberate style he had.

"Evening, Slim. Everything okay?" Uncle Jesse asked. "Midnight didn't give you any trouble, did he?"

"None. He is a good horse," Slim said.

"And I see the barn is still standing."

"It is," Slim replied with a slight smile.

"Good man," Uncle Jesse said.

"What did you do while we were gone?" Zeke asked. "Where'd you go?"

"I took a ride. Nowhere in particular," the Tarngatharn said, exchanging looks with each of the men.

"So now that you've had a chance to ride him, which do you like better? Hellfire or Midnight?" Zeke asked, fighting off a yawn.

"I like them both," Slim said.

"But which is faster?" Zeke asked, confident he knew the answer.

"Midnight is very fast," Slim admitted. "But speed is not everything. Where I come from, the forests have many dangerous beasts and traveling by foot is hard. The yerka is one of the most fearsome beasts, and other creatures stay away from it because they are afraid. It is in their nature. When they smell the yerka or hear its growl, they move deeper into the forest. So it is easier to travel safely.

"Midnight is fast but other animals would not fear him. Beasts, like the yerka, would lie in wait to attack, and Midnight would have to use his speed to escape. For this reason I think it is safer to ride a yerka, even though it is slower than the horse. It is better to ride an animal that other animals fear and try to avoid, than to ride an animal that must run away in order to survive."

Zeke hadn't thought of the question in those terms. "What about here? Which is better?" he asked.

"For here, I think the horse is better," Slim admitted.

"Then I guess that makes them about even," Zeke said, and Slim laughingly agreed.

"Time for bed, everyone," Uncle Jesse declared, stretching with an audible yawn. "We have a big day tomorrow."

Then Uncle Jesse turned to Zeke. "I'm expecting that you're gonna have to work a little harder around here until we get back. You need your rest to get all those extra chores done."

Zeke was too tired to argue. "Goodnight, everybody."

When Zeke opened the door to his room he saw a drawing propped up against his pillow. It was a detailed portrait of Midnight and looked just like the Andalusian.

"Whoa!" he exclaimed. "This is amazing!" Then it occurred to him to check under his mattress to see if that weird-looking pipe was still there. Sure enough, it was gone! Zeke couldn't help but feel guilty and wondered if he shouldn't have just given the object back to Slim right away. He always intended to give it

Chapter Six

back and hoped Slim wasn't mad at him.

Zeke knocked on Stumpy's door to show him the drawing. "Look what Slim left me while we were gone."

"*Hmm* . . . Not bad," Stumpy said as he held out the drawing at arm's length. "That Slim's a good artist."

"He never mentioned he could draw," Zeke observed.

"It wouldn't surprise me if he could do a lot of things he hasn't told us about," Stumpy said. "This is something special, all right. We'll talk about it more in the morning."

The old cook waited until Zeke closed his door and it was quiet before walking back to the kitchen. Uncle Jesse and Bull were still up, laughing and talking about the party.

"Slim's been snooping around," Stumpy whispered. "He was looking for something."

"How do you know?" Bull asked in a serious tone.

"He found some paper and pencils I keep in my room. I had them inside an old bed roll. He must have gone through my things. He drew a picture of Midnight, of all things, and left it in Zeke's room."

"Paper and pencils? That doesn't make any sense. What's he looking for? Is anything else missing?" Uncle Jesse asked.

"Not from my room," Stumpy answered. "You may want to check to see if he took any of your things."

"I will," Uncle Jesse agreed. "I think we all better sleep with one eye open."

Chapter
Seven

I t was after midnight when ten Cragnon warriors and their prisoner reached the outskirts of D'Allesandro's land. They rode single file through the darkness toward the Crossed Swords Ranch on the backs of the feathered dinosaurs that the rancher's men had nicknamed "war birds." They carried the weapons of their people—the spear, axe, hammer, knife and shield—decorated with large colorful feathers.

Although Slim had told Uncle Jesse and the boys the beasts were similar to the chickens he had seen scratching around the Double R, war birds weren't birds at all. They were a species of raptor. They had feathers and clawed feet like their distant avian cousins, but some of them stood almost ten feet tall and weighed as much as a full grown horse.

War birds were meat-eating dinosaurs that relied on a

combination of stealth and speed to chase down smaller creatures for food. Instead of wings, they had arms and claws for holding their prey, and long, whip-like feathered tails that helped them maintain their balance when they ran.

The plains people lived in harmony beside the war birds for thousands of years. Over generations, they bred a new strain of the beasts, a variety that was big enough to carry a warrior and fast enough to hunt triceratops, yet less ferocious and unpredictable than their wild counterparts. That didn't mean this new breed was tame; it just meant they wouldn't bite your leg off if they missed a meal.

When D'Allesandro's men first discovered the plains people's homeworld and began to explore the planet's vast grasslands, they found themselves under constant attack from the raptors. Professor Kornbluth warned the ranch owner and Cable Cooper not to let the men shoot too many of the feathered dinosaurs or it might attract unwanted attention, but Cooper called the Professor a coward, and told his boys they could do whatever they wanted. Wild war birds were a deadly nuisance, and getting rid of them was a priority.

D'Allesandro's men shot the creatures on sight for sport and left them to rot where they dropped. They made it into a contest to see who could kill the most, and the Professor implored D'Allesandro to make them stop. As it turned out, the Professor's instincts were right.

When the Cragnon discovered the bodies of the dead war birds and saw the animals' nesting grounds destroyed, they were outraged. They revered the creatures and killing them was forbidden; a crime punishable by death.

Chapter Seven

So they laid a trap and captured five of D'Allesandro's men.

The Cragnon were curious to learn who these men were, where they came from and why they'd come to their grasslands. When the men refused to cooperate, they were tortured until their bodies and wills were broken, and eventually they revealed D'Allesandro's plans to hijack the trikes. From that moment on, the Cragnon declared war on the strangers.

Of the five captives, only Tom White survived and the Cragnon forced him to lead them to the Crossed Swords Ranch. If their plan worked and the Cragnon gained the upper hand in the conflict with D'Allesandro, they would be merciful and Tom would be spared a slow, painful death. He would still be killed, but it wouldn't be slow and painful.

Tom was cheered and relieved to be back in the glorious State of Texas and to breathe the dry, clean air. He had been scheming to escape from these plains people since the day he was captured. When he stepped back onto Texas soil he made up his mind that there was no way he was going back to wind up as bird feed.

Escape wouldn't be easy. He had suffered mightily while in captivity. His clothes were tattered, his body was covered with scars and bruises, all of his joints hurt from the abuse he'd suffered, and he'd barely eaten or slept in days. That wasn't all.

His captors had tied one end of a rope around his neck, and the other end to a collar fashioned out of jagged shards of stone which they placed around the neck of a war bird. It was a devilish contraption. If Tom pulled too hard on the rope for any reason, the collar would dig into the neck of the war bird, and it would turn on him. If he managed to solve that puzzle with

Rex Riders

both of his hands tied together, he still had to escape the armed warrior that was guarding him.

As the band of marauders approached the Crossed Swords, they reviewed their battle plan. The first step was to cut the enemy off from their horses by setting them free. One group would take the corral and another would take the barn. Without their horses, the cowboys would be helpless against the Cragnon's attack.

The horses got wind of the Cragnon warriors before anyone else did. They could smell the war birds and became increasingly skittish as the dinosaurs approached. By the time the plainsmen reached the gate to the corral, the horses had moved to the opposite side and were making a terrible racket, whinnying and neighing in fear of the deadly beasts. And as the sounds of the horses carried through the night, the small crew of four sleeping in the Crossed Swords bunkhouse stirred.

"Carlos, get your butt out there and see what's up with those horses," Archie Turner said.

Carlos pretended to be asleep, but Archie wouldn't have it. "Carlos!" he shouted. "It's your turn. Move it or we'll throw you out."

"Aw, there's nothing going on," Carlos grumbled.

It was a losing argument, and Carlos knew it. The horses were making a racket, and someone had to go outside and investigate. The reluctant ranch hand got out of bed and slowly pulled his jeans over his long underwear.

"Move it along, will you Carlos? The boys and I need our beauty sleep."

"I'm going, I'm going," Carlos said.

Chapter Seven

He pulled his boots on, grabbed his holster and headed for the door.

"Call if you need us," Archie shouted as Carlos closed the door to the bunkhouse and walked stiffly toward the corral.

Carlos hadn't gone far when he saw what the commotion was all about. The gate to the corral was open, the horses were gone, and there were odd-looking people on top of equally strange two-legged animals inside the corral.

"What the heck is that?" Carlos exclaimed. "Where'd the horses go? Hey! *Hey!* What are you doing there?" He started trotting toward the riders until he was close enough to see them more clearly. Then he turned and ran back toward the bunk house to get help. He didn't get far. An axe flung by a warrior struck Carlos in the back and sent him sprawling facedown in the dirt. He tried to rise but a spear pinned him to the ground and ended his life.

When Tom White saw Carlos go down, he knew his friend wouldn't get back up, and had to turn away. It felt like someone had hit him in the gut. Tom knew all along that this is what the Cragnon were planning, and it killed him that he'd shown them the way to the ranch. This was the last straw. He'd find a way to escape or die trying. There was no way he was going back.

The warriors had split up into two groups to carry out their murderous plan. That left Tom against just one warrior. It was time to make his play.

The rope around Tom's neck was too thick to break, but there might be another way. He took the reins of his war bird and yanked them in the direction of the warrior who was sitting next to him. The war bird reacted instantly by moving to the side, and it collided with the guard's mount. At the moment of impact Tom jerked the rope attached to the collar around his dinosaur's neck, and the war bird he was sitting on reached over and bit the animal next to him. It was pure instinct and it happened so fast that the warrior could do nothing to stop it.

The guard tried to pull his war bird back, but it was too late. The animals set upon one another in a fight to the death. And each time Tom yanked the rope, his war bird increased the viciousness of its attack. He had gotten exactly what he wanted, but now the trick was to stay alive and avoid being clawed, bitten, thrown or crushed to death.

As Tom and his guard struggled to control their dinosaurs, the guard repeatedly jabbed his spear at Tom. It was impossible to aim the spear accurately on a bucking war bird, and Tom deflected it several times by hitting the shaft with his bound hands, but the rider got lucky and caught Tom in the side. It wasn't a very deep wound but it hurt like crazy.

Then it happened. The makeshift collar around the neck of Tom's dinosaur was torn in half just as he'd hoped.

Tom's war bird locked its jaws around the neck of its enemy, forcing it to the ground. Seizing the opportunity, Tom leapt from his dinosaur onto the rider of the fallen war bird, and they tumbled to the ground in a death match of their own.

His hands were still tied together, and the wound in his side was leaking blood, but that just made Tom fight harder. A blood-lust came over him, and he clasped his fingers together into a single solid fist, knocking the Cragnon warrior unconscious with several hard blows to the face.

Tom thought of his dead friends in the other world and

Chapter Seven

the savage killing of Carlos. He thought of what the Cragnon planned to do to the innocent people of Dos Locos and the blood bath that would follow when they unleashed their war birds on the town. He ripped a knife from the warrior's belt and raised it over his enemy's chest. He wanted to kill him for all of the things the Cragnon had done; make him pay with his life for all the pain he had endured as their prisoner.

But as Tom stared down at his unconscious foe he couldn't do it. The warrior was no longer a threat to his escape, and killing wasn't in Tom's nature. He staggered to his feet and stumbled off to find a safe hiding place where he could cut the rope that bound his hands together and tend to the wound in his side.

Back inside the bunkhouse, Archie stared at the ceiling and listened for Carlos's return.

"Something's wrong, boys. I'm going out to find Carlos."

Archie got dressed and strapped on his gun belt and holster. "Look for me if I don't come back."

He hadn't gone far before he found poor Carlos's body and began to sound the alarm.

"Attack! Attack! We're under attack!"

Archie's warning cries did their job, and the two cowboys in the bunkhouse leapt out of bed, grabbed their guns and took positions on either side of a window. They managed to bring down one of the warriors, but couldn't defend the sides of the building without windows, giving the Cragnon an opening to set fire to the bunkhouse. In the end they were overcome by smoke and never made it out.

* * *

Archie's cries also caught the attention of the attackers, and one of them broke from the group setting fire to the barn. Archie saw the warrior heading toward him and ran to the main house. He bound up the steps of the porch and hit the latch to the door just as a spear flew by, barely missing his shoulder.

Luck was with him!

He threw himself inside and managed to squeeze off two shots through the open doorway as he skidded across the floor. The rider sagged to one side with a mortal wound. Archie slammed the door shut and bolted it.

Maria sat up. A moment ago she was sleeping peacefully, and now her eyes were wide open. *What were those crashing sounds in the foyer? That was gunfire!* she thought.

And someone was shouting from the foyer at the top of his lungs: "Wake up! We're under attack!"

Maria yanked her dresser open and pulled out a pistol that was hidden underneath a pile of clothes in the top drawer. She checked the cylinder to make sure it was loaded before running into her daughter's room.

"Angelina, wake up."

Angelina sat up. "What's wrong? What's happening?"

"I heard shots," Maria said. "We're being attacked."

"Attacked? By who?"

"There's no time to explain. You have to hide." Maria scanned the room. "The wardrobe."

When Angelina first arrived at the Crossed Swords, her uncle had teased her about where she'd keep all the clothes she'd brought since her room had only a small dresser with a mirror and no closet. But less than a month later, an ornately-carved,

Chapter Seven

mahogany wardrobe with mirrored doors arrived and solved the storage problem. Now, it would serve as a hiding place.

Maria stripped the bed, stuffing the blankets and pillows underneath. Then she opened the wardrobe doors and began to throw Angelina's clothing onto the floor. Angelina looked at her mother like she was crazy.

"What are you doing?" she asked.

"This room needs to look empty. I don't want them to search it. Help me!"

Together they finished emptying the wardrobe and kicked everything under the bed.

"Get inside," Maria ordered.

"Please don't make me," Angelina pleaded. "Let me go with you." She began to cry and her mother put her arms around her.

"Everything's going to be okay. Just do as I say. Come on, I'll help you."

Angelina did as she was told and squeezed inside.

"Now, don't come out until I tell you to, no matter what!"

Maria kissed her daughter on the cheek and closed the door. She briefly considered locking it shut to make it more difficult for anyone to search inside, but then there would be no way for Angelina to get out.

"Stay there!" Maria shouted, and she ran back to her bedroom to get dressed.

With the horses scattered and the bunkhouse and barn in flames, the Cragnon converged on the main house. Their leader grabbed the head of a crude sledge hammer strapped to his back and shouted orders to the others, as he jumped down from his mount.

Several warriors joined him, each taking turns raining blows against the front door.

As the booming sounds of the hammers echoed through the halls of the house, Maria fumbled with the buttons on her blouse and told herself to remain calm and concentrate; just a few more buttons. The war birds screeched, and Maria felt a cold shiver of fear. She had never heard a sound like that before.

Angelina pushed herself against the back of the wardrobe. She knew something was coming, and there was nothing she could do but sit and wait.

Archie had shoved as much furniture as he could manage in front of the door, and shot the lock off D'Allesandro's gun cabinet to get at the stockpile of weapons and ammunition inside. He was loading his rifle when Maria joined him.

"Mrs. Con Fuego, take your daughter and get out of here. I'll hold them off as long as I can," he shouted.

"I'm staying. Pass me a rifle," Maria ordered.

"You know how to shoot one of these?" Archie asked as he held up one of D'Allesandro's hunting rifles.

"Just give it to me," Maria demanded impatiently. "At this range it's hard to miss." Maria was playing the odds. It was impossible to know whether taking a stand was the best thing to do, but she believed her daughter's chances of survival were better if she defended the house with a large cache of weapons than if she took Angelina and they ran outside into the darkness where their attackers awaited.

Even though Maria had never actually fired a gun at someone, she raised the rifle to her shoulder and swore to herself that

Chapter Seven

she'd shoot anyone who came through that door.

The door caved in, and the first dinosaur ducked its head and squeezed through, screeching at the top of its lungs, with two more right behind it. The furniture that Archie had stacked up might have slowed the warriors down if they had been on foot, but those chairs, end tables and couches were no obstacle for the powerful, long-legged war birds. What they didn't step over, they bulled their way through.

Archie shouldered his Winchester and fired two rounds, hitting the first beast in the chest. The animal howled in pain but didn't fall, and tore into Archie before the ranch hand could fire again.

Maria was knocked off her feet by a chair that went flying when the first dinosaur crashed into the barricade. She managed to hang onto her rifle but was unable to fire a single shot. A second war bird lunged at her and just missed tearing off an arm.

"Back! Back!" she screamed as she swung the weapon wildly in an effort to keep the beast at bay. But the animal was too fast and caught the Winchester in its jaws. Maria tried to wrestle the rifle free, but the dinosaur jerked it out of her hands and snapped the gun in two.

Maria ran for the stairs but the war bird caught her by the pant leg. She tried desperately to grab onto something—the railing, *anything*—as the creature dragged her down the staircase and lifted her off the floor.

From inside the wardrobe, Angelina could hear the sounds of gunshots and screams. She prayed for her mother's safety and blocked out the sound by sticking her fingers in her ears and humming to herself. Panic was the enemy now, and Angelina knew she had to control her fear or she was finished.

The newspapers back east were full of sensational stories of violent encounters between Native Americans and settlers. Although these accounts read like fiction, many of them were based on true stories.

Angelina remembered mentioning the articles to her mother before they moved west and asking her what to do if they were ever attacked. Her mother scoffed at the idea that they would be in any danger in Dos Locos since the town wasn't close to any Native American tribes, but they talked about the importance of remaining calm in an emergency and paying attention to what was happening at all times.

Angelina knew she had to remain hidden where she was and be patient. Opening the door of the wardrobe just a crack to peek outside could give her away if a hinge squeaked too loudly.

The problem was that she smelled smoke. And if the ranch house was on fire, she had to get out of there as fast as possible. Fire was extremely dangerous in the old west since ranchers had no way of putting it out, and even a small fire could quickly become a catastrophe if the conditions were right.

When the screaming stopped, Angelina waited. The smell of smoke got stronger, and she decided to take a chance. She barely opened the wardrobe door and sniffed the air. There wasn't any smoke in the bedroom, but something was definitely burning.

A loud bang against the door to her room startled her, and she pulled the wardrobe closed, pressing an ear against the inside to listen. Another bang, and she heard the door break into pieces.

It was quiet for a moment; then Angelina heard something

Chapter Seven

strange. It was the kind of sound a dog's paws made on a wooden surface when its nails were too long, except this was louder, and the floor boards were creaking so much it couldn't possibly be a dog. And it was coming closer.

The feathers on the back of the war bird's neck stood up as it walked toward the wardrobe. Something had caught its attention. The warrior raised his spear, ready to strike anything that moved. Then the rider saw his mount's reflection in the mirror.

The beast thinks there's another u'har in the room, he thought.

He banged the end of his spear on the floor two times and shouted to his companions that the room was clear.

Angelina exhaled as the room became silent once again. Whatever it was, it was gone.

After finishing their search, the Cragnon regrouped outside the ranch house to take stock of the casualties. They'd lost two of their own and one u'har, though two others were missing. There was also a prisoner unaccounted for, but presumed dead. The warriors had killed four cowboys and taken one new captive. Their dead comrades would be carried back home, but the carcass of the war bird would be left behind.

Two riders were sent to recover the bodies of their dead comrades. They found one of the missing u'hars in the back of the barn where it had torn a hole in D'Allesandro's shed and was trying to get at something inside. The other war bird was feeding on the remains of an injured horse it had taken down.

With everyone accounted for, the Cragnon began their trek home. They had struck a powerful blow at D'Allesandro, and had a new prisoner. Maybe the woman would get the rancher's attention. If not, they would kill her and find another way. Even more important, the Cragnon had discovered how D'Allesandro and his men were able to travel back and forth from his land to theirs. With that secret in their grasp, there was nothing to stop the Cragnon from returning and exploring what riches this new land had to offer. After all, it was a matter of survival.

Angelina closed her eyes and tried to rest. It was impossible. She hummed to herself and prayed, trying to keep up her spirits. The screaming had been horrible, but the silence and waiting that followed were just as excruciating. The smell of smoke from the burning barn and bunkhouse had grown stronger, and all she could think about was that the house was going to burn down with her in it. Her legs and back cramped up, and tears streamed down her face from the pain. Making matters worse was the uncertainty; the constant thought that her mother had been killed and she did nothing to stop it.

She waited as long as she could once things had quieted down before opening the door to the wardrobe a second time to let herself out. She had no idea how much time had passed. She stretched her back and legs, and her muscles began to unknot.

Angelina tiptoed to the doorway and looked down the hall, making sure it was quiet, before retrieving her clothing from under the bed. She changed quickly out of her nightclothes into something suitable for riding, then crept to her mother's room.

"Mother," she whispered. The bedroom was empty, and tears welled up in Angelina's eyes. She had the sinking feeling her mother was gone and she'd never see here again, but

Chapter Seven

forced herself to be optimistic nonetheless.

My mother is still alive, she repeated to herself. *She has to be.*

Angelina ran to the end of the hall and looked down from the balcony at the shattered front door and Archie's lifeless body, lying amid the destruction. She closed her eyes and stifled a sob. This was a nightmare.

As she ran downstairs she forced herself not to look at Archie. There was blood everywhere, and she found herself starting to cry again. She ran out the front door and looked around. It was silent except for the crackling of the dwindling fires. The bunkhouse was gone, but the barn suffered only minor damage. The siege on the ranch house had distracted the warriors from burning it to the ground. Then she noticed Carlos's body. It hit her that she was the only one left alive at the Crossed Swords, and an overpowering sense of panic set in. She had to get out of there and get help!

Angelina ran to the corral, but the horses were gone. Now what? The barn was smoking and any horses that had been in there had either run away or were dead. She ran to the back of the house and saw several horses standing in the darkness. They'd been run out of the corral, but didn't run off the grounds! But despite several attempts, she couldn't catch a single one of those danged horses. This was hopeless. Angelina felt like giving up when she heard someone call her name.

"Angelina, is that you?"

"Who is that?" she called. "Where are you?"

"It's me, Tom White. I work for your Uncle!"

Tom crept out from the place he'd been hiding and staggered toward her. "It's okay, they're gone."

"Are you okay? What's wrong?" As Tom drew closer, Angelina winced at the sight of the blood stains on his shirt and pants. "You're hurt. What can I do?"

"I'm okay," Tom replied. "It isn't that deep."

"Can you ride?" Angelina asked.

"I think so."

"Then I'll get us some help." Tom's injury had a galvanizing effect on Angelina and made her more determined to get out of there. It took several more tries, but Angelina finally caught one of the horses. After struggling to get Tom up into the saddle, she made up her mind to head to the Double R.

It was a miserable ride and the going was slow due to Tom's fragile condition. Having never actually visited the Double R, Angelina had only a vague sense of which way to go and was nervous they would get lost. Tom tried to help, but he kept drifting in and out consciousness, and it was all he could do to keep from falling out of the saddle. And the whole trip Angelina couldn't shake the feeling they were being followed, though she knew better.

It was past three in the morning when Angelina and Tom arrived at Uncle Jesse's doorstep. Angelina helped Tom off the horse and half carried him up the steps. He was pretty far gone by that time from exhaustion and blood loss. Angelina was ready to collapse herself, and it took her remaining ounces of reserve to pound on the door and cry for help. Still her knocks carried little weight and her shout was more of a whimper. She hoped it would be enough.

* * *

Chapter Seven

Inside, Stumpy was the first to respond, which was typical. Uncle Jesse could never understand how the lame-footed, hard-of-hearing old cook did it.

"I think I heard somebody at the door," he said, hobbling past the others' rooms on the way to the kitchen, Uncle Jesse right behind.

The next moment, everyone was crammed into the narrow hallway, talking at the same time.

"What the heck is going on?" Bull asked.

"I think I heard somebody at the door," said Stumpy.

"Maybe D'Allesandro found out that Slim's here," Zeke said.

Uncle Jesse shook his head. "Zeke, you know better than to say something like that around Slim. It's only going to get him riled up."

Sure enough, Slim tensed like he was getting ready for a fight and let out a weird kind of growl.

"There's that breath again," Bull said as he waved his hand in front of his nose.

"Everybody, quiet down," Uncle Jesse demanded. "Would you all let me handle this? D'Allesandro is not at the front door. He's in Santa Fe. Or some other place."

"What if he ain't? What then?" Stumpy asked, and Slim released another growl.

"You know what? I don't really care where he is. If he's at the front door, I'm telling him to get the heck off my property and go home. Slim, stay out of sight. Zeke, get back in bed and don't mention D'Allesandro again! Bull, Stumpy, come with me. And make some room here for goodness sake? I can't even get down the hall with all of you standing in my way."

Rex Riders

Uncle Jesse opened the front door, and Angelina practically collapsed under Tom's weight. They were a ghastly sight. Tom's blood covered Angelina's clothing, and it looked like both of them had been mortally wounded.

"Mr. McCain, we were attacked. Tom's hurt bad. You have to help us, please."

Without a word, the men sprang into action. Bull hoisted Tom into his arms and placed him on a couch in the sitting room, while Stumpy boiled a pot of water to tend to their wounds.

"Best seat in the house, Tom," Stumpy called. "We'll get you fixed up."

While Stumpy prepared to minister to Tom's wounds, Uncle Jesse and Zeke took Angelina into the kitchen and gave her some water. She told Uncle Jesse in the most sorrowful way that her mother was missing and she had to find her. But when Uncle Jesse asked her for details about what happened, she said she didn't know and started to cry. It was frustrating for both of them, so he decided it was better to let her rest than to badger her with a lot of questions. He hoped that Tom would be more helpful, and was relieved when Tom felt well enough to hobble into the kitchen under his own power and ask for a cup of coffee and something to eat.

"He'll live," Stumpy declared.

For the next hour Tom held them all spellbound with a tale that would have seemed impossible to believe just a few days before. The boys took it all in and said nothing until he was finished.

"Were there any survivors other than you two?" Uncle Jesse asked when Tom had finished.

Chapter Seven

"No. They killed everyone." Tom looked down at the floor as he tried to hold his emotions in check.

Angelina stared slack-jawed at Tom and tears ran down her face. "Everyone?"

"I beg your pardon, miss," Tom said, looking up. "Everyone but you and your ma."

"What!" Angelina exclaimed. "My mother is alive?"

"They took her with them. She wasn't moving, but they wouldn't have taken her if she wasn't still alive. I'm sorry, but I wasn't in any kind of shape to try to stop them. I must have passed out and when I woke up, I saw Miss Con Fuego and called to her. She got me here."

"You need sleep," Uncle Jesse said. "Take the couch in the sitting room and rest up. Stumpy will call you for breakfast and get you into town afterward."

"Thanks, Jess. You were always a good man. Oh, one more thing."

"Yep."

"I ain't going back there."

"I know. And I wouldn't ask you to."

Stumpy got Tom a blanket and he drifted off to sleep in the sitting room, leaving the group alone in the kitchen.

"I guess that settles it," Stumpy said.

"It surely does," Uncle Jesse replied, looking at Angelina. "We're going after your ma. We'll bring her back."

Angelina jumped out of her chair toward Uncle Jesse and hugged him with all her might. "Thank you," she whispered.

"Bull, get dressed. As soon as you and I are packed, we'll ride out to the Crossed Swords Ranch and pick up the trail."

"I'm going with you!" Angelina said, wiping away her tears.

"I am too," Zeke chimed in.

"No, you're not," Uncle Jesse said firmly as he looked first at Zeke and then Angelina. "Neither one of you is coming. It's too dangerous. You'll stay with Stumpy and wait for us to come back. Is that understood?"

Uncle Jesse looked directly at Zeke. "I didn't hear you answer me. I said, is that understood?"

"Yessir," Zeke answered grudgingly.

"I need you to saddle the horses and help Stumpy get our bags packed, while Bull and I get our gear ready."

"Which horse do you want to take?" Zeke asked.

"Midnight," Uncle Jesse replied. "And check with Slim to see if he needs any help."

Slim had stayed out of sight while he listened to Tom's story, but when he heard his name mentioned he stepped into the doorway to the kitchen.

"Please get Hellfire ready too," Slim said.

Angelina gasped out loud when she saw the Tarngatharn, and everyone in the room had exactly the same thought at exactly the same time: how could they smooth this over and calm her down?

As usual, they all started talking at once.

"Ah, it's only Slim," Stumpy said in a reassuring tone as he glanced back and forth at Slim and Angelina, trying to gauge how upset she was. "Nothing to be scared of. Slim, come in and say howdy to Miss Angelina."

"Angelina, Slim. Slim, Angelina," Zeke said quickly. "It's okay. He's a friend."

"Slim's from . . . Europe," Bull added.

Chapter Seven

Uncle Jesse closed his eyes and grimaced. "Slim, you see what just happened? That's why I've been telling you to stay out of sight."

"I'm sorry I frightened you, Angelina," Slim said gently.

Angelina was oblivious to everything except for the monstrous being standing in the doorway. She pointed a finger at the Rider and whispered, "You can talk. Who are you?"

"It's kind of a long story," Zeke said. "See, Stumpy and I were down by Small's Stream and—"

"Son, that's enough," Uncle Jesse interrupted. "We all have work to do, including you. Why don't you get Angelina out of here and tell her all about it while you get the horses ready?"

"I'll help," Angelina said, jumping to her feet.

"Good. When you're done, bring the horses around to the front of the house."

As they walked outside, it occurred to Zeke that maybe he should say a word or two about the T-rex in the barn. "Now don't be nervous when you see Hellfire, he's just a lot of noise."

"What kind of girl do you think I am? I'm not scared of horses, Zeke Calhoun."

"Well, he's not exactly a horse."

For the next hour the Double R was abuzz with activity as everyone pitched in to get the men ready for what lay ahead. Zeke introduced Angelina to Hellfire, and she had the same reaction the others had when they saw Hellfire for the first time: a mix of awe and fascination, with a dose of terror thrown in after she heard him roar the first nine or ten times and got a load of those teeth.

Rex Riders

It didn't take the men long to get ready, and they were waiting on the porch dressed like a couple of outlaws when Zeke and Angelina walked the rex and the horses out front. Uncle Jesse was wearing two bandoleers loaded with ammunition criss-crossing his chest and had a fine-looking, pearl-handled pistol at his side. Bull was wearing two gun belts with holsters tied to each leg.

"I haven't worn these in a while," Uncle Jesse said as he adjusted the ammunition belts.

"Me, neither," Bull said.

"And all this time you had me believing you two were just a couple of old farm boys," Stumpy joked. Uncle Jesse and Bull grinned.

"That's us; just a couple of farm boys," Bull repeated, and they all laughed uproariously.

Seeing his uncle and Bull armed to the teeth, laughing at the idea that they were farmers, made Zeke realize that there was a lot more to these men than he knew.

He leaned over to Stumpy and pointed to the bandoleers: "Where did those come from?"

Stumpy pretended not to hear him, and Zeke let it drop. He could always ask again later after they'd left, but the boy had a feeling he wasn't going to get an answer and he might never find out.

"You ready?" Uncle Jesse asked.

"Looking forward to it," Bull said.

Slim walked out the front door and stretched his long arms. Stumpy's eyes immediately went to the leather pouch that was hanging from his belt. Sure enough, the Tarngatharn had recovered what he was looking for. Whatever it was, Stumpy knew Slim had found it in Zeke's room.

Slim walked over to Zeke and took the reins of his rex.

"I may not see you again. I am grateful for all you have done for us. You would make a fine rider."

Stumpy handed Slim a set of saddlebags, the same ones he stored his old pencils and paper in.

"I don't know whether Zeke had time to thank you in all the confusion, but that was a pretty good picture you made of Midnight. I thought you might have a use for these. And I see you found what you were looking for."

Slim stared at the bags for a moment and then looked Stumpy in the eye and shook his hand. "I did. He is young and curious. Thank you. I hope we meet again."

Slim slung the saddlebags on top of Hellfire, and they looked right at home.

"I put some jerky in there in case Hellfire gets hungry. I know *you* won't eat it!"

Slim hopped up on Hellfire, and the T-rex looked over at Midnight and growled. He still hadn't gotten over the fact that Slim rode the big stallion. The Rider laughed and patted the dinosaur on the neck.

"Stumpy, give us three days—four at the most," Uncle Jesse said. "If we aren't back by then, tell the Sheriff and Doc what happened."

"Good luck," Stumpy said.

"And Zeke, that barn better still be standing when I get back."

"It will be," Zeke said, before breaking into a big smile.

"Good man. Angelina, keep these boys in line for me, will you?"

Angelina smiled weakly. "I will, Mr. McCain."

"Adios, señores and señorita," Uncle Jesse said, and they rode off into the dark.

Zeke and Angelina watched from the porch until they couldn't see them any longer. Zeke wished he could have joined them on their adventure, but Tom's story about the torture he endured at the hands of the Cragnon was sobering. He remembered what Slim had told him when he compared Midnight to Hellfire, and it made a lot more sense to Zeke now. He doubted anyone could take Slim captive with Hellfire there to protect him.

Angelina was exhausted. From the time she and Tom fled the Crossed Swords Ranch, she'd been running on pure adrenaline, and now she suddenly felt so tired she could have gone to sleep where she was standing. When she first saw Uncle Jesse, Bull and Stumpy, she felt everything would be okay, but now that Uncle Jesse and Bull were gone, she was overcome with feelings of desperation and foreboding. Would she ever see them again? And what would become of her mother?

She didn't have long to dwell on those feelings. Stumpy took her by the arm and said, "All right, Miss Con Fuego, it's off to bed with you."

"But it's almost morning," Angelina protested.

"I know what time it is, miss. It's best that you get some rest. You had a long night," Stumpy said firmly, walking her toward the bedrooms. "You'll take Zeke's room. Don't pay any attention to the dirt. We'll clean it up for you."

Chapter Seven

"Wait a second. Where am I going to sleep?" Zeke asked.

"You'll take Slim's room," Stumpy replied.

Zeke sighed and began to walk in that direction, but Stumpy reached out and put his hand on Zeke's shoulder. "Where are you going?"

"Back to bed," Zeke said as if the answer were obvious.

Stumpy raised an eyebrow and looked at him. "No you ain't. We got chores to do. It's almost 5 A.M. We should have started by now."

"But I'm tired," Zeke whined. "I hardly got any sleep."

"Neither did I. A little hard work will wake us both up. Now get moving."

Zeke groaned and shuffled out the door.

"Nobody said life on a ranch was easy, young fella," Stumpy said, chuckling to himself.

The sun was coming up when the Crossed Swords Ranch came into view. It was a depressing sight. Just days earlier the ranch was bustling with life and energy, and now buzzards circled overhead and smoke rose from the blackened ruins of the smoldering buildings. Uncle Jesse spat in disgust. Those danged birds meant death. Whatever bad blood existed between D'Allesandro and McCain, Uncle Jesse took no pleasure in seeing a neighbor's ranch in ruins.

"It looks deserted," Bull said.

"Slim, you know these Cragnon. Do you think they left any of their men behind?" Uncle Jesse asked.

"It is doubtful."

"We better stay together."

Rex Riders

They found the remains of the ranch hands killed during the attack lying on the grounds and in the ruins of the bunkhouse. Bull carried Archie Turner's body out of the foyer and gently laid him alongside the others. Although Uncle Jesse was anxious to gain ground on the Cragnon, he insisted that they take the time to give the men a decent burial. It was the right thing to do. He picked a spot around the back of the bunkhouse, and when they'd finished, Bull constructed several crude markers out of wood. Uncle Jesse said a few words in memoriam and they saddled up.

It wasn't hard to pick up the trail left by the Cragnon. They made no effort to cover their tracks. The trio rode in silence for hours at a steady pace. The horses and the rex got along well as they settled into a rhythm. The time they spent together in the barn had helped them get used to one another, and Hellfire even stopped growling at Midnight.

This was the first time they had seen Slim ride his rex, but it looked perfectly natural to their eyes. He rode the animal with the same self-assurance with which they rode their horses and were surprised to see Hellfire respond better to commands than their horses did.

Uncle Jesse had no idea how fast the Cragnon's dinosaurs were in comparison to a horse, so he didn't know how far ahead they were. He would have run the horses full out to catch up with them, but Hellfire wouldn't have been able to keep pace. The horses were better at running at sustained speeds over long distances than the rex was, so Uncle Jesse and Bull held their rides back.

Chapter Seven

"I'm sorry we didn't leave earlier like you wanted," Uncle Jesse said to Slim.

"It wouldn't have made a difference. D'Allesandro brought this on himself. Let us hope we are not too late to stop him."

The trail led into the mountains to an area known for unusual rock formations that were shaped by the force of rushing water eons ago. There were arches, columns and projections in every shape and size, all sculpted out of red and brown stone. This part of the trail was clearly the work of D'Allesandro's men. It was wide enough for a wagon and showed signs of recent heavy use. There were tracks left by men and horses, and deep indentations from wheels carrying heavy loads. And laid on top were fresh tracks left by the war birds.

They were getting closer.

They reached the entrance to a cave and found the bodies of two of D'Allesandro's men. Uncle Jesse wondered if they were guards. It was too big a coincidence for these men to have been out in the mountains when the Cragnon rode through, and yet, it surprised him that D'Allesandro had gone to such extraordinary lengths to protect his discovery.

Wouldn't it be something if this were the cave that held the legendary D'Allesandro family fortune? he thought. *Whatever was inside must have been incredibly valuable to the ranch owner.*

"Is this the place?" Uncle Jesse asked Slim

"This is it," the Rider confirmed.

"Did you ever see this before?" Uncle Jesse said, turning to Bull.

"No. I've been all through these parts at one time or another, and this wasn't here. There might have been openings in the rock, but nothing this big. It looks like they blasted it with TNT, then dug it out and shored it up with supports to keep it from caving in. I wonder how deep it goes."

"Only one way to find out," Uncle Jesse observed. "We're going to need light."

"There must be lanterns or torches inside the cave," Bull said. "I'll take a look."

Bull found several wooden crates full of supplies, including lanterns. They took what they needed along with some extra kerosene.

"Let's go," Uncle Jesse said.

They rode into the darkness, and the tunnel made a sharp turn. But instead of descending into a mine shaft as Uncle Jesse and Bull expected, they traveled straight into the mountain. They hadn't gone far when they emerged on an enormous stone ridge that overlooked a breathtaking sight. In the center of a cavern of immense size—surrounded by massive stalagmites and hanging stalactites laced with sparkling malachite—lay a transporter.

Chunks of its carved stone façade had fallen off to reveal an underlying structure that was constructed of metal and synthetic materials. Two of the three stone walkways that led to the circular platform were intact, and it looked like someone was preparing to repair the third using stones and logs. Three towering metal sauropods remained perched on their hind legs as their builders had intended.

"What is that thing?" Bull asked.

"This is the machine I told you about. It was used to bring things from your world to mine."

"What kinds of things?" Bull asked.

"All kinds of things."

"And that contraption will take us to where you came from?" Uncle Jesse asked skeptically. "It doesn't look like much."

"I don't get it," Bull added. "It doesn't have any wheels and there isn't any way out other than the way we came in. I don't see how that thing can take us anywhere."

"I'm afraid I can't explain how it works," Slim responded with a laugh. "But I can show you."

"Lead the way, Slim," Uncle Jesse said.

As they rode toward the base of the transporter, Bull gestured toward one of the towering metal long-necks on the edge of the platform and jokingly asked, "Are the critters this big where we're going?"

"Some are," Slim replied. "Some are even bigger."

Bull looked at Slim like he was crazy, and shook his head. "*Hmmph*. I'd like to see the critter that's bigger than that thing. Heck, I'd pay to see a critter as big as that one!" Bull muttered to himself.

"The machine starts to work when you step on the platform," Slim explained. "The power comes from underneath. I don't know how deep it goes or how it works. It was designed to protect against accidents, and there are timers that can be reset depending upon what is being transported and how much time is needed to load the platform. We will have sixty seconds to reach the top from the time I step on the walkway."

"What happens if we don't get up there in sixty seconds?" Uncle Jesse asked.

"I will leave without you."

Chapter Seven

Hellfire stepped onto the walkway, activating the generators. Almost instantly, the cave filled with a humming noise that grew louder by the second. Uncle Jesse and Bull covered their ears as it echoed through the cavern.

The metal dinosaurs began to glow as they became charged them with power and lit up the inside of the great cave. Their eyes sparked and crackled at first, but within seconds progressively longer bolts of blue lightning shot forth until they streamed out and leapt from one dinosaur to the next. In seconds, what began as bolts of energy coursing between each sauropod grew into a swirling, fifty-foot tall, blue vortex that resembled a tornado and extended from the base of the platform over the heads of the metal dinosaurs.

"What the heck is that?" Bull shouted to Uncle Jesse.

"Looks like a twister, but there's no wind. I don't get it," Uncle Jesse cried.

When Slim and Hellfire reached the top of the walkway, Slim turned and looked back at the two men. Then he rode the rex directly into the path of the swirling power field and stopped. Waves of blue energy enveloped them, and it appeared as if Slim and Hellfire were on fire.

"What's he doing?" Uncle Jesse yelled.

"Come on," Slim shouted, waving the two men to join him. Rider and mount passed through the energy field, and Uncle Jesse and Bull lost sight of them.

Uncle Jesse looked at Bull with a serious expression: "Bull, are you sure you want to go? This ain't your fight, you know."

Bull looked at him for a second and nodded gravely. Then both men burst out laughing.

"It ain't yours either!" Bull said. "And anyway, since when did that ever matter? A fight's a fight. If *you're* in it, *I'm* in it and vice versa."

Bull stuck out his hand, and they shook.

"Just like old times, partner," he said with a grin.

"It surely is," Uncle Jesse agreed, laughing.

"I just hope the food's good." Bull tugged on the reins of his horse, let out a yell, and charged straight up the walkway into the blue vortex. Uncle Jesse could barely hear his friend calling to him from inside. "Didn't hurt a bit! Come on, Jess."

Well, here goes, thought Uncle Jesse. He put the spurs to Midnight and . . . the big stallion chose that exact moment to get cold feet! He refused to budge, and when Uncle Jesse pulled on the reins to get his attention, the horse reared up in defiance. Uncle Jesse was livid. *This is a fine time for you to get skittish on me,* he thought.

"Oh, come on, dang you!" Uncle Jesse yelled, but the stallion would not move.

"They ain't leaving without me," Uncle Jesse declared, getting off Midnight and walking around to his front end to look him in the eye.

"You better knock it off. This ain't your decision. We're going, and that's final. Now git!" Midnight snorted and shook his head. By now Uncle Jesse was so annoyed he'd lost all patience, "Keep this up and you're going back to D'Allesandro, *comprende?*"

That last threat did the trick, and Midnight's legs started moving. Uncle Jesse looked back over his shoulder as he walked the stallion up the platform, "You know, you could take some lessons from Hellfire."

Chapter Seven

When they reached the top, Uncle Jesse closed his eyes as they stepped through the blue energy field. Bull was standing next to Slim about fifty yards away, looking up at what was happening around them. It was like being in the eye of an electric tornado. The energy beams were revolving so quickly now they were just a blur, and you couldn't look at them for too long or you'd get dizzy. It was a sight you'd never get used to no matter how many times you experienced it.

"What happens next?" Uncle Jesse shouted.

Slim pointed up, and Uncle Jesse saw the opening at the top of the vortex closing. The Tarngatharn yelled something, but Uncle Jesse couldn't hear a word of it because his ears started ringing.

And then it happened: the vortex collapsed in on itself, and Uncle Jesse felt everything go blank. It was a strange sensation. Not so much like passing out as it was like time froze, and life suddenly stopped.

He had no idea how much time had passed before he sensed sound and movement again, he became aware that he was standing on a different platform. When he opened his eyes and looked around, he knew they were no longer in Dos Locos.

Chapter
Eight

"We're back!" Slim roared, and Hellfire let loose with a roar of his own. The Tarngatharn was accustomed to the nauseous feeling that accompanied the use of the transport device, but Uncle Jesse and Bull didn't know what they were in for and that first ride was a doozy. They both felt sick to their stomachs, and the intense midday heat didn't help matters any. The feeling didn't last long, but the memory of it left them in no hurry to take another trip. Even the horses were a little wobbly.

When they felt better, they walked to the edge of the transporter and surveyed the surrounding area. They were standing in the middle of a great forest on top of a platform similar to the one they had just left. The main difference was that the three metal sauropods that originally served as conductors had long ago been destroyed, leaving only remnants of the alloy that was the key to the device's operation.

An eighty-yard circular area around the machine had been cleared of trees, and untold centurys' worth of dirt, vines and vegetation had been removed from the platform itself. Within this cleared area, about thirty feet from the transporter, logs had been driven into the ground every five feet to form a crude barrier that ringed the device. The space between the logs was wide enough for a horse or a small T-Rex, like Hellfire, but a large adult dinosaur wouldn't be able to squeeze through. The only break in the circle opened at the mouth of a freshly-cut trail.

"Woo-wee! What's all this for?" Uncle Jesse asked.

"These are new," Slim said, pointing to the logs that encircled the platform.

"Get a load of those tree stumps!" Bull said excitedly. "I bet some of them are ten feet across. I've never seen trunks that big in my life."

"Me neither," Uncle Jesse said as he shook his head in amazement. "Remember those towers on D'Allesandro's land? I knew those logs weren't from Dos Locos."

Bull nodded. "Let's go down and take a look."

Piles of sawdust, wood chips, dead branches and wilted leaves covered the ground where the trees were cut. Some of the stumps were so big a cowboy and his horse could stand on them. In many cases D'Allesandro's men were only able to cut partway through the trees before they began to topple and snapped off at their bases, leaving jagged pieces of wood standing in the air as tall as a person .

"What kind of trees are these?" Uncle Jesse asked Bull.

Chapter Eight

"Hard to say," he replied as he rode around one of the stumps and examined its bark. "That's the kind of thing Stumpy would know. It looks like maple, but it's bigger than any maple I've ever seen. I'll bet those trees over there are more than two hundred feet tall. What do you make of all this?"

"I don't know."

Uncle Jesse pointed to the opening in the forest a couple of hundred yards away. "It looks like D'Allesandro had his men clear a trail into the woods. You think it's wide enough to run a herd of those three-horns through there?"

"It might be."

"Nobody needs a trail that big just to get a wagon into camp."

Meanwhile, Slim was busy examining the tracks left by the Cragnon. Given their head start, it would be hard to catch them before they reached their village. As the Rider contemplated the group's next move, he picked flowers. When he had a good size bouquet, he held it up to his nose, closed his eyes and inhaled.

"Ahhh," Slim said, savoring the perfume. Then he opened his cavernous mouth and stuffed the whole bouquet inside; roots, stems, flowers, and all.

Bull elbowed Uncle Jesse. "Did you see what he just did? That ain't natural."

"I'm starting to get used to it," Uncle Jesse said. "Hey, Slim, where does that trail lead?"

"The Sulant River," Slim said between chews. "Following it upstream will take you to Mujar, the Cragnon village. But the warriors we pursue have taken a route through the forest. It is safer that way. Too many adult yerka hunt along the shoreline."

"How big a river are we talking about?" Uncle Jesse asked.

"Maybe a hundred yards wide in spots," Slim answered, as the hungry Tarngatharn bent to pick a second course.

"You think D'Allesandro might be planning to attack the Cragnon from the river?"

"Perhaps," Slim replied, before stuffing more foliage into his mouth.

Bull turned to Uncle Jesse, "He can't be thinking about floating those big three-horned critters down the river. That would be crazy."

"You're probably right," Uncle Jesse said. "But he could have built a heck of a raft out of the logs he cut. Maybe he floated some of the logs to his camp and used them there. That would explain the pikes in his barn; he'd need them once he got the trees in the water."

"He could be moving supplies to his camp by river," Bull suggested.

"But then why'd he cut the trail so wide?" Uncle Jesse argued." Seems like a lot of extra work considering the size of the trees."

"Maybe it was Cooper's idea. He ain't too smart," Bull offered.

"If you're ready, we should go. Do you want something to eat before we start?" Slim held out a handful of flowering plants that he'd just pulled from ground. Some of them still had clods of dirt hanging from their roots. "They're delicious."

"I'm sure they are, Slim, but no thanks," Bull said. "Um, you got something there in your teeth."

Slim carefully worked a large green stem from between his teeth. "Thanks," he said, before popping it into his mouth.

Chapter Eight

"How far ahead of us are they?" Uncle Jesse asked.

"Maybe half a day," Slim replied. "But I don't believe we can catch them before they reach Mujar. They are too far ahead."

Uncle Jesse gritted his teeth. He expected to take on a dozen warriors at most, not a whole village! "So what do we do now?"

"We could shoot our way in," Bull suggested.

"Too obvious," Uncle Jesse said.

"How about we scout the area and when we find out where she is, we break her out at night like we did in Juarez," Bull offered.

"Too dangerous. Slim, you know these Cragnon better than we do. What's the plan?"

"I will seek an audience with their Chief and plead for mercy."

Uncle Jesse and Bull were taken aback. This was not what they had in mind when they left Dos Locos armed to the teeth.

"I don't think I heard you right," Uncle Jesse said, shaking his head. "Did you say 'plead for mercy'?"

"I thought we were going to rescue her," Bull said.

"We are," Slim said.

"And what if that doesn't work?" Uncle Jesse asked with more than a little doubt in his voice.

"Then we ride to D'Allesandro's camp," Slim replied.

"And?"

Slim looked at the two men, "That's where you come in."

Uncle Jesse was stunned. This was Slim's plan? Was it possible he never expected to overtake Maria's kidnappers and only brought him and Bull along to deal with D'Allesandro in case he failed to rescue her from the Cragnon? It would be smart to leave dealing with D'Allesandro and his men to them, but Uncle Jesse felt deceived. Slim should have told them that was his intention all along. What else hadn't the Rider told them?

"We might as well take these off," Uncle Jesse said, and he and Bull removed the extra ammunition belts and tied them to their saddles.

For the next several hours they followed the trail left by the raiding party through the forest, while Slim described the Cragnon's customs. Uncle Jesse and Bull were eager to learn as much as they could and stopped Slim at different points to offer their insights based upon their experiences with Native Americans.

The Cragnon were hunters and gatherers. Their village, Mujar, was built atop a rocky bluff that faced the Sulant River. Crops were grown in low-lying areas near its fertile banks and tended to by the women and children. The best hunters of the tribe lived outside the village, leading a nomadic life following the triceratops as the great beasts migrated in search of plants to graze on. They made their homes in temporary grass-and-branch huts that blended into the environment and were easy to take down and move.

When a kill was made, the animal was skinned and the hide was hung out to dry in the sun. Runners of the tribe carried the majority of the meat back to Mujar on rigs pulled by war birds. Some of it was eaten, while the rest was preserved with salts and spices, and stored. Cragnon tanners used the trike's hide to make clothing and shoes, and other useful items, like tents and

Chapter Eight

drums. The creatures bones were ground to a fine powder, some of which served as fertilizer, the rest incorporated into the food as a vital source of calcium. Not a single part of the dinosaur was wasted.

In times of war the hunters abandoned the plains and returned to protect Mujar, which was heavily fortified against attack. The tribe lived off the stores of trike jerky, supplemented with fish from the Sulant, during these periods.

The leader of the Cragnon was an elderly chief named Braknar. He had been a great warrior in his youth, but as he grew older he advocated diplomacy in the tribe's relations with its neighbors. This change created a split among some of the younger warrior-hunters who felt that Braknar was violating ancient traditions and weakening the tribe. They wanted the Cragnon to dominate the lands and inspire fear in their enemies as they had done for thousands of years. There was no doubt in Slim's mind that many of the younger warriors would be in favor of war with D'Allesandro.

The wild card was Shugath, the tribe's shaman. According to Slim, Shugath was a medicine man and magician rolled into one and wielded great influence among the superstitious Cragnon. To convince Chief Braknar to release Maria, he would also have to win over Shugath.

The forest they were traveling through was full of wild-life and while they talked Slim kept a watchful eye for anything that moved. Most of the animals they saw were small: rodents, reptiles, and animals with feathers that looked sort of like birds, and all kept their distance.

Uncle Jesse and Bull were curious about everything they saw

Rex Riders

and Slim shared what he knew. There were a couple of times when Slim heard the sound of a large animal moving in the distance or Hellfire began to growl and they changed their route to avoid whatever it was. Sometimes Uncle Jesse and Bull caught glimpses of the animals that were making the noises, and the two men were stunned by their tremendous size.

When they stopped to rest the horses, Uncle Jesse asked Slim to draw him a map in case the Tarngatharn was separated from them and he and Bull needed to find their way back to the transport machine by themselves. Slim started to sketch one on the ground with a stick until he remembered Stumpy's gift. Retrieving some paper and a charcoal pencil from his saddle-bag, he laid out the transporter; Mujar and the route they were taking to the Cragnon village; their relation to the river; and the location of D'Allesandro's camp.

The nausea from the transporter had long since past, replaced by the stirrings of hunger. So Uncle Jesse and Bull dipped into their supplies for some of Stumpy's jerky to snack on. Hellfire watched closely when the men approached their horses as if the yerka knew what they were doing. The second the dried meat strips came into view, the T-rex gamboled over and nudged them for some. When Hellfire didn't get what he wanted he started to growl, so Uncle Jesse and Bull wound up sharing with the persuasive yerka.

"Don't give him too much," Slim said, keeping an eye on Hellfire, though never scolding the beast. "If you let him, he will eat everything you have. Let him growl; there will be meat for him when we reach Mujar."

* * *

Chapter Eight

They reached the edge of the forest and before them lay a vast expanse of rolling hills that stretched to the horizon. The ground cover was much thicker here than it had been in the forest, and much different from the tall grasses that covered the prairies back home. Flowering plants dotted the plains, and the air was fragrant with their scent. The flowers attracted all kinds of strange flying insects that flitted from bud to bud, the air filled with their soft buzzing sounds.

"There are a lot of bugs around here," Bull said, as he whacked a big one with his hand.

One landed briefly on Slim and tried to bite through the armored plate that covered his shoulder, but the Tarngatharn's skin proved too thick, and it flew off. "Stay away from those," he cautioned, pointing to an insect that looked like an unusually large yellowjacket. "They make their nests in the trees. If you are stung by one, you will die."

"Good to know," Uncle Jesse said. "Are there any more bugs like that? You know, the poisonous kind?"

"*Hmm* . . . That would be most of them."

The men noticed that many of the trees seemed to suffer from a strange affliction: the foliage looked normal up to a point about thirty to forty feet off the ground and then there was a fifteen foot band that was devoid of leaves. Above that level the foliage appeared normal again.

"What happened to those trees over there?" Bull asked. "Are they sick?"

"Xenolopticoi," Slim said, pointing to a row of large tracks some of which were three feet across!

"That a disease?" Bull asked.

Rex Riders

Slim smiled. "Come on, I'll show you."

The Rider led them to a small hill topped by a cluster of trees. As they neared, the head and neck of a dinosaur appeared to rise out of the ground itself, and seemed to have no end.

Hellfire started to growl, so Slim signaled the men to stop. They watched from a distance as a full-grown Sauroposeiden slowly made its way up the opposite side of the hill. It caught sight of Hellfire and trumpeted a warning. More long-necked brachiosaurids from the same group joined the first one and took positions around the trees to feed. There were six of them, and they varied in size from thirty to a hundred feet in length. The biggest member of the group must have been fifty feet tall!

Neither man could believe what he was seeing.

"Look at the size of those things," Bull exclaimed. When Slim told them there were creatures bigger than the metal sauropods back in the cave, he wasn't kidding!

The adult Sauroposeidens stretched their necks to reach the higher branches, while the juveniles fed on the lower ones. While young and old ate continuously, the adults were more efficient at stripping the branches of their leaves and had bigger appetites than the juveniles, so the branches the adults munched on tended to lose more of their leaves than the lower branches on which the young fed. When the adults finished an area, they moved to another. The result was a clear fifteen-foot zone like the ones on the trees that Uncle Jesse and Bull thought were sick.

"See how they stretch to reach leaves that are up high, but avoid lowering their necks to eat leaves on the lower branches?"

"Seems strange," Bull said. "How come?"

"They move slowly because of their size. Their long necks

Chapter Eight

help them to spot danger in the distance and move away before it can reach them. Notice how they watch us? They never take their eyes off my yerka. One of them is always watching. If they lowered their heads to eat the ground cover, they would lose the advantage that their height gives them and become more vulnerable to attack. A strong bite on the neck from an animal like a yerka would kill them. Keeping their heads and necks up high, also keeps them out of reach."

"What do you call them again?"

"It may be easier for you to call them 'long-necks.'" Slim said with a laugh.

"Are they dangerous?" Uncle Jesse asked.

"They can be, but they won't attack unless they feel threatened."

"Hellfire has been growling since he first saw them," Uncle Jesse observed.

"Yerkas prey on Xeno— on long-necks," the Tarngatharn explained. "I try to avoid them because yerkas make them nervous, and sometimes an adult will attack to protect the herd. Full grown long-necks like these can kill a yerka. It is best to stay clear of them."

"Funny we ain't seen any of those three-horns," Bull said.

"We should have seen them by now," Slim agreed. "These lands are usually full of them. Something has moved them away from their grazing grounds. This is not good." The tension in Slim's voice was unmistakable.

"How much longer until we reach Mujar?" Uncle Jesse asked.

"We're very close. There is a route we could take across these plains, but I don't want their warriors to see us and send word to

Braknar. I want to reach the village without anyone knowing we are coming."

Uncle Jesse agreed with Slim's strategy but he wasn't happy. Taking a roundabout way to the Cragnon village through unfamiliar territory could be a problem. It would be hard to retrace their steps. It was a good thing he had that map. Crude as it was, it was better than nothing. Best to press on and hope for the best. If D'Allesandro's men could navigate their way across this land, they could too.

Slim's route took them to the Sulant River, and Slim was visibly shocked at what he saw. The water level had dropped so dramatically that travel by boat or raft was impossible. This was the first time that Slim allowed himself to appear worried. Once again something was seriously amiss and D'Allesandro apparently had a hand in it. Although Slim said nothing to Uncle Jesse and Bull, they could tell the odds were poor the Tarngatharn's appeal for mercy would work.

The sun was beginning to set when they reached the outskirts of the Cragnon nation. Mujar was built on a huge bluff that was carved out of the land by the Sulant eons ago. It was connected to the riverbank by a strip of land that was less than a hundred yards wide. The side facing the riverbank was protected by a massive wall made of blocks of rough-hewn stone. Sharpened logs had been placed strategically throughout the wall in the spaces where the corners of the stones met, and any gaps between the larger stones were filled with smaller ones. Together, they formed a barrier that prevented even the largest predator from breaching the walls and entering the city.

Chapter Eight

As they studied the layout both men realized that there was no way to approach the wall without being seen, and trying to cross the strip of land that bridged the riverbank would leave them fully exposed to attack. That made a secret rescue operation virtually impossible.

"How do we get in? That wall looks solid," Bull observed.

"It can be opened from the inside. But something is wrong. It is usually open."

"Any other way in?" Uncle Jesse asked.

"The only other approach is from the side of the bluff that overlooks the river, but the bluff is over thirty feet high there. The Cragnon use rope ladders to reach the Sulant. They dock their canoes against the bluff and pull the ladders up when they're not being used. It would be difficult to scale without being noticed. We'd have to do it at night."

"Then we wait 'til dark and go up the back way," Bull said, shrugging his shoulders.

"We may be too late," Slim said grimly.

"I don't see as we have much choice," Uncle Jesse said. "We can't just walk out there in the open and ask them to let us in. We'd be sitting ducks. What's to stop them from picking us off one by one?"

"They will not harm us," Slim declared confidently.

Uncle Jesse glanced over at Bull and the big man frowned. *Famous last words.* "So you're saying we just ride up to the front door, and they'll let us in?" Bull asked.

Slim nodded.

"All right," Uncle Jesse said, sighing. "You got us this far, Slim. Lead the way, and we'll follow."

Rex Riders

Slim nudged Hellfire into the open. Uncle Jess and Bull followed drawing up beside the Tarngatharn and yerka. As they drew closer to the ridge the grass showed signs of heavy traffic, mixed with an abundance of feathers and animal droppings.

Slim signaled them to stop. "I will go first. You follow," he ordered, then spurred Hellfire onto the ridge.

They were little more than halfway across when a warning volley of spears sailed over the wall and landed in front of them. They were not to come any closer. Hellfire roared his disapproval.

"Easy," Slim whispered to calm his yerka.

"I thought you said they wouldn't shoot at us," Bull said.

"I said they wouldn't harm us. I never said they wouldn't throw spears at us."

Slim raised his arms and called out in the language of the Cragnon, his booming voice echoing against the bluff face.

"I am the Rider. I am here to see your chief, the great warrior Braknar. Open the gates that I may pay him homage and meet with him about a matter of great importance."

The horses were restless, but Slim and Hellfire stood motionless, staring at the great wall.

There was no reply, so the Rider repeated himself.

The high-pitched screeching of great stone wheels grinding against one another shattered the silence, and an opening in the wall appeared.

Slim urged Hellfire through the wide entrance into a grassy area, followed closely by the two cowboys. As the wall closed behind them, they were surrounded by Cragnon warriors, armed with war clubs and long poles, atop their war birds. Their hatred for the cowboys was obvious, and as they rode

Chapter Eight

around the trio, they shouted insults and deliberately poked Uncle Jesse and Bull.

"Quit it," Bull yelled, as he swatted a pole away and struggled to control his nervous horse.

"Put down your weapons and leave these men alone. They mean you no harm," Slim growled imperiously. "I seek an audience with your Chief."

The leader of the warriors addressed Slim. "We welcome you, Yerka Rider. But these others are not Riders. They are from the tribe of strangers who desecrate these lands. Tell us why we should not kill them."

A warrior leaned in close to Uncle Jesse and snarled at him.

"They are with me," Slim said menacingly. "That is reason enough. None may harm them while they are under my care. I owe you no explanation."

Slim placed his hand on the leather holster around his waist. It was a small gesture but it had an immediate effect on the leader who backed away and ordered his warriors to do likewise.

"That's more like it," Bull whispered.

"Come forward then and follow me," the leader ordered.

The warriors surrounded the trio of outsiders and led them through the village.

The buildings were made of stone, wood and animal hide. The Cragnon lived simply, but the availability of unusually tall trees coupled with hides that were many times larger than even the biggest buffalo skins made it possible for them to construct elaborate structures unlike anything the two men had ever seen.

As they rode through the village into a large market everyone stopped what they were doing and stared. An eerie quiet descended upon the crowd. Uncle Jesse locked eyes with a teen-ager whose curious expression immediately changed to a scowl the second he saw him. The disgust on the young Cragnon's face was so intense that Uncle Jesse sensed that something ugly was about to happen.

"Watch yourself," he shouted to Bull.

Suddenly, the boy picked up a rock and threw it at Uncle Jesse. He managed to duck in time, but the stone hit one of the war birds, unleashing a wave of pent-up fury that swept through the crowd. In seconds the villagers were showering the cow-boys with rocks. Others pressed forward shaking their fists and shouting threats. As Uncle Jesse and Bull tried to protect them-selves from the stones, they were forced to slow down, and the angry mob swarmed around them. "This doesn't look good," Uncle Jesse shouted.

Fists flew as villagers tried to separate the men from the over-whelmed warriors, and pull them off their horses. For an instant, Uncle Jesse thought about firing a warning shot in the air, but decided it was too risky and kept his gun holstered.

As the situation spun out of control, Slim had to fight to re-strain Hellfire whose natural instinct when attacked was to rip someone's arm off. That problem was shared by the Cragnon warriors who struggled to control their war birds to prevent them from harming the villagers they were supposed to protect.

This was part of the risk of bringing predatory dinosaurs into a community. They were useful precisely because they were deadly wild animals, which made them an effective means of protection. The down side was that if anyone was stupid enough to deliberately provoke one of the creatures, there was a good

Chapter Eight

chance the animal would lash out no matter how much training it received or how "domesticated" it seemed to be.

The leader of the warriors barked out a series of orders, and two Cragnon at the rear of the group wheeled around to create a barrier to stop the crowd from following them. But that only made things worse! Uncle Jesse turned to see the villagers shouting and straining to break past the two warriors, who were striking them with their clubs.

Then it happened!

One of the warriors was dragged off his war bird and beaten, while the second was almost knocked unconscious after being hit in the head with a large stone. Now, adding to the general chaos was an out of control war bird!

The big dinosaur did exactly what it was trained to do when its rider was hurt: remain at his side and attack anything that came near! The teenager who threw the rock at Uncle Jesse was at the front of the crowd waving a club at the war bird, which lunged at the boy. The youngster tried to back up but the crush of bodies made it impossible to retreat.

"Come on!" Uncle Jesse shouted to Bull, but the big cowboy was already in motion, fighting the mob to turn his horse in the opposite direction.

They came at the war bird from two different directions, ropes at the ready. If they were going to save the youth, they had to pull the animal away. Bull threw his lasso around the war bird's neck. Uncle Jesse scooped up a lid from a fallen basket and rode between the dinosaur and the teen just in time to save the boy from being torn to pieces. He parried the animal's thrusting jaws by using the lid as a shield, distracting it long enough for Bull to wrap his rope around his saddle horn.

The beast's claws ripped through the air as the rope tightened around its neck, and the animal roared as Bull pulled it away.

They had managed to save the teen, but it was only a matter of seconds before the animal would turn on Bull. Uncle Jesse drew his gun and aimed at the animal's head, but before he could fire, Slim pulled the metal device he was carrying out of its holster and pointed it at the war bird while his great fingers moved over its surface in rapid succession.

A bolt of what looked like lightning surged from the device and hit the rampaging beast in the back. The war bird dropped in its tracks, its legs and arms twitching uncontrollably, its tail thrashing up and down. The fighting came to a sudden halt as the crowd stared in amazement. Bull noticed that the dinosaur's back was scorched, and the burned feathers smelled awful, but the creature was still breathing.

Uncle Jesse turned to face the young Cragnon who had sparked the riot, and whose life Uncle Jesse had saved. "You okay?" he asked.

The youth didn't speak English but understood that Uncle Jesse was expressing concern, and nodded. Slim and Bull helped the warrior who had been beaten by the crowd back to his feet. He was glassy-eyed, but okay.

The leader of the Cragnon garrison rode through the crowd and grabbed the teen by the front of his vest. Before he could carry him off, however, Slim stepped in and pointed out that the crowd might riot if he didn't release the young one. The warrior looked around and relaxed his grip enough that the teen was able to squirm free and disappear into the crowd.

Chapter Eight

There was no point taking a chance.

Just as suddenly as it began, the riot ended and the crowd dispersed. The warriors regrouped around the men and continued their journey through the village without further incident.

"Nice shooting back there," Uncle Jesse said, turning to Slim. "You'll have to show me how that thing works some time. I wouldn't mind having one myself."

"Maybe you will," Slim replied with that weird kind of smile of his, which bared his massive teeth and scared the heck out of most people.

Before long they came to a stone platform. A flight of steps lead to a large wooden structure at which stood Braknar, the eldest chief of the Cragnon nation and leader of the tribespeople who lived on the bluff. He was dressed in leather skins and held an ornately-carved wooden staff decorated with colorful raptor feathers. Next to him stood Shugath, the shaman.

The garrison leader who had led the trio through the village ran up the steps and bowed before Braknar before telling him about the riot in the marketplace. The chief and shaman listened attentively, nodding every so often. When the warrior had finished, Braknar invited Slim and the cowboys to approach.

"Greetings, Chief Braknar. We seek an audience with you and your war council."

Chief Braknar grasped Slim's hand. "We know why you are here, Yerka Rider, but you are too late. The council has already made its decision. The Cragnon are preparing for war."

"If you are only preparing for war, then I am not too late. I respectfully repeat my request for an audience with the council."

Rex Riders

"There is no harm in listening to what the Rider has to say," Shugath whispered to his chief.

Braknar nodded.

"Come, Rider, let us talk." He turned and led the visitors inside.

The room was lit with small torches and crude lamps. Chief Braknar and Shugath took their places at a long table, joining the council members, who were already seated. Slim stood before them, with Uncle Jesse and Bull behind.

"You have come a long way, Rider," Braknar began. "And have brought two of the outlanders with you. Why have you come?"

"I want the woman you hold prisoner. Release her to me."

The council members were startled that Slim knew about their prisoner. How was this possible?

"You seek much. What do you offer in exchange?" Braknar asked.

"I will go to the strangers and tell them to leave these lands and never return."

"I don't understand. Two of the strangers ride with you. Why are they here? Do they wish to negotiate with us for this woman?"

"These men are not part of the tribe that threatens you. Their tribe seeks peace and wishes to help me persuade your enemy to give up the lands he has taken and return to the place he came from. I propose to bring the prisoner with me as a sign of good faith."

Shugath looked at Slim and a cunning smile crossed his face. "Tell us Rider, why is this prisoner so important to you?"

"I know of your attack on the strangers' world. I have seen the bodies of those who were slain. This prisoner was not among the invaders. She took no action against you. The others will seek revenge if this innocent woman is harmed. The violence between your tribe and the strangers will increase, and peace will be more difficult to achieve. If I can obtain her release, I may be able to stop this from happening."

Shugath was impressed. "You know a great deal, Rider. But if this prisoner is as important as you say, then our leverage is increased by keeping her. Remember, we did not start this war. We struck at them as repayment for the crimes they committed against us."

"And I would not argue otherwise," Slim said quickly. "But I urge you to give diplomacy a chance. To declare war now is premature . . ."

The second he used the word "premature," Slim knew he had made a mistake. His comment made it sound as if the harm the Cragnon had suffered up to that point was insignificant, and the Rider could tell from the expressions of the council members that he had made a serious blunder.

"*'Premature'*? Have you seen the Sulant, Rider?" Braknar demanded angrily.

"I have," Slim admitted. "And I know your people suffer."

"Then you must also know that the three-horns have begun to migrate toward the flooded area near the outlanders' village," Braknar continued. "Our warriors are killed by them when they try to hunt. Our crops suffer for lack of water, and the fish are few. Yet, you say that war is premature. I ask you how much more we must endure before we are justified in defending ourselves and driving the outlanders from these lands?"

"Your people's suffering grieves me greatly, Chief Braknar,"

Rex Riders

Slim said. "My choice of words was poor. I know that what I ask requires sacrifice and faith on your part. It is not a request I make lightly."

"You ask for a prisoner but offer nothing in return," Shugath said. "Mighty Braknar might agree to release the prisoner you seek if you give him something of value in exchange."

"What is it he wishes, shaman?" Slim asked warily.

"That one of you remains here in her place. An outlander for an outlander. Is that not fair?"

"That is impossible—" Slim began, but Braknar interrupted him.

"You ask our people to sacrifice for peace. Are you unwilling to sacrifice something of value as well? I will grant your request, but these are my terms. In two nights the red moons will rise. Convince the outlanders to relinquish their lands and depart. If you succeed, then the prisoner will be released and given safe passage back to their world. If you fail, we will sacrifice the prisoner to the gods and ask the holy Shurah to bless us in battle."

"What is your answer, Rider?" Shugath hissed.

The eyes of every member of the council were on Slim. He knew it was fruitless to try to change the terms of the bargain he was offered. He had been outfoxed.

"I must speak with the outlanders," the Rider answered. He turned and made his way out of the chamber, motioning for Uncle Jesse and Bull to follow.

"How'd it go?" Bull asked.

"They are willing to release the prisoner," Slim answered.

"Great work!" Uncle Jesse cried as he gingerly slapped Slim on the back.

Chapter Eight

"There is more," Slim said, holding up his hand to cut off Uncle Jesse's celebration. "They are only willing to release the woman, if one of you stays in her place. Then, whichever one of you does not remain will accompany me to D'Allesandro's camp. We'll have two days to convince him to leave. If we succeed, the prisoner will be released."

"*What?!*" Bull exclaimed. "Who the heck agreed to that?"

"No one as yet," Slim said. "That is what they are asking."

"And what if D'Allesandro refuses?" Uncle Jesse asked.

"Then, they will kill the prisoner."

The men were stunned. "This ain't happening," Uncle Jesse said angrily. "We're leaving. We came here to spring Maria. This wasn't part of the deal. *'Plead for mercy'*—what kind of stupid plan was that? Come on, Bull. We'll figure something out on our own."

"I will not try to stop you," Slim said.

"Don't, because you won't be able to," Uncle Jesse said.

Uncle Jesse and Bull stormed past the guards and walked down the steps toward their horses. "We're getting out of here one way or another," Uncle Jesse said as he fingered his gun. But when they reached the horses, Bull didn't saddle up.

"Jess, maybe I ought to stay."

"What are you talking about?"

"If I stay, the odds of you and Maria convincing D'Allesandro to leave peacefully are better than if I go with you."

"Bull, we've been in jams before . . ."

"I know, but those times we only had to worry about you and me. Jess, we can't take on this whole village. That won't work. Not with just two of us. That leaves only one choice. I'll take her place. You and Maria go with Slim."

Uncle Jesse looked at his old friend; his expression was resolute.

"All right," Uncle Jesse finally said, with a sigh.

The men walked back into the hall and told Slim their decision. Slim looked Bull in the eye and said, "We'll be back."

When the war council heard that the men had agreed to the exchange, Chief Braknar ordered Maria's release. The warriors escorted them to a circular pit that was carved into the rock, and a crowd gathered to watch.

Suspended over the pit was a large wooden cage that once held D'Allesandro's men. Just out of range of the cage were half a dozen war birds tied to logs embedded in the floor of the pit. Atop each log was a human skull.

The war birds seemed calm. Several were standing; one sat, staring into space; and another slept.

Shugath shouted something at them and tossed a rock toward the cage. Then he laughed uproariously as the war birds leapt at the rock thinking it was food.

Shugath looked at Bull contemptuously, then spoke to Slim. "Tell him to keep his arms inside the cage."

The warriors restrained the raptors while the cage was lowered. When it touched the ground, two of the warriors entered and pulled Maria out. She was too exhausted from lack of sleep to offer any resistance, and her limp body was dragged up a flight of stairs out of the pit.

When Maria saw Uncle Jesse she couldn't believe it was him and started to sob. "Am I dreaming? Where is my daughter? Is she alive?"

Chapter Eight

"She's fine," Uncle Jesse said. "She's at the Double R."

"Oh, thank goodness," Maria said.

"You're coming with us."

Now it was Bull's turn to take her place. Bull turned all of his weapons over to Uncle Jesse while the Cragnon watched, and then they searched him. "Good luck," Bull said, shaking hands with Uncle Jesse.

Uncle Jesse had a grim look on his face. "I'll see you in two days. Stay sharp." Then the two cowboys exchanged winks.

Uncle Jesse handed Bull's gun belt and holster to Maria and told her to put them on. Shugath gave the signal to close the cage door, and the warriors raised the wooden cell in preparation for releasing the war birds.

"Let's get going," Uncle Jesse said to Slim.

"It's dark. We should wait until morning. Riding at night is not safe."

"We ride tonight," Uncle Jesse insisted.

"This woman needs rest and water or she will be useless to us," Slim countered.

"Then we'll camp near the city. I don't trust these Cragnon, and I'm not spending the night here."

Uncle Jesse and Slim exchanged hard looks, but the Yerka Rider could see in the rancher's eyes that this was one battle he was not going to win. It was useless to try to convince him to stay inside the village, and Slim wasn't sure it was safer inside than outside, so he agreed to leave.

They made camp at a point that overlooked the Sulant. From that spot, they could keep an eye on the ridge that led into the walled village and take note of anyone going in or out. This allowed Uncle Jesse to make sure they weren't followed.

Maria was too tired to even carry on a conversation and she went right to sleep.

Uncle Jesse and Slim took turns keeping watch. It was after midnight when Uncle Jesse saw four riders leave the city. He doused the camp fire and woke Slim, but they never heard or saw them again.

The next morning Maria felt much better, and they set out early for D'Allesandro's camp. She was full of questions about her daughter, and Uncle Jesse told her how Angelina had escaped from the Double R and saved Tom White's life.

At first, Uncle Jesse held back asking Maria about her brother. But he couldn't stop thinking that she had lied to him about the whereabouts of D'Allesandro the night of the square dance, and it bothered him. Finally he just came out and asked,

"How much did you know about what your brother was doing here?"

Maria turned away.

"I've got two days to convince your brother to head back to Dos Locos or Bull is dead," Uncle Jesse persisted. "Are you going to let him die or will you tell your brother to pack up his tent and head back home?"

"Dante is a stubborn man, Mr. McCain. You know that."

"So am I. And you didn't answer my question. You'd still be back there if Bull hadn't taken your place. You owe him."

"I will do what I can," Maria replied curtly.

Chapter Eight

Slim made a growling sound like something you'd expect to hear out of Hellfire, and his face contorted into something animal-like. "See that you do," he said, and no one missed the menacing tone in his voice.

By the time they reached the outskirts of D'Allesandro's camp, Slim was having some serious second thoughts about having freed Maria. He was unsure whether she would succeed in persuading her brother to go back to Dos Locos or whether she would even ask him to do so. And that meant that he had to be prepared to take more aggressive action.

Then there was the matter of the explosions the group heard in the distance as they neared the camp.

"You hear that?" Uncle Jesse asked.

Slim nodded, and they both looked at Maria.

"You have any idea what's going on?" Uncle Jesse asked her.

When Maria didn't answer, Slim decided to take a detour and see for himself.

"My brother's camp is in this direction," she said, as the Rex Rider turned Hellfire away.

"I know," he said. "We're heading toward the river."

They rode to the edge of a canyon that overlooked the Sulant. There Slim found what he was looking for: a wall of rock more than fifty feet tall, damming the river. D'Allesandro's men had blasted the sides of the canyon and sent tons of stone tumbling into the water, all but stopping the river's flow. It was crude, but it worked. No more than a trickle crept out from the base of the fallen rock, and that was sure to stop as the men continued blasting. Armed guards patrolled the sides of the canyon, while several others were stationed at the base of the dam. Things were starting to fall into place.

"They must have gone through a half dozen crates of TNT already," Uncle Jesse observed. "And they ain't done yet."

"TNT?" Slim asked.

"Explosives; you know, to blow things up?"

Slim nodded.

"But why build a dam, Slim?" Uncle Jesse asked.

"I am not sure. The Sulant is the Cragnon's lifeblood. It's possible that once D'Allesandro controls the flow of its waters to Mujar, he'll either drive the tribe off their lands or they will be forced to make peace with him on his terms. Or he may have something else in mind."

Uncle Jesse glanced at Maria to see her reaction. She was staring at the dam impassively with her arms folded. Uncle Jesse leaned closer to Slim. "Be careful what you say around her," he whispered.

"Let's go," Slim said.

"I know the way from here," Maria said sharply.

"I'll bet you do," Uncle Jesse said under his breath.

As they neared D'Allesandro's camp, they saw several towers identical to the ones on his property in Dos Locos, except that these were manned by one or two cowboys using spyglasses. The men in the closest tower spotted them first and sent out a signal by ringing a bell. The trio could see him pointing at them and shouting to someone on the ground.

"Looks like they're forming a welcoming party to say *howdy*," Uncle Jesse said. "Let's not keep them waiting."

They quickened their pace, and it wasn't long before they

Chapter Eight

were met by a gang of roughnecks led by Cable Cooper.

"It's Mrs. Con Fuego, boys!" he shouted.

As Cooper's men circled them, Uncle Jesse noticed they kept their distance. It was clear they recognized Slim and Hellfire.

"Ma'am, it's good to see you!" Cooper said, tipping his hat to Maria. "What are you doing here with these two? How'd you get here?"

"It's a long story. Where is my brother?"

"Back at camp. We're getting ready to leave. He's been pretty busy."

"Busy," Maria said scornfully. "Yes, my brother is a very busy man."

Cooper acted as if Uncle Jesse and Slim weren't even there.

"How about taking us to see him?" Uncle Jesse interrupted.

"How about you hold your horses, McCain?" Cooper spat. "I'll take you when I'm good and ready."

Cooper looked Slim up and down. "I thought you were dead," he sneered.

The Rex Rider's eyes narrowed, and his hands balled into fists. He had a score to settle with Cooper but he had to bide his time. "It is good to see you again too, Cable Cooper."

"Follow me, Mrs. Con Fuego. A lot's happened since you last visited."

Uncle Jesse and Slim exchanged knowing looks. As they'd suspected, D'Allesandro's sister knew far more than she was saying. She rode alongside Cooper, while Uncle Jesse and Slim trailed behind, surrounded by D'Allesandro's men.

Uncle Jesse gestured to the men that surrounded them, "Are these the same men who ambushed you at Small's Stream?"

"Shhh," Slim cautioned quietly before nodding toward Maria and Cooper. The Rider was staring at them intently. Uncle Jesse looked at Slim and wondered if he could possibly hear what they were saying. That would explain a couple of things.

As they rode toward a cluster of buildings, Slim whispered to Uncle Jesse, "Where can I get TNT?"

"TNT? Do you mean around here? D'Allesandro must have wagonloads of it somewhere," Uncle Jesse answered, also maintaining the appearance that he and Slim were innocently riding along. "But you can bet it's heavily guarded. Why?"

"Can Stumpy get some?"

"Yeah, I guess he could."

"Give me the map I gave you. When I give the signal, I'll need you to distract them. Can you do that?"

Uncle Jesse smiled as he reached into his shirt pocket and handed the map to Slim. "No problemo."

Cooper led them to a barrier constructed of wood, metal and barbed wire that was nearly twenty-five feet high. Two gates stood side by side, one slightly wider than the average doorway only much higher. This provided easy access to horsemen and anyone traveling on foot. The second extended the full height of the surrounding fence, and was wider still to allow the passage of any wheeled vehicles. Thick wooden posts served as the support frame for the barrier, with a pair of logs crisscrossing the center of the larger gate to form an X. Sharpened poles protruded along the entire line, with pointed metal bars woven into the gates for additional security

Both entrances were open, and men and horses moved in and out. On each side of the gate armed men in towers kept watch.

Chapter Eight

Inside the barrier was something resembling a small town. There were corrals for the horses; a barn and blacksmith's shop; a huge bunkhouse that appeared as if it could sleep a hundred men; a large dining hall; and many other buildings of various shapes and sizes. The living quarters and the dining hall were built on stilts.

But the most surprising sight was the two medium-sized trikes joined together by a heavy wooden yoke that had been carved to fit their massive necks. The two horns on the top of their frill had been cut down in length, but it didn't seem to affect them any. They were pulling logs that would have taken a team of horses to move, and were doing it effortlessly. McCain was awed by their power.

So this is how D'Allesandro built all this, Uncle Jesse thought. The rancher had an unparalleled lumber supply and animal power that moved trees and boulders with ease. Animals this size could pull farm equipment that was far bigger than anything anyone had ever built and clear land in a fraction of the time it would take other creatures. It was no wonder D'Allesandro wanted to bring the trikes back to Dos Locos.

The group stopped in front of a large square building in the center of the compound. It was a good six feet off the ground and the only way up was by ladder. There was a hitching post in front of the building. "Tie your horses there, McCain" Cooper ordered.

Slim started to loop Hellfire's reins around the hitching post, but Cooper stopped him. "Not you. I don't want that thing near the horses."

Hellfire growled in response.

Cooper pointed to another post a dozen yards away that was empty. "Use that one. And settle down that overgrown lizard of yours before my men shut him up for good!"

Slim smiled as he rode Hellfire away. Cooper was playing right into their hands.

When the Tarngatharn reached the hitching post, he dismounted and opened his saddlebag. He removed some of Stumpy's jerky and held the food in front of Hellfire's snout. As he whispered in the rex's ear, the animal licked and began to nibble the meat. Slim opened his fist, and Hellfire took the jerky out of his hand and swallowed it. Then Slim scribbled something on a piece of paper and stuffed it inside the saddlebag. From Cooper's vantage point, it looked like nothing more than the rider quieting his animal with a treat and pat on the neck.

Then Slim looked at Uncle Jesse and nodded.

"Hey Cooper, is your boss home? I'm tired of waiting." Uncle Jesse said, deliberately brushing against Cooper and starting up the ladder.

Cooper screamed at Uncle Jesse to get down, and Uncle Jesse told him where to go. As the argument got louder, men came running from every direction to see if a fight was going to break out.

Slim quickly turned Hellfire in the direction of the compound entrance, which luckily remained open. He hit the T-rex on the rump and sent him on his way. Several men stopped in their tracks and stared as the dinosaur trotted through the gate into the forest, but most were too busy trying to get a look at the fracas between Cooper and Uncle Jesse to question what was happening or try to stop it. Slim, meanwhile, walked back to the

Chapter Eight

scene of the argument as if nothing had happened.

D'Allesandro stepped out of his cabin and leaned over the railing. "What's going on, Mr. Cooper?!" he shouted angrily. "Get these men back to work!"

"It's McCain, Mr. D'Allesandro," Cooper said. "I told him to get down but he won't listen."

"Mr. McCain! Maria! I was told you were here! Come up and join me!" D'Allesandro spotted the Rider towering over the men at the rear of the crowd. "The Rider, too! This *is* a surprise. "Tell him to come up, as well. It's been a long time."

D'Allesandro's cabin was Spartan but well-used. The log walls had windows cut into them, each covered with metal poultry netting and heavy wooden shutters that could be bolted shut from the inside. A hunting rifle hung from every wall, and open boxes of ammunition lay on the floor. There were several tables and enough benches for a dozen men.

D'Allesandro and Professor Kornbluth had been working on an account of their exploration of the world. Maps covered with notes were tacked on the walls, and several leather-bound books sat open on the tables nearly hidden by pages of more notes and drawings of the wildlife the two men had encountered.

The Professor straightened his collar and greeted each of them in turn. He was wearing a short-sleeve shirt, and his right arm was severly discolored. He'd been bitten by an insect that got into his cabin while he slept, and his condition was worsening.

Maria rushed to her brother and embraced him.

"Maria, what are you doing here?" D'Allesandro asked.

"Dante, the Cragnon attacked the Crossed Swords. They

killed the men and kidnapped me," Maria replied, choking back tears. "Mr. McCain and Mr. Whitman rescued me."

"Where is Mr. Whitman?" D'Allesandro asked.

"He stayed behind. They wouldn't let me go unless he agreed to take my place."

"What do the savages want?"

"They want you to leave and their lands returned to them."

"The game is up, Mr. D'Allesandro," Uncle Jesse interjected. "The Cragnon know how to find your ranch and how to get to Dos Locos. If they don't get what they want, they'll burn the town to the ground. Slim bargained with their medicine man, last night. If I'm not back in forty-eight hours, they're going to kill Bull."

"By 'Slim,' you mean the Rider, I presume. What a colorful nickname. You say he spoke to their medicine man?"

D'Allesandro closed his eyes and began to pace.

"I know this will come as a disappointment to you, Mr. McCain, but I'm afraid I'm not leaving. And neither are you."

"What are you talking about?"

"You're staying here as my guest."

The tension in the room was inching up to unbearable proportions. Uncle Jesse and Maria had no idea what D'Allesandro was talking about, but Slim could see where it was going.

"Did you hear what I just said?" Uncle Jesse asked defiantly.

D'Allesandro nodded to Cable Cooper, "I think so." Cooper drew his gun and pointed it at Uncle Jesse, and his men did the same.

Slim reached for his holster.

"Make a move Rider, and McCain is dead," Cooper sneered

Chapter Eight

as he cocked his revolver. "We ain't making the same mistake we made last time."

"What are you doing? Dante, what's going on?" Maria shouted.

"Mr. McCain is going to be our guest for a few days while we finish our work here. After that, whether he stays or goes back home will be entirely up to him."

"A few days?" Uncle Jesse cried. "If I don't get back to the Cragnon village, they're going to kill my friend! Dos Locos is in danger!"

"No, Mr. McCain," D'Allesandro said calmly. "It is you who are in danger, if you don't do exactly as I say.

"We've been here less than a year, and have made tremendous progress. The wildlife, the plants—so many new species. They will be incredibly useful in ways I can't begin to imagine. I'm not throwing all that away because one of your men was captured by a group of savages."

"Don't you get it? They're coming in a matter of days and will kill everyone here. You can't win, D'Allesandro."

"Is that so? Do you think that I did all of this without help?"

D'Allesandro looked at his pocket watch, then out the window. A smile crept over his face as he turned to face Uncle Jesse and Slim. "Allow me introduce a friend of mine. Or should I say, business partner?"

The last person Uncle Jesse or Slim expected to see walking into the room was Shugath, the Cragnon shaman. Cable Cooper burst out laughing when he saw the expressions on their faces.

Uncle Jesse couldn't process what was happening. "Your

ranch . . . We saw your ranch. It was destroyed," he stammered, dumbfounded.

"Yes," D'Allesandro sighed. "That was not part of the plan. But the war council demanded retaliation, so Shugath had no choice."

"If I don't return, they will attack this camp," Uncle Jesse repeated.

"Yes, they will attack this encampment. But I have altered the balance of power, Mr. McCain. I provided the tribesmen who are loyal to Shugath with guns. When the Cragnon leave their village, those tribesmen will kill those faithful to Braknar. Shugath will become the new Cragnon chief, and we will have an alliance. His tribe will once again rule these lands, and there will be peace between us. He will have what he wants, and I will have what I want. And the town of Dos Locos will be perfectly safe."

"But what about Bull? If I don't go back, he's dead."

"He will be killed regardless of whether or not you return, because I have no intention of leaving by Braknar's deadline. I intend to settle these lands, Mr. McCain. This minor skirmish is just the beginning. The conquest of this land will take time, and there will be casualties on both sides. It is unavoidable. But in the end, mankind will reign with its new partners."

"You're loco," Uncle Jesse shouted.

Out of nowhere, Cooper slugged him across the face. Maria gasped.

D'Allesandro shook his head. "You will never understand the ways of business, Mr. McCain. And thus, never be anything more than a hired hand." He turned toward Slim. "I was told you were

Chapter Eight

dead, Rider, but your arrival may prove helpful. Give me the device you wear around your waist or my men will shoot Mr. McCain in the head. And unlike you, he will not survive."

"Don't . . . ," said Uncle Jesse weakly.

Cooper snapped his fingers and gestured toward Slim. Two of the men approached the Tarngatharn, guns drawn.

"Don't make a move, ugly," the first man ordered. "*Ugh,* he stinks! Smells like onions and grass."

When the man turned back his head to share in the rest of the men's laughter, Slim grabbed his outstretched arm. There was a horrible cracking sound as the arm was wrenched out of its socket, and the man collapsed in pain on the floor.

In a flash, Slim backhanded the second man, sending him flying across the room. The other men rushed the Tarngatharn, but Slim moved quickly, striking with both hands and knocking several of them down.

A gun roared, followed by the sound of a body dropping to the floor. All eyes turned toward Cooper who had his boot on Uncle Jesse's chest, while he writhed in pain from a gunshot wound to the shoulder.

"Make another move and McCain's dead," Cooper declared, leveling his gun at Uncle Jesse's head. "Did you think we were kidding, McCain?"

Slim released the men in his grasp and dropped his hands to his sides.

"Hold him," Cooper ordered.

While several men held Slim's arms, Cooper strode over to the Tarngatharn and snatched the powerful device from its holster.

"Looks like this ain't your lucky day," he said, holding the force generator in Slim's face before turning it over his boss.

D'Allesandro couldn't believe his good fortune. "It seems I have altered the balance of power once again," he whispered as he studied the device.

A chill ran through Shugath. He wondered if D'Allesandro realized the power he now had at his command. He had done something no Cragnon had ever dared: taken a Rex Rider prisoner! Braknar would never have been so bold.

The shaman knew it was risky to ally himself with D'Allesandro, but all the signs had foreseen the arrival of strangers, followed by a period of great upheaval and conflict. It was not clear to Shugath who would prevail, but he was now sure that the time of great change had begun.

"Tell me how to operate this," D'Allesandro demanded.

A stream of gooey spittle squirted out of the Tarngatharn's mouth and landed on D'Allesando's shirt.

"You son of a . . ." Cooper roared, as he punched Slim in the face. The blow had no effect on the Tarngatharn, but everyone in the room winced when they heard the sound that Cooper's hand made when it struck the bony plates on Slim's head.

"*Yow!*" Cooper screamed, clutching his hand.

D'Allesandro shook his head as Cooper howled in pain. "Mr. Cooper, when will you learn? Professor, take this device and tell me how it operates."

"Mr. D'Allesandro," the Professor pleaded, "You know I'm not well. I don't have time; there is other work that needs my attention."

D'Allesdandro gently placed a hand on Kornbluth's shoulder,

Chapter Eight

"You are the only one here who has a chance of figuring out this device."

"But I'm a paleontologist, not an engineer!"

"You are a man of science and on my payroll," D'Allesandro said firmly. "You have until tomorrow. If you fail, I will have to convince my friend the Rider to tell me its secrets, and that will be very unpleasant for Mr. McCain. Now, go and do as I say."

The Professor was shaking. "I'll try."

"Mr. Cooper, the Professor needs quiet. Remove these two. Put the Rider in chains."

"What about McCain?"

"He won't give you any trouble. He'll be fully occupied trying not to bleed to death. Put him someplace where he won't escape, but don't harm him any further. We may need him if the Professor fails. And when he's feeling better, thank him for taking care of my horse. Now, where is the Rider's tyrannosaur? I want it killed."

"It's tied out front, Mr. D'Allesandro. I'll do it myself." Cooper grinned at Slim. "It'll be good to get rid of another one of those things."

Cooper walked out onto the porch only to return a moment later in a state of panic. "Where is it?" he roared in the Rex Rider's face. "Tell me or so help me I'll kill McCain right now."

Slim just laughed. "I set it free. It's in the woods. Go find it yourself."

Cooper clenched his fist, but thought better of using it to hit the Tarngatharn. Instead, he walked over to Uncle Jesse. "Here's what happens when you don't do what we say," he sneered as he punched Uncle Jesse in the gut.

Slim flinched at the sight of his friend in pain and clenched his massive fingers. Cooper would pay for this.

"Get them out of my sight," D'Allesandro ordered. "Shugath, send your warriors to kill the rex. And tell them not to damage the head. I want it for my wall."

"My warriors will not fail you," Shugarth promised. "Tonight, we will feast on its flesh!"

Chapter
Nine

Angelina was relieved and grateful to be able to stay at the Double R while she awaited the return of the men with her mother. Although it wasn't necessary, Stumpy forbade her—and Zeke—from going back to the Crossed Swords Ranch.

As Zeke had feared, Slim's room had acquired a stinky smell during the Tarngatharn's brief visit, and the odor permeated everything. To make matters worse, Zeke had the uncomfortable feeling that he was beginning to reek from sleeping in the room, although he wasn't positive. Stumpy brushed off the boy's concerns and told him that he smelled fine, and anyway, the room assignment was only temporary until Uncle Jesse got back. Then the old cook cautioned that if Zeke didn't keep his door shut, he'd nail it closed and winked at him, leaving Zeke utterly confused about the state of his body odor.

Zeke thought that living under the same roof with Angelina would give him a chance to get to know the girl better and bring them closer together, but that didn't happen. Angelina was withdrawn and unfriendly, and Zeke's efforts to coax her out of her shell were met with a cold response. Even when Stumpy brought Tom White to Doc in town, leaving Zeke and Angelina alone at the Double R for a few hours, she did nothing but stay in her room the whole time. At first, Stumpy thought to take Zeke aside and tell him to give the girl some breathing room, but eventually decided to let the teens work it out on their own.

Angelina's first few days at the Double R were especially hard. She couldn't get the thoughts of her mother's abduction out of her mind, and her sleep was plagued by nightmares. Zeke and Stumpy tried to reassure her that everything would turn out fine, but when Uncle Jesse and Bull didn't return right away, everyone began to feel a little edgy.

"When do you think they'll be back?" Zeke asked over dinner one night.

"Can't say for sure," Stumpy said between mouthfuls of steak.

"It'll be three days tomorrow," Zeke observed.

"Yes, it will. And there's no sense getting our guest upset over nothing," Stumpy said firmly. "Make no mistake about it; your uncle Jesse and Bull can take care of themselves. Those boys have seen it all."

"I know," Zeke said. "It's just that the last time you said that, things didn't work out too well."

"You don't say," Stumpy said evenly. "And when was that?"

"The time Uncle Jesse and Bull tangled with Slim and got their butts whipped."

Chapter Nine

"And what happened after that?"

"Well, we all got to be friends."

"Like I said, those two know how to take care of themselves," Stumpy said, winking at Angelina.

The following morning, Stumpy awoke with a taste for bacon. He was on his way to cut himself a piece when he saw a familiar tail sticking out of the smokehouse door!

"*Dadblastit!* What are you doing here?" the old cook yelled, waving his cast iron skillet at Hellfire's rump. "Get out of there, you!"

The T-rex gave Stumpy a look and grunted before going back to sniffing and licking the tasty cuts of meat. Stumpy whacked the rex across its hindquarters with his skillet, but the big meat eater was so intent on choosing its breakfast that it didn't notice. When Stumpy hit Hellfire a second time even harder, the rex instinctively shifted its hips and swung its thick tail, knocking him down. As the old cook struggled to his feet he felt a sharp pain in his hip. In the meantime, Hellfire settled on the very same piece of pork that Stumpy had his sights on and backed out of the smokehouse with the prize locked in its jaws.

"Put that down!" Stumpy shouted. "I was gonna cook that for breakfast."

After another disinterested look and grunt, the big animal trotted off toward the barn to enjoy its meal, leaving Stumpy to simmer in his own juices, so to speak.

"Zeke!" he cried. "Get out here!"

"What is it, Stumpy?" the boy called, as he ran toward the smokehouse with Angelina following close behind.

Stumpy had a pained expression on his face and was rubbing his hip.

"What happened to your leg?" Zeke asked. "You okay?"

"Hellfire hit me with his tail pretty good, but I'm fine."

"Hellfire's back?! Where is he? Is Slim with him? What about Uncle Jesse and Bull?" Zeke asked excitedly.

"And my mother? Is she with them?" Angelina interjected.

"Hold on a minute, you two. I ain't sure where they are, or if they're even here at all," Stumpy said soberly. "Hellfire was alone."

"We've got to spread out and look for them," he continued. "You two go to the barn and see if Midnight's in his stall. And Zeke, make sure Hellfire's tied up so he can't get out. I'll take a walk around and see if I can find your uncle or Bull, or Angelina's mother. If you see them before I do, holler."

When they met later on the front porch, Stumpy looked worried. "Something's wrong," he said. "They ain't here. Is Midnight in the barn?"

"No," Angelina answered.

"And neither is Bull's horse," Zeke added quickly.

"That's what I was afraid of." Stumpy sighed and stared at the ground. This was a bad development, and they all knew it. Things had gone from happy to depressing in a matter of minutes. "Let's go back inside," he said.

They shuffled back into the kitchen and gathered around the table.

"What do we do now?" Zeke asked glumly.

For a long while no one spoke.

Angelina looked ashen, worse than when she arrived at the

Chapter Nine

Double R. "I don't think my mother's coming back," she said softly, averting her gaze.

"Now, there's no reason to start talking like that," Stumpy said encouragingly.

Stumpy took a deep breath, and Zeke suddenly noticed how old he looked. Nothing fazed the old cook, and he was always ready with a funny story or a snappy one-liner, regardless of how bad a situation appeared. But now, he seemed to be at a loss.

It didn't last long. "I'm going after them," he said finally.

"You can't go by yourself, Stumpy. Let me go with you," Zeke begged.

"Son, somebody has to stay here and mind the Double R, and keep Angelina company until I get back. I wish you could go son, but I can't take you with me."

"But how are you going to find them?" Zeke said.

"If I know your uncle, he marked his trail as he went along, just in case he ran into trouble."

Stumpy stretched his leg and winced. *Isn't this just my luck?* he thought.

"What's the matter?" Zeke asked worriedly.

"I already told you I'm okay. Hellfire knocked me down when I wasn't looking, that's all. I'm fine."

Zeke could tell from Stumpy's pained expression he was lying. "Stumpy, your leg isn't good. You told me plenty of times that you can't ride for hours like you used to. Let me go instead."

"I'll take Hellfire," the boy continued. "He'll let me ride him. Slim and Uncle Jesse must've sent him back here to get me. I'll be okay. You remember what Slim said? It's a lot safer to ride a critter like Hellfire where he comes from, than a horse."

Stumpy had to admit Zeke had a point. The boy had a bond with the animal, and it was possible that Slim had sent Hellfire back deliberately to get help.

"Let's say you take Hellfire and leave your horse here. How are you gonna get back? Once you've found Slim, you'll have to give the critter back to him."

"I'll ride with Uncle Jesse. Or Slim will take me. Don't worry about that. Let me find them first. Then we can figure out how to get back together. If I can't find them, I'll return on Hellfire, and we can all go for help."

"Let me think about it," Stumpy said.

Yes! Zeke thought. This was progress. If his uncle had been here, the boy knew he'd never have gotten this far.

Angelina watched Stumpy intently. She wanted to see how this was going to turn out before she made her play.

Stumpy was quiet for a long moment. He was staring into space thinking about something Zeke had said. Surely, the boy's uncle didn't intend for Zeke to gallop to the rescue on that beast. He barely allowed the boy to ride the sorrel when he wasn't around and was adamant that Zeke remain at the Double R while he was off with Bull and Slim. But then why send Hellfire back, unless . . .

"Zeke, did you notice if Hellfire had on those saddlebags that I gave to Slim?"

"I'm not sure," Zeke replied.

"He did. I saw them," Angelina interjected.

"Good. Go out to the barn and bring them here. I want to see something."

* * *

Chapter Nine

Soon Stumpy had the contents of Hellfire's saddlebags strewn across the kitchen table. The beef jerky he'd wrapped as a snack for the T-rex was gone, but the writing paper and pencils seemed to be intact. Stumpy rifled through the sheets, and sure enough, there was a map drawn on one with a note written on another.

"This is it," Stumpy said, studying the map.

Slim had penciled in a route from the transport device to the Sulant, and upriver past the Cragnon village to D'Allesandro's camp.

Angelina looked over Stumpy's shoulder and read the notes aloud. "'We okay. Follow river. Take yerka.'"

"And this drawing looks like sticks of TNT and a rope," Zeke added.

"It must have been Slim," Stumpy observed. "This is a pretty good drawing."

Angelina and Zeke looked at each other.

Stumpy stared at the message as he rubbed his chin.

"Son, it looks like you were right. They sent Hellfire back here to get our help, and like you said, you're the only one who can ride him."

"Then I can go?" Zeke asked excitedly.

Stumpy hesitated. "Yes, you can go."

Zeke let out a cheer. Considering the seriousness of the situation, it really wasn't appropriate, but this was the vote of confidence the boy had been waiting for since he first arrived at his uncle's ranch, and he just couldn't help himself!

Angelina had been quiet while Zeke made his case about why he should go in Stumpy's place and was impressed that he'd gotten this far. Now it was time to make her move.

"If he's going, then I'm going too," she announced, folding her arms across her chest.

Zeke grimaced. This was exactly what he was afraid of. If Angelina made an issue of going, Stumpy might change his mind and decide that it was easier if neither one of them went. Here was Zeke's chance to prove himself to Uncle Jesse after the barn incident, and Angelina was going to screw it up!

"No, you're not. I earned the right," Zeke said, his voice rising in anger. "Isn't that right Stumpy? I'm going, and I'm going alone!"

"You're going to need help," Angelina said.

"What are you talking about? I can do just fine on my own. You're not going, and that's final."

"Yes, I am. And you can't stop me."

Zeke and Angelina looked at Stumpy. "Well?" they said in unison.

Stumpy's eyes darted from one to the other. This was tricky business. Angelina may have been only fourteen, but it wasn't like Stumpy was her father. She didn't have to do what he told her. Angelina had just as much of a reason to want to go as Zeke did. The real question was whether the girl would be a help or a hindrance to Zeke. And based upon what the old cook had seen, Stumpy felt he knew the answer.

"Angelina, I'm not gonna say you can't go. It's up to you. It's gonna be dangerous. You heard what Tom White said, and you saw what those Cragnon did to your uncle's ranch. But if you want to go, you can."

Angelina whooped and hollered just as much as Zeke had, while Zeke dropped his face into his hands and groaned.

Chapter Nine

Stumpy just shook his head. These young people had no idea what they were in for, but if they set aside their differences and worked together, everything might work out.

"The next thing we have to do is find some TNT," he said, once Angelina had settled down. TNT was commonly used in mining operations. It wasn't generally needed by ranchers, and Uncle Jesse didn't have any.

"Where are we going to get TNT?" Zeke asked.

"My uncle's ranch," Angelina volunteered.

"Figures," Zeke mumbled, rolling his eyes.

"That'll work," Stumpy said. "You know where he stores it?"

"Well . . . not really," Angelina admitted. "But I know he has some. I heard them talking about it."

"We'll find it. As long it didn't blow up in the fire there's only a few places it could be," Stumpy said. "Now both of you get your things together, and we'll ride out to the Crossed Swords Ranch. We'll pick up the trail there and see where it leads."

"I'll get Hellfire ready," Zeke said, as he shot Angelina a dirty look.

"And I'll take my Uncle's palomino," Angelina said defiantly.

"No need to bring a horse," Stumpy said, looking first at Angelina, then Zeke. "You'll be riding together . . . on Hellfire."

"What?" Zeke and Angelina shouted in unison for the second time that day.

"You heard me. If Hellfire can carry somebody as big as Slim, he can carry you two string beans. Together you don't weigh but a fraction of what he does. He'll feel like he's getting a day off."

"It won't work! Hellfire won't let anybody ride him but me," Zeke protested.

"And he smells bad!" Angelina said, pointing at Zeke.

"That's not my fault," Zeke shouted defensively "If it wasn't for you, I never would've had to stay in Slim's smelly room to begin with!"

Zeke looked at Stumpy and frowned. "You told me I smelled fine!"

Stumpy just chuckled. This was going to be fun. "You two get ready. We leave in an hour."

As Angelina headed from the kitchen to pack her gear, Stumpy put a hand on Zeke's shoulder. "You may want to borrow a clean shirt from your uncle and wash up a bit," he whispered. "You two are gonna be kind of close for a while."

Stumpy made good time refitting Slim's saddlebag with everything Zeke and Angelina would need for the trip. The same, however, could not be said for the teens who wouldn't stop feuding. And their bickering continued throughout the trip. Stumpy wondered what had happened to the kids that had a crush on each other at the square dance.

It was late afternoon when they finally reached the Crossed Swords Ranch. Stumpy was riding his horse; Zeke was seated on Hellfire wearing one of Uncle Jesse's clean shirts; and behind him was Angelina. Stumpy would have preferred avoiding the ranch house entirely if he could have helped it, but Angelina had asked if she could pick up some clean clothes and other lady things. Since they didn't have what she needed at the Double R, he agreed, even though he knew that stopping there was sure to bring back a lot of bad memories for Angelina.

Chapter Nine

The front door to the building was gone, and there wasn't a sound. It was sad to see the ranch house empty, and it reminded Angelina of her mother. She quickly wiped away a tear when no one was looking. Zeke wasn't real comfortable either. Just being in the vicinity of the Crossed Swords Ranch made Zeke nervous, despite knowing Cable Cooper was gone.

As they rode closer, Hellfire's demeanor began to change. The rex seemed to be on alert. He lowered his head and began to sniff the ground, and his gait was more deliberate.

"He must smell those critters Tom told us about," Zeke said. "I hope they're not still around."

"They're gone," Angelina said. "Or they'd have been on us by now."

Zeke frowned. *Little Miss Know-It-All had become quite an expert on these birdy riders,* he thought. *"Bird rider;" the whole idea is ridiculous.*

"Look here," Stumpy said, interrupting Zeke's musings. Below them were dozens of unusually large tracks that looked as though they'd been left by a giant bird.

"Wow," Zeke exclaimed, staring at the huge indentations. "Those were some big animals!"

"And over there, a feather," Stumpy said.

The feather was at least eighteen inches long, and the closer they got to the house the more of them they saw.

"How many war birds did Tom say there were?" Zeke asked.

"Don't recall," Stumpy said. "Angelina, before you go inside, we're gonna check the perimeter to make sure the place is empty."

As they made their way around the big house, Stumpy

periodically called out, but there was no response.

"Why are you calling out like that?" Zeke whispered. "If there's anybody in there, they know we're here for sure now."

"Son, if there were anyone inside that house that meant us harm, they would've known we were here long before we got this close."

From a distance they saw the row of graves that Uncle Jesse, Bull and Slim had dug, and the markers Bull had made. Angelina bit her finger to keep from sobbing. It was a sad sight.

"Stay here," Stumpy said. He rode over to the makeshift cemetery and got down off his horse to take a closer look at something that caught his eye. The earth on several of the graves had been disturbed, like something was digging around the bodies. *That's strange,* he thought. *No sense saying anything about it; probably just an animal.*

"What do you see?" Zeke shouted. "Want me to come over?"

"You stay where you are," Stumpy said. "Everything's fine."

When they reached the front porch, Zeke helped Angelina down off Hellfire.

"I don't understand why we have to stop. We've wasted enough time already," he commented.

"I'll only be a minute," Angelina snapped. "I want to get some clean clothes. I've been living in these for the past week."

"You want me to come with you?" Zeke asked with just enough disapproval in his voice to let her know he really didn't want to.

"Don't bother," Angelina answered.

"Suit yourself."

"Angelina, you take your time," Stumpy said patiently. "We

Chapter Nine

can spare a few minutes. Zeke and I will wait out here."

Angelina stopped short when she reached the doorway and peered inside the darkened foyer. She could hear the screaming and anguished cries that rang through the halls the night the war bird riders stormed the house and shuddered.

I hope they're not inside, she thought.

"You need me to go inside with you?" called Stumpy.

"No, I'll be okay," Angelina replied bravely.

"Holler if you need us," Stumpy said.

Zeke reacted to Angelina's hesitation with a disgusted expression and a loud grunt just to make absolutely sure that his feelings were known. But as soon as Angelina went inside and was out of earshot, Stumpy turned toward the boy and looked him in the eye.

"Son, you have to go easier on her," he said. "You're starting to remind me of somebody."

"Who's that?" Zeke asked defensively.

"Your uncle! And I don't mean that in a good way!"

Zeke was shocked and embarrassed to hear Stumpy compare his behavior to Uncle Jesse's. He was about to come back with something when he thought better of it and bit his tongue. If that was how he was coming across, maybe it was time to lighten up.

"All right," Zeke said after a moment. "I'll try."

Stumpy was prepared for an argument, so Zeke's reaction to his criticism took him by surprise. But he said nothing. Maybe some of those late night walks did some good after all.

"Stumpy, if it's okay with you, I'm going to check out the barn," Zeke suggested in a suddenly mellow tone. "Maybe I can find where they've stored the TNT."

Rex Riders

"Go ahead, but be careful. If you find some, don't do anything. Just come and get me, and we'll look at it together. That stuff is dangerous, and I don't want you blowing yourself up."

As Angelina carefully navigated through the debris strewn around the foyer, her eyes darted from side to side searching for any sign of movement. *The best thing for me to do is head straight for my room and pack a small bag with some clean clothes,* she thought. *Don't look in any of the rooms, don't waste any time and don't make a sound.*

The floors were a mess, covered with broken furniture, weapons, dirt, blood and the occasional dino-dropping. *Uncle Dante will have a fit when he sees this. He's such a perfectionist. He'll have people cleaning for days.*

Angelina climbed the stairs to the second floor and stared down the hallway. Hers was the last room on the right, and at that moment it seemed like it was very far away.

There was a sound. She stopped to listen. There it was again! Faint, like something was running across the floor. *Probably just a small animal,* she thought. *You leave a door open and animals are bound to come in. Yeah, that's all it is.*

Angelina started down the hall, glancing sideways into each room she passed and picking up the pace with every step. *I have to get out of here,* she thought. She paused in the doorway to her bedroom. Her things were scattered across the floor, just as she'd left them and it appeared to be empty.

There it goes again! The scurrying sound was right behind her, but when she turned around, there was nothing there. *What was that noise?*

Chapter Nine

Angelina didn't wait to find out. She ran into her room and grabbed a pair of riding pants, a flannel shirt, a belt, some underwear and a hair brush. It wasn't much, but a change of clothes would come in handy, and she wasn't about to waste any more time in the house than she had to.

She stuck her head out the doorway and looked down the hall.

Empty.

She felt something brush against the back of her blouse, and let out a small scream. She didn't bother to look back as she ran toward the stairs.

Stumpy was approaching the front door with his gun in hand when Angelina nearly collided into him.

"What's going on? You okay?" he asked.

"I'm fine," Angelina panted. "There was something upstairs."

"You want me to take a look?"

"No. I got my clothes. Let's just get out of here. Where's Zeke?"

"He's over in the barn."

Stumpy watched as Angelina bolted toward the barn. This was a bad sign. Angelina hadn't even gotten out of Dos Locos, and it looked like her nerves had already gotten the better of her. He couldn't blame her for being scared, but how would she react when things got rough? On the other hand, maybe he'd take a look around and make sure they really were alone.

He climbed the staircase and started down the hallway. He pushed open the first door he came to. Nothing. When he got to Maria's room, he stepped inside. It was quiet and the afternoon shadows were getting longer. Maybe that's what spooked her.

Otherwise, there was nothing, just like he thought. Stumpy sighed and walked back downstairs. He never saw what was crawling on the back of the door in Maria's bedroom.

As Zeke rode toward the barn, he noticed something lying on the ground in the distance. Hellfire started to growl as they got closer, and Zeke saw it was the body of a dead war bird. It was huge and bizarre looking. The feathers and skin had collapsed around the bones, and it looked dried out and emaciated from lying in the open.

Zeke gave the carcass a kick, and the skin seemed to throb. He didn't want to touch it so he found a broken board and jabbed at it. He squatted down to get a better look and lifted up the skin with the board.

Zeke was stunned. The creature's body was crawling with insects that looked like grubs, but were at least a foot long and four inches in diameter. The boy had never seen bugs this big in his life! He poked one of them, and it grabbed hold of the piece of wood with its jaws. Zeke tried to shake it off, but when it didn't let go, he dropped the board entirely and hustled back on top of Hellfire.

Zeke shuddered. Those bugs gave him the creeps. Where did they come from?

The front half of the huge barn had been heavily damaged by fire the night of the attack, but it was still standing. When the riders swept through, they freed the few cattle and horses that were inside, so the building was empty and eerily quiet.

"Hello," Zeke called, as he slowly rode through the barn

Chapter Nine

looking into each of the stalls. The boy was glad to have the big T-rex with him. It stepped through the cold, charred wreckage cautiously and every so often stopped to sniff the ground and growl.

When Zeke reached the back of the barn, he noticed the strange shed that had caught Uncle Jesse's eye during his tour of the ranch. When he rode toward it, Hellfire started growling again and Zeke could feel the T-rex's body tensing beneath him. *That's odd*, he thought. *Why is he growling at a shed?*

"What is it, boy? It's okay; there's nothing here."

The door was bolted shut. Zeke thought about trying to open it by himself, but decided against it, thinking Stumpy would be angry if he did. The pikes leaning against the shed during Uncle Jesse's visit were scattered on the floor. It wasn't the kind of tool a rancher needed, and Zeke had never seen one before.

He was about to ride back when he saw Angelina walking quickly toward him, and Stumpy riding behind. She looked agitated, and Zeke thought it was best not to say anything that would upset the girl.

"Everything all right?" he asked.

"Fine," Stumpy said evenly. "Angelina thought she heard something back in the house. I think it might be best to find that TNT, and get you both on your way."

He turned to Angelina. "Assuming you still want to go."

Angelina nodded, but when Stumpy looked into her eyes, he wasn't convinced.

"There's a shed in the far corner, but it's locked," Zeke said. "I'm guessing that's where they store the TNT."

"Angelina, is that where it's kept?" Stumpy asked.

Rex Riders

"I don't know," she replied. "But it's definitely in the barn. I heard my uncle telling his men where to put the explosives when the supplies he ordered came in."

"So the TNT could be in the shed?" Stumpy asked.

"Maybe. My Uncle Dante told me never to go near it because it was dangerous. That's all I know."

"Then that's probably where it is," Zeke said. "Let's go see."

But Stumpy didn't move. "It's possible he took the TNT with him," he said.

"I guess that's possible," Zeke agreed. "I still think we ought to check. It can't hurt."

Stumpy stared at the shed and rubbed his chin. You didn't need a shed that big to store the amount of TNT that was needed on a ranch. What could D'Allesandro be using it for?

"Ride Hellfire closer to the shed," Stumpy ordered. Sure enough, the closer the rex got, the more it growled.

"Aw, that doesn't mean anything. He's been growling since we got here. We found a dead war bird outside, and he growled the whole time. It probably just means he smells something left by those bird riders. Heck, it could be that big pile of birdy-doo over there," Zeke said, pointing to a large pile of droppings. "Or these feathers. They're everywhere."

Stumpy said nothing. Maybe he was just feeling over-protective because of Angelina, but something seemed off about this whole situation. The problem was he couldn't put his finger on anything specific.

"Go ahead and open the door. Angelina, why don't you give Zeke a hand? You two are gonna be working together, so you may as well get started."

Chapter Nine

Zeke got off Hellfire and walked up to the door of the shed.

"Are you going to give us a hand?" Zeke asked Stumpy.

"I'm gonna stand over here and give orders. That's what we old-timers do best."

"Angelina, I'll slide the bolt open, and you go inside and see what's in there," Zeke said, dismounting.

"Got it," Angelina said. She hoped that Zeke hadn't noticed her voice quaver. She was still uneasy about the events at the ranch house, but she wasn't going to let him know.

"Ready? On a count of three. One, two . . ." Zeke pushed against the bolt as hard as he could and it slowly moved to one side, unlocking the heavy wooden door. Then he braced himself and pushed against the door until it slid open enough to allow Angelina to stick her head inside and take a look.

Sure enough, Hellfire started growling again.

"Ah, you be quiet," Zeke ordered.

"I can't see too well. It's pitch black," Angelina said as she squeezed inside. "Oh lord, it stinks in here! It's disgusting! *Eeeew.*" She stuck her head out and started to gag. She needed several deep breaths to clear her lungs.

"Maybe we ought to get you a lantern," Stumpy said. "Give me a minute. Can you see anything in there?"

"Let me take another look," Angelina said.

She pinched her nose and plunged back inside.

"I'm starting to see a little better; my eyes are getting used to the dark," Angelina called after a few moments. "There are some old clothes lying on the floor and somebody's hat."

Zeke looked at Stumpy with a quizzical expression. *Old clothes?* "What about the TNT?" Zeke asked. "See any? It's probably stored in wooden crates, right Stumpy?"

Inside, Angelina picked up a filthy civil war hat. "Take a look at this," she said, as she handed it out the opening to Zeke.

"It looks familiar," he said.

"Give it here," Stumpy said, limping over from the opposite side of the barn where his search for a lantern had taken him. "*Hmm* . . . This looks like Shorty's old hat. What else is in there?"

"Bones. Real big ones. Some of them are huge. Wait a minute; I think I see boxes. They're toward the back. That might be what we're looking for. And there are these big black things on the floor. They're all over the place."

Then Angelina shrieked. *"They're moving!"*

It suddenly dawned on her what she was looking at. "Omigod, they're bugs. Giant bugs!" she cried. "This place is filled with them!"

The beetle in front of Angelina sprouted wings and flew straight at her face. She waved her arms but the beetle dodged and hovered overhead. Then a second one took flight, and a third.

She smacked one of the flying beetles with her hand. "Get it away from me," she screamed "Get it away!"

"Get her out of there, and shut that door!" Stumpy shouted.

Zeke stepped into the shed, but couldn't tell what was happening because it was too dark.

"What's that sound?" he cried, as he tried to figure out where the buzzing noise was coming from. Angelina whacked him across the face. "*Ow!* Watch what you're doing for Pete's sake." Zeke grabbed Angelina's wrist and pulled her out of the shed.

"Shut the door!" Stumpy ordered as a beetle escaped and soared out of sight in the rafters.

Chapter Nine

Zeke threw himself against the door, shoving as hard as he could, but several more bugs made it out before he could close it. The door slammed shut on a two-foot long roach, leaving half of its wiggling body sticking out.

As the beetles flew overhead and circled them, Zeke cursed under his breath and grabbed a pike that was lying on the floor. This was not going the way he expected. Hellfire added to the confusion by roaring as he tracked the flight of the beetles hovering overhead.

Even though the barn was huge, the three of them were so close together they kept bumping into one another. The air was filled with so much buzzing, it was impossible to tell which direction the bugs were coming from. It was also getting darker by the moment and the black beetles were hard to see against the rafters of the barn.

Zeke swung his pike and hit one. It landed on the back of his shirt, and he yelled as it clung to the fabric and pulled at his hair.

"It's on me!" he cried hysterically. "Get it off!"

Zeke swung the pike over his head to try to strike the insect, but the handle was too long and he wound up hitting himself. *"Ow!"*

"Give me that," Angelina ordered, grabbing the pike from Zeke's hands. "You're going to hurt yourself!"

Angelina brandished it like it was a spear and lunged at Zeke's shoulder. He barely managed to get out of the way in time to avoid being run through.

"*I'm* going to hurt myself?" he shouted in a panic. "Don't *stab* the danged thing! Hit him with it." He spun around so Angelina could swat the big beetle on his back.

The girl gasped when she saw the size of the bug. It was huge! She closed her eyes and swung the pike with all of her might. Unfortunately, she missed the beetle and hit Zeke's lower back, instead.

"Yow!" he screamed in pain, falling to his knees. "Not me; the bug!"

"I'm sorry," Angelina cried, as she wound up for a second try.

This time she struck the insect in the center of its body, smashing through its hard exoskeleton and spraying herself with viscous, yellow bug blood. The big beetle dropped to the ground, its legs twitching and clawing at the air.

For a moment, Angelina just stood there trembling uncontrollably from the cold, shivery feeling you get when you've just been frightened. But she calmed herself down right away and regained her composure. "Okay," she said as she brandished the pike with renewed determination. "Where are the rest of those little buggers?"

Chapter Nine

Stumpy had been shaking his head watching the two of them in action waiting to see if they could coordinate a plan of attack, and this looked encouraging. He decided to give them a little help.

His gun roared and a second flying beetle fell to the ground and landed in front of Hellfire. The bullet had pierced the body and gone out the opposite side, but other than damaging its wings, it seemed none the worse for wear and began hobbling away. It didn't get far.

Hellfire lunged and snapped the bug up. It made a sickening, crunching sound as the big rex crushed it between its teeth, and the disgusting yellow liquid overflowed from its jaws as it chewed on the insect's chitenous body. When he was done, he lowered his head and spit out the remains on the ground. Then he stepped on it for good measure. Although the beetle's gooey blood had absolutely no effect on Hellfire, Angelina and Zeke felt like they were going to puke.

"That was gross!" Angelina cried.

Hellfire barely missed a third beetle that flew by its snout, but Angelina speared it with her pike, pinning it against the wall of the shed.

"Die, you stinking bug!" Angelina used so much force she had to put her foot up on the side of the building and brace herself in order to pull the pike out of the wall.

Suddenly the buzzing stopped, and all was quiet.

"They're around here somewhere," Zeke said as he searched the rafters of the barn. "I say we forget them and get out of here."

"We can't just leave. We have to kill those things," Angelina said.

"Why? They'll probably just die anyway," Zeke argued. "What difference does it make?"

"It'll make a big difference if they get inside the house," Angelina insisted.

"I don't think it's gonna matter much, Angelina," Stumpy interrupted. "Come take a look at this."

The old cook led them to a spot on the opposite side of the shed and pointed to an opening near the base that had been scratched, clawed and chewed open by one of the war birds on the night of the attack. "I have a feeling these bugs are already in the house. That's most likely what you heard upstairs."

Angelina looked crestfallen. "So what do we do now? Leave?"

"You two get the TNT out of the shed," Stumpy said, as he looked them both in the eye. "And this time work as a team. Heck, I've seen coyotes and chickens work together better than you two. We'll take care of the bug situation when you get back. For now, grab some wood while I get a lantern. We're going to plug up this hole."

Angelina was quiet for a moment. Then she looked at Zeke, "Okay. Let's get that TNT."

This time things went much more smoothly. First, Angelina lit a lantern that Stumpy had found. When Zeke opened the door to the shed, she set the lantern down on the floor so they could see what they were doing and have both her hands free. Then Zeke used the curved end of the pike to pull a box of explosives toward them without stepping too far inside. When the bugs approached, they pushed them back using the pikes, and batted away any flying beetles the same way. When they the job was done, they locked up the shed and congratulated

Chapter Nine

each other. Stumpy couldn't have been more pleased. They had begun to operate as a team!

Stumpy hefted one of the pikes and pretended to jab an unseen enemy. "Looks like these things came in handy."

"They sure did," Zeke agreed.

"Why don't you take some with you."

"How many should I take?" Zeke asked.

"Better ask your partner over there."

"Take two, one for each of us," Angelina suggested.

As Stumpy predicted, Uncle Jesse had marked his trail, so it wasn't hard to follow. As they rode away from the Crossed Swords Ranch, Angelina looked back but this time there weren't any tears. She made a promise to herself that when she returned she'd help get rid of those bugs and restore the house to its former beauty.

The sun was just beginning to set when they found the entrance to the cave that housed the transporter. Zeke and Angelina did not want to stop, but Stumpy knew they were still pumped from the excitement at the ranch house, and once the adrenaline wore off, they'd be too tired to continue. He wanted them to pace themselves, so the old cook insisted they bed down for the night just inside the mouth of the cave. Besides, taking a break gave him a good opportunity to talk to them about their little adventure at the ranch.

That night as they sat around the campfire, Stumpy reviewed what Angelina and Zeke had done right and wrong earlier in the day, and gave them pointers on how to work better as a team. He also taught them how to safely handle TNT to keep from being blown up. There was a lot to cover, and Stumpy was glad he had the chance to see them in action before they started their journey.

"Now, when you hear Hellfire start growling, don't ignore him and don't tell him to be quiet," Stumpy said. "Zeke, are you getting this? Figure out what he's growling at. And another thing; when Hellfire starts acting up, that ain't the time to get off him. The safest place to be is on top of him. You two got that? That critter's better than any gun for getting you out of trouble, and don't forget it!"

By the time Stumpy was done with his critique, Angelina's and Zeke's eyes were closed from exhaustion. The old cook covered them with blankets and bid each goodnight. Then he threw some wood on the fire and kept watch.

As the fire burned he remembered he had stuffed Shorty's hat under his saddlebag during all the commotion in the barn and took it out to examine it. He stuck his finger through a hole in the back of the hat and wasn't surprised to see blood stains on the inside. Shorty never made it out of town.

There were several times during the night when Stumpy thought he saw something or heard something in the darkness that caused him to reach for his gun, but he never fired a shot. He didn't know for sure if there was really anything out there or if it was just his imagination. But one thing was certain: the Wild West suddenly seemed a lot wilder.

Chapter
Ten

"**I**t's about time you woke up," Stumpy said, when Zeke finally opened his eyes. "Get yourself something to eat. You have a big day ahead of you, and your partner is waiting."

Zeke looked over at Angelina and she waved to him.

She's smiling, thought Zeke. *That's a good sign.* He smiled back.

As they ate breakfast, Stumpy gave them some final words of advice. Angelina paid close attention, but Zeke was only half-listening because he had something important on his mind and was waiting for the right moment to bring it up. When Stumpy asked if they had any questions, Zeke seized the opportunity.

"Stumpy, are you going to let me carry a gun?"

"I've been thinking about that very thing and have come to a decision."

This was the moment Zeke was waiting for. Although he'd used a rifle for hunting plenty of times and had fired a pistol with supervision, he'd never been allowed to carry one on his own. But this was a bona fide emergency. If there was ever a situation that screamed out "sidearm," this was it.

"And?"

"The answer is no. I watched the two of you in the barn yesterday, and neither one of you is ready to handle a pistol."

"What!" Zeke shot Angelina a dirty look. This was all her fault. Here was another thing she ruined. "Why not?"

"You ain't ready. That's all there is to it. And don't be looking at Angelina. I said *you're* not ready. She didn't ask me if she could carry a gun, you did. This has nothing to do with her."

"You're letting us bring TNT!" Zeke shouted. "That's ten times more dangerous than a gun."

"No, it has the potential to do more damage, but that's an entirely different thing. I've seen plenty of accidents involving guns. But I've never seen anyone blow themselves up just by carrying a stick of TNT where the detonator ain't attached. I'm not saying it can't happen; just that I ain't never heard of it happening."

"But what if we run into something we can't handle?" Zeke asked. "How are we going to defend ourselves? Throw a stick of dynamite at it?"

"First off, I don't believe you'll be running up against anything without Hellfire letting you know about it long before it reaches you. But if something like that does happen, I want you to hightail it out of there and come back and get me. Is that understood? You shouldn't be taking on anything you'd need a gun to defend yourself against. And if you find yourself cornered,

Chapter Ten

let Hellfire deal with it. From what I've seen, there ain't much he can't handle."

"I can't believe you! This is so stupid!"

Uncle Jesse would have lost his temper at that remark, but Stumpy didn't react at all. "That's enough talk about guns," he said matter-of-factly. "It's time to saddle up." Then he turned his back on Zeke and went to work getting the boy's and Angelina's horses ready for the trip.

"I can't believe you! This is so stupid!"

Zeke stared at Stumpy, as the old ranch hand packed up the gear, and then it hit him. Here he was asking to be treated like an adult and the minute he didn't get his way, he reacted like an angry little boy. He'd yelled at Stumpy and made a scene in front of Angelina, and the day had barely begun. He couldn't have handled things any worse. All at once the anger drained out of him.

Zeke walked over to Stumpy. "I'm sorry," he said. "That was out of hand. I shouldn't have said that. If you don't think I'm ready, then . . . I'll just have to prove to you that I am."

Stumpy smiled, and then he turned around and faced Zeke. He had a feeling that Zeke was going to ask about carrying a gun and wasn't sure how the boy would react. He was a little disappointed when Zeke lost his cool, but Zeke's apology more than made up for it. "Son, what you just said shows me you're on your way."

Angelina cleared her throat. "Um, if you guys are done, maybe we can get moving?" ·

"Uh, right. I'll get my things," Zeke said sheepishly.

They followed the trail through the tunnel and into the large cavern that housed the transporter, stopping at the foot of one of the ramps. "The tracks end here," Stumpy observed, as he stroked his chin and stared at the platform.

"You want me to see what's up there?" Zeke asked.

"In a minute. Let's take a look at this thing first. Angelina and I will go this way. You take Hellfire in the other direction, and we'll meet in the middle. Take your time and pay attention."

Stumpy rode while Angelina walked beside him.

"These carvings look like some kind of writing," she said, pointing to images at the base of the machine. "Can you read it?"

"No, but I think you're right."

Stumpy stopped his horse and lowered his voice, "Angelina, you and I haven't had any time alone. It may turn out that your uncle is the cause of all this trouble with your ma. I ain't taking sides, but it could be that what happened back at your uncle's ranch was revenge for something he did. You understand what I'm saying?"

"I know," Angelina said. "And I still want to go."

"Just as long as you understand that."

"I do."

Stumpy regarded Angelina for a moment. *I hope so,* Stumpy thought. *Or there's going to be trouble.*

They met Zeke on the opposite side of the platform and they all walked back together. "So what did you see?" Stumpy asked.

"Not much. Just some carvings," Zeke answered. "You think it might be writing?"

"That would be my guess," Stumpy said. "It might reveal what this thing was built for and how it works. But Slim's the only one who could've told us for sure, and he ain't here. So we're

Chapter Ten

gonna have to figure it out on our own."

"How?" Zeke asked.

"First, we'll see what's on top of this platform," Stumpy answered.

"I'll go," Angelina volunteered.

"Good. Go on ahead, but be careful!"

Angelina activated the machine when she started up the walkway, and the noise took everyone by surprise. Stumpy shouted at Angelina to take cover, and she ran back down and hid behind some rocks. The transporter didn't explode as Stumpy feared and when he looked over at Hellfire, he noticed that unlike the horses, the rex was not the least bit bothered by the sound.

"I think I know how your Uncle Jesse and Bull got out of this cave," he said. "Let's try something. Zeke, I want you to run up and throw your hat on top of that platform. Then, get back down here, and we'll wait and see what happens."

"My hat? Why are we using my hat?"

"We need to see how this contraption works. I'm guessing it'll take the both of you to wherever it is your uncle and Angelina's mother are. If I'm right, you'll get your hat back when it's your turn to step up there."

"It makes sense to me," Angelina said, nodding in agreement.

"Thank you, miss," Stumpy said with a tip of his hat.

"What if he's wrong?" Zeke asked Angelina.

"Then your hat will still be waiting for you on the platform, silly," she answered.

Zeke looked confused. "Wait . . . ."

"Zeke, we don't have all day," Angelina said impatiently.

"Could you get going?"

"I like the way you think," Stumpy said.

Zeke's mouth fell open a little as he looked at one and then the other. It was useless to argue. A little more than a minute later Zeke's hat was gone, and they had themselves a plan.

"Time to go," Stumpy announced.

He shook hands with Zeke, and gave Angelina a buss on the cheek. "Which one of you has the map?"

"Right here," Angelina said.

"Any chance you'll change your mind about what we were talking about before, in light of my maturity and all?" Zeke asked hopefully. Zeke mimed shooting a pistol with his hand.

"Not a chance," Stumpy replied sternly.

"I didn't think so."

"Good luck you two. Remember to act like a team. And if there's trouble—"

"'Don't get off Hellfire,'" Zeke said before Stumpy could finish.

"I'll make sure we don't," Angelina said, as she elbowed Zeke for being impolite.

"Who put you in charge?" Zeke said.

"You're both in charge," Stumpy said firmly. "And don't forget it!"

Zeke held the reins with Angelina sitting closely behind, as Hellfire stepped onto the walkway and activated the generators that powered the huge machine. Zeke turned around and looked at Angelina.

"You know, there's still time to change your mind and go back," he said.

Chapter Ten

Angelina frowned and pinched him on the arm. "Fat chance. Turn around and keep riding, mister."

"Ow! Okay!"

Zeke urged Hellfire forward, and the T-tex trotted up the ramp without hesitation.

Stumpy steadied his horse as he watched the blue electric curtain grow. It may not have shown on his face, but he was nervous about what was unfolding in front of him. Whatever this thing was, it looked like the key to reuniting the two teens with Uncle Jesse and Bull. The old cook could barely see the kids waving at him, as the energy field rose. Then it fell back in on itself, and the platform was empty.

Stumpy sighed. The only thing he could do now was make camp by the mouth of the cave and wait. He'd give them a couple of days, and if they weren't back by then, he'd organize a search party. In the meantime, he'd have a look around the cave and see what else was in there.

"That was quite a trip," Zeke said, trying not to retch from the waves of nausea he was experiencing.

"I feel a little dizzy," Angelina said. "Maybe we should sit for a minute and figure out where we are while our stomachs settle down."

Zeke retrieved his hat and sat down next to Angelina as she studied Slim's map.

"We're supposed to head toward the river," she said. "Which way is that?"

"This seems to be the only ramp that leads directly to a path," Zeke observed, pointing to the trail cut by D'Allesandro's men.

Rex Riders

"That certainly narrows our choices," Angelina said. "Let's try it."

The trail was easy to follow and wide enough to accommodate two stagecoaches with room to spare. Anything that may have been in the way had been cut down, pulled out, or blown up, and then smoothed over. The teens weren't sure the route they had chosen led to the river, but they were encouraged that someone had invested a considerable amount of time and energy to build it. Although neither one of them mentioned it, they both knew it had to have been Angelina's uncle.

By the time Zeke and Angelina reached the Sulant, they needed a break from the heat, so they decided to stop and cool off. The riverbed was less than a hundred feet across at this spot and the water was only hip deep in the very deepest ruts. They threw off their boots and socks, and led Hellfire down the embankment.

"That feels good," Angelina said, as they stepped into the cool water. "I'm glad we found this river. I needed a break. My butt's killing me."

Zeke was a little flustered by that comment, and wasn't sure how to reply. "Um, yeah. You know what? Let's refill the canteens." He pointed to several large rocks along the shoreline that were stained by the water when the level was much higher. "It looks like the river is down a lot."

"Drought, maybe?"

"Maybe. Everything looks pretty green, though. If there were a drought, the plants around here would be dried and brown. Strange."

"Should we tie Hellfire up?" Angelina asked.

Zeke looked at the T-rex. "Nah, he won't go anywhere.

Chapter Ten

He probably needs a drink."

While Angelina and Zeke refilled their canteens, Hellfire lapped up the water, then waded into a deeper part of the river. Abruptly, the dinosaur stopped and stared intently into the Sulant.

"What's it doing?" Angelina asked.

"I don't know. Maybe it sees something."

Suddenly, Hellfire thrust his head under the water and emerged with a huge fish clenched between his teeth. The catch whipped violently as the rex made its way back to land. Once ashore, the dinosaur dropped the fish on the ground and proceeded to eat it, putting a foot down on the creature's tail to hold it in one place while ripping it in half.

"*Ugh,* that's disgusting" Angelina said. "Does he always do that?"

"Do you see the size of that fish?" Zeke exclaimed, ignoring Angelina's question. "Maybe we can catch one. We could cook it for lunch and save the jerky for later."

"Yeah, but how do we do that? We don't have any fishing poles."

Zeke thought for a moment. "Easy. I'll use one of the pikes and spear one."

Hellfire finished his lunch, plopped down in the shade and stood watch over the riverbed. Zeke walked over to where the rex was lying and unhooked one of the pikes.

"I'm ready!" Zeke shouted, holding it over his head.

"Did you ever do this before?" Angelina asked.

"No, but it can't be too hard. If that ole boy can catch a fish, so can I."

Rex Riders

Zeke waded to the spot where Hellfire caught his meal. The water was clear and he could see the bottom of the riverbed. A fish swam by, and Zeke raised the pike over his head.

"Wow, there are some big fish in here!"

Zeke thrust the pike into the water and screamed in pain. *"Auughh!"*

"What happened?" Angelina cried, jumping to her feet.

"My foot!" Zeke yanked but the pike appeared as if it was stuck.

Angelina ran toward him, "Are you okay?"

"No, I'm not okay! I just stabbed my foot!"

But when she reached Zeke, he held up the pike and started laughing.

"Just kidding," he said with glee. "You should have seen your face!"

"You jerk!" Angelina shouted angrily, smacking him on the shoulder. "I thought you were really hurt!"

"Ow!" Zeke cried as if he were in pain.

"Oh come on, you big baby. I didn't hit you that hard."

"Not you. Something just bit me."

"Yeah, right! Like I believe that!"

Zeke jerked his foot out of the water, and there was a small fish hanging from it.

"Get it off me!" he screamed. He ran to shore and stamped his foot on the ground until the creature finally released its grip.

"That hurt," he said, as blood trickled down his toes.

"Let me take a look," Angelina said, examining the bite. "It's not so bad. That'll teach you to play a trick on me. Now give me that pike and go start a fire."

Chapter Ten

Zeke watched as Angelina waded into the water. Did she actually think she'd be able to spear anything? He stifled a laugh as she floundered about in her first few attempts.

"I got one!" Angelina yelled proudly.

Zeke couldn't believe it. But sure enough, at the end of the pike was a good-sized fish. He was impressed but he didn't want to let on.

"Nice job," he called back.

Neither one of them knew what kind of fish it was, but after it was cleaned and cooked, it tasted as good as any fish either of them had ever eaten.

"When we start moving again, how about I take the reins for a while?" Angelina suggested.

Zeke started to laugh.

"What's so funny?"

"Hellfire won't listen to you. Slim and I are the only ones who can ride him. And I almost got killed the first time. Trust me; you don't want to try it."

Angelina was hurt and annoyed by Zeke's high-and-mighty attitude and ignored him when he tried to continue the conversation. Of course, Zeke assumed she was mad because she couldn't ride Hellfire, but what was he supposed to do? It's just the way things were, and she'd have to get over it.

Zeke extinguished the fire and buried the ashes along with the remains of the fish. "I'm going to look around for a minute. You want to come?" he asked, trying to patch things up.

"No, I'm going to stay here and cool off," Angelina said. "As soon as you get back we should get going."

"I'll be fast. I promise."

Rex Riders

* * *

Zeke walked along the riverbed. *It's beautiful here,* he thought. *And so quiet.* In the distance something big stepped out of the woods. Zeke froze. It was pretty far off and staring into the water, so it hadn't seen the boy as it walked toward him. Whatever it was, it was looking for fish. And it was much bigger than Hellfire.

Zeke squatted to lower his profile. He shielded his eyes from the sun so he could get a better view of the animal. Had Dr. Kornbluth been there, he would have been able to tell the boy that he was looking at a Baryonyx.

The Baryonyx had a long, narrow snout packed with teeth that was similar in shape to a crocodile's. It didn't get as big as a T-rex when full grown, but this one was more than twenty-feet long. It had long arms and claws, which it used to grab fish and small prey, like lizards.

This expanse of the Sulant and its immediate surroundings were the animal's feeding grounds, but pickings were few since D'Allesandro dammed the river. With the resulting decrease in the water level came a shortage of food, creating problems for dinosaurs like Baryonyx that relied on the Sulant as their primary food supply. What little water still flowed came from streams that fed the river further down from the dam.

Large herbivores that fed off the plants normally growing along the banks of the Sulant were leaving the area where the level had dropped and the foliage had receded, and migrating to places where water was plentiful. This migration caused problems for predators that relied on the big herbivores for food. All of the carnivores along the river were hungry, and as their

Chapter Ten

hunger grew, they became more aggressive and began to encroach on one another's territory for sustenance.

The Baryonyx Zeke was watching suddenly plunged its head into the water.

Good time to leave, Zeke thought. He cautiously started backing up, but had scarcely gone a few feet when the dinosaur reared up with a fish in its jaws and water streaming off its head and neck.

Zeke stopped, but not quickly enough. The Baryonyx paused a moment when it caught sight of the teen, only taking its eyes off him to swallow the fish it had caught.

It sees me.

Zeke recognized the creature's behavior. It was considering whether to attack him, but it didn't want to scare its prey—Zeke—by making any sudden moves. He tried to stay calm, reminding himself that running was generally not a good idea.

No sense getting it upset, he reasoned. *Maybe now that it's eaten, it'll just walk back into the woods.*

Zeke backed up very slowly. But when it started walking toward him, Zeke knew the beast had made up its mind to come after him. It was time to run.

"Angelina!" Zeke shouted.

Angelina stood up quickly and felt lightheaded. She had been sitting in the shade next to Hellfire trying to stay awake in the midday heat when she heard Zeke's cry.

"What's going on?" she mumbled, rising. She trotted to the riverbed and saw Zeke running toward her in the distance.

"Get on Hellfire!" he screamed.

Angelina could barely make out what he was saying. "What?"

Rex Riders

"Get on Hellfire! *Now!*"

Angelina hesitated for a moment. *'Get on Hellfire?' What for?*

"You told me not to!" she cried.

"Just do it!" *Why did I tell her not to ride Hellfire? Why am I so stubborn?* Zeke thought.

The Baryonyx rounded a bend in the stream and roared.

Oh, that's what for! Angelina turned and raced for Hellfire.

The T-rex was on its feet the second it heard the big dinosaur roar and answered with one of its own.

When Angelina was just a few feet away, the rex whipped its big head around and roared at her. She stopped and stared at him.

He's not reacting to you, Angelina told herself. *He knows you. He's reacting to the big dinosaur charging over there.*

"I have to get on you, okay? I'm your friend," she said, her voice quivering.

Hellfire looked back at the Baryonyx racing its way and roared again, stamping its feet in anger. The rex looked ready to attack.

"I'm getting in the saddle now," Angelina continued. She took hold of the reins and eased her foot into the stirrup.

"Yes, *yes!*" Zeke shouted when he saw Angelina take the reins. "That's it!" *Please cooperate with her, Hellfire, don't go all crazy.*

"Steady now. We have to get Zeke, okay?" Angelina's heart was racing, and her voice was barely above a whisper. She tugged gently on the reins, and Hellfire began moving. "That's it, boy. Just a bit faster now, okay?"

She gave its ribs a light kick with her heels, and the rex took

Chapter Ten

off down the embankment toward Zeke. *Did it understand me?*

Hellfire was moving fast, faster than Angelina thought possible. *I have to keep him away from deep water,* she thought. *He won't be able to run as quickly, and I'll never get to Zeke in time.*

"Stay out of the water!" Angelina shouted, but she had no idea if Hellfire understood. Angelina weaved back and forth across the riverbed trying to stay in the shallowest areas. Zeke was doing the same, but that big fish-eater's stride was so long it was gaining on him quickly.

She was heading straight toward Zeke but had no clear idea what she was going to do, and the Baryonyx was directly behind him. They would collide in seconds.

Angelina reached down and grabbed one of the pikes. If she could hit the beast, she might cause enough pain to distract it. She'd have to time this just right. Angelina tucked the pike under her arm and held it out like she was holding a lance in a jousting tournament. She'd seen pictures of medieval knights doing this; maybe it would work.

As she rode toward Zeke, Zeke could think of only one thing: *she's going to run me through!*

"Dive!" Angelina screamed, as she careened toward him.

Zeke dove face-first into the rocky riverbed without a second to spare. He could have sworn he felt the end of the pike tickle his hair as it passed over his head.

Angelina struck the Baryonyx squarely in the chest. The blow may not have had enough force to penetrate the animal's bony chest cavity, but it certainly hurt enough to get the dinosaur's attention. The mighty meat-eater reared up and roared in pain, flailing its arms, and dislodging the pike.

As Angelina rode past, she cut in behind the massive beast and circled back.

Zeke was back on his feet and running from the big predator as fast as he could. The Baryonyx whirled around to try to catch Angelina, and as it did, its long tail whipped around and headed straight for Zeke's head. But with his back to the dinosaur, Zeke so had no idea the tail was swinging toward him.

Angelina screamed a warning, and Zeke ducked just in time to avoid being knocked off his feet.

Angelina was riding next to him now. "Jump on!" she shouted, as she swung her arm down and grabbed Zeke around the waist, swinging him up onto Hellfire's saddle in one fluid motion.

"Where'd you learn to ride like that?" Zeke gasped.

"Lessons! Hang on."

Hellfire raced down the riverbed with the Baryonyx in pursuit. It was hard work maneuvering around the deeper rivulets that would slow Hellfire down and staying on the drier areas. She cut back and forth, jumping over logs and rocks, and splashing through puddles.

"'Guns are dangerous,' Stumpy said. Remember?" Zeke shouted. "'If you come up against something you have to use a gun on, come and get me.' *Ha!* Like that'll work!"

"Would you shut up? I'm trying to concentrate."

Zeke looked over his shoulder, and the baryonyx was snapping at the rex's tail. "Faster! Faster!" he yelled.

Up ahead, Angelina saw what appeared to be a giant rock formation, but it seemed to be throbbing as if alive. "There's

Chapter Ten

something up ahead. What should I do?"

"Well, don't stop! That thing is right on top of us!"

As they rode closer the shapes came into focus, and the Baryonyx slowed to a halt.

"We're getting away! We're getting away!" Zeke cried.

They were midway between their pursuer and the mass of rocks when it suddenly became clear why the Baryonyx had stopped. The pulsating formation was in fact a hunting pack of tyrannosaurs, huddled over and enjoying the remains of a freshly killed lambeosaurus.

Lambeosaurs were large duck-billed herbivores with colorful bony crests on top of their heads. They could grow as much as thirty feet in length, ideal for a hungry band of T-rexes. The smaller members of the pack attacked from the rear and drove the panicked plant-eaters into the path of the female who lay in wait on the shore. Ordinarily, even a full-grown tyrannosaur wouldn't have targeted an adult lambeosaurus, but the threat of starvation had increased the beast's ferocity and daring.

The other T-rexes joined the female after the kill, and were eating together peacefully when the intruders arrived. Now, as they stared at Hellfire and the Baryonyx, the question running through their dinosaurian minds was whether to attack the newcomers. And that depended on whether any of them was foolish enough to challenge the dominant female for control of the kill.

Although the female had eaten her fill, that didn't mean she would yield the carcass to some other predator. If either Hellfire or the Baryonyx started forward, she was ready to defend her territory with an all-out attack.

Rex Riders

Angelina brought Hellfire to a stop. Zeke noticed that the water flowing around the rex's feet was red from the blood of the lambeosaur.

"What are they?" Angelina whispered.

"I don't know," said Zeke. "They look like Hellfire, only bigger."

"A lot bigger," Angelina said, as she stared at the female.

"Look at those little ones. They have feathers." Among the group were three small tyrannosaurs that were so young they hadn't yet lost the feathers they'd hatched with. They stayed close beside their mother who made sure they weren't attacked by another T-rex.

"That big one must be twenty feet tall," Zeke said quietly.

Angelina looked back over her shoulder at the Baryonyx. It hadn't moved. They were caught in the middle with no way out.

The adult female moved toward them, while her offspring stayed behind with the kill. She was bigger than the other members of the pack and significantly larger than the Baryonyx.

"What do we do now?" Zeke asked under his breath. "We're trapped."

"We stay on Hellfire, and remain still," Angelina replied softly. "And don't make a sou—" Before Angelina could finish, Hellfire roared.

"Shut up! *Shut up!*" Zeke ordered in an urgent whisper. He reached back and smacked the T-rex on the rump, but it roared again.

"He never listens," Zeke groaned.

The big female stopped in her tracks and grunted. Her eyes

never left Hellfire as she returned the roar. The sound was deafening. The massive beast continued her cautious approach until she was directly in front of Hellfire and the teens, but it wasn't Zeke and Angelina she was interested in. She bent down and sniffed Hellfire. The smaller T-rex lowered its head submissively, and big female roared again in approval. Hellfire had shown deference, and was no threat to her dominance over the group.

She raised her head and growled at the Baryonyx. The other rexes left the kill and fanned out on either side of her, walking past Hellfire toward the baryonyx. The Baryonyx roared and hissed at the T-rexes as it backed up, but it was outnumbered and had no hope of surviving an adult tyrannosaur, let alone a group. It had no choice but to retreat.

As the Baryonyx lumbered off, the smaller T-rexes turned their attention back to Hellfire. The teens were terrified, as the dinosaurs encircled them. One ran its tongue along Angelina's leg and stared at her curiously, but apart from that and a lot of sniffing, none moved to attack. The teens may not have looked anything like T-rexes, but Hellfire's scent was all over them, making them brethren in the eyes of the pack.

Having satisfied their curiosity, the T-rexes walked back to the remains of the lamboeosaurus and resumed eating.

"One of them licked you," Zeke whispered. "Maybe it liked you."

"I think it was tasting me."

"Let's get out of here," Zeke said.

Angelina tugged on the reins to head back in the direction they came from, but Hellfire pulled back and refused to budge.

Chapter Ten

"What's going on?" Zeke asked nervously. "We have to get out of here."

"He doesn't want to go."

"Do you want me to try?" asked Zeke.

"He wants to keep going upriver."

"What do we do?" Zeke said.

"We can either walk past them or we can wait here until they leave and hope they aren't still hungry."

"Bad idea," Zeke said.

"Which one?"

"The one where we wait until they're done and see if they're still hungry. If he won't go back, try going around them. Just don't get too close."

"Fast or slow?" asked Angelina.

"Medium."

The pack of rexes had returned to their meal and weren't paying any attention to Hellfire or the two teens. Angelina nudged the rex forward at a medium clip. They stayed as far away from the tyrannosaurs as they could, but couldn't help staring as they rode past. The lambeosaur carcass was huge but it was impossible to tell what the animal had looked like before the rexes got to it. What was left was one big, disgusting mess.

When they were safely beyond the pack, Angelina picked up the pace. It wasn't the smartest thing to do considering the heat, but she wanted to put some distance between them and the tyrannosaurs. The whole experience with the rexes had seriously rattled their nerves.

They traveled in silence for much of the afternoon. Neither one of them said a word. They were terrified that the sound of their voices might attract an animal that was hiding in the woods and couldn't shake the fear that something else was awaiting them around every bend in the river. Whatever this place was, it was far more dangerous than they could have dreamed!

"Do you think those animals back there were related to Hellfire?" Angelina asked finally.

"I don't know," Zeke answered, relieved to be talking again. "Did you see the little ones? I never saw an animal that had feathers like that."

"Do you think Hellfire will get as big as the one back there?"

"Maybe. I always thought he was full grown," Zeke admitted. "Maybe he's just a baby."

"'A baby,'" Angelina repeated, as she turned the thought over in her mind. It was mind-boggling that a creature this size could be a baby! She started shaking uncontrollably. "Do you mind if we stop a minute?"

"Are you okay?" Zeke asked. "What's wrong?"

"I don't know," she said a little tearfully.

Zeke felt awful seeing Angelina so upset but didn't know what to say or do. He was just as scared as she was, but was trying hard to keep it together and not show it. "Do you want to go back home?" he suggested weakly.

"I'm okay. I just need a minute." She got off Hellfire and started to walk away, but stopped and returned to the T-rex's side when she realized what she was doing was dangerous. "I want to give Hellfire something."

Angelina opened the saddlebag and took out a lump of beef jerky. The T-rex gingerly took it from her hands as she stroked its neck.

Chapter Ten

"We never would have made it back there without you," she said. "We owe you our lives."

"Stumpy was right all along. It's a good thing we have him with us," Zeke said. "And thanks for coming back for me. That took a lot of guts. If it weren't for you, I would have been a goner. I'm glad you came." Zeke stuck out his hand. "Partners?"

"Partners," Angelina agreed, and shook Zeke's hand firmly. She thought he might be teasing her again when he winced, until she looked at his palm. It was pretty torn up.

"How did that happen?" she asked.

Zeke pulled his hand back and shoved it into his pocket. "I'm okay," he replied. "I scraped it on some rocks when I dove into the riverbed."

"We should get going," he continued, eager to change the subject. He didn't want to make a big deal of it. Anyway, the alternative would have been a lot worse.

"Do you want to take the reins for a while?" Angelina offered.

Zeke looked at her and smiled. "Nah. You know what you're doing as much as I do. Maybe more. I'll take over when you get tired."

He assisted Angelina back into the saddle and the two hurried on their way. After the delays they'd suffered, they were anxious to get the dynamite upriver as quickly as possible.

"Do you think Hellfire would ever turn on us?" Angelina asked.

"You mean attack us?"

Angelina nodded.

"No. But if he does, he ain't getting any more jerky!"

* * *

Rex Riders

Slim had drawn a circle on his map to indicate the location of the Cragnon village along the Sulant, but it was not labeled as such. All Angelina and Zeke knew was that they had to pass something big on their way to D'Allesandro's camp. By dusk the teens could hear the sound of drums and reasoned that they must be coming from the home of the Cragnon. Why else would Slim mark its location so boldly?

Drums weren't necessarily a bad sign. They could mean that a celebration or a ceremony of some kind was taking place. But the teens also knew that the sound might signal impending war.

When Hellfire abruptly stopped moving and started to growl, they knew there was danger ahead.

Zeke took Stumpy's spyglass out of his bag and studied the village on the bluff. "There's a stone wall surrounding the village," he noted. "I can't see anybody, but they must be inside."

"Anything else?" Angelina asked.

"I see a lot of smoke. Something's going on," Zeke continued. "There are a few guards watching the front, but I don't see anybody at the back. We could wait until dark and try and to sneak by."

"What if Hellfire starts to roar? Then they'll know we're here and come after us."

"We could tie his jaws shut," Zeke suggested.

"How do you do that?"

"Easy. My Uncle Jesse did it once. You get a rope and you just tie a noose around his snout."

"I don't know . . ."

"It won't be for long; just until we get past the Cragnon. Then we'll untie him. Unless you have a better idea." And this time

Chapter Ten

Zeke was serious about being open to anything Angelina might suggest.

"No, but I'm trying to think what Stumpy would say if he were here right now. I have a feeling he wouldn't like this plan."

"Angelina, Stumpy isn't here, and we have to figure out some away around the village if we want to get to your uncle's camp," Zeke said impatiently.

Angelina shifted uncomfortably. "What if Hellfire doesn't like it? What if he tries to bite you?" she said. "Or what if we need him to protect us? If his jaws are shut, he won't be able to."

"My Uncle Jesse did it, and it worked fine. You just have to be firm with him."

Zeke knew that wasn't completely true. He purposefully left out the part about Hellfire removing the rope with his claws, figuring that detail would only make Angelina more nervous. Besides, he intended to tie the rope tight enough so the T-rex couldn't tear it off.

"Let's wait until it gets dark. If it doesn't work, we can try something else."

Angelina agreed.

They climbed out of the riverbank and made their way into the woods. They didn't go too far because it was getting dark and they were afraid they wouldn't be able to see anything. They settled on a spot just inside the tree line so they couldn't be seen, and sat down to wait. Zeke had trouble keeping still.

"I'm going to see if anything's happening," he whispered.

Angelina knew better than to try to stop him. "Be careful."

Zeke crept out to the edge of the riverbank and lay down. The red moons were rising in the night sky, their light so bright it lit up the forest and the riverbed, making it easier to see what was happening on the bluff. But it also made traveling down the riverbed without being seen more difficult and dangerous. Folks back home used to say that the light from the full moon made animals nervous. Creatures that were normally active under the cover of darkness were suddenly exposed, and their behavior became unpredictable.

Zeke heard the sound of voices and ducked down. Two Cragnon warriors rode slowly up the river dragging something behind them. It was only when they were just past his hiding place that Zeke dared to raise his head and take a look. This was his first look at a Cragnon warrior and a live war bird. They were a scary enough sight in the daylight, but in the moonlight they were absolutely terrifying. Zeke couldn't take his eyes off them.

Even more remarkable was their cargo: wooden crates marked with logos in English. It seemed impossible, but they were dragging crates with weapons!

As he watched, the warriors turned and disappeared into the woods upriver from where he was lying. He made sure no more riders were coming, then scrambled back to where Angelina was waiting.

"I saw them," Zeke said breathlessly. "Riders from the tribe that took your ma. They rode past me, then went into the woods."

"Which way were they going?"

"They were heading toward the bluff. And they were pulling boxes of guns and ammunition behind them."

"*Guns?* Where did they get guns from?"

"Maybe they stole them from your uncle when they raided his ranch."

Chapter Ten

"Zeke, my mother is on that bluff. We have to try to rescue her."

"How? We have no idea where she is."

"She's up there," Angelina replied.

"We can't stop now. We told Stumpy we'd get this TNT to Uncle Jesse. He needs it. What if we get caught?"

"You said before that Stumpy wasn't here, and we had to think for ourselves. What if it was someone from your family who was up there? What would you do?"

Now this is a surprise, Zeke thought. *Angelina's starting to sound like me, and I'm starting to sound like her!*

"I don't know," Zeke said. "But even if we wanted to do something, how would we get in there?" he asked. "A wall surrounds the whole city."

"What about the ladders where the boats are tied up? We could get in that way."

"But then we'd have to leave Hellfire behind. I thought we agreed that was a bad idea."

"Then I'll stay with Hellfire, and you go up," Angelina continued undeterred. "If you can't find my mother, we'll leave. If you do, we'll figure out how to get her out."

"Angelina, we don't have any guns," Zeke said finally.

"We have Hellfire . . . and TNT. Two teens with a yerka and a box of TNT can accomplish a lot."

Zeke looked at her in the moonlight and started to laugh. She had a point! "Okay. What do we do about Hellfire?"

"We tie his jaws so he doesn't roar, like you said. We can't take a chance. If he starts roaring while you're up there, they might hear us."

Rex Riders

Zeke agreed and they shook on it. He pried open the lid of the wooden crate holding the TNT and stuck three sticks into his belt. Then took six detonators and fuses from his saddlebag and stuffed them in his pockets.

Angelina was suddenly nervous as the reality of what they were about to do sunk in. "What are you doing?" she asked nervously.

"Insurance," he explained.

Zeke unhooked the rope and quickly tied a noose. "Now I'm gonna have to tie your jaws up, big fella," he said, turning to Hellfire.

"Be careful," Angelina said.

Zeke approached the rex, "This will only be on for a short time," he said soothingly. "I promise it won't hurt."

Hellfire growled, but allowed Zeke to slip the rope over its snout. Zeke knew from firsthand experience that the rex had an amazingly flexible neck and could reach the muzzle with its claws, so the teen also tied one end around Hellfire's neck.

This might not stop you from getting that rope off, Zeke thought. *But it'll slow you down a little.*

As he knotted the rope, Zeke looked into Hellfire's eyes. He had the uncomfortable feeling that the rex was not happy about what he was doing, and that made him nervous.

"What's the matter?" Angelina asked.

"Nothing," Zeke replied, turning away.

This is stupid, he thought. *It's for his good, too. If he makes too much noise we'll all get caught.*

"Let's go," Zeke finally announced. Then he cautiously rode Hellfire out of the tree line, looking carefully around before

Chapter Ten

stepping into the riverbed.

They kept to the shadows as they rode toward the bluff, and neither of them said a word. Hellfire growled as they drew closer, but it couldn't roar like it usually did.

As darkness fell Zeke and Angelina heard strange insect noises and caught glimpses of low-flying animals, as the creatures of the night emerged from their hiding places. They couldn't make out what they looked like, but they were much bigger than bats. Every so often one of them would swoop down near Hellfire, and the rex would whip his head around to get a better look.

Zeke kept an eye out for the spot where the two Cragnon warriors disappeared into the woods. It wasn't difficult to find. The crates they were dragging were heavy enough to leave a clear impression in the muddy riverbed. Angelina dismounted just long enough to build a small pile of rocks to mark the spot so they'd have no trouble spotting it later.

The drums were quiet now, and the fires had gone out. The only sound came from Hellfire's steps in the riverbed and the occasional splash when he stepped into a puddle. The shadow of the ladders against the rock wall soon came into view.

"I'm going to take the rope," Zeke whispered, and he slung it over his shoulder. "If you see anyone, get out of here and keep going upriver. Don't wait for me. Wish me luck."

Angelina leaned over, and they hugged. "Good luck."

Zeke grabbed hold of the nearest ladder and started climbing. It was plenty strong enough to support his weight, and he made it to the top without any trouble. As he pulled himself over the wall, his heart skipped a beat. He was inside the Cragnon village!

So far, so good, he thought.

Zeke thought it was strange that the ladders were left down and unattended, since anyone could climb up, but didn't waste time questioning his good fortune. He had to find where they were keeping Mrs. Con Fuego and get out. He waved to Angelina, and watched her ride to safety, as they'd agreed, before continuing.

When Angelina saw that Zeke had made it safely to the top, she headed back to the hiding spot beyond the tree line. She hadn't gone far when she saw someone in the shadows of the riverbed coming toward her. And there was no doubt that whoever it was saw her as well.

Zeke crept through a maze of huts and buildings, searching for any sign of Angelina's mother. When he reached the center of the village and saw the wooden cage suspended over the pit, he guessed that had to be where the prisoners were kept.

"Mrs. Con Fuego," Zeke called quietly, praying he wouldn't be overheard by the wrong set of ears. "Are you in there?"

"Zeke, is that you?"

"Bull?" Zeke replied, confused "What are you doing here?"

"I took Mrs. Con Fuego's place," Bull explained. "Now, get out of here. If they catch you, they'll kill you or throw you in here with me."

Zeke couldn't hear a word Bull said. A moment ago he was so nervous he thought his heart would bust out of his chest it was pounding so hard. Now he was tingling with excitement.

Chapter Ten

For the first time in his life Bull needed his help! Here was a chance to save Bull and prove to himself and Uncle Jesse that he was a man.

"Zeke, did you hear me? Get out of here, now!"

"Nothing doing," Zeke answered. "I'm getting you out."

Bull sighed and shook his head. He was afraid of that, but there wasn't much he could do inside the cage to stop him. "All right," he agreed finally. "Have you got a gun?"

"No, but I think I can get one. I've got some sticks of TNT, though, if that'll help."

"What did you just say?"

"I have three sticks and Angelina's got more."

"I think my hearing's going on me, son. Did you just say, 'Angelina'?"

"Yeah. She's with Hellfire."

Bull couldn't believe this was happening: *Zeke was standing inside the Cragnon village of Mujar with three sticks of TNT, and Angelina was with Hellfire! Where the heck were Uncle Jesse and Slim? How did all this happen so fast? Best to just go with it.*

Bull had been planning to escape from the moment Uncle Jesse slipped him a knife as they were shaking hands, and told him to "stay sharp."

"Son, do me a favor and toss me one of those sticks of TNT."

"You want me to attach the detonator?" Zeke asked.

"No, no, don't do that," Bull replied quickly. "I'll do it."

Soon Bull had a stick of TNT, primed with a detonator and fuse in his possession. All he needed now was a spark to light it, and he could generate that easily enough with the small piece of flint he always kept in the pocket of his jeans.

Rex Riders

Bull told Zeke where to find the winches that operated the cage and controlled the raptors. He had no idea how much power it took to work the devices or if Zeke was strong enough to do it himself, but Bull figured it was worth a shot. If the boy couldn't do it, Bull was stuck, and maybe then Zeke would listen to reason.

Zeke pushed and pulled with everything he had but couldn't budge the winch.

"I can't do it," he whispered in frustration.

Bull wasn't surprised. It took several Cragnon to turn the massive wheels and they were bigger and stronger than Zeke.

"That's okay, son. What I need you to do now is get out of here and find your uncle and Slim. They'll be able to help."

Zeke considered the situation. If he left now, he'd be giving up his best shot to save Bull and be a hero. On the other hand, if he stayed and got caught, he'd have done more harm than good. "I'll be back. I promise."

"Good man," Bull said. "I know you will. Now git!"

It felt awful leaving Bull behind, but Zeke realized that the best way to help the ranch hand was to do as he asked.

Zeke retraced his steps and climbed down the ladder to the riverbed. When he reached bottom, he looked in both directions to make sure no one had seen him before blending into the shadows and taking off downriver in the direction he last saw Angelina riding. He ran a couple of hundred yards at a steady pace, stopping every so often to whisper her name, but heard nothing in response. It was right about then that he saw two figures standing beside Hellfire in the distance. And he was pretty sure the one holding the long club wasn't Angelina.

Chapter Ten

* * *

It was past midnight, and D'Allesandro was pacing. Shugath had sworn that his warriors would bring him Hellfire's dead body before the end of the day, but now—on the eve of D'Allesandro's departure—there was no sign of the shaman.

"Where is he?" D'Allesandro growled, as he stared out the window of his now-empty cabin. The clutter that was there just two days before was gone, and the walls were bare. D'Allesandro had carefully packed away the maps, papers and journals in anticipation of his return to Dos Locos. All that remained was some unfinished business.

"I ain't surprised," a smug Cable Cooper sneered. "You should have listened to me." Cooper was dead set against D'Allesandro's alliance with Shugath and made no secret of it. He didn't trust the Cragnon and especially didn't trust their medicine man. But D'Allesandro had his own ideas about how to get along with the indigenous people in this new world and hadn't asked for Cooper's opinion.

Before D'Allesandro could fire back a response, one of the sentries standing guard in a watch tower shouted a warning and rang the alarm bell.

The powerful ranch owner flew out the cabin and ran to the gate. Sure enough, someone was riding toward them in the moonlight on a war bird, with two more trailing behind. "There he is. That has to be Shugath. And look. They killed it!"

"Well, I'll be. It looks like they did," Cooper admitted grudgingly.

"Open the gate," D'Allesandro ordered.

"Welcome Shugath," D'Allesandro said in the language of the

Cragnon. "What have you brought me?"

The shaman gestured to the war birds behind him. Each carried something, concealed by blood-stained, hand-woven tarps. D'Allesandro walked to the first, rubbing his hands together in anticipation. But when he pulled back the cover, instead of Hellfire's head and neck, he uncovered the badly mangled body of a Cragnon warrior.

D'Allesandro gasped and stepped backward. "What is this?"

"Pull the other blanket back," he ordered one of his men. The cowboy did as he was told and revealed the lifeless body of a second warrior.

"What happened to the third?" D'Allesandro demanded.

Shugath shook his head solemnly.

D'Allesandro was furious. "You swore to me that your warriors would kill the beast," he shouted angrily. "My men delivered the weapons as promised, but you have not held up your end of the bargain. I hold you to your vow. Destroy the beast and bring me its head. Do you understand, shaman?"

Shugath seethed. D'Allesandro had shown no respect for the dead, not even a hint of sorrow for their sacrifice!

Waving his arms wildly, his eyes bulging out of his head, the Cragnon medicine man jumped from his mount and approached D'Allesandro. "The beast is cursed," Shugath hissed. "Give the Rider to me, and I will put an end to his sorcery!"

With barely the slightest motion, Cooper slipped his pistol out of its holster and cocked the trigger. If Shugath attacked D'Allesandro, he'd have the excuse he needed to drop the shaman in his tracks.

But D'Allesandro refused to be bullied and stood his ground.

Chapter Ten

"No. The Rider was not part of the bargain. He is mine."

Shugath and D'Allesandro stared at one another. The rancher knew the risk he was taking. He needed the shaman to lead the Cragnon away from the river. Otherwise, all his plans would be ruined. Even worse was the possibility that Shugath would betray him to Chief Braknar.

But this was no time for weakness. If D'Allesandro gave in to Shugath and handed over the Rider, the shaman would gain the upper hand, a position D'Allesandro might never recapture. There could only be one leader, and whoever won this showdown would be it. Besides, D'Allesandro needed the Tarngatharn alive in case the Professor failed to figure out how to operate the force generator.

Shugath cursed D'Allesandro with every imprecation the shaman could think of, but the calculating rancher refused to budge. Finally, the Cragnon medicine man spit on the ground at D'Allesandro's feet and remounted his war bird.

"It will be done as you command," he said with a scowl.

"Good. Your reward will be great," D'Allesandro said. "The Cragnon will bow before you as their king, and together we will rule this land. Now go."

D'Allesandro's men couldn't understand what their boss and the shaman had said to one another, but could tell from the tone of their voices and facial expressions that D'Allesandro had won the round and the next morning they'd move out on schedule.

Later that night, as D'Allesandro walked with Cooper back to their cabins, Cooper couldn't pass up the opportunity to take a poke at Shugath. "Looks like they didn't do any better at killing that beast than my men did," he observed with a snort.

"You're correct, Mr. Cooper," D'Allesandro replied. "You have all lived down to my lowest expectations."

"Huh?"

"Good*night*, Mr. Cooper."

The twin moons made the woods uncomfortably bright, as Shugath rode back to Mujar with the two rider-less war birds and their cargo in tow. The reek of death from the dead Cragnon put the creatures on edge, and Shugarth was uneasy that the scent might attract other predators, so he had to hurry.

As the shaman rode, he reflected on the events of the past several days. The fact that Hellfire had proved difficult to kill was no surprise. The Yerka of the Riders were highly trained by their masters, and more deadly than their untamed counter-parts. The methods used by the Tarngatharn were shrouded in secrecy, and the full extent of the abilities of their mounts was unknown.

Although D'Allesandro was worried that Hellfire might be prowling the woods searching for Slim, Shugath believed the dinosaur was the least of their problems. From Shugath's perspective the Rider was far more problematic than his rex.

The key question was whether he could trust D'Allesandro to finish off their common enemy. The rancher was ruthless, but if the Rider somehow managed to escape and Chief Braknar learned of Shugath's treachery, retribution would be swift and painful.

No, Shugath couldn't afford to take a chance. He would have to prepare a back-up plan of his own.

Chapter
Eleven

Come daybreak, D'Allesandro paid a visit to Professor Kornbluth. The Professor looked up at D'Allesandro from the work table where he was dozing with the expression of a man who was caught doing something he shouldn't.

"Good heavens, what time is it?" he asked, embarrassed.

"Time to leave, Professor," D'Allesandro answered sternly. "When I didn't see you at breakfast, I had a feeling you were still here. Take a moment to collect your thoughts and tell me what you've learned about the weapon."

"Yes, of course," Kornbluth agreed as he took a sip of coffee from the tin cup D'Allesandro offered him. "From what your men have told me about their encounter with the Rider, it seems he activated the device pressing the buttons that line its side in a precise sequence. I've tried hundreds of combinations, and kept track of them in this notebook, but I haven't found the right one.

"Part of the problem is the grip," Kornbluth explained. "It fits the Rider's hand, which is much bigger than mine, but the buttons are spaced too far apart, so I have to hold the instrument with one hand and press them with the oth—"

"May I see your notebook?" D'Allesandro interrupted.

"Of course."

The Professor felt his stomach tighten into knots as he handed it over.

"What do the stars you've placed beside some of the entries mean?" D'Allesandro asked.

"Some combinations caused the device to react. It would glow or hum, but nothing further happened."

"I see."

Although D'Allesandro's face was expressionless as he reviewed Kornbluth's notes, the Professor knew that this was not what D'Allesandro wanted to hear.

D'Allesandro closed the book and smiled. "It appears that I will have to pay the Rider a visit after all. I'll take that now, please."

"What are you going to do to him?" Kornbluth asked uneasily as he handed back the instrument.

It made the Professor physically ill to think that his failure would cause someone to suffer at the hands of D'Allesandro's men. Uncle Jesse's shooting and mistreatment was just one of many similar episodes Kornbluth had witnessed during the expedition that upset him, and he turned a blind eye to them all. Although D'Allesandro tried to convince him that they were mere "sacrifices" that had to be made in the name of science, the

Chapter Eleven

Professor never agreed. But rather than argue, he made up his mind to concentrate on the job he'd been given and stay out of D'Allesandro's business.

"I hope you won't harm him," he added after D'Allesandro ignored his question.

"You concentrate on packing your things. We have only a few hours."

The Professor hesitated.

"May I speak candidly?" he finally asked.

"You may."

"Please understand that I am not ungrateful for all that you've done," Kornbluth began, "and I would never think of questioning your authority in these matters. But I am not sure that imprisoning the Rider is the right approach. We know nothing about him; where he comes from; what he's doing here. I don't have to tell you he has a very high level of intelligence despite his outward appearance. That device of his; the crafts-manship is remarkable. I couldn't begin to duplicate it."

"What is your point, Professor?"

"I was just thinking . . . Perhaps if you proceeded differently; suggested to the Rider that we exchange ideas; spoke to him as an equal. I'm sure he can be reasoned with. It might even turn out that this instrument is more valuable than these animals."

D'Allesandro nodded approvingly. "Your suggestion is a good one, Professor."

"I hope I have not spoken out of turn."

"No, you haven't. Your thoughts echo my own."

Kornbluth was relieved by D'Allesandro's positive response. He had no way of knowing, however, that everything he had said about Slim's intelligence reinforced D'Allesandro's belief that the Rider was too dangerous to remain alive.

Getting Slim out of D'Allesandro's cabin hadn't been easy. None of the men wanted to get too close to the Tarngatharn, because they were afraid of him. They couldn't anticipate what he might do because his physical abilities were so different than theirs. When they pushed him to climb down the ladder, he jumped off the top instead, and landed on his feet ready to fight. If D'Allesandro hadn't held Uncle Jesse prisoner, there was no way of predicting what might have happened, but that changed the equation dramatically. Whenever Slim moved in a threatening manner or tried something they didn't like, they threatened to harm Uncle Jesse. The threat of further injury to his friend proved mighty effective in keeping the Rider under control.

Then there was the problem of what to do with Slim once they got him outside. Cooper suggested throwing him in the stockade with Uncle Jesse, but D'Allesandro nixed that idea. He wanted them kept apart so they couldn't work together in planning a move against him. D'Allesandro was also concerned that they wouldn't be able to keep an eye on Slim inside the windowless stockade.

They finally settled on chaining Slim to a pile of boulders in a rocky corner of the compound using the same heavy chains they used for hauling logs, and posting a guard on him.

Slim was sitting on the ground when D'Allesandro approached the cowboy who was on sentry duty.

"What has he been doing?" the rancher asked.

Chapter Eleven

"Not much, sir. Mostly, he just sits there."

"Find Mr. Cooper and tell him to meet me here. I'll watch the prisoner until you return."

D'Allesandro waited until the cowboy was gone and then held up the force generator he'd taken from Slim. "Tell me how to use this, and you and Mr. McCain will be freed. You have my word," D'Allesandro said.

Slim rose to his feet and walked as close to D'Allesandro as his chains would allow. "Give that back to me, and you will be spared," he countered. "You have my word."

"You are the one who is shackled, Rider."

"For now."

"'For now.' Yes, 'for now,'" D'Allesandro said with mock laughter. "I could have you killed with a snap of my fingers, but as I said, I'm willing to let you go. Just tell me how the device works. You will have your freedom, and I will return to Dos Locos."

"It is not that simple."

"Why? What is stopping you?"

"It is forbidden."

D'Allesandro frowned. "If you don't tell me what I want to know, your friend, Mr. McCain, will die."

"Then he will die," Slim replied matter-of-factly.

The callousness of Slim's response surprised D'Allesandro. It was only because of his concern for his friend's life that the Rider was at D'Allesandro's mercy. Yet, now Slim was acting as if he didn't care what happened to McCain.

Why the sudden change in attitude? D'Allesandro thought. *Is it possible he doesn't believe I'm serious?*

Rex Riders

"Perhaps I should have Mr. Cooper drag Mr. McCain out here," he suggested.

Slim glared at his captor and growled.

D'Allesandro decided to change his approach.

"A moment ago you said it is forbidden to tell me how this device works," he began. "Forbidden by whom? Who sent you? Where are you from?"

Slim simply stared at D'Allesandro.

"Rider, you accomplish nothing with your silence. You may threaten me all you want, but I see no risk in defying you. You are in chains and your threats are empty."

"Release me now and I will show you mercy."

"And if I don't?"

"Others will come. You have more to fear from them than you do the Cragnon."

"I see."

Up until that moment, D'Allesandro only suspected that Slim was not acting on his own but as an agent of some larger group. Now, things made sense. Slim's loyalty to whoever sent him was greater than his concern for Uncle Jesse. The fact that the Rider was willing to sacrifice his friend's life rather than reveal how the force generator functioned was proof of the device's value. There was no way D'Allesandro would give it up now.

Slim's warning confirmed something else D'Allesandro had suspected: as long as the Rider was alive, he was a danger. Even worse, there were others like him who would try to reclaim the weapon by force, provided they could find it.

The guard's sudden return with Cable Cooper interrupted D'Allesandro's thoughts.

Chapter Eleven

"You wanted to see me," Cooper said.

"Yes, Mr. Cooper. I was just chatting with the Tarngatharn. We were negotiating the terms of his and Mr. McCain's release."

"Is that so?"

Cooper cleared his throat and leaned close to D'Allesandro. "The men are ready to leave. What are we gonna do with McCain and ugly here?"

D'Allesandro cast an eye in Slim's direction before turning his back on the Rider. "Negotiations have not gone as well as I'd hoped," D'Allesandro said, lowering his voice. "They're staying."

"So I get to shoot them in the head, right?" Cooper said, slapping his holster.

"Assign that task to someone else, Mr. Cooper. You have other duties that are more urgent. Tell your men to wait until we've broken camp. And make sure the bodies are burned, not buried. There is to be no trace of either of them.

"As far as the other men are concerned," D'Allesandro continued, "the Rider and Mr. McCain decided to stay behind and will be released as soon as we're gone. No one other than the men who take care of this is to know what really happened. Is that understood?"

"Yes sir, Mr. D'Allesandro," Cooper said with a smile. "I'll take care of it right away."

D'Allesandro turned back to Slim and smiled. "I am glad we spoke. I feel that we finally understand one another. I'll be back shortly."

Slim nodded and narrowed his eyes. "I understand you much better now as well."

"Come with me, Mr. Cooper. We're going to pay a visit on Mr. McCain." Then lowering his voice again, "Maybe he can loosen up our friend here."

As they walked to the stockade, Cooper looked over his shoulder at Slim and sneered. *That big goon's time is almost up; only he's too stupid to know it,* he thought.

Slim had heard every word of D'Allesandro's orders to Cooper. Time was running short. The Tarngatharn stared at his shackles and smiled. The chain was the type used to anchor ships and was unusually heavy. Given enough time and energy, Slim knew he could break it, but there was a simpler way to escape and conserve his energy for when he needed it. He just had to be left alone long enough to execute his plan.

Following the melee in D'Allesandro's quarters, Uncle Jesse was locked in a windowless cabin commandeered to serve as the compound's stockade. The building offered little air, and the heat was stifling. Uncle Jesse was rapidly becoming dehydrated. It wouldn't be long before delirium set in, and then death.

Uncle Jesse did his best to stop the bleeding from the gun-shot wound to his shoulder by applying direct pressure, but the pain was excruciating. The bullet had to come out soon before it became infected.

Making matters worse, the smell of blood attracted all kinds of carnivorous insects that crawled along the outside of the walls searching for gaps between the logs big enough to squeeze through. The safest place was in the center of the floor, but Uncle Jesse was constantly on alert to even the faintest sound. It was nerve-wracking to sit in the dark and hear them coming for him,

Chapter Eleven

but he had no way to plug up the holes.

He was lying on the floor when the door was unbolted, and in walked D'Allesandro, followed by Cooper carrying a pail of water.

"You smell something, Mr. D'Allesandro? It stinks in here."

D'Allesandro ignored Cooper. "How are you holding up, Mr. McCain?" he said. "You don't look well."

"He looks thirsty," Cooper said, bringing a ladleful of water to his lips and slurping loudly as he drank. "And it looks like he's had some company," Cooper added, pointing to the dead insects littering the floor that Uncle Jesse had killed.

"What do you want, D'Allesandro?" Uncle Jesse asked.

"I'm here to renew my offer. It would be such a waste for a man of your capabilities to die suffering on the floor of this room, when I can get you medical attention. Join me. I can use a man like you."

"I'm all ears. What do I have to do?"

"Persuade the Rider—'Slim,' if you prefer—to reveal the secrets of the device I took from him. He's very loyal to you. He may not show me, but he might tell you."

Uncle Jesse started to laugh. He couldn't help himself. The heat was getting to him, and as D'Allesandro was speaking the absurdity of the situation sunk in. "Is that all?"

"I don't understand what's so funny," D'Allesandro said angrily. "This is not a joke, Mr. McCain. I'll make it worth your while."

Uncle Jesse tried shaking his head to regain his composure but couldn't stop laughing. His life depended on whether he would agree to convince an eight foot tall, talking monster, who he'd known for only a couple of days, to tell him how to use a piece of metal pipe he'd only seen from a distance. And if he didn't agree, he'd likely be shot or left to die from dehydration or blood loss, whichever came first.

"You're loco, D'Allesandro, you know that?" He said, finally getting control of himself. "This whole place . . . this plan of yours . . . What's the point? We don't have enough cattle in Texas for you? You need to come here and start a war with the Cragnon; destroy their world. For what? A bunch of three-horns or whatever you call them?"

"The West does not have a monopoly on cattle or the land that's needed to raise them, Mr. McCain. There is no good reason why other territories north, east and west of Texas cannot be used. Our whole way of life—yours and mine—is not only dying; it's in danger of extinction.

"Look around, Mr. McCain. Have you seen what these animals are capable of? I have. Imagine plowing a field behind a beast of this size. How big a plow could you use? Think of how much faster you could get the job done. Think of everything mules or oxen do; then picture these creatures doing the same things. Hauling timber; moving boulders to build roads and dams; pulling heavy wagons full of provisions. Work that requires a team of animals can be done by one triceratops—just one! They will revolutionize agriculture.

"You see these boots I'm wearing? They're made from the hide of a triceratops. Do you know how many pairs can be made from one of these creatures?

"Have you seen any cattle in this compound, Mr. McCain? Or hogs? Or chickens? A single triceratops provides enough

Chapter Eleven

meat to feed a hundred men for a week."

"You grill 'em right, and they taste just like longhorn, McCain," Cooper said, grinning. "Which kind of makes sense when you think about it, since they both have long horns and all, don't it?"

"The best part?" D'Allesandro finished. "I alone will control the supply of these creatures."

"That may be true, but who's gonna control *them*? You saw what just one of them did to the town."

"Yes, I will grant you that," D'Allesandro conceded. "Right now, they are dangerous. But what's to stop me from breeding a less aggressive strain? They're doing it now back east. Ranchers pick the traits they want their cattle to have, and selectively breed animals with those specific traits. Any with undesirable characteristics are cut from the herd and slaughtered. It works. All it takes is time.

"I'm offering you an opportunity to do something that will insure that the west—*our* west—has a future. If you won't do it for yourself, then do it for the people of Dos Locos. This is my vision for Dos Locos. Tell me what you see, Mr. McCain."

"What do I see? I'll tell you what I see," Uncle Jesse said, the anger rising in him. "I see a no-good, double-dealing carpet-bagger. On top of that, you want to use me to get on a friend's good side only to stab him in the back. Or am I missing something?" Uncle Jesse spat on the floor in disgust. "I think you know my answer."

D'Allesandro grimaced. "I pity you, Mr. McCain. You have absolutely no vision. You are doomed to be swept under the wheels of progress.

Rex Riders

"If you think to insult me by calling me a 'carpetbagger,' you are mistaken. I consider it a compliment. True, I'm not from this place, but I see a land before me that offers great opportunity. I intend to take advantage of it before someone else does. That is what men of ambition do, Mr. McCain. And that is what they have always done. They seize the opportunities that are before them, and they do it before someone else seizes them first."

There was a knock on the door.

"The men are ready, sir," a guard announced from the doorway.

D'Allesandro sighed. It was clear that his discussion with Uncle Jesse was going nowhere. And without Slim's cooperation, he would have to either fall back on Professor Kornbluth to unlock the secrets of the force generator or find someone else to do it.

"Mr. McCain, whether you agree with me or not, I can still use your help. And I'm willing to pay you handsomely for it. Will you help me?"

"Don't waste your breath."

"Good luck, Mr. McCain. You are a man of principles. I suspect that you will soon be taking them with you to the grave. Perhaps they will be of some comfort. I regret that I will not see you again, at least not in this life."

D'Allesandro pulled a gun from the pocket of his vest. Uncle Jesse tensed up, expecting the unscrupulous rancher to put him out of his misery.

"Relax, Mr. McCain. I have no intention of firing the weapon."

D'Allesandro opened the cylinder of the gun and emptied all but one of the bullets into his hand. "We've found out the

Chapter Eleven

hard way that men with open wounds tend to have short life spans in this country. As you can see, the local wildlife has an uncanny ability to sniff out blood, especially the insect-life. You may wish to consider the quick and painless death of a bullet to the temple. The alternative is much worse."

D'Allesandro placed the gun on the floor and walked out.

"Here, McCain, have a drink on me." Cooper sneered, as he heaved the bucket of water at Uncle Jesse. It was a cruel thing to do, but the cold water felt good in the heat.

"Thanks, Cooper!" Uncle Jesse shouted, just as the ruthless right-hand man slammed the door shut.

It took a moment for Uncle Jesse's eyes to readjust to the darkness before he could locate the gun. He opened the cylinder and felt each chamber with his fingers. There was one bullet as D'Allesandro had promised. It would have to do.

D'Allesandro looked out over the compound from the railing of his personal quarters. Cable Cooper stood close behind. D'Allesandro was disappointed that his conversations with Slim and Uncle Jesse hadn't worked.

"Such a waste," he said to himself. "It's time to leave, Mr. Cooper. Our work here is done . . . for now."

"How soon before we come back?"

"I don't know. I spoke to my sister last night about the attack on the Crossed Swords, and the damage was quite extensive. It may take months to repair everything. Which reminds me, where is my dear sister?"

"I locked her in the cabin after she turned in, just like you asked."

Rex Riders

"Good. I don't want her poking her nose where it doesn't belong. Send someone to let her out. And tell him to be careful. She may take a swing at him."

"Already did."

Below, Professor Kornbluth came into view. He was carrying a leather bag, and seemed to be walking with great effort.

"All packed and ready to go, Professor?" D'Allesandro shouted from the railing.

"I have my journals here," he called back, patting his bag. "And my instruments and specimens I left with the luggage in my cabin."

"Fine. Mr. Cooper will send someone to get it."

"Thank you. Will I be riding with you, sir?" Kornbluth asked, gasping. "I don't think I have the stamina to ride a horse."

"I wouldn't hear of it. You'll ride in the coach with me and my sister. The men are getting it ready. Go and make yourself comfortable. I will join you in a few minutes."

As the Professor turned toward the stagecoach, he nearly collided with D'Allesandro's sister, who strode by in a huff followed by two of Cooper's men.

"Good morning, Maria," D'Allesandro called. "It's good to see you up. Have you eaten, yet? We're almost ready to leave."

"How dare you lock me in my cabin! And where is Jesse McCain?" Maria demanded. "You told me he was coming with us."

"He will not be joining us after all," D'Allesandro answered in a pleasant tone, refusing to be drawn into an argument in front of his men. "I offered him a job as you and I discussed, and he declined. His decision entirely, I assure you. You know

Chapter Eleven

full well, I would have preferred it if he had accepted for several reasons."

"Where is he?" she persisted. "You said you'd release him."

His sister's public display of disrespect irritated D'Allesandro to no end. The nerve of her shouting at him in front of the men! But the powerful rancher kept his emotions in check as he climbed down from his cabin to confront her.

"Maria, would you please lower your voice?" he asked firmly.

"I want to speak to him."

"That's not possible. We are leaving, and he is to remain in the stockade until after we're gone."

"How dare y—?!"

"I had no choice," D'Allesandro interrupted, in a stern voice that made it clear he'd had enough. "Mr. McCain is in a very agitated and unstable state of mind. There is no telling what he might do if left to his own devices."

D'Allesandro turned to Cooper, refusing to make further eye contact with Maria. "Mr. Cooper, I'll be walking the grounds. Make sure my bags are packed and the carriage is ready."

As D'Allesandro proceeded past Maria, he was confronted once again by his sister.

"Mr. McCain and his friend freed me," Maria shouted at his back, as he walked past.

"I know," D'Allesandro replied, without breaking his stride.

"We owe them!"

"No. You do. *I* owe them nothing," D'Allesandro said, as he whirled around to face her. "Let us not forget that they came here to stop me. What would you have me do? Abandon all my work, because Jesse McCain doesn't approve? What business is it of his?

Rex Riders

Why should his opinion matter more than mine? I've considered the risks, and they are acceptable to me."

"And what if those risks involve innocent people, Dante?"

"What of it? When Professor Nobel invented TNT and shared his discovery with mankind, he involved innocent people. How many of them have been hurt or killed as a result of his work? Is he personally responsible for all those deaths and injuries? What should he have done, Maria? Should he have burned the results of his research?"

Maria said nothing.

"Now, if you'll excuse me, I have work to finish."

As her brother strode away, Maria simply stared, shaking her head. *Same old Dante: always right about everything,* she thought. *The only person that ever mattered to him was himself.*

An hour later, D'Allesandro took his seat across from his sister and Professor Kornbluth. The custom-built stagecoach in which they sat was D'Allesandro's lone concession to the comforts of civilization. The rancher had it built and delivered to the compound for what he hoped would be a triumphant trip home. It was unusually opulent by Dos Locos standards with its heavily-padded, crushed velvet interior and fold-down bar, and totally impractical as a means of regular transportation in this primitive world. But the vehicle was never intended for everyday use.

"I'm looking forward to returning to the Crossed Swords," D'Allesandro said pleasantly.

"What's left of it," Maria muttered.

"I'm sure we'll all sleep better tonight," the Professor offered.

Chapter Eleven

"Open the gates!" Cooper shouted from his horse.

With a squeal of metal, the large gates to the compound slowly moved aside.

"After the last transport leaves, make sure the camp is locked down," Cooper ordered as D'Allesandro's carriage started its journey.

Cooper turned to One-Eyed Jack, Tall Bill and Thom Jackson, who waited by him on horseback. "You boys know what to do."

"Sure do, boss," One-Eyed Jack replied.

"We'll take care of everything," Tall Bill confirmed, grinning.

"Make sure you do. And take care that nothing happens to Mr. D'Allesandro's horse or there'll be hell to pay."

Still concerned for Uncle Jesse, Maria looked back at the stockade as the carriage trundled past Cooper and his men on its way out the gate.

"What were they talking about?" she asked her brother suspiciously. Something was going on, and she was sure it involved Uncle Jesse.

"Just a few last minute details that need to be taken care of," D'Allesandro replied blandly.

"You're lying. I can always tell when you're lying. What's going on?"

When D'Allesandro did not answer, she moved to get out of the cab, but D'Allesandro grabbed hold of the handle.

"Sit down, Maria. There is nothing going on, I assure you."

As the gates closed behind the caravan, D'Allesandro's henchmen got to work shutting down the compound. There was nothing Maria could do now but go along for the ride.

* * *

The cowboy who was guarding Slim left with the others. The Tarngatharn was finally alone.

It is time, he thought, testing the chains attached to his wrists.

The ends of each chain were connected to iron rings attached to heavy iron spikes that had been driven into the rock with a sledgehammer. Though the spikes were too difficult to pull free, their tips could be snapped off if hit hard enough. There were plenty of stones nearby, too heavy for D'Allesandro's men to lift, that would work fine. There was no time to lose.

Cooper told his henchmen that they could do whatever they wanted with Uncle Jesse and Slim once D'Allesandro's carriage was well clear of the compound, as long as there was no trace of the bodies. Tall Bill, Thom Jackson and One-Eyed Jack were perfect for this kind of dirty work since they still bore a grudge against McCain for what had happened months before at the Double R when Bull had throttled them.

Cooper warned them that McCain was armed, but that wouldn't be a problem for those three snakes. They knew plenty of sneaky ways to disarm him. They could make a big show of releasing Uncle Jesse and then shoot him in the back as he walked out. Or maybe they'd trick him into surrendering his gun before they shot him. Heck, they could even open the stockade door and let loose with a hail of bullets. That uppity rancher would never know what hit him!

"I've been looking forward to this for a long time," Tall Bill said eagerly.

"Me, too," One-Eyed Jack agreed.

"Shame Cable ain't here to enjoy it," Thom Jackson added.

Chapter Eleven

When they reached the door to the stockade, the men drew their guns and positioned themselves on either side of the entrance before knocking, determined not to be taken off-guard if McCain fired a shot before the door was opened.

"Hey, McCain, you remember us?" Tall Bill announced. "It's Tall Bill and One-Eyed Jack and Thom Jackson, come to pay you a visit. McCain, you in there?"

"You think maybe he's dead?" One-Eyed Jack whispered.

"Maybe he's just playing possum," Thom Jackson said. "I'll unbolt the door, and you boys go in and check."

"Us? Why should we go in? He's got a gun. You go in."

"You boys looking for someone?" The men whirled around to find Uncle Jesse, rifle in hand, standing on the ground looking up at them.

"McCain!" all three cried in unison.

"How'd you get out here? The door's locked," Tall Bill asked, shocked.

"A friend of mine let me out the back door."

The three scoundrels looked at one another.

"There ain't no back door," One-Eyed Jack observed.

"There is now."

The wooden boards the men were standing on exploded upward as a support pole burst through the floor and knocked them off their feet. The whole structure began to creak and shake as another corner support of the porch was ripped from its moorings. Now the whole porch began to sag toward the ground, threatening to collapse at any moment. The men jumped back and clawed at the walls of the stockade, but there wasn't anything to grab onto.

"What's happening?" One-Eyed Jack shouted.

"You boys are in for an early fall," Uncle Jesse said, as a third support was wrenched free.

The floor finally collapsed, and the men crashed to the ground amid a pile of boards where they lay too stunned to move.

Slim strode into the mess dragging his wrist and ankle chains behind him. He picked two of the men up, one in each hand.

"We're taking your horses," Uncle Jesse said.

"How will we get back?" Tall Bill asked.

"Looks like you'll be walking. Now hand over your guns."

The trio surrendered their weapons and ammunition, and Uncle Jesse gave them a count of ten to make themselves scarce or he'd start shooting.

"Let's find the horses," Slim said.

"Before we do that, we better get those shackles off. You're going to hurt your horse if you try and ride with those chains hanging down. They must have a blacksmith shop around here somewhere."

"How is your shoulder?" Slim asked.

"It'll do," Uncle Jesse answered, wincing as he moved his arm.

"Can you ride?"

"Try and stop me."

"Would you like me to remove the bullet?" Slim asked.

Uncle Jesse stopped in his tracks. He knew Slim was smart, resourceful and tough, but he had no idea that he also knew how to perform surgery! "You know how to do that?"

"I've never tried, but it can't be that hard. Let me take a look . . ."

Uncle Jesse took a step back. "Um, no offense, Slim, but I

think I'll wait on that. We don't have a lot of time, so maybe we ought to concentrate on getting those chains off for now. But thanks for the offer." Slim shrugged his shoulders

"You got a plan, yet?" Uncle Jesse asked.

"I'm working on it," the Rider replied with a wink.

"You're starting to sound like me."

They found the building that housed the camp smithy and removed the manacles around Slim's ankles. But the Rider insisted on keeping the ones around his wrists, together with the four-foot lengths of chain that were still attached to each. All he'd say was that he might need them later. Then Slim wrapped the chains tightly around his forearms to keep them from dragging. He reminded Uncle Jesse of a picture of a Roman gladiator he'd seen in the Bible once.

The horses were tied up near the gate, and it put a big smile on Uncle Jesse's face to see Midnight again. He was surprised to see that his saddlebag had remained untouched. He opened it, and sure enough, there was a lump of Stumpy's jerky inside.

Midnight perked up when he heard Uncle Jesse's voice, and it made Uncle Jesse think of Zeke and the Double R. It was funny how things had turned out. First Zeke was accused of stealing the Andalusian; then Uncle Jesse owned him; then D'Allesandro stole him; and now, Uncle Jesse had the stallion back!

Uncle Jesse planned to let Slim ride Midnight because the big Andalusian was better suited to the Tarngatharn, and Slim had ridden the horse before. He'd ride one of the remaining two horses and take the last for Bull.

"This one'll do," he said. He secured the third to his horse's saddle before setting his foot in the stirrup. But before he could pull himself up, Slim put a hand on his shoulder.

"You take Midnight. I'll take this one," the Tarngatharn offered.

"You sure?" Uncle Jesse asked.

Slim nodded.

"That's mighty thoughtful, Slim. I owe you one."

Even though he was down to one good arm, Uncle Jesse pulled himself into the saddle effortlessly and grabbed the reins. Then, tucking the injured arm into his shirt, he adjusted his hat so it wouldn't fall off and clenched his jaw.

"Let's get Bull!"

D'Allesandro's stagecoach wound its way through the forest to a narrow trail that led down to the riverbed near the foot of the dam. Cooper rode out front with two of his men and another six men behind.

"Where are the rest of the men?" Maria asked.

"They'll be meeting up with us shortly," D'Allesandro answered.

At the base of the dam, Maria marveled at its size. It was an amazing feat. Her brother may have been a self-centered jerk, but he knew how to get things done against odds that other people would have found overwhelming.

They continued down the riverbed for approximately a hundred yards when D'Allesandro abruptly rapped on the roof of the carriage.

"We'll wait here," he called to the driver.

"Why are we stopping?" Maria demanded impatiently.

"We're waiting for the rest of the men to join us."

Chapter Eleven

No one spoke as the minutes passed. While D'Allesandro sat quietly, his face was expressionless, Maria fidgeted nonstop. She fanned herself, sighed loudly and did everything she could think of to show her displeasure.

"I'm getting out," she finally said, and this time she reached the door handle before D'Allesandro could stop her.

"Where are you going?"

"For God's sake, Dante, where do you think? I'm going outside for some air! It's too hot in here."

Maria stepped out of the coach and walked toward the dam. She was still upset with her brother, but thoughts of Angelina helped ease those feelings. With luck she would be reunited with her daughter that evening. But what would she tell Stumpy and Zeke about Uncle Jesse and Bull? She considered telling them they'd stayed behind, but realized Stumpy and Zeke would never believe that. Maybe she'd tell them that there'd been an accident. It was bound to be awkward, but it didn't really matter if they believed her or not. They'd never find out the truth. The most important thing was to get her daughter back.

A distant rumbling interrupted Maria's musings. The ground began to vibrate as the sound grew louder. Maria looked about to see where the noise was coming from, but it seemed to be closing in from everywhere at once.

"What is that?!" she cried.

Maria looked upriver, worried that the vibrations might be coming from the dam. Even at such a great distance, she could see small stones jarred loose from their positions, falling into the riverbed, and water began pooling at the base.

"The dam is going to burst!" Maria screamed in panic, as she ran back to the carriage and hopped onto the running board.

"Relax, Maria . . ." D'Allesandro said firmly.

"We have to get out of here," she insisted through the window.

"I said relax," D'Allesandro ordered. "Now, get back in here so we can get going."

Two triceratops joined by a massive wooden yoke lumbered onto the riverbed a dozen yards ahead of the carriage. They were pulling a wagon on which the men had mounted a Gatling gun. On each side of the weapon sat a row of men, and the platform was surrounded by a railing.

"Maria, please get back inside," D'Allesandro urged. "We have to get into position."

The driver gave the order, and the horses started toward the pair of trikes.

As they pulled up behind the yoked beasts Maria could see down the trail the trikes had taken to the river. It was far wider than Maria had envisioned, but it wasn't the size of the trail that shocked her. Just inside the tree line, as far as the eye could see, row after row of triceratops stood, awaiting their turn to enter the riverbed.

One of the men gave the signal, and D'Allesandro's men began to herd the trikes down the trail. Despite the creatures' awesome size, there was room enough for cowboys to patrol the perimeter, keeping the ceratopsids moving and preventing any of them from straying outside the herd. The triceratops continued to flow into the Sulant until a sea of several hundred animals of different sizes filled the riverbed.

At the rear a team of four horses pulled a wagon left over from the Civil War that was full of heavily-armed men ready for battle.

Chapter Eleven

"Anybody seen Tall Bill, One-Eyed Jack or Thom Jackson?" Cooper shouted as he rode down the line, but the only replies he got were blank stares and shrugs.

This was not a good sign.

"Trouble, Mr. Cooper?" D'Allesandro asked, when Cooper rode up alongside his boss's coach.

"The boys I left behind ain't arrived yet. You want me to go back and see what's keeping them?"

"We are not waiting, Mr. Cooper. Your men know how to find us. Now, move 'em out."

"They've got Midnight."

D'Allesandro was plainly annoyed. "I said to move out."

Cooper galloped to the head of the caravan, where he could be seen by the men manning its outermost edges, and gave the signal. Each man in turn signaled the one behind until it reached the end of the herd. Soon, the trikes began to lumber down the riverbed. The sound of their feet on the hard earth, mixed with their cries, was so loud that conversation was impossible unless you yelled directly into the ear of the person next to you.

But that wasn't a problem for cowboys. They operated by an unwritten set of rules when they were on a drive, and didn't do a lot of talking that wasn't absolutely necessary while they were working. Each man counted on the man across from him to do his job automatically, without being told.

"They ain't no different than longhorns, just bigger," Cooper remarked to himself, as he rode down the line to check on the men. The Sulant was so wide at this point that the triceratops could move freely, and the cowboys could cut in and out of the herd without much danger. Occasionally one animal would bump into another and set off a shoving match that had to be stopped before it escalated, but those conflicts weren't hard to handle.

D'Allesandro leaned out the window to get a better look. Massive horned heads bobbed up and down amid a cloud of dust as far as the eye could see. The canny rancher allowed himself a small smile. Everything was proceeding according to plan; these trikes were going back to Texas!

They continued for hours at a slow, steady pace. There was no reason to push the herd, and they stopped often to let the animals rest and drink.

Maria had fallen asleep but woke suddenly when she heard something in the distance. "What's was that?" she said.

"You heard something?" D'Allesandro asked doubtfully.

"There it goes again."

D'Allesandro's eyes narrowed as he concentrated, trying to shut out the noise from the stagecoach and the trikes. The sound was low and deep, like the lowing of a bull moose. And it was coming closer.

D'Allesandro sat up. "Cragnon?"

"No, something different. I've heard the sound before," Professor Kornbluth exclaimed, as he poked his head out the window of the stagecoach. "There, up ahead!"

A large group of lambeosaurs walked toward the caravan on their way upriver to a place where water was more abundant. D'Allesandro leaned out of the window on the opposite side of the cab to get a look, and even Maria managed to squeeze her head out to see what was going on.

The cowboy riding shotgun alongside the driver fired once into the air in an attempt to drive off the giant creatures, but

Chapter Eleven

D'Allesandro shouted at him to stop. There was no reason to chase them off. Though each was far greater in size than a triceratops, the lambeosaurs would soon yield to the sheer volume of the trike herd. Why not enjoy the majestic view of the dinosaurs until then?

"Magnificent beasts!" the Professor declared excitedly.

"We'll have to capture a couple of specimens on our next trip back," D'Allesandro said.

"Capital idea," Kornbluth agreed.

One of the trikes at the head of the caravan bellowed at the advancing lambeosaurs, and a large male bellowed back.

"There it goes again! Did you hear it?!" the Professor cried. "That sound is made by the creature's exhalations through the crest on its head. Watch, maybe he'll do it again!"

As D'Allesandro and Kornbluth expected, the gentle giants moved into the woods well before the procession reached them.

The experience revived and exhilarated D'Allesandro, and he was suddenly in a mood to celebrate.

"Professor, may I offer you a glass of sherry?" he asked, pulling a bottle from the bar compartment in the cab and uncorking it.

"That would be lovely," the Professor said, as he took the glass from D'Allesandro.

"Maria?" She ignored him and stared out the window.

"A toast to the future Professor! May it bring us both success beyond measure!"

"To the future," Kornbluth repeated, and the two men clinked glasses.

"I promised you that if you joined me, I would secure your

place in the annals of science, did I not?"

"You did, sir, and it has been the experience of a lifetime."

"And your journals?"

The Professor pointed to the roof of the stagecoach where the luggage was stowed. "Packed safely inside my bag."

"Good. Mine too. We must safeguard our notes and findings. The information they contain—the record of our explorations thus far—is priceless."

"What will you do first when you get back to your ranch, Mr. D'Allesandro?"

"I think I shall take a hot bath and wash off the dirt of this place. And I won't be the least bit surprised if I emerge ten pounds lighter!"

"That sounds tempting," Kornbluth said, laughing.

"And you, Professor?"

"I shall take a room at the hotel in town and sleep for a week! It will be the first good night's rest I've had since I arrived here."

"I'd have insisted you stay at the Crossed Swords, but I'm afraid it's in desperate need of repairs."

The Professor shook his head. "I'm looking forward to some solitude. I need to get away for a time and reflect on everything that's happened these past months. I want to reread my journal entries and begin to edit them while everything is still fresh in my mind."

"I understand completely. I shall be doing the same."

The sun was setting as they approached the outskirts of the Cragnon territory. Here, they would stop and make camp for the night. The next step was up to Shugath.

* * *

Chapter Eleven

As the caravan settled in, Chief Braknar and his chiefs conferred in the war room to finalize their plan to attack D'Allesandro's compound. Shugath had made sure that the scouts who had seen or heard D'Allesandro's caravan moving down the Sulant River reported nothing to the tribe. So far, everything was under control. All that remained was to lead the warriors who were loyal to Chief Braknar into the trap.

"As I foretold, the promises of the Rider and the invaders were empty," Shugath spoke with great solemnity. "The secrets of what is to come have been revealed to me. We cannot afford to wait any longer. Tomorrow at dawn, we will journey to the strangers' village and burn it to the ground!"

The war chiefs howled their approval, and Chief Braknar smiled. "Your powers of prophecy are great, shaman. Long will the people remember your name for what you have done."

Shugath bowed. "You honor me, great chief. The people are gathering to hear your words in the plaza. It is time to make an offering to the gods so they may bless our tribe in battle."

"Send for the prisoner," Braknar announced with a clap of his hands.

Inside the wooden cage Bull watched and waited. There was a strange tension in the air. Bull knew the tribe was planning an attack on D'Allesandro's camp, but there were signs that something else was brewing. He had noticed an unusual number of Cragnon, looking around to see who was watching or listening, as they whispered to one another throughout the day.

As sunset approached, torches were lit and the activity level in the city increased. Bull knew it was only a matter of time before they came for him. He'd come up with a plan involving the stick of TNT he'd hidden in his clothing, but it was risky. When the Cragnon gathered to get him, he would light the fuse and hide the explosive in a narrow space between the floorboards of the cage. He'd allow himself to be taken without a struggle, lulling his captors into thinking he'd given up. When the TNT exploded, he'd fight his way out using the knife Uncle Jesse had given him.

The full moons would help him escape. The problem was the fuse. If the timing wasn't perfect, he might blow himself up before he was out of the cage. No. Maybe there was another way. But he had to make a decision fast. Should he ignite the TNT or not? Once he lit the fuse and left it behind, there would be no turning back.

The warriors pulled back the war birds and lowered the wooden cage to the bottom of the pit. When the door was opened, Bull walked into the rough hands of the Cragnon. He was paraded through the square on his way to a crude ceremonial alter built out of stones. Along the way the people shouted insults, and hurled sticks, stones and garbage at him.

Chief Braknar stood atop the altar with Shugath at his side and addressed his tribespeople. "Tomorrow we take back what is ours. No longer will these outlanders plunder our lands."

Shugath descended the steps and stood before the roaring crowd. He raised his arms to call for silence; then made a show of walking in front of Bull as if the shaman were deciding the prisoner's fate.

He abruptly stopped and pointed at Bull's chest. A roar went up from the crowd. Two stocky warriors grabbed Bull's arms and dragged the struggling cowboy up the steps, with Shugath

Chapter Eleven

leading the way. At the top, Bull's arms were yanked behind his back, and he was forced down onto the stone altar.

"Easy boys, you're hurting my shoulders," Bull grunted.

Shugath looked gleeful as he raised an axe over his head, pausing in dramatic fashion when the weapon reached its apex. The Cragnon screamed their approval. But before the axe could start its deadly descent, gunshots rang out and ricocheted off the axe head, nearly knocking the weapon from Shugath's grasp.

The stunned shaman ducked backward to protect himself. Where did those shots come from? Had D'Allesandro double-crossed him? Then he heard the unmistakable roar of a T-rex from the back of the crowd and knew the Rider had returned!

The sea of Cragnon parted as Slim and Hellfire made their way toward the foot of the sacrificial altar. Behind the Rider rode a boy and a girl atop a war bird, and a young Cragnon on another. Both were dragging wooden crates behind them.

Shugath recognized the boxes immediately. They held the weapons D'Allesandro's men had given his warriors! How did the Rider find them? And who was that young Cragnon? Was he a prisoner?

Bringing up the rear was Uncle Jesse on Midnight, and there was no question about where the shots came from. Uncle Jesse was aiming a brand-new Winchester repeating rifle at Shugath.

"Drop the axe medicine man," he shouted. Uncle Jesse figured Shugath must have picked up a little English from his dealings with D'Allesandro and the rancher's men. "Make another move and you're dead. *Comprende?*"

Shugath understood exactly what Uncle Jesse was saying, but the axe remained in his hands.

He wouldn't dare shoot me in front of this crowd, he thought. *They'll tear him limb from limb.*

Shugath's eyes were fixed on Slim's belt. If the Rider didn't have that accursed weapon of his, this interruption would be over in minutes, and the shaman could get on with slaughtering Bull, along with McCain and the other humans. But Slim was a step ahead of him.

"Hear me, Cragnon," the Rex Rider roared, as he rode closer to the altar. "One among you is a traitor!"

"You have betrayed your people!" Slim continued, pointing at Shugath.

Slim then turned his attention to the young Cragnon sitting atop the war bird. "Come forward, boy, and tell your chief and people what you told me."

The youth dismounted and stood beside the Rider.

Shugath thought he recognized the boy. Then he realized it was the same youth who threw the stone that started the riot just days before; the one who was saved by Uncle Jesse and Bull. The boy hated the outlanders! What could he possibly have to say?

"I saw him," he said in a quavering voice, pointing nervously at the shaman. "I saw him take weapons from the outlanders. I heard him speak of a plan to kill Cragnon warriors and rule the Cragnon himself."

"These are the weapons Shugath was given by the men who have dammed the river," Slim said, gesturing to the crates. "They were the reward for his treachery. At dawn, he plans to lead his warriors into battle, against all those loyal to Chief Braknar!"

Unrest swept through the crowd as everyone looked at their neighbors and wondered if they were part of the plot. Chief

Chapter Eleven

Braknar raised his arms and called for silence to preserve order.

"What do you say to these accusations, Shugath?" the Chief demanded.

Shugath turned toward Braknar, his head bowed, as if he were too ashamed to look upon the chief. But instead of saying something in his defense, the shaman reared back and hurled his axe, hitting Braknar in the chest. The old chief screamed in agony and fell to his knees.

"Attack!" Shugath shouted. "Attack!"

The square erupted in pandemonium as warriors who were loyal to Shugath rampaged through the crowd battering Chief Braknar's followers. The element of surprise was on their side, and many warriors who were loyal to the chief were killed in the first minutes of battle.

"I have seen the future Braknar, and you are not in it." Shugath spat, pulling the axe from the chief's chest. But when the duplicitous shaman raised it to deliver the final blow, Bull socked him in the jaw and sent Shugath tumbling down the stone steps. One of the warriors, who'd been holding down Bull just moments before, now clutched the big cowboy's arm in a gesture of thanks.

Afraid for the young Cragnon's well-being, Slim pushed the youth behind him. But instead of remaining there, the boy hurtled past the fallen shaman straight up the altar steps. Slim followed, and the two stood by Chief Braknar to protect him from further attack.

In the square, Uncle Jesse and the kids had no idea what to do, as Cragnon men, women and children scattered, and the civil war between the warrior factions raged around them. They couldn't tell the two sides apart. To make matters worse, both sides considered Uncle Jesse and the kids their enemies! The best thing to do was to grab Bull and get out of there.

Despite being bruised and bleeding from his fall down the stairs, Shugath struggled to his feet and began to shout orders to his followers. Then his eyes locked onto the crates that the Rider and his allies had dragged into the village.

"Get the weapons!" Shugath screamed.

From atop Midnight, Uncle Jesse saw Shugath's warriors fighting their way through the surging crowd to reach the weapons. They had to get out of there, but the war bird on which Zeke and Angelina were riding was hitched up to the rig they used to pull the crates.

"Cut her free, Zeke! We have to get out of here," Uncle Jesse shouted.

"Stay here. I'll be right back," Zeke told Angelina before jumping off the war bird. He tried desperately to untie the leather harness and ropes that tethered the rig to the beasts, but the humid air had made the knots wet, and he couldn't do it.

"They're stuck fast!" he cried.

"Hold them up," Uncle Jesse ordered.

Zeke held one of the ropes as high above the fracas as he could and winced in anticipation. Uncle Jesse took aim with his good arm and fired, cutting it in two.

"Now the other," Uncle Jesse shouted.

But before Zeke could get into position, a Cragnon grabbed him from behind, locking his arms around the teen's chest and lifting him off the ground. Zeke struggled to free himself but the warrior was much larger and had Zeke's arms pinned at his sides.

Chapter Eleven

Uncle Jesse tried to get a clear shot at the Cragnon, but Midnight started to buck, and Uncle Jesse had to work to stay in his saddle. Just as he managed to get the Andalusian under control, however, another warrior grabbed Uncle Jesse's leg, bringing his full weight to bear on the injured cowboy. Uncle Jesse leaned hard against the saddle horn in the opposite direction in a desperate effort to keep from being pulled off, but he knew he couldn't hold on for long with just one arm.

Cragnon swarmed on top of the crates. One of the warriors vaulted onto the war bird Angelina was sitting on, and grabbed her in a choke hold from behind.

Even within the mighty embrace of his assailant, Zeke saw that both Angelina and his uncle were in trouble. He had to free himself, so the teen tried a different tactic. He kicked his opponent's shins with the heels of his boots, connecting twice. The Cragnon loosened his grip just enough for Zeke to regain his footing and slip under the warrior's grasp. "Hang on, Uncle Jesse! Angelina! I'm coming!" he shouted.

Angelina was about to pass out from lack of oxygen, when she saw Slim and Hellfire racing toward her. The big rex charged through the crowd, bowling over Cragnon, like they were corn stalks, and leapt onto the crates, scattering warriors in every direction. The combined weight of Slim and Hellfire caused the wooden contraption tied to the crates to crash to the ground, dragging down the war bird that was still harnessed to it.

Angelina and her attacker hit the ground, and the impact loosened the Cragnon's grip on her throat. Hellfire did the rest, grabbing the attacker's leg in its jaws and jerking him into the air.

She looked up in horror as the rex shook him furiously, before tossing him aside.

Now Slim had their attention. Warriors swarmed around the Rider and his rex, striking from every direction with heavy wooden clubs, trying to knock him off his mount. Slim's long arms were a blur as he deflected most of the enemies' blows using forearms that were still wrapped in heavy chains, and few of the blows reached their targets. In a flash, he plucked a pair of cudgels from the hands of two attackers and struck back at them with savage force.

Hellfire lunged at Shugath's warriors with frightening speed, first in one direction, then the other, and the Cragnon flung themselves backward to avoid being caught in the predator's mighty jaws.

Several assailants rushed in and poked at the rex with long poles to draw its attention, while a comrade attempted to smash the beast's skull. But Hellfire was too canny. When the warrior approached swinging his club, the big rex delivered a fatal bite to his exposed midsection. After that, the group drew back to a safe distance and formed a circle around Slim and his allies.

Uncle Jesse fought off his attacker and positioned Midnight between the crowd and the teens to protect them, as Slim and Hellfire kept Shugath's followers at bay.

"Keep behind me," Uncle Jesse shouted to Angelina and Zeke.

"Where's your rifle?" Zeke cried.

"Lost it," Uncle Jesse replied.

"I should've brought a gun," Zeke muttered.

Shugath's forces had routed the loyalists, and were now regrouping to reclaim their weapons and complete their conquest

Chapter Eleven

of Mujar. The warriors closest to Slim and Hellfire jeered at them while they called for reinforcements with spears, so they could finish off the fight from a safe distance.

From his vantage point atop the altar, Bull saw that his friends were in trouble. He'd done what he could for the chief. Now it was time to help the others. He used one of the ceremonial torches that lined the altar to light the stick of TNT he had hidden inside his clothing.

I knew it was a good idea to hang on to this, he thought as he ran down the stone steps.

A pair of Cragnon tried to tackle him at the bottom, but Bull put his head down and knocked them aside.

"Get down!" he screamed, hurling the dynamite into the air.

Shugath turned in time to see a tiny yellow flame against the night sky, tumbling toward his warriors. Slim forced Hellfire into a sitting position, covering the rex's head with his body, while Uncle Jesse did the same to Midnight, seconds before the blast.

The force of the explosion rocked the battlefield and brought the fighting to a halt, as rocks and debris flew in every direction, and dozens of warriors collapsed. There was a brief period of silence, followed by the moans of the wounded. Slim took advantage of the lull to lead Hellfire and the others across the still-smoking blast site.

When Shugath saw the crater left by the explosion and the bodies of the dead, he ordered his men to retreat. He was ill-prepared to oppose such otherworldly magic and couldn't afford to have his forces suffer further casualties. Besides, his men had already crippled the tribe's ability to defend itself and demoralized its people. They would be too afraid to oppose him, and he would have little trouble taking control of the village upon his return.

Shugath spied the youth who exposed his plan beside the dying chief, and vowed the boy would die a slow, painful death when next their paths crossed. But first the shaman would make absolutely certain that no one followed him and his warriors again.

The shaman spread his arms wide, and his eyes rolled back in his skull as he began to chant an ancient curse. Uncle Jesse and the others stared transfixed as he slipped into a trance. Suddenly a twenty-foot tall wall of flame erupted from the earth, engulfing Shugath and his forces.

"Whoa!" Zeke shouted as he shielded his eyes from the intense light given off by the fire. "Where did that come from?"

"That ain't normal," Bull shouted.

When the flames had died down, Shugath's warriors were gone, and they had taken the crates with them.

Although everyone was relieved the fighting was over, the mood inside the village was somber. No one suspected that Shugath would turn on his own tribe and mastermind the murder of so many innocent Cragnon.

Braknar was carried to his hut and gently laid on his bed. He was dying and knew it. He summoned the youth to his side and asked his name—Kesma. Although the pain was great the chief wanted to thank the boy for his bravery.

Kesma knelt beside the bed, and Braknar placed his hand upon the young Cragnon's head, an honor reserved for only the tribe's greatest warriors. Braknar barely touched Kesma before his hand fell away, and the chief was dead.

Chapter Eleven

"What do we do now?" Kesma asked. "So many warriors who were loyal to Braknar were killed. There aren't enough left to defend the village. What will become of us?"

"The shaman's warriors will return," Slim said quietly. "If the people stay, they will have two choices: bow before Shugath or be killed."

"Someone must warn them," the youth observed.

Slim smiled. "No, someone must *lead* them."

"Then we are doomed," Kesma replied grimly. "There is no one left to lead."

"You can," Slim said.

"*Me?* They won't listen to me. I am just a beggar. How can I lead them?"

"The people need someone brave. It took great courage to come forth against Shugath in defense of a handful of out-landers. And the tribespeople listened. They will do so again. Tell them to gather their belongings, then lead them away from the village. Do it tonight. Those that wish to stay can remain behind."

"No one will choose to follow me," Kesma laughed.

"We will see."

Kesma grew quiet as he thought over Slim's suggestion.

"Will you go with us, Rider?" he finally asked.

"I will go with you, tonight. But I must leave by morning. We have different tasks before us."

"And what is your task, Rider?"

"When a door opens, it is my task to close it."

Kesma's puzzled expression did not go unnoticed by the Tarngatharn.

"You will understand one day," he said "Come. It is time for you to address your people."

As Slim predicted, some of the older Cragnon, and the sick and wounded, refused to leave, insisting it was no more dangerous to live under Shugath's reign than it was to wander the plains until a suitable site to rebuild their village could be found. But the shaman's betrayal had shaken the rest, and they decided to take their chances in the wild. The Cragnon were a hardy race and males were used to living outdoors among the animals. It would be a challenge, but one that they would face together.

Under Kesma's guidance, the people gathered their belongings and whatever provisions they could carry, and loaded them onto war birds. Then they said goodbye to the ancient city and the protection it provided, and marched by moonlight out of its gates across the plains.

Slim on Hellfire rode with Uncle Jesse and Bull up front. Soon, they were joined by Zeke and Angelina.

"We wanted to ask you about some critters we saw in the riverbed," Zeke began.

"We thought they might be related to Hellfire," Angelina continued.

"Tell me about them. What did they look like?" Slim asked, intrigued.

"They were in a group. They looked like Hellfire, only bigger; one, a lot bigger. And there were three babies," Zeke explained.

"And the babies had feathers," Angelina added.

"Where did you see them?" Slim asked.

"A couple of miles upriver from the end of the trail that

Chapter Eleven

Angelina's uncle cut through the forest, where it meets the riverbed," Zeke replied.

Throughout Zeke's recounting of their confrontation with the baryonyx, the flight atop Hellfire, and the unexpected encounter with the pack of feeding Tyranosaurs, which resulted in the teens shocking escape, Slim's expression changed from curious to concerned.

"Try to remember; how many of them were there?" he asked.

"Maybe six or seven," Angelina replied.

"This is not good," the Rider muttered.

"Why?" Angelina said.

"The river cuts across a yerka hunting ground. Yerkas do not generally hunt in packs, but will do so when food is scarce. I am afraid that when they smell the three-horns, they may attack the herd."

Angelina's voice started to rise: "But my mother is with them. And my uncle . . ."

"Is there anything we can do to stop it?" Uncle Jesse interjected.

Slim shook his head. "Not without my *gun*."

"Well, where is it?" Angelina blurted.

"Your uncle took it from me."

"But I don't understand. Why would he . . ." Angelina stopped when she noticed the stern expressions on the faces of Uncle Jesse, Slim and Bull.

Uncle Jesse had avoided telling Angelina how he got shot, but now the time was at hand. He had to tell her the truth before she got her hopes up that her uncle would cooperate.

He asked Zeke and the others for some privacy while he took

her aside. Uncle Jesse minimized her mother's involvement in the telling, and Angelina said nothing as he recounted what actually happened at her uncle's camp.

When he finished, Angelina looked crestfallen. She thanked Uncle Jesse; then walked off to be by herself. Uncle Jesse told Zeke to let her alone, but to keep an eye on her in case she needed anything. After a time, Zeke approached her.

"Hey, you okay?" he asked quietly.

"We can't sit by and do nothing, Zeke," Angelina said firmly.

Zeke looked over his shoulder to make sure no one could overhear. "I know what it does. I got it to work once."

Angelina gave him a puzzled look.

"Slim's *gun*," he explained. "You know, that thing he was talking about."

"You did? How? What does it do?"

"It's kind of hard to say. First there was this light and there was this . . . it was like . . . Maybe I better just tell you what happened."

Zeke recalled how he originally found the device and hid it, and later accidentally turned it on.

"What if we got it back? Do you think you could do it again?" Angelina asked excitedly.

"I think so. I don't know for sure. I only did it once, and then Slim took it back."

"Zeke, if we can get it away from my uncle, we can save my mother."

"Angelina, we can't just ride off."

"We have to! If we don't, they could all be killed. I can't do it by myself, but we can if we work together. We're partners, right?"

Chapter Eleven

"You bet," Zeke agreed without hesitation.

Zeke thought about what Angelina was asking, and what would happen if they skipped out without telling Uncle Jesse. There'd be hell to pay, for sure. But then again, if they managed to get Slim's *gun* back . . .

"Let me sleep on it," he suggested, and they shook.

Meanwhile, Bull was doing some catching up of his own. A lot had happened in the short time that he'd hung suspended over the war bird pit in Mujar, not the least of which was Uncle Jesse's and Slim's escape from D'Allesandro's compound.

When the Rex Rider and the cowboy reached the outskirts of Mujar, Slim used the hollowed-out tooth around his neck to call Hellfire. Imagine their surprise when the rex appeared with Zeke and Angelina on its back, accompanied by Kesma!

Kesma, they learned, had followed Shugath's warriors when they left the village after he'd overheard a couple of them discussing the shaman's plan. He saw Shugath accept the crates of weapons from D'Allesandro's men and was shocked to hear Shugath's promise to help the outlanders.

The young Cragnon was returning to Mujar when he encountered Angelina and Hellfire. Since he didn't know whom of his own people to trust, he sought Angelina's help, thinking she could summon the Rider.

When Slim and Uncle Jesse were reunited with the teens, no one was happier than Kesma. He took the outlanders to the spot where the weapons were hidden and told them what he had overheard. It was then that Slim formulated a plan. After that, they made their way to Mujar to stop Shugath and rescue Bull.

Rex Riders

"That's quite a story," Bull commented. "It's too bad Shugath got away with all those guns, though. That's gonna make him even more dangerous."

"I don't think we have to worry about that," Uncle Jesse said.

"What are you talking about? The crates are gone."

"The kids took the guns out and hid them," Uncle Jesse explained. "All Shugath and his warriors got were a lot of rocks."

Bull burst out laughing. "Well, don't that beat all?"

They rode for several hours before making camp. Zeke and Angelina said nothing more about Angelina's idea to steal away to find her mother and uncle. Zeke wanted to say yes, but he was worried. They couldn't take Hellfire, and the rex was the reason they had gotten to this point safely. If they had struck out on this journey with just their horses, they wouldn't have made it.

To go back to the Sulant without Hellfire—knowing that a pack of rexes were hunting the river—would be suicide. But how could he say no to Angelina? What if the situation was reversed, and he needed her help to save Uncle Jesse? He decided the best thing to do was to sleep on it.

Some time before dawn Uncle Jesse woke up. He knew something wasn't right. Then he noticed an empty spot among the bedrolls. Zeke and Angelina were gone.

Chapter
Twelve

D'Allesandro's men had bedded down the herd for the night and were taking turns keeping watch, when a loud explosion downriver awakened them. D'Allesandro knew instantly that Shugath had begun his attack. It was earlier than expected, but the shaman must have had his reasons. His victory over Braknar would insure the caravan's safe passage past Mujar and provide D'Allesandro with a powerful ally.

D'Allesandro said nothing about the blast during breakfast, and Maria did not bring it up. It was possible she slept through the explosion, but D'Allesandro wasn't interested in finding out, since he had no intention of discussing it with her.

It was just before noon when they reached Mujar, and Cooper signaled the caravan to stop. So far, their journey had been uneventful. If Shugath's warriors had prevailed, it would stay that way. But if something went wrong and Braknar's forces had defeated the shaman's, D'Allesandro and his men were in for a war.

Cooper planned to send a small company ahead in order to determine the status of the Cragnon. The worst case would be if Shugath had failed to overtake Braknar's command and the advance group came under attack from the ramparts overlooking the Sulant. If that happened, they could try running the trikes past the village but they risked losing control of the herd.

Braknar's warriors might choose to confront the caravan in the riverbed. If the chief was foolish enough to try that, then running the trikes downriver would be the perfect strategy. Anyone standing in their way would be trampled. Of course, these strategies would not be needed if everything went according to plan and Shugath was victorious. But D'Allesandro was not one to take anything for granted.

With weapons drawn, the scouts rode ahead. Mujar was quiet and the men didn't see a single face peer over the stone barricades at the top of the bluff. Once past the village, they returned the same way.

Nothing happened.

Cooper ordered the cowboys to make another pass. They came back moments later and reported no sign of resistance by the Cragnon.

"Excellent," D'Allesandro said. "Take us out, Mr. Cooper. From here on we're home free."

Maria remained quiet as the carriage lurched forward. Her mind was filled with thoughts about the exchange of prisoners that resulted in her freedom. At the time she was in such a state of shock, she wasn't completely aware of what was going

Chapter Twelve

on. Now, she wondered what had happened to Bull. He was probably dead. She felt her eyes well up with tears. No, she had to put such thoughts out of her head. She couldn't do a thing to help him, and that was that.

As the trike drive rolled past Mujar, Maria closed her eyes and tried to visualize her daughter, hoping that might lessen the guilt she had over Uncle Jesse's right hand man. But it was impossible.

Cooper was the first to spot the remains of the lambeosaurus that the Tyrannosaur pack had downed several days earlier. He signaled the men to stop while he rode ahead to take a look. There wasn't much left of the giant beast. After the rexes ate their fill of muscle and entrails, and abandoned the carcass, smaller dinosaurs took their turn, followed by a parade of reptiles and insects. What little remained was a mess, but at least it didn't smell. When Cooper returned he rode straight to see D'Allesandro.

"What is it, Mr. Cooper?" D'Allesandro asked.

"Something I think you and the Professor ought to take a look at," Cooper replied.

D'Allesandro's smile hid his concern. He knew that if Cooper insisted he take a look at something it signaled trouble.

"What is it?" Maria asked.

"Ah, it's nothing, ma'am," Cooper lied. "Just some dead critter I thought the Professor might get a kick out of taking a look at. And Mr. D'Allesandro might want to add the skull to his bone collection."

"Sounds interesting," D'Allesandro said, seeing right through Cooper's subterfuge. "Come join us, won't you, Professor? It will give us both a chance to stretch our legs."

The second D'Allesandro saw the size of the carcass, he understood Cooper's concern. Kornbluth's sigh confirmed his suspicions that all was not well.

"What do you think, Professor?" D'Allesandro asked as they walked around the remains.

"The shape of the skull gives it away," Kornbluth answered. The professor was so caught up in the excitement of the find that any worry he may have had was temporarily replaced by his overwhelming curiosity as a scientist. "This dinosaur was a member of the group we saw yesterday. Notice the bony crest here at the top. This is the source of the sound we heard. Quite amazing, really."

D'Allesandro nodded. "Fascinating. Any idea what killed it?"

The Professor stopped at different points to examine the remains, poking at it with a long stick. A swarm of insects took flight and had to be beaten off.

"Look at this area," the Professor observed, pointing to a section of splintered backbone. "This animal was struck along the spine and here at the base of the neck. Judging from the extent of the damage and the size of the lambeosaur, I would say the creature that did this was extremely large. If I had to make a guess, I'd say it was an adult tyrannosaurus."

D'Allesandro's men had killed, and been killed by rexes since they arrived in this place and were familiar with the great beasts' hunting prowess and killing power. They had seen them attack and kill adult trikes on the plains, and heard the horrible crunching sound of bones being crushed between their mighty jaws. The war birds were a deadly nuisance, to be sure,

Chapter Twelve

but the tyrannosaurs were a different kind of problem; a thirty ton kind of problem.

"How many animals are we talking about?" Cooper asked.

"I'm not sure," Kornbluth replied.

Cooper frowned. "Give me your best guess. The boys need to know what they're up against."

"A lot of the flesh is gone. Does that tell you anything about the number of predators in the group?" D'Allesandro pressed.

"Not really. These woods are full of scavengers that would have fed on the remains long after the tyrannosaurs had finished. They would have stripped the flesh off its bones. What you see here is not indicative of what the rexes ate. I simply can't tell you anything more based upon these remains."

"Mr. Cooper, would you check for tracks?" D'Allesandro suggested with an exasperated sigh.

"I'll get Frenchy up here. It'll give him something useful to do for a change."

Maria joined them. "You've been here a long time. What's wrong?"

"Something killed the animal that is lying here, and there's a remote chance that it's still in the area," D'Allesandro replied.

"When you say 'something,' what do you mean?"

"A predator; a big one," volunteered the Professor, nervously.

"Then we have to get out of here," Maria said, her voice rising.

"Yes, we know that," D'Allesandro said. "Now, try to remain calm."

"I am calm," Maria snapped.

Cooper rode back to the men and called for Jean-Claude Pinchot. Although Cooper and Jean-Claude didn't get along, the French-Canadian trapper had proven to be valuable to the Professor and D'Allesandro in their field work. Jean-Claude wasn't a scientist and didn't know anything about prehistoric animals, but his knowledge of the habits of North American wildlife was vast, and his instincts concerning dinosaur behavior were right more often than wrong.

Cooper led the wily trapper to the area surrounding the kill to search for tracks, while D'Allesandro continued to question Professor Kornbluth.

"How old would you estimate the kill is?" D'Allesandro asked.

"Two or three days. No more than that." The professor bit his lip and looked around nervously. "How much farther are we going?"

D'Allesandro was deliberately vague. "Not far. Ah, Mr. Cooper, what have you learned?"

"It's hard to say. Frenchy spotted a lot of tracks."

"Oui," Jean-Claude agreed. "I counted at least six of these, how you say, rexes. What I cannot tell is if they were here at the same time or different times."

"How big were they?" D'Allesandro asked.

"I saw the tracks of a tiny baby and a grownup mademoiselle. The big one, she could be fifteen meters long."

"Meters? What the heck is a meter? Would you talk English, Frenchy?" Cooper ordered.

"Never mind, Mr. Cooper. I understand," D'Allesandro interrupted before turning to Kornbluth. "Professor, what is the likelihood they will attack the herd?"

The Professor was staring into space and didn't seem to hear

Chapter Twelve

D'Allesandro. At the moment, all he knew was that he wanted to be back safely in Dos Locos. If he had to die, he wanted to do it in Texas, not here.

"Professor, did you hear me?"

"I'm sorry. Yes, yes, I heard you. I'm not sure. I don't know their habits well enough. I have seen lone tyrannosaurs stalk herds of triceratops and attack from the rear, but they usually target the vulnerable—the young, sick, old or injured. They're patient and smart. But I've not seen them hunt as a pack, so I have no idea how they would behave as such."

"Then guess," D'Allesandro said sharply.

The Professor swallowed. "Well, I imagine they would follow the same pattern as other animals which hunt in packs: smaller members would try to segregate a member of the group and drive it toward an adult lying in wait. But it's all just conjecture."

"What would the herd most likely do if that were to occur?" D'Allesandro pressed.

"On the plains the males would try to defend the group, but this riverbed would make that difficult. They might just run."

"A stampede," Cooper said grimly. "Sounds like fun."

A stampede would be a disaster, D'Allesandro thought. *It would destroy everything I've worked for.*

"What if the men fire their guns into the woods to drive the rexes off?" D'Allesandro continued. "Do you think the sound will frighten the triceratops? I don't want them upset."

Kornbluth stared blankly at D'Allesandro.

D'Allesandro stepped closer until he and the Professor were nose to nose. "Give me your assessment, Professor. Which risk is greater? Are the trikes more likely to panic from an attack by a pack of rexes or the sound of guns being fired?"

"I—I don't know," Kornbluth stammered. "I just don't understand why this is happening now, that's all."

"Go back to the stagecoach, Professor," D'Allesandro ordered in disgust. His patience had worn out. He scanned the woods and considered his options. The fact that they hadn't actually seen any rexes meant nothing. The great beasts surely knew where the trikes were, unless they moved upriver to follow the lambeosaurs.

A sudden commotion down the line interrupted the rancher's thoughts.

"Someone's coming," one of the men shouted.

D'Allesandro looked at Cooper, but Cooper had already drawn his gun from its holster.

The last two people anyone expected to see riding toward them were Angelina and Zeke Calhoun. The teens rode together on one of the horses Uncle Jesse took from D'Allesandro's compound. Zeke felt terrible taking it without asking, but riding into D'Allesandro's caravan on war birds would have gotten him and Angelina shot the minute they stepped into view of Cooper's men. Showing up on horseback tied into the story they planned to tell D'Allesandro and Maria about how they got there.

Maria shrieked with joy and ran toward her daughter. Angelina jumped from the horse into her mother's arms. Tears of happiness streamed down their cheeks as they hugged each other.

Zeke was happy for Angelina and started to get a little choked up until he noticed Cooper staring at him, and all of those warm feelings gave way to cold fear.

Chapter Twelve

"I was so afraid I'd never see you again," Angelina said.

"How did you get here?" Maria asked. "How did you find us?"

"Yes, tell us," D'Allesandro said with an icy touch of menace in his voice. "Tell us everything."

Angelina didn't hesitate. "After the ranch was attacked and mother was kidnapped, I rode to the Double R and asked Mr. McCain for help. He and his hired hand, Mr. Whitman, promised they'd look for mother. When we didn't hear back from them, Stumpy—I mean, Mr. Gibbons—was going to go, but he hurt his hip. So he sent Zeke and me to look for you."

"Did anyone else come with you?" D'Allesandro asked.

"No, just us," Angelina answered.

"That was extremely brave of both of you," D'Allesandro remarked. "Mr. Calhoun, did you find your uncle and his friend?"

"No, sir," Zeke said, clearing his throat. "We rode upriver and camped overnight a little ways from here."

"When we heard you coming, we were afraid, so we hid until we saw who it was," Angelina added quickly.

"I was hoping you could help me find him," Zeke said.

D'Allesandro looked at Zeke and then Angelina. "We'll organize a search party immediately."

Zeke smiled. "Thank you, sir. I'm grateful for the help. I'm really worried about them."

"Of course you are. I understand completely. These forests are filled with all kinds of dangerous creatures. We were just examining the remains of one such beast," D'Allesandro said, patting Zeke on the back. "If your uncle and Mr. Whitman are in these woods, we'll find them. I'm once again in your debt, young man, for taking such good care of my niece."

"I am too," Maria said, choking back tears.

Angelina rushed to D'Allesandro and hugged him. "Thank you, uncle. Thank you."

D'Allesandro returned her embrace weakly. "Mr. Cooper, come with me. We'll send a group of men to search upriver for any sign of Mr. McCain and his partner."

"Got it, boss," Cooper said. "We'll find them."

D'Allesandro freed himself from his niece's embrace and walked back to the stagecoach with Cooper.

"We'll take the boy with us," D'Allesandro said, once he was sure he and Cooper were far enough away not to be overheard.

"Why bother?" Cooper asked. "Why not leave him here? Tell him his uncle is upriver and send him on his way. We'll never see him again."

"No, we're going to bring him back to Dos Locos with us," D'Allesandro ordered. "He and my niece will tell the townspeople we saved them. That way, no one will ask any questions.

"Have the men keep an eye on him, though," D'Allesandro added. "If he does anything suspicious, let me know right away. But don't do anything without speaking to me first. I'll handle it. Understood?"

"Where's he gonna ride? With you?" Cooper said with a laugh. The stagecoach was spacious with three people. But adding two more bodies was going to make it crowded.

"He'll ride with the men. The last thing I need is two sweaty teenagers leaning on me."

"I'll take good care of him," Cooper sneered.

"Make sure he doesn't have an *accident*, Mr. Cooper," D'Allesandro said firmly.

Chapter Twelve

"Don't worry. He'll make it back alive."

"And in one piece. With all of his fingers and toes."

Angelina pointed to the body of the lambeosaurus. "Mother, what is this thing?" she cried in mock alarm.

"It's nothing to be afraid of," her mother said reassuringly, as she embraced her daughter. "You're safe with me now."

As Maria led Angelina away from the remains, Angelina looked back over her shoulder at Zeke and winked. Neither one had said a word, but they both knew what the other was thinking: *so far, so good.* The next step would be to let her mother in on their plan. But how and when?

"Come with me, Calhoun," Cooper said. "You'll be riding with the boys."

Zeke said nothing as he rode along the riverbed behind Cooper. The combination of Cooper and all the trikes was giving Zeke a bad case of déjà vu. The last time he saw a three-horn was in Dos Locos on the same day that Cooper threatened him in the alley. Zeke was hoping the ornery cuss had forgotten the episode.

Cooper pointed to a teenager not that much older than Zeke who was killing time whittling a stick with his knife. From the look of his clothing, Zeke figured the teen to be a vaquero. Stumpy had told Zeke stories about vaqueros— Mexican cowboys—and their horsemanship. But he'd never met one until now.

"You stay by him," Cooper ordered.

Zeke was about to turn his horse toward the teen, when Cooper grabbed the reins. "I got my eye on you Calhoun," he added ominously. "Don't make me shove you in front of one of them long-horns."

"Mr. Cooper, sir, are the men going to look for my uncle?" Zeke asked timidly.

Cooper had to stifle a laugh. "Oh, yeah. I almost forgot about that," he said, dropping the reins. "I'll take care of it myself, Calhoun. I wouldn't want anything to happen to the town hero."

With Angelina at her side, Maria was more relaxed. "You look worried, Professor," Maria observed. "Is everything alright?"

D'Allesandro narrowed his eyes at Kornbluth, who understood the look and kept his mouth shut. "The Professor is not feeling well, my dear. It's the heat, I'm sure."

"Yes, the heat," the Professor agreed weakly and started to bite his fingernails.

Cooper spread the word that the men were to keep watch for the rexes. If they saw anything, they were to fire their weapons and drive them off. None of the men acted concerned. There was strength in numbers, and the group was well armed. Nevertheless, as the trikes lumbered down the riverbed the men paid less and less attention to watching the herd and more time staring into the woods along the river banks.

Then the gunfire started.

At first, there were just a few sporadic shots, but soon more and more men on both sides of the river were firing into the woods. No one could tell what anyone was shooting at, but every time a gunshot was heard, the anxiety level went up a notch. Had the man who fired actually seen something? Or was it just a false alarm? No one knew for sure.

Chapter Twelve

"What are they shooting at?" Zeke asked nervously.

"They're looking for los depredadores—those big meat eaters," the young vaquero answered. He didn't look the least bit worried and hadn't joined in the shooting. "Word is that a bunch of them may be in these woods. Where's your gun, amigo?"

"I lost it," Zeke lied. "In the woods a ways back."

"That's not good! Take this," the vaquero said, handing Zeke a pistol. "You may need it. Just make sure you don't lose it, okay? That's my lucky pistol. My initials are carved on the handle. See?"

Carved into the bottom of the ivory grip were the initials "R.R." What a strange coincidence, thought Zeke. Same as my uncle's ranch. Zeke wasn't superstitious, but he wondered if that meant something.

"I won't lose it," Zeke said quickly. "You sure you don't need it?"

"Yeah, I've got a rifle. You hold onto it. My name's Roberto Rodriquez, but folks call me Ringo. What do they call you?"

"Zeke. It's short for Ezekiel. Thanks for letting me borrow your gun, Ringo." Zeke examined the pistol like it was the most precious thing he'd ever held.

Ringo noticed Zeke staring at the gun. "Look okay to you?"

"Oh, yeah," Zeke said, sticking the pistol inside his belt at the back of his pants. "This is just fine."

Angelina sat next to her mother and smiled. She avoided looking at her uncle because every time she did, a rage started to build inside her. He had lied to her and Zeke about seeing Uncle Jesse and Bull, and done it so smoothly that, if she hadn't know better, she would have believed every word.

Rex Riders

As the miles went by, Angelina and Zeke thought about when they would have an opportunity to speak to each other. Surely, the caravan would stop at some point to give the horses and dinosaurs time to rest, and everyone else time to respond to nature's call.

After several hours, the convoy reached the last leg of their journey home: the trail into the forest that led from the Sulant to the transporter. While the dinosaurs drank and rested, Cooper sent a team of men ahead to secure the log corral that encircled the machine. They would be responsible for maneuvering groups of trikes onto the platform to be sent back to Dos Locos and controlling the trikes that were waiting inside the pen for their turn to make the trip. Cooper also repositioned the wagon with the Gatling gun at the back of the convoy to defend it from an attack from the rear.

The logs that ringed the transporter protected the forward end of the caravan, leaving cowboys to patrol the sides of the trail that led from the river to the pen. In theory, they had everything covered.

Cooper rode up and down both sides of the herd chatting with his men and making sure everyone stayed on their toes. They were almost home. This was no time to let their guard down.

As D'Allesandro's ranch boss galloped past Zeke, he felt Cooper's eyes boring into him and was sure Cooper knew he was carrying a gun. Zeke breathed a sigh of relief once Cooper was out of sight, and took the opportunity to ride to the front of the herd to speak with Angelina and her mother before the caravan started moving again.

For her part, Angelina told her mother she wanted to stretch

Chapter Twelve

her legs and then made up a story about how she was nervous going alone. "Stay with me," she implored as she pulled her mother by the arm.

When they were a safe distance from the stagecoach, Angelina looked her mother in the eye and whispered, "Where is the Rider's device?"

Maria was startled by the question. "What are you talking about?"

"We're all in danger, mother. I know what's going on. There's a pack of rexes hunting these woods. I saw them."

"You saw them?" Maria said, panicked. "When? Where are they?"

"A few days ago. The only way to stop them is with that metal thing that Uncle Dante stole from the Rider. Where is it?"

Maria looked around nervously to see if anyone was listening. Then she pulled Angelina further into the woods. "I don't understand."

"Mr. McCain is alive and so is Mr. Whitman," Angelina started to explain.

"How do you know all this?" Maria asked, shaking her head in disbelief.

They heard D'Allesandro calling for them and turned in the direction of his voice.

"Mother, there isn't time. Tell me where it is!"

"He's carrying it in his jacket. Please don't say anything. Promise me."

"Does he have a gun?"

"I don't know. Maybe."

Angelina released her mother's arm. "We have to go back."

Rex Riders

As they stepped out of the woods, Angelina noticed Zeke looking for her. She also saw her uncle standing by the carriage with his hands on his hips, eyeing them angrily. Zeke rode over to Angelina and her mother with a stern look on his face. He leaned over and pointed toward the caravan as if to convey that he was telling the pair they were holding things up.

"It's in his jacket. But he might have a gun," Angelina said in a low voice, before waving to her uncle.

Zeke sat back up on his horse and said in a loud voice, "Well, I'll see you back at the ranch." Then he tipped his hat to Angelina's mother and galloped away to retake his position.

D'Allesandro studied the faces of his sister and niece as they returned to the carriage. There was something strange about Maria's expression. Try as she might, Maria could never hide anything from her brother.

"Uncle Dante, can Zeke go with us?" Angelina pleaded.

"Mr. Calhoun will go with the next group," D'Allesandro replied pleasantly. He had already decided the teens should be kept apart until he figured out what they were up to.

"Why can't he go with us?" Angelina insisted.

"He'll go when I say he goes," D'Allesandro said sharply.

Angelina folder her arms across her chest and shot him a nasty look but said nothing in reply.

Leading the way, D'Allesandro's stagecoach was first to break out of the forest into the clearing surrounding the transporter. As the driver maneuvered the stage to the foot of a ramp, a group of cowboys herded a half dozen trikes into position to follow. The log posts surrounding the transporter helped

Chapter Twelve

contain any triceratops that tried to wander off. The men weren't too worried about these mavericks. They weren't going anywhere and could be moved into place later.

"They're ready, Mr. D'Allesandro!" Cooper shouted.

"Then it's time to say goodbye, Mr. Cooper. We'll see you in a few hours."

Cooper raised his arm over his head and whistled. The cowboys positioned by the walkway did likewise. Then Cooper dropped his arm.

With a hearty *"Yee-ha!"* the driver snapped the reins, and the stagecoach lurched forward, as the horses began their climb up the ramp. D'Allesandro counted to himself . . . *one . . . two . . .*

The destruction of the metal sauropods had slowed the platform down dramatically and it took much longer to generate the energy field that was necessary for it to function, giving D'Allesandro's men plenty of extra time to move the trikes into position.

D'Allesandro smiled as the generators fired up. "Right on schedule."

Maria covered her ears. "I forgot how loud this thing was."

Angelina bit her lip. She wondered what Zeke was doing and whether he was okay. Maybe they would all make it across safely after all.

D'Allesandro had gambled that the beasts would tolerate the noise from the generators because the trike in Dos Locos had made the trip, but no one had tested the theory on a group of the beasts until now. D'Allesandro drummed his fingers against his leg anxiously. "Almost there," he whispered to himself.

The stagecoach crested the platform and the driver shouted to a cowboy leading the first line of trikes. "Looking good!"

The driver maneuvered the stagecoach to the middle of the platform, while the men driving the trikes positioned the creatures around its edge, doing their best to keep them clustered together. The idea behind keeping the carriage centered was to ensure it wouldn't be knocked over the side if something excited the trikes. But it also meant the stagecoach was cut off from a speedy exit should something go wrong.

Despite the great size of the triceratops and the number of the beasts driven onto the machine, there was still plenty of room for the coach. One of the cowboys on the platform shouted down to Cooper that there was room for more trikes, but Cooper waved his arms to signal *no*. This was a mixed load of people, vehicles and animals. It was too dangerous to crowd them. He had already told the men to keep the first couple of trips light to get a routine going. He wasn't going to take any chances by rushing things. There was plenty of time to get all of the creatures over.

The men on the ground stared at the platform as it continued to power up. Most of them had made only a single trip, and it was such an incredible sight that they couldn't tear their eyes away.

D'Allesandro stepped outside the carriage.

"Where are you going?" Maria asked.

"I want to savor the moment," he explained. "You're welcome to join me. What about you Professor?"

"I'll stay inside, thank you," Kornbluth replied.

Maria joined D'Allesandro. It was all happening just as he'd planned. There were a halfdozen triceratops on the platform now, and even a number this small was enough to start a herd as long

Chapter Twelve

as there was a breeding pair in the group.

D'Allesandro patted his jacket pocket to make sure the Tarngatharn force generator was still there. Whatever powers the device held, they'd soon be back at the Crossed Swords outside the grasp of his enemies. The thousands of man-hours and dozens of lives lost on both worlds was about to payoff.

D'Allesandro suspected that this was how his ancestors felt when they brought their treasures back to Spain from North America centuries before. And now it was happening all over again: the beginning of a new era of exploration and conquest in the tradition of Cortez and Pizarro. Where it would all lead was impossible to tell.

"That's something, ain't it, Zeke?" Ringo said, as he looked up at the platform.

Zeke didn't answer. He caught a glimpse of something on the edge of the forest beyond the perimeter of the log corral, but a trike moved into his field of vision before he could make out what it was. When the animal moved, there was nothing there, and Zeke wondered if he had imagined it. After all, everyone's nerves were on edge.

"Something wrong, amigo?"

"I'm not sure," Zeke replied as he stared into the distance. "We might have been followed."

Zeke looked around at all of the faces staring at the platform, and it dawned on him that no one was watching the woods!

"Ringo, the depredadores we were worried about, they're here. You have to get out of here now."

"Where? Where are they?" Ringo asked, reaching for his gun.

"I'm sorry, Ringo, but I have to go. I'll meet up with you later.

I'll give you your gun back, I promise."

Zeke maneuvered his horse through the men and dinosaurs awaiting their turn at the base of the transporter, but Cooper blocked his way up the ramp.

"Where do you think you're going?" Cooper demanded above the din of the transporter and the dinosaurs.

"I forgot to tell Angelina something," Zeke replied.

"You'll wait your turn. Now, get back." Cooper growled, shoving Zeke so hard the teen almost fell off his horse.

Zeke looked at the stagecoach and then at Cooper. *It's now or never*, he thought. He started to pull his horse away just enough for Cooper to lose interest and return his attention to the transporter. Then Zeke whipped around and kicked his ride into high gear, galloping past Cooper up the walkway.

"Calhoun!" Cooper shouted.

Zeke pierced the veil of power and saw D'Allesandro and Maria standing in its center. As he jostled around the triceratops, he checked to make sure Ringo's gun was still at his back. He'd need it in a few seconds.

Cooper was close behind. That snot-nosed kid was finally going to get what was coming to him just like his uncle had, and this time there wasn't anybody to stop him.

"We'll be home soon," D'Allesandro remarked. "And all of this will be a distant memory."

D'Allesandro thought he heard someone call his name. He turned to see Zeke riding toward him with Cooper close behind. Before D'Allesandro could respond, however, the energy field collapsed and everyone on the platform vanished.

* * *

Chapter Twelve

Slim, Uncle Jesse and Bull were riding down the Sulant when the bracelet on the Rex Rider's wrist started to beep. The sound could have meant that the force generator was disabled or destroyed, but Slim knew better. D'Allesandro had crossed over to Texas and the generator was now outside the range of the tracking device! Slim let loose with one of the animalistic roars that scared the bejeezus out of anyone nearby.

Uncle Jesse glanced back at Bull and raised an eyebrow; someone was in for a world of trouble.

Zeke's and Cooper's horses were in full stride as their atoms were blasted apart. When they re-materialized in Dos Locos, Zeke's horse stumbled slightly but remained erect, while Cooper's fell, and he was tossed to the platform.

The men stationed in the cave were caught completely unawares. They expected D'Allesandro's stagecoach and a dozen or so triceratops, but not Cooper chasing some kid on horseback. They froze when they saw Zeke draw Ringo's gun and level it at their boss.

"What's going on?" Maria exclaimed when she saw the weapon in Zeke's hand.

Zeke had never pointed a gun at anyone in his life, and his hand was shaking so much he could hardly control it. This was exactly what Stumpy was afraid of! A man never pointed a gun at anyone unless he had grounds to use it and wasn't afraid to pull the trigger.

"I need that thing you're carrying Mr. D'Allesandro. And I need it now. Give it to me."

"I don't know what you're talking about."

"The device you took from the Rider. It doesn't belong to you. Give it here."

"And what if I don't?"

Zeke gulped. "Then I'll shoot."

Cooper signaled his men to stand down, as he struggled to his feet and strode toward Zeke. Calhoun had defied him and caused him and his horse to take a tumble. And now the teen was pointing a gun at Mr. D'Allesandro. If it was anyone else, Cooper would have shot him dead on the spot. But in this case it would be more fun to terrorize the little whelp. Besides, he was positive Zeke would never shoot. The teen didn't have the guts.

Zeke saw Cooper in the corner of his eye, but was so frightened he didn't dare point the gun directly at D'Allesandro's ornery ranch hand. Zeke just waved it around in his general direction. "Get back," he ordered.

"Give me that gun," Cooper snarled. It was an order and a threat rolled into one. Cooper's tone confirmed what Zeke already knew: it didn't matter whether he handed over the gun or not. Either way he was in for a beating.

"Those big critters you were looking for? I saw one of them. It was near the tree line," Zeke said, his voice rising. "They followed the trikes. They're going to attack!"

Cooper was circling now. "You're crazy, Calhoun. They didn't follow us. No one saw a thing."

Zeke turned to D'Allesandro and pleaded, "They're there. I swear it. I need the thing you took from Slim. If we don't go back your men are dead. It's the only chance to stop those critters before they—"

Cooper lunged at Zeke while the teen's head was turned and

Chapter Twelve

grabbed the barrel of the gun. He twisted it up and back, so the trigger finger was bent in the most painful position, and Zeke screamed.

"Let go or I'll snap your finger."

Zeke released the gun, and Cooper smashed him across the face with it. He fell to the platform, unconscious. Angelina started for him, but her mother held her back.

Cooper looked down at Zeke and kicked him in the gut for good measure.

"Stop it!" Angelina screamed.

Cooper looked up with a big smile on his face and laughed. "You're all safe, now. He's out cold."

He turned to his men who hadn't moved a muscle. "Don't just stand there," he sneered. "Get him off here. We'll deal with him later."

"Wait," D'Allesandro said. "He said he saw something."

"He was lying, Mr. D'Allesandro," Cooper insisted impatiently. "None of us saw anything, and neither did the men. He just wants that thing so he can give it back to his buddy. He doesn't know he's wasting his time."

"He needs it to save your men!" Angelina shouted. "They're all going to die back there."

D'Allesandro stared at Angelina. "What do you mean 'he needs it'?"

"When Zeke found the Rider he found the device with him. He figured out how it works."

"You can't be suggesting he knows how to operate it," D'Allesandro scoffed. "He's nothing more than a thick-headed mule, like his uncle."

"He's a lot smarter than you think. Let him go!" Angelina cried.

This news was literally beyond belief. D'Allesandro stared at Zeke in amazement. "Who would have dreamed that the answer was right here under my nose," he muttered under his breath.

He looked at Angelina. "If you're lying to me, Master Calhoun will pay a heavy price."

"What do you want me to do with him?" Cooper asked.

"Tie him up and put him in the stagecoach. When he awakens, I'll deal with him."

"If you say so," Cooper said, disappointed.

D'Allesandro started back to the stagecoach, but stopped and looked at his sister and niece. Angelina and Maria stepped back as D'Allesandro instead walked toward them with a menacing expression on his face. He knew they were up to something when he saw them together on the side of the river.

"Which of you told him I had it?" D'Allesandro demanded. Then he fixed his eyes on his sister. "You told him."

"No, Dante, I never said a word. I don't know how he knew." D'Allesandro knew she was lying. "I'll deal with you later."

Angelina stepped between them. "Don't you threaten my mother."

D'Allesandro slapped her across the face. "How dare you! You will speak when you are spoken to. You and your meddlesome mother have been nothing but trouble since the moment you arrived."

When Zeke came to, he was in a great deal of pain. He had a splitting headache, a throbbing nose, and his stomach hurt from

Chapter Twelve

where Cooper kicked him. To make matters worse, his hands were numb from being tied behind his back. He opened his eyes to find he was inside D'Allesandro's stagecoach sitting across from a smiling, middle-aged man that he didn't recognize.

"Who are you?" Zeke asked.

"I am Professor Kornbluth."

"Nice to meet you, Professor. I'd shake your hand except for this rope around my wrists. Could you do me a big favor and untie me?"

"I'm afraid I can't do that."

"Yeah, that's what I thought you'd say. Where's Angelina?"

"Outside with her mother. They went for a walk."

Zeke leaned his head against the seat cushion and looked out the window. He had no idea how much time had passed. Where was Angelina? What happened to Uncle Jesse and Bull? And what was going to happen to him?

Outside the window triceratops grazed contentedly on Texas grass in the warm sunshine. D'Allesandro's men had made a lot of progress while Zeke was unconscious. Every so often a trike would raise its head and bellow.

D'Allesandro stood at the edge of the herd talking to several cowboys on horseback. There was no sign of Cooper, and Zeke couldn't see Angelina or her mother.

"Do you know if anything happened back there?" Zeke asked, turning his attention back to Professor Kornbluth.

"As far as I know, everything is fine."

"Where's Cooper?"

"I think he went back."

"Good. Maybe he'll stay there."

The Professor laughed. "He frightens me too, and I'm a lot older than you are. I overheard you say that you understand how to operate the device."

"Yep," Zeke replied, trying to sound confident.

"My hat's off to you, young man. That's quite an accomplishment."

"It's no big deal."

"But it is. It's kept you alive. If it were up to Mr. Cooper, you'd be dead by now. A word to the wise young man: *cooperate*. If you don't, things will get ugly. Trust me; I know."

D'Allesandro started walking back to the stagecoach. Zeke felt himself becoming more and more nervous, so he closed his eyes and pretended to be asleep.

"It's a perfect day," a cheerful D'Allesandro said, stepping inside the cabin. "We'll be moving shortly."

"Do you think it's safe? Shouldn't we wait for the rest of the men?" Kornbluth asked.

"No need my friend. According to the men, the herd is adjusting well. They're calm and grazing."

"Good show," the Professor replied.

"You'll be joining us for dinner, Professor. We're having a picnic. And I believe steak is in order; *beef* steak, that is. I don't know about you, but I've quite enough triceratops for awhile. How is Mr. Calhoun? Is he awake, yet?"

Zeke cleared his throat. "Yeah, I'm awake."

Maria and Angelina squeezed into the opposite side of the coach.

"How do you feel?" Angelina asked, relieved to hear Zeke's voice.

Chapter Twelve

"I'm okay."

The stagecoach lurched into motion. With trikes as far as the eye could see, it was difficult for Zeke to tell exactly where they were headed. Although the teen could see out the side window, he couldn't tell where the stage was in relation to the trikes or what route they were taking.

"Where are we going?" Zeke asked.

"Back to my ranch," D'Allesandro replied pleasantly. "I realize you may be in a great deal of discomfort, but it's not that far. I'm hoping that when we get there, you'll tell me everything you know about the Rex Rider and his device. I offered your uncle a reward for it not too long ago when he paid us a visit. If you cooperate with me, the reward is yours."

"What if don't?"

"Then I will have you arrested. You attacked my sister and me with a gun, and threatened to shoot me if I didn't hand over something that doesn't belong to you. That is attempted armed robbery. If it hadn't been for Mr. Cooper—"

"Something you stole." Angelina interrupted, her voice dripping with sarcasm.

Maria elbowed her daughter in the ribs. "Stop it," she demanded through tightly pursed lips.

Angelina was livid, but when she saw her mother's anguished expression, she decided to say nothing further. This wasn't the time. She'd figure out what to do, once they arrived home.

Several hours had gone by, and Ringo was still puzzling over Zeke's abrupt decision to ride onto the platform. As much as the vaquero wanted to think otherwise, everything pointed to Zeke making up the story about the rexes stalking the trike drive in order to run off with Ringo's lucky gun.

Ringo couldn't blame Zeke for wanting to get back home on the first trip out of there. Zeke wasn't one of the crew, yet Cooper put him to work and gave him a hard time. Then Cooper made him wait to return home. Zeke should definitely have been treated more like a guest than a hired hand.

Still, Ringo was annoyed that his reward for doing a good deed was having his pistol stolen. But such was the life of a cowboy. Somebody was always trying to take advantage of your good nature and generosity. The funny part was, if a similar situation were to come up again someday, he'd probably handle it the same way.

The tyrannosaur pack began stalking the convoy soon after it passed Mujar. Triceratops were a favorite prey of rexes, and this herd of three-horned beasts looked no different to them than any other. The presence of humans riding horses added an element of danger and unfamiliarity, but the rexes were too hungry to let that stop them.

The predators' mottled tan hides made them practically invisible in the woods as the female led the pack downriver, waiting for just the right moment to strike. The number of trikes had steadily shrunk as the creatures were transported to Earth, but so had the number of men and vehicles that protected them. And now, conditions finally looked right.

Denny Wilson was working the trail when he noticed a change in the trike's behavior and rode over to talk to Les Conrad about it. Throughout the trip the animals had maintained a respectable

Chapter Twelve

distance apart from one another, but now they were bunching up and bumping into each other, as an unseen fear spread from one animal to the next. It was the creatures' natural instinct to move away from danger, and they couldn't help but be in each other's way as they tried to maneuver away from the forest along both sides of the trail. And when they knocked together, they became surly and aggressive, making them a danger to the other members of the herd and the cowboys watching over them.

Les agreed with Denny that the herd was acting funny. He was also concerned, because he'd lost sight of Bill Murphy who was working the opposite side of the trail.

"I'll go see if I can find him," Denny volunteered.

"I don't know about that," Les said as he scanned the woods. "Something doesn't feel right."

"There you go. That's another reason to check up on him. I'll see if I can get across and ask him if he's seen anything."

Les shook his head. Trying to cross a riverbed packed tight with unruly triceratops was a stupid thing to do, but every cowboy loved a challenge, especially one that involved horsemanship, and the high degree of danger made the trip that much more exciting.

The dinosaurs were generally okay with the men riding in their midst, but Denny found the trip to the opposite side much harder than usual. After several near misses, he made it and was relieved to see Bill in the distance. But just as Denny started waving to him, a twenty-foot tall tyrannosaur dove out of the woods and plucked Bill off his horse before he knew what hit him.

Another even larger rex emerged, followed by a third and

they looked straight at Denny. Denny remained calm and drew his gun to alert the other men by firing a warning shot into the air. But an angry male trike rammed his horse to the ground as the herd began scrambling to get away from the rexes. In seconds both horse and rider were dead, trampled by thousands of pounds of triceratops gone amok.

By attacking the middle of the convoy, the tyrannosaurs split the trikes and drove them in opposite directions, either toward the transporter or back toward the Sulant. The forest wasn't their natural environment and woods were difficult for them to traverse because of their size.

At the rear of the caravan the driver of the gun wagon was sitting with his hat pulled over his eyes when the two yoked trikes tethered to the wagon began to struggle against each other. The driver pulled the reins to control them as the wagon rocked from side to side, but the beasts were caught up in the fear that had overtaken the herd and wouldn't obey his commands.

As the triceratops tried to turn around and head toward the river, the combination of the yoke, the wagon, and the stampeding trikes that were pushing against them caused the vehicle to get stuck and block the trail. The driver yelled for help as the sheer weight of the beasts pressing against the wagon caused it to buckle and shatter, and the men on the wagon disappeared under a sea of trikes.

Up by the transporter, the platform had powered down and was temporarily inoperable while the cowboys back in Texas moved the latest load off to prepare for the next group. It was a safety feature built into the operation of the machine, and it wouldn't restart until all of the trikes were removed from

Chapter Twelve

the platform on the opposite end.

The triceratops on the loading side were becoming more agitated by the moment as the wave of hysteria from the tyrannosaur attacks further back worked its way forward. At the base of the walkway the beasts became more difficult to keep in line, and the men were growing uneasy. They moved many of the animals into the crude corral that encircled the transporter, but that area was now full.

The logs that made up the pen had been driven into the ground and braced for stability, but they were never intended to be strong enough to withstand the impact of a full grown trike smashing into them. As long as the animals remained calm the pen would hold, and the cowboys could maintain order. If things got out of control, there was enough distance between the logs to let the men escape on their horses and ride on the outside.

Two cowboys circled the log corral looking for an opening amid the roiling trikes to jump back inside, when they spotted the big female tyrannosaur burst from the tree line and charge across the clearing toward the pen. Any order that was left before the big rex appeared was now gone. The trikes' instincts took over, and they were consumed with trying to avoid an attack that would be there in seconds.

The big predator slammed into the log posts, sending two of them hurtling through the air as if they were a pair of skinny two-by-fours. The logs bounced off the trikes, but one wiped out a cowboy who couldn't get out of the way fast enough.

Triceratops began to pour out of the enclosure and into the clearing, running in every direction.

Ringo was one of three cowboys on top of the platform when

the big rex attacked. From their elevated position, it looked to the men like the entire convoy of trikes was surging toward them from the trail, and they knew there must be more rexes further down the line. If the machine fired up, they stood a chance of getting out of there, provided they weren't crushed by the spooked trikes on the platform. Right about then, one of the cowboys alongside Ringo started firing at the rex.

"What are you doing? *Stop!*" Ringo yelled. The last thing they needed was to attract the attention of the female tyrannosaurus. But it was too late. When the dinosaur felt the sting of the bullets and heard the sound of the gun, it looked directly at the cowboy responsible and made for one of the ramps.

The trikes atop the transporter slammed into one another as they rushed to get away. The shooter yanked desperately on the reins to turn his horse around and escape, but a triceratops blocked his way. There was no place to go, and jumping off on horseback was out of the question. He was trapped.

The angry rex reached the top of the platform and charged the cowboy with its massive jaws open wide. It hit the horse full force, knocking it down. The cowboy managed to jump free and avoid being pinned underneath, but the rex stomped on the fallen steed and clamped its massive jaws around him as he tried to run.

Ringo and his horse teetered on the edge of the transporter, trying not to topple off. The rex was swaying, trying to decide what to take down next. Ringo knew he had to get out of there. Then he heard the drone of the underground generators. The transporter was recharging! There was no way he was going back with this thing. He had to get off. This was going to take guts!

He lowered himself on one side of the horse so it looked like

Chapter Twelve

it was riderless and rode straight toward the ramp the rex had just come up. The rex was caught off guard and snapped at them as the horse ran past, but it was too slow.

Down the ramp they flew, but the trikes at the bottom blocked their way. Ringo hoisted himself back into the saddle, and horse and rider jumped to the ground. He ducked his head and swung the horse under the edge of the platform. The rex roared, and when Ringo looked up, a triceratops' tail waved back and forth overhead. He gulped at its huge hindquarters. Heaven help him if the beast fell off; it would crush him *and* his horse.

The vaquero tried to navigate his horse away from the platform, but there were too many triceratops. He was hemmed in!!

Ringo saw one of the trike's huge rear feet dangling over the edge. He jumped to the ground, dug his boots into the soil and pressed his horse against the side of the transporter's base as hard as he could. The trike lost its balance and tumbled off the platform. It bounced off two other trikes just a few feet from where the vaquero was standing and hit the ground.

You would have thought with all that mass that there would have been a tangle of bodies and broken bones! Instead, the beast sprung to its feet unhurt and shook its head. Then it joined the crush of bodies trying to move away while the big rex loomed over them. D'Allesandro was right about one thing: those trikes were tough and durable!

By now the noise of the transporter was deafening. Ringo covered his ears just as a curtain of energy flashed above him, followed immediately by a strange lull. The lowing of the panicked trikes continued, but the roar of the tyrannosaur had quieted. The rex was gone!

Rex Riders

Back in Texas, the platform was firing up and the men were poised to greet the next group of cowboys and triceratops. It had been an uneventful day, and as the operation began to draw to a close, everyone started to relax and goof around.

As the rex materialized in front of them, all hell broke loose. Though they'd been warned of trouble, no one actually planned what to do in an emergency. So every man had a different idea on how to respond. A dozen thoughts flashed through a dozen minds at the same time: save the horses; shoot the rex; get out of there; warn the others; move the herd out of the way; hide; and more! Had Cooper been there, he would have taken charge and directed the men in a coordinated way, but since he wasn't, it was chaos.

The rex was momentarily disoriented by the sudden change in its environment, but that did little to help the cowboys in the cave who suffered their own moment of shock when the beast appeared. When it saw the men, the rex strode to the edge of the platform and roared. Its instincts told it to attack. It bound down the ramp, scattering the cowboys in every direction, and raced through the cave down the trail that D'Allesandro's men had cut.

As it ran, the rex picked up the scent of the trikes. It wasn't hard to follow. The gigantic animals left a fragrant trail of manure behind them wherever they went and anyone with a working nose could follow it.

Cooper had said goodbye to D'Allesandro not long before, and was taking a break at the mouth of the cave, talking to a couple of the boys, when he heard the roar of the T-rex echoing through the mountain.

Chapter Twelve

"What the heck is that?!" one of the cowboys cried, but they all knew exactly what it was.

Cooper didn't dwell on how the dangerous creature made it through the transporter. His main concern was warning his boss, who was in a carriage bringing up the rear of the triceratops herd. And it didn't take a tracker like Frenchy to know that the tyrannosaur was on the scent of its dinner, and would have to pass through D'Allesandro to reach its prey.

"Try and hold it for me, boys," Cooper ordered, as he prepared to ride. "I'll warn the boss. And don't get yourselves killed. Let's hope it's a small one!"

As the stagecoach continued its meandering journey to the Crossed Swords Ranch, the only two people that did any talking were D'Allesandro and Professor Kornbluth. They both agreed that because of their great size, the number of trikes they would lose to predators, like wolves, would be low. Rattlesnakes? Gila Monsters? They'd crush them underfoot. There wasn't an animal in all of North America that could challenge them. And without predators, there was little chance of their being spooked into running like cattle sometimes were.

Zeke was in a great deal of discomfort. His hands had been tied behind his back for several hours, and he was clenching his fists, wiggling his fingers, doing whatever he could to keep them from getting numb. The rest of his body wasn't doing too much better. His shoulders and back ached from the strange position he was forced into, and try as he might, he couldn't ease the pain in his joints. In a cramped cabin, someone who is fidgeting is going to make everyone uncomfortable. And being tied up for such a long time created another obvious problem.

"Mr. D'Allesandro, sir, would you mind if we stopped so I could, you know"—Zeke looked at Angelina and her mother before continuing in a whisper—"Pardon me ladies . . . relieve myself?"

When D'Allesandro hesitated, the Professor joined in Zeke's request. "A brief stop would be most welcome."

D'Allesandro signaled the driver to stop, and everyone piled out. D'Allesandro allowed Angelina to untie Zeke's hands but warned him not to run. Zeke opened and closed his fingers, and felt the circulation return to his arms.

"I'll be right back," Zeke said as he left to find a little privacy.

"Are you happy to be back, Professor?" Maria asked.

"I'm not only happy to be back, I'm relieved to be back. As much as I enjoyed my excursion, it's time to rest. I'm going to try to regain my health."

"I'm sorry."

"Don't be. The exploration of the unknown involves risk. It was an adventure I undertook willingly. I just hope I live long enough to finish my account of the expedition."

Maria pointed to a cowboy who was just a speck in the distance. "Someone is coming toward us. I wonder who it is."

"I'm afraid my eyesight isn't good," Kornbluth replied.

Cooper could finally see the stagecoach and the triceratops herd, but they had chosen the worst possible time to stop! He had to get them moving again.

"*Go! Go!*" Cooper screamed, frantically waving his arm. He knew it was useless to shout from this distance, but he had to try.

Chapter Twelve

He drew his gun and began firing into the air.

"Is that Mr. Cooper? Why is he shooting?" Maria asked.

The cowboys heard the gunfire and instinctually drew their weapons as they turned to see what was happening. The same questions crossed all their minds: who is that guy and why is shooting in the air?

Soon something else appeared on the horizon behind Cooper, and it was very, very big!

"Whoa! What's that thing following him?" Maria asked.

"A tyrannosaurus . . ." Kornbluth replied slowly, as the gravity of the words sunk in. ". . . in Texas!"

"He's leading it to us!" Maria shouted.

"I can't believe this is happening." D'Allesandro said angrily. Before he could say anything else, a group of cowboys from the herd rode toward them.

"What now?" D'Allesandro muttered.

Mickey Strong, the acting trail boss, told D'Allesandro that his men would abandon the trikes to make a stand and defend them from the rex, but D'Allesandro would have none of it.

"You men stay with those animals, do you understand me? Get them back to my ranch. We will be fine. The Professor will guide us. He knows these beasts."

It was a lie, and everyone knew it. Kornbluth had barely held it together when they were examining the dead lambeosaurus. D'Allesandro knew he'd be useless in the face of real danger, but the rancher was determined not to lose any trikes.

"Now, get those animals moving!"

Strong and his men whipped their horses around and raced to move the herd out, but the triceratops had already caught the rex's scent and begun to move on their own.

It was obvious to the men what was about to happen next. Regardless of what D'Allesandro wanted, the trikes were going to stampede, and there was no way to stop it.

"Stay with 'em boys," Strong shouted.

As the men rode off, Maria confronted her brother in a state of panic. "Where are they going? What did you tell him?"

"I told him to protect the herd."

"What? Are you crazy?!"

Maria grabbed her brother's arm. "We need those men. This stagecoach is too slow. We'll never make it!"

"Unfortunately," D'Allesandro said, jerking himself free, "it's the only one we have. Quickly, Professor, inside."

"Where are the kids?"

"I'm not risking all our lives because of a couple of stubborn children, Maria! Get in the stagecoach now! We're leaving."

Angelina and Zeke stood together on a small hill watching as the rex drew closer.

"That looks like the same one we saw in the river. I wonder what happened back there," Angelina said.

"I'll bet it was bad," Zeke said, somberly. "Too bad we don't have Hellfire with us."

They looked at the stagecoach and saw the adults piling in.

Then Angelina held out her hand; this was going to take teamwork. Zeke took her hand in his, and they started running.

"Do you think you can work that thingamajig, Zeke?"

"Count on it."

* * *

Chapter Twelve

The horses could sense the impending danger and were skittish to leave. The carriage lurched into motion, quickly picking up speed.

"Dante, no!" Maria cried.

The driver looked over his shoulder and saw the kids running toward the coach. "There they are, Mr. D'Allesandro!" he shouted.

"Do not stop!" D'Allesandro commanded.

The driver didn't exactly stop, but he eased back on the reins to slow the vehicle down. Angelina reached the door just as her mother pushed it open so she could scramble inside, while Zeke ran past and climbed up beside the driver. There was no way he was letting anybody tie him up again.

"Where does he think he's going?" D'Allesandro demanded. With Zeke up top he couldn't keep an eye on him.

"I'll ride shotgun," Zeke shouted to the driver, holding out his hand for a weapon. He wasn't sure he'd get one but it was worth a try, and it might even the odds a bit.

The driver looked at Zeke suspiciously, since he'd seen what happened back at the platform, but seeing as how they were in a pretty bad situation, he nodded and passed Zeke a shotgun.

Zeke returned the nod and smiled. *Yup, this evens up things quite nicely,* he thought, as he confirmed the gun was loaded. Of course, he wasn't sure what was more dangerous: D'Allesandro or the rex.

"Which way do we go?" the driver shouted.

Zeke pointed toward an abandoned ranch house in the distance. "That way. Head for the barn."

"Hang on, everyone!" the driver yelled, putting the lash to the horses.

Rex Riders

Cooper understood what D'Allessandro was trying to do when he saw the stagecoach veer away from the herd. So he decided to further confuse the rampaging beast by riding in a third direction in the hope he could lure it away from the others.

"Is it still coming?" Maria asked.

D'Allesandro stuck his head out the window and to his horror, saw that the rex was now following them. Cooper's ploy had failed.

"Yes, it is," he replied.

"Don't worry mother, we'll be okay," Angelina said, as the stage bounced up and down.

The ranch they were heading toward had been abandoned by its owners a few years before, and nature had taken its toll. The buildings were in a terrible state of disrepair. This wasn't unusual. When settlers moved on, they didn't bother to tear down the buildings they left behind. There was no reason to; the elements did it for them. In the meantime, the structures served a useful purpose by providing temporary shelter for travelers.

There were four altogether: a one-story log house, a small barn, a shed and an outhouse. It wasn't much, but it gave them a place to hide on the wide expanse of the open range.

Maria was right about the stagecoach that her brother had commissioned. It was never intended to carry a full load of passengers over rough terrain at a high rate of speed. It was a punishing ride as the vehicle bucked along, and everyone was thrown about the cabin.

The tyrannosaur followed at a steady pace. The carriage looked interesting and was slower than the triceratops. Maybe she could catch up to it . . .

Chapter Twelve

The stagecoach careened into the barn, and the driver and Zeke jumped down to close and lock the barn doors. They only had minutes to come up with a plan before the rex reached them.

From his experience with Hellfire, Zeke knew the rickety old barn would be destroyed in short order by an animal as massive and powerful as the one that was chasing them. Their only hope was to get the Tarngatharn force generator away from D'Allesandro and activate it. But first he'd try to create a diversion to buy them some time.

"Unhitch the horses," he cried, but no one made a move to help him except for Angelina. Although they were accustomed to being around trikes, they hadn't developed a tolerance for predators and started bucking and whinnying. Once the tyrannosaur reached the barn, there'd be no way of controlling them, and they'd either hurt themselves trying to escape while hitched together, or the rex would kill them all.

"Come on," Zeke shouted. "Help me release them!"

A look of horror suddenly crossed Angelina's face.

"What's wrong?" Zeke asked.

"Both of you, put your hands up and get away from the horses," D'Allesandro ordered, pointing a small gambler's pistol at Angelina and Zeke. "And hand me that shotgun."

"Dante, what are you doing?" Maria shouted.

D'Allesandro ignored her. "You heard me. Move! I will not allow you to release our only means of escape."

"Are you crazy?" Angelina screamed. "If we let them loose, they'll lead it away from here. Don't you see?"

"It'll go after the horses but it won't be able to catch them. They're too fast," Zeke explained. "We'll get out the other way.

Trust me, Mr. D'Allesandro. I know what I'm talking about."

"You know nothing," D'Allesandro spat. "You are a stupid farm boy. When that beast realizes it can't catch the horses, it will return, and we can't outrun it on foot. Now, get away from them and kick the shotgun to me."

"It's coming!" the driver yelled from the barn doors, where he was keeping an eye out for the rex. But when he turned around and saw D'Allesandro holding a gun on Zeke, he balked. This was a repeat of what happened earlier on the platform. Whatever was going on, he wanted no part of it. Let those fools kill one another. He had to get out.

The driver ran to the back of the building and kicked out several loose boards until he was able to squeeze through. Then he took off running across the field behind the barn.

"What are you doing? Get back here!" D'Allesandro shouted.

"That coward left us!" Maria screamed hysterically.

Enraged, D'Allesandro fired after the driver, even though he was already gone. Zeke was appalled. D'Allesandro was wasting ammunition! He was out of control.

Zeke thought back to the advice that Stumpy gave him the night before he was supposed to be shipped back East many months ago, words the teen had turned to in the Cragnon world. *"A man controls his emotions, not the other way around."* He had to stay calm and overcome his fears, if he was going to survive this ordeal and save the others.

"We'll never make it out of here," Professor Kornbluth declared.

"Oh yes, we will," Zeke whispered to himself, as he charged D'Allesandro, knocking him to the ground.

Chapter Twelve

* * *

As it approached, the tyrannosaur caught sight of the driver running through the grass behind the barn and immediately detoured around the structure after him.

The driver saw the fearsome creature coming for him. Then he made a mistake no one skilled in handling a gun should ever make. As he was running and looking behind him, he tried to draw his pistol out of its holster and cock it. The driver tripped, and the gun went off, hitting him in the leg. He writhed in pain, knowing his cries and movement would draw the huge animal to him. His eyes teared up as he clenched his jaws to stop from crying out. He told himself to stay down, thinking that in the tall grass the rex would be unable to find him.

But because of their height, tyrannosaurs had an advantage over smaller animals that tried to hide in tall grasses. Unless their quarry lay perfectly still, the big predators could see the movement of the grass when their prey tried to escape.

When the driver fell and disappeared in the grass, the rex stopped and scanned the field for any sign of movement. Then it lowered its head and sniffed the ground to pick up the scent of its prey.

The driver lay still on his back, barely breathing with his revolver at the ready, hoping the big dinosaur wouldn't find him. But the driver's leg wound gave him away. The rex could smell the blood.

The tyrannosaur walked slowly toward him. Even though the beast had size and strength on its side, it could be cautious and stealthy when circumstances called for it. When the rex got a fix on where it thought the driver was hiding, it became very still and listened while its eyes scanned the grass.

The driver knew the rex was near, but between the creature's lower stance and the tall grass, he had no idea how close the animal was. Then the driver made his second and final mistake. He cocked his pistol.

Click!

That was all the Tyrannosaur needed to lock in on its target. It pounced. The driver managed to squeeze off a single shot before the beast's mighty jaws closed on him. He didn't even have a chance to scream.

It was over in moments. When the T-rex finished licking the ground where the driver had fallen, it turned toward the barn. It could hear the sound of the horses desperately trying to kick the barn door open. There was no reason to wait any longer.

D'Allesandro was bigger and stronger than Zeke, but Zeke had youth and endurance on his side. He was used to physical labor and running around, while D'Allesandro rarely exerted himself. Maria and Angelina screamed at the two fighters, as they rolled around on the floor of the barn, while Professor Kornbluth worriedly turned in circles and talked to himself.

Suddenly, there was a tremendous crash. The tyrannosaur had used its head like a battering ram against the rear of the old barn. The rotting boards gave way and the back of the roof collapsed, killing the Professor instantly and knocking the horses to the ground.

The horses struggled to get back on their hooves, but the tyrannosaur was upon them. It locked its jaws around one and lifted it off the ground, dragging the others with it. It was a

Chapter Twelve

horrible scene as the horses tried to defend themselves against the rex, and the beast tore into them

D'Allesandro was on top of Zeke, punching the teen in the face, when the roof collapsed. Zeke saw it coming and protected himself as best he could, but D'Allesandro wasn't so lucky. As debris fell on him, the rancher's body actually shielded Zeke from serious injury.

Zeke pushed a dazed D'Allesandro off him and crawled out from under the wreckage. D'Allesandro was bleeding from a head wound where a board had gashed his scalp. He'd lost his pistol and started groping around to find it.

Maria had been knocked to the ground by a falling beam and lay facedown on the floor. Only Angelina had managed to escape injury by sheer luck and was at her mother's side, trying to pull her out from under the support. Her mother was not responding.

"Come on," Zeke whispered to Angelina. "It's too late."

Before D'Allesandro could stop them, Zeke and Angelina squeezed out between the barn doors and ran toward the ranch house. The tyrannosaur saw them but it was too busy feasting on the horses to stop what it was doing. It would find them as soon as it was done.

They pushed open the front door and looked inside. Light streamed in through the opening and a dozen small holes in the roof. There wasn't much; just a table, a couple of broken chairs, and a small fireplace—no place to hide. It looked hopeless. Zeke closed the door behind him, anyway.

They heard D'Allesandro scream and the rex roar, and then the shotgun went off. Angelina closed her eyes and reached for Zeke's hand. Without Slim's force generator, which was in

D'Allesandro's jacket pocket, there was no way out.

A shotgun blast blew open the door to the ranch house, and D'Allesandro staggered in, wild-eyed and beserk. Another moment and the rex would be there.

Zeke picked up a leg from a broken chair and charged D'Allesandro. The crazed rancher deflected the blow with the shotgun, and Zeke stumbled, giving D'Allesandro enough time to level his weapon at the teen. But before he could pull the trigger, Maria staggered through the doorway. D'Allesandro was distracted for only a split-second, but that was all the time it took for Zeke to bring the hunk of wood down over D'Allesandro's head. The rancher crumpled to the floor.

Angelina was upon him in an instant, rifling through his jacket pockets, desperately searching for the Rider's device.

"I found it!" she yelled. But there was no time to celebrate.

The tyrannosaur rammed the front of the house, sending debris in every direction. Angelina thrust the force generator into Zeke's hands, and his fingers flew over the keys, as the rex's head burst through a hole in the ceiling, stopping just short of where they were standing.

Nothing happened.

"No, no, that wasn't it. Wait . . ." He tried the sequence again, and this time he heard a familiar beeping sound.

"Yes," he shouted. "I got it."

Suddenly the device started to whine and emitted a greenish light, which encircled them in a strange glowing bubble.

The tyrannosaur struck again, but this time it hit the force bubble. The elastic field crackled with energy, as it absorbed the force of the impact.

Chapter Twelve

"It can't get through!" Angelina shouted triumphantly.

Again and again the huge dinosaur struck, but it couldn't penetrate the protective shield. The beast roared in anger and shook its head. It lifted its leg and clawed at the glowing sphere, as if it were trying to climb on top and crush them. Then it got quiet and stared at them. The rex was frustrated and thinking about what to do next; how to attack them.

Zeke put the generator on the floor and backed away. He didn't want to risk shutting off the device accidentally.

Angelina and Zeke looked up at the tyrannosaur looming over them. They walked to within six feet of its giant head and both dinosaur and humans contemplated one another.

Close up, their suspicions were confirmed. Yes, this enormous dinosaur and Hellfire were related. They were too frightened to see it the first time they encountered her, but they could see the resemblance now. This is what their jerky-loving friend would someday become. And even though it was bigger and deadlier than any animal Zeke and Angelina had ever seen, and they knew how much damage and pain it was capable of inflicting, the teens weren't afraid of it any longer. They saw the rex for what it was: an animal like any other, with a strong instinct for survival. And like the triceratops, it didn't belong in Texas.

The tyrannosaur was bleeding from several gunshot wounds, but didn't look hurt. At least it didn't show any signs that it was. It shook its massive head and snorted; then turned and slowly walked back toward the barn where it sniffed around for any leftovers.

Angelina threw her arms around Zeke and hugged him. "You did it! I knew you would!"

Zeke was dazed and overwhelmed. He shook his head to clear the cobwebs. "I guess I did."

"Congratulations," a voice said from the damaged front entry. It was Slim with Hellfire! And there was Stumpy, all smiling and looking at them through the bubble.

"Do you know what to do next?" Slim asked quietly.

"I think so," Zeke said. Then looking in the direction the rex had gone, he asked, "Is it safe?"

Slim assured Zeke he would take over and deal with the tyrannosaur so it wouldn't cause any more damage.

Zeke picked up the force generator and hit a different sequence of buttons, which caused the field to disappear.

"Good. You are learning." Slim said, sounding pleased.

Zeke handed the device back to Slim, and the Tarngatharn rode Hellfire after the rex. Zeke watched as Slim produced another force field, but this one surrounded the barn with the rex inside. The creature didn't even notice it was trapped.

"I'm glad to see you," Zeke said, pumping Stumpy's hand. "That was close." The teen felt like a huge weight had been lifted off his shoulders.

"I'm proud of you, son," Stumpy said, beaming. Then he gave Angelina a big hug, and whispered, "And I'm very proud of you."

"I hope Uncle Jesse and Bull aren't too mad at me and Angelina for taking the horse and sneaking away from them," Zeke said.

"Hmm . . ." Stumpy began, stroking his stubbly chin. "Well, I can't speak for your uncle, but I'm guessing he'll get over it . . . *someday*."

"Where are they?" Zeke asked.

Chapter Twelve

"They went to help D'Allesandro's men round up them three-horns."

Zeke nodded. "What about Cable Cooper? Where did he go?"

Stumpy looked thrown by the question. "We ain't seen him."

To get to the Crossed Swords Ranch, the herd had to pass by Henry Poole's place. Months before at the square dance, Maria had tried to convince Poole to sell his spread to her brother because of its close proximity to the mountains where the transporter was located, but Poole resisted her sales pitch, and when he found out that Uncle Jesse wasn't moving, he declined D'Allesandro's offer to buy.

It was late afternoon, and Henry and his son, Caleb, were out fixing fences. It had been a long day in the hot sun, and they were looking forward to finishing up and taking it easy. Henry's younger kids were playing outside the Poole's simple cabin, while inside their mother was preparing the evening meal.

"You hear that, pa?" Caleb asked.

Henry scanned the skies. "It sounds like thunder, but I don't see any rain clouds."

"Look," Caleb said, pointing to a cloud of dust in the distance. "Something's coming."

"Go round up your brothers and sisters," Henry ordered. "I'll get your ma."

The triceratops were running at a fast clip, but Uncle Jesse and Bull had caught up. Along the way, they passed the bodies of several of D'Allesandro's men, who'd been crushed attempting to slow the stampeding herd. There wasn't much left, other than their blood-stained clothes.

"We have to stop them," Uncle Jesse shouted to Bull as they approached the rear of the herd.

"How are you gonna do that? You only have one arm!"

"I ain't. *You* are! Come on!" Uncle Jesse hunched over Midnight's neck, dug his boots into the Andalusian's chest, and pulled ahead.

Oh, lord, Bull thought. *Here we go again!*

Uncle Jesse had a plan in mind. If he and Bull could get a rope around the horns of the trike that was out in front, Bull was strong enough to use the rope like the reins on a horse. He'd steer the leader away from Poole's farm, and the herd would follow. There were all kinds of animals this technique worked on. They just had to figure out how to reach the lead trike without getting themselves killed.

The men had two options to get close enough to lasso the leader. They could ride either outside the herd and try to cut in when they reached the front or straight up the center and take their chances, bobbing and weaving through the jostling pack. Both choices were fraught with extreme danger. Even a slight bump from the enormous creatures would send a man and his horse careening to certain death underfoot. And then there were several hundred sharp horns to watch out for.

Uncle Jesse nodded toward the herd, and Bull understood. No sense playing it safe. They'd ride up the middle!

Uncle Jesse went first. He steered Midnight through the herd, passing smaller trikes running alongside their mothers, and elderly ones that were having trouble keeping up. It wasn't safe to ride alongside another horseman in a stampede, so Bull kept a safe distance behind.

Chapter Twelve

They were closing in on the front of the herd when Bull heard the sound of a gun. But that was impossible. Shooting wouldn't stop the critters; it would only spook them further.

Bull glanced over his shoulder and couldn't believe what he saw: Cable Cooper closing in on them with his gun drawn. That psycho was going to try to kill them inside the herd where there wouldn't be any witnesses!

He lowered his head and rode up beside Uncle Jesse. "It's Cooper!" he shouted, pointing behind him.

Uncle Jesse looked, but Cooper was gone.

"I just saw him," Bull yelled.

Uncle Jesse nodded. "Drop back."

In theory, Uncle Jesse and Bull had the advantage, since there were two of them against one Cooper. Since Uncle Jesse's injured arm prevented him from shooting, he would be the decoy, while Bull held back and waited for Cooper to make his move. The only problem was, if anything happened to Bull before Cooper revealed himself, Uncle Jesse would be a sitting duck, unable to use his gun to defend himself without taking his good hand off the reins.

Bull drew his revolver and slowed his horse, so it fell back to the rear, but couldn't see Cooper. Worse: he lost sight of Uncle Jesse! The massive animals were shifting from side to side, their patterns constantly changing as they ran. Gaps between them would open up for a few seconds and then close just as quickly.

"Blast it!" Bull shouted. He moved to his right. Nothing.

Cooper couldn't believe Uncle Jesse and Bull were still alive and seethed with anger. They had to be part alley cat seeing as how

many lives they had. But now, the end was at hand for both of them. This was the perfect time and place. All Cooper needed to do was find a way to knock them down. No one would ever know he was involved in their deaths after the three-horns trampled their bodies. Heck, it would be tough to even find their bodies after these animals were through mashing them into the ground.

He had just missed Bull, and that son of a gun had fallen back out of sight, which was fine with Cooper. He wanted to take out McCain first anyway. Cooper spurred his horse forward, dodging recklessly between the trikes. He had trouble spotting Uncle Jesse because he couldn't see over them and had to wait until

Chapter Twelve

there was a break between their massive bodies to see around them. Suddenly, a gap opened up and Cooper saw Uncle Jesse. He took aim, but before he could fire, he heard a shot from behind.

Bull was coming up on Cooper fast. Now, Bull was directly behind the ornery cuss, aiming his gun straight at him. Bull knew it was life or death; he couldn't risk Uncle Jesse's life by giving Cooper a second chance.

Cooper turned and fired at Bull, but missed. It was difficult enough hitting a man chasing you on horseback on open terrain, never mind while trying to navigate through a stampede of triceratops!

Rex Riders

Then Cooper had an idea. As Bull charged, he deliberately fired at the trike running next to Bull, grazing its rear hip. The instant the triceratops felt the sting of the bullet it bellowed angrily, tossing its head and driving into Bull's horse, just as Cooper had planned.

Luckily, Bull saw the maneuver coming. He pulled hard on the reins, and the injured trike slammed into the animal next to it instead. Bull barely made it out from between them and was fortunate that he didn't get impaled on the horns of a triceratops coming up from behind when he abruptly slowed down.

Cooper laughed. That plan almost worked! As much as he wanted to forget McCain's lackey, Cooper realized he'd have to take care of Bull first. He pulled back, allowing his horse to fall behind Bull. He'd get him next time no matter what!

Bull was still righting himself and didn't notice Cooper's quick maneuver, until he looked up. Cooper had disappeared! Where'd he go? Then he heard a gunshot and felt a bullet whistle by his ear. Cooper fired again and hit Bull in the arm. The bullet only winged him, but it hurt!

Bull winced in pain. He had to get out of the line of fire. The next shot could be fatal. There was an opening up ahead and he went for it.

Cooper saw Bull's desperate charge and was not about to let him escape again. Then someone grabbed him from the left.

It was McCain!

Uncle Jesse had been closing in on the lead trike when he heard gunfire, but he couldn't make out where it had come from. Between the pounding of the feet and constant bellowing, the

Chapter Twelve

noise level of the stampeding trikes was tremendous.

He didn't figure any of D'Allesandro's men would be stupid enough to shoot at the animals, thinking that might stop them, so it had to be Cooper. He cut to his left and drifted back among the herd, and that's when he saw Cooper wing Bull.

Uncle Jesse had the reins of his horse in his teeth and was trying to pull Cooper off his horse with his good right arm. Uncle Jesse figured if he was going to die because of Cooper, he'd take that slime bucket down with him!

Cooper fought back as their horses rode side-by-side between the giant creatures, bouncing off one another. He struck Uncle Jesse in the face. Once, twice . . .

Uncle Jesse was hit hard. He felt light-headed but held on to Cooper. If he could just keep his grip on him . . .

Cooper's head suddenly flew forward, his eyes rolling backward.

Wielding a wood slat he'd retrieved from the old barn, Zeke had come up from behind on Hellfire and hit Cooper on the head. Cooper went limp from the blow and slumped across his horse's neck. A small shove would have sent him to his death, but Zeke held back. Cooper was helpless and a cowboy didn't hit a man after he was down.

As Cooper's horse slowed and fell behind, Zeke maneuvered Hellfire next to Uncle Jesse and helped prop his uncle back up. He was a mess.

"Thanks," Uncle Jesse shouted. "I'm okay."

He smiled, as blood dripped from his nose and lips, then gave Zeke a small nod, and the teen knew exactly what his uncle had in mind. If they were going to stop the triceratops from

Rex Riders

destroying Poole's ranch, the three of them would do it together!

"Come on," Uncle Jesse cried, and Zeke followed, with Bull bringing up the rear.

Poole's farm lay in the distance, and they were closing in fast! They galloped hard through the herd and emerged beside a tremendous male trike, leading the pack.

Lord, he's a big one, Zeke thought.

"We have to get closer," Uncle Jesse yelled.

Zeke started moving to his right toward the big bull, when another triceratops cut between them. But Uncle Jesse wouldn't be denied! He put the spurs to Midnight, and the mighty Andalusian pulled ahead of the trike blocking their way, moving directly in front of it. Zeke followed, and for a moment, he and his uncle were riding less than ten feet ahead of the charging creature!

Uncle Jesse swung Midnight over so he was next to the lead bull, and Zeke did the same on Hellfire.

"Tie one end around your waist. Then lasso the horns and hang on!" Uncle Jesse shouted.

Zeke did as he was told and let his lariat fly, but missed. He had to reel it in fast before an animal stepped on the loop. Otherwise, its foot might get caught and Zeke would be yanked off Hellfire.

"I'm gonna try again," Zeke cried. He took a deep breath. The rope spiraled through the air and landed around one of the trike's horns. The big triceratops shook its head but the lasso stayed in place.

"I got it!"

Zeke let the rope go slack. The next move had to be timed just right.

Chapter Twelve

He put his hands on top of Hellfire's neck, leaned forward and pulled his legs up under him so he was squatting on top of the rex's back. Uncle Jesse stretched out his good arm to help steady him.

Zeke looked down for a second and felt dizzy.

"Don't look down," Uncle Jesse warned.

Zeke snapped his head back up and kept his eyes on the triceratops.

"Steady . . ." Jesse cautioned.

Zeke leapt!

He landed across the trike's massive back, but there wasn't anything to hold on to and he started to slide off. Then he felt a hand grab the back of his shirt and pull him forward onto the neck of the beast so he was able to grab his lasso.

Where did Bull come from? Zeke thought. *And how in the heck did he do that with just one hand?*

When the triceratops felt Zeke land on its neck, it snapped its head back, and the bony edge of its huge frill hit Zeke across the top of his nose.

"Yow!"

Zeke saw stars as he grabbed the frill so he could keep his head out of the way. With his free hand he worked the rope tied around his waist over his head. Then Zeke tossed the loop around the trike's other horn so the two ends resembled the reins on a horse.

"Pull!" Jesse shouted.

Off in the distance a yellow dog stood in the middle of a huge expanse of grassland barking at the approaching herd.

Zeke grunted and braced himself. He pulled back on both

ends of the rope with all his might.

Nothing happened.

"Pull it to the side!" Uncle Jesse yelled.

Zeke suddenly realized what he was doing wrong. The key to stopping the stampede was to turn the herd so it was moving in a circle, instead of a straight line. And to do that, Zeke had to turn the lead triceratops. If Zeke could do that, the other dinosaurs would follow and eventually slow to a stop.

Zeke wrapped the rope around his right arm and took a deep breath. For a split second he remembered how he couldn't budge the wheel that lowered the cage in which Bull was imprisoned in Mujar and felt sick. What if he couldn't do this? He couldn't fail again! He wouldn't allow himself!

The muscles in his neck bulged, and the lariat dug into his forearms as he pulled. The triceratops felt the rope tugging on its horn and fought back. Even though Zeke wasn't nearly strong enough to overcome the power of the trike's massive neck, the pressure on the right side was enough to cause the animal to turn in that direction!

"Keep pulling!" Uncle Jesse shouted.

The trike moved away from the field, and the others followed. The herd turned in a broad arc and finally slowed down. Zeke had done it!

Bull and Uncle Jesse were whooping and hollering when a stray triceratops suddenly shot out from the pack. Bull barely avoided colliding with the animal, but Uncle Jesse and Midnight never saw it coming. It smashed into Midnight, sending Uncle Jesse and the big stallion tumbling to the ground!

Chapter
Thirteen

When Bull reached Uncle Jesse, he was sprawled on the ground and looked like he was dead. His legs and arms were at odd angles, and his shirt was soaked with blood from his shoulder wound, which had reopened when he was attacked by Cooper.

Henry Poole had seen everything and immediately drove his buckboard to the scene of the accident to help. Neither Bull nor Henry wanted to move Uncle Jesse, but they didn't have a choice.

By the time Zeke caught up with the two men, they had gently placed his uncle in the buckboard and secured his limp body as best they could so the ride wouldn't jar him too much during the long trek into town. Zeke wanted to go with them, but he had to return Hellfire to Slim, who had his own emergency to deal with.

Uncle Jesse was still unconscious when they arrived at Doc's place. Luckily, Doc was gardening out back, instead of making the rounds among his far flung patients as he usually was, and came running when he heard Bull calling.

"Got a patient for you, Doc!" Bull shouted.

"Don't tell me that stranger got himself shot up again," Doc said as he hurried to the front of the house.

"It's Jesse."

"What happened to him?"

"One of them three-horns knocked him off his horse," Bull replied.

Doc shook his head in disbelief. "I'll ask you about it later. What about the blood on his shirt? Did that happen in the fall?"

"That's from where Cooper shot him."

Doc sighed. This was going to be one heck of a story! "You two go on inside and get my stretcher. I'll stay here with the patient."

After his examination, Doc concluded that Uncle Jesse had suffered a serious concussion from the fall, but didn't appear to have a fractured skull or any broken bones. He speculated that what saved Uncle Jesse from further injury was the fact that his body was relaxed at the moment of impact. Since Uncle Jesse hadn't seen the trike coming, he didn't tense up like people do when faced with danger. That was a big relief, because Uncle Jesse needed immediate surgery to remove the bullet that Cooper put in his shoulder, and additional injuries would have delayed the procedure.

After the operation, Doc told Zeke and Bull that Uncle Jesse

Chapter Thirteen

would have to remain in his care until he was well enough to return to the Double R. It was just as well. There was so much unfinished business to take care of that Zeke, Bull and Stumpy couldn't spare anyone to look after Uncle Jesse.

"Send me the bill," Henry insisted when Doc was through. "Whatever it is, I'll pay for it. These boys saved my place."

Back at the Double R, everyone, including Angelina, was helping Slim deal with the angry tyrannosaur. He made it clear that killing the beast was not an option, and no one dared question him. But getting it back home seemed impossible until Angelina came up with the idea of knocking out the animal, and carrying it back using the same wagon that her uncle had used to move the triceratops that had ravaged Dos Locos.

Slim thought it a brilliant plan and was impressed by Angelina's creativity.

D'Allesandro had a very different reaction. He was livid. His niece had betrayed him again! Angelina had no right to give anyone permission to use property that belonged to him, and D'Allesandro refused to cooperate unless Slim agreed to leave behind a small herd of trikes.

Tempers skyrocketed. Everyone had a score to settle, and D'Allesandro's gamesmanship in the face of a problem for which he was responsible was too much for anyone to take! Just when things were about to get even uglier, the Sheriff arrived with a posse of armed men carrying warrants for the arrest of D'Allesandro and Cooper on suspicion of murder.

Unbeknownst to anyone, Stumpy had alerted Sheriff Healy to the human remains and blood-stained Civil War hat that were found inside the shed in D'Allesandro's barn, when everyone was in the world of the Cragnon. Upon further investigation the Sheriff discovered that the location of the bullet hole matched up with a similar hole in a skull he found in the shed. Under the circumstances Sheriff Healy felt he had enough evidence to charge D'Allesandro and Cooper with Shorty's murder. It wasn't the strongest case, since there were no eye-witnesses to the crime, but justice required it.

The Sheriff told D'Allesandro that if he didn't agree to provide the wagon and manpower to move the rex, he'd declare a public emergency that the rex posed a danger to the townsfolk of Dos Locos, commandeer the wagon himself and lock up D'Allesandro indefinitely. D'Allesandro was beside himself with anger and warned Healy that he'd have his badge, but in the end D'Allesandro backed down and the Sheriff got his way.

The threat of being jailed may have kept D'Allesandro in line, but no one, including the Sheriff, expected the powerful rancher or Cooper to be convicted. Even if D'Allesandro hadn't been so politically well connected, the evidence against him and Cooper was only circumstantial.

D'Allesandro accompanied a crew of men back to the Crossed Swords Ranch to retrieve the wagon and saw for the first time the devastation the Cragnon had wrought. He was shocked at the sight of his beloved home in ruins and insisted on staying behind to survey the damage.

Slim knocked out the T-rex by feeding it a hunk of Stumpy's barbecue laced with a powerful sedative. It wasn't hard to get the giant predator to eat it. There was just something about Stumpy's smoked meat that drove rexes wild! Once the animal

Chapter Thirteen

was asleep and safely enclosed inside a force bubble, Slim and Hellfire, with help from Zeke, Bull and some of D'Allesandro's men, rounded up a team of triceratops. Then they hitched the trikes to the wagon and carted the tyrannosaur home.

That evening, Maria and Angelina returned to the Crossed Swords to gather some things so they could spend the night in town. There was no trace of D'Allesandro. He had left without a word to anyone. It was later rumored among the townspeople that he and Cooper had gone south to start a cattle ranch in Mexico, but Maria and Angelina knew better. They were sure the two men had returned to Ismalis.

In the wake of her brother's unexpected departure, Maria suddenly found herself in charge of the Crossed Swords Ranch! The spread was in a terrible state of disrepair from the damage wrought by the Cragnon marauders, and someone had to exterminate the bugs that escaped from the shed. Even the business was faltering. D'Allesandro had neglected the ranch's cattle operations while he built his outpost.

To complicate matters, Maria had no idea where her family's cash and gold were hidden. Despite all D'Allesandro's wealth, she had no idea how to get hold of it. It was a strange position for Maria to suddenly find herself in. The family fortune made her rich, but she had no money! Fortunately, the people of Dos Locos rallied around her, promising to help her rebuild. After all, it was the neighborly thing to do.

Before long, it was time for Slim to return home. Bull and Stumpy said goodbye to their friend outside the mouth of the cave that housed the transporter and assured him that once he was back home, they would close it. Permanently.

Then, Zeke and Angelina accompanied Slim inside to say their own goodbyes.

"I guess we won't be seeing you again," Angelina said as she stood on the ledge that overlooked the machine.

"That depends," Slim said.

"It does?" Zeke said, surprised.

"On what?" Angelina asked, but before Slim could answer Hellfire began to growl.

Zeke muttered something under his breath about not having a gun to protect them; then suddenly smacked himself in the head with his fist. "Ringo's gun!" he blurted. "I was supposed to return it!"

"Where'd you leave it?" Angelina asked.

"Cable Cooper took it from me here in the cave. I don't know what happened to it after that."

"I wouldn't worry about it," Angelina said. "It's not like you'll ever see Ringo again."

"That's not the point. I promised him I'd return it."

Then Angelina noticed some feathers on the floor of the cave. They were smaller than those found on a war bird. "These look familiar," she said, but couldn't place where she'd seen them before.

"There's your answer," Slim said, holding up the torch he was carrying to illuminate a corner of the cave. Three small dinosaurs scampered across the floor and hid behind a pile of rocks.

"How'd they get here?" Zeke asked.

Slim shook his head ruefully.

Chapter Thirteen

"They probably came through the transporter looking for their mother. When I found Hellfire he was no bigger than they are," Slim explained, as they walked down to the machine. "Zeke, do you have any of Stumpy's dried meat?"

Slim took a piece of jerky from Zeke and told the teens to watch. As he neared the young rexes' hiding place, three sets of eyes peered out over the top of the rocks, lured by the smell of the meat. One of the little beasts walked forward, but instead of biting the jerky, it tried to nip Slim's finger. Slim was prepared. He caught the rex by its neck and hoisted it off the ground. It squealed and snapped its jaws, while its feet clawed the air.

"Make sure you hold it with its head turned away from you," Slim explained. "This one is a fighter, just like her mother. Now, watch closely."

Slim took a small metal disk that resembled a bottle cap from his saddlebag and positioned it near the rex's backbone at the base of its tail. He pressed the disk into place, and small prongs emerged that dug into the creature's flesh through its feathers. Trickles of blood seeped out where the device penetrated its skin, and the rex cried and thrashed about.

"Do you see where I placed it?" Slim continued. "It has to be in a spot the animals can't reach with their legs or jaws. They're very good at removing these things."

"What's that for?" Angelina asked.

"It will help us track them."

Angelina and Zeke looked at each other and mouthed the same word: 'us'?!

"Now, bring the other two to me," Slim directed. "Do it the same way. Hold out the food and wait for them to come to you.

Rex Riders

It's important that you don't show fear. Go on."

The teens did as they were told and offered pieces of jerky to the hungry juveniles. One of them approached Angelina slowly. She stayed very still and softly urged it closer, until it took the meat out of her hand. Then she reached down and carefully picked it up exactly as she had been instructed. The rex squirmed a little but Angelina had the situation under control.

"Looks like you got a good one," Zeke observed.

The other rex stayed back and eyed Zeke suspiciously. When Zeke held out his hand, it fled behind a rock. "And I got a cowardly one," Zeke said, laughing.

Zeke casually stepped around the rock, expecting to find the creature cowering in fear, but instead it leapt out and attacked him! Zeke jumped back and fell on his butt. The rex pounced on his chest and snapped at his face.

"Augghh!"

Zeke knocked the youngster off his chest and sprang to his feet. The two squared off against each other. Now it was personal.

"You cannot show fear," Slim reminded.

"I'll show it fear. Come on over here and get some of this." Zeke ripped off his bandana and wrapped it around one of his hands. He held the fist in front of him, inviting the rex to strike. When it did, he grabbed its neck with his free hand. The beast put up quite a fight, and Zeke had a hard time controlling it.

"Good," Slim said. "Now, bring them to me."

"You got the bad one," Angelina whispered, suppressing a laugh.

"It's not funny," Zeke scolded. "I almost got my nose ripped off."

Chapter Thirteen

Slim handed them both a tracking device and walked them through the process of attaching it. When they finished, Slim touched his wrist band and a holographic image of Angelina's rex appeared over his bracelet in the center of a three-dimensional grid.

"These symbols tell me where the yerka is, so I can find him whenever I need to. But when they are trained correctly, all you will need is one of these," Slim explained, holding the tooth around his neck. "And the animals will come to you."

"Can we keep them?" Angelina asked tentatively.

"Not here," Slim replied, and both teens looked crestfallen. "It's too dangerous."

Slim told the teens to put their rexes on the ramp while he said something to Hellfire. Before the little beasts could run back into the cave, Hellfire roared at them, and they fled to the top of the platform, triggering the machine.

As the transporter fired up, Zeke and Angelina said goodbye to Hellfire. The rex had saved their lives, and they had grown very fond of it. Hellfire was like a horse, a grizzly bear and a friend all rolled into one. They wrapped their arms around the rex's neck and hugged it tightly, as tears welled in their eyes.

"It's time to go," Slim said. "This door will be closed. But if it is meant to be, you will find a path back to me where Hellfire and I will be waiting for you."

It was several weeks before Doc sent word to the Double R that Uncle Jesse was well enough to have company. The next day when he awoke from a nap, there was Stumpy, sitting at his bedside, staring at him.

"What are you looking at?" Uncle Jesse growled.

"Are you talking to me?" Stumpy said, looking around the room.

"There ain't anyone else in here."

"In case you're interested, your horse is fine," Stumpy snapped.

"I was getting around to it."

"I saved you the trouble," Stumpy replied curtly.

"So how is he?"

"I already said he's fine."

Stumpy stood up. "Let's take a look at your shoulder."

Uncle Jesse winced as Stumpy pulled the front of Uncle Jesse's shirt away and lifted the dressing on the bandaged wound.

"Careful you old coot, that stings!" Uncle Jesse yelled.

"Quit whining."

"How's it look?"

"Ah, it's nothing," Stumpy scoffed. "I've had splinters worse than that."

"So?"

"So *what*?"

"So what happened with the three-horns and that overgrown . . . you know."

"Yerka?" Stumpy offered.

"Right. Where'd they all end up? And what about Slim and Hellfire? What's Bull been up to?"

"You want to keep asking me questions or do you want me to tell you what happened?"

"Well, fill me in. I can't lie around here all day and talk to you. I have to get back to work."

Chapter Thirteen

Stumpy told Uncle Jesse everything that happened to Zeke and Angelina, from the time the teens snuck away and joined D'Allesandro on the triceratops drive, to the moment Uncle Jesse was blind-sided by the trike. The old cook also filled in Uncle Jesse on what happened while he was convalescing.

After an hour, Doc poked his head in and told Stumpy that visiting hours were over, and Uncle Jesse needed to rest.

Stumpy was almost out the door when he turned around. He looked like he had something important on his mind. "By the way, Zeke asked me to tell you to take it easy and not rush to get back."

"That's nice of him," Uncle Jesse said. "How's he working out? Is he giving you any trouble?"

"Nope. He and Bull have things running pretty smooth. He's doing your old job, only a lot better than you ever did it. But he said you're welcome back any time, as long you can pull your weight. Otherwise, you may want to start thinking about getting an easier job in town. Mr. G has an opening for a stock boy. I'm thinking you should probably look into it."

Uncle Jesse started yelling before the door closed.

THE END